Cooking Up a Storm

Sue Welfare

To
Jacqui
with lots of love.
Happy writing!

Sue

This book is dedicated to the fabulous friends who have supported and helped me get it up off the kitchen table, to Sarah Allen, Susan Opie, Jane Dixon-Smith and Rebecca Emin, without whom this book wouldn't have been possible, and to my agent and friend, Maggie Phillips.

Thanks too to the lovely people who sent me recipes and suggestions for food-related content. Where possible I have added links to their blogs, Facebook pages and websites.

And last but in no way least, to Phil for loving me, keeping me in tea and being the best friend and husband a girl could ever want – oh, and to Jake and Beau, who have turned my office into a kennel with a keyboard.

Foreword

Cooking Up a Storm is a romantic comedy with extra added cookery.

Some of the recipes are my own favourites and standbys. Other recipes in the book come from family, friends and strangers who kindly sent me their favourite simple dishes. None of them are tricky – all of them are delicious.

Although the recipes are dotted throughout the text, they are also collected together at the end of the book. There seems to be a lot of cakes...

The amounts, weights and quantities are written exactly as they were sent to me – so they swing between imperial, metric, American-style cups, personal tastes and guesstimations.

I've tried most of them and taken the rest at face value.

I hope you enjoy the story and the food.

With lots of love,

Sue
x

Chapter One
Ice-cream in Alex

'So, the thing is,' said Rosa, their editor and boss, during the regular Monday-morning meeting, 'like every other company, I'm afraid we are going to have to make some changes here at Hanleys over the next few months. There are going to be cuts across all the stores, so we up here in the in-store magazine can't expect to be spared.'

Rosa re-organised her face into something meant to suggest compassion, although with that much Botox and her spray tan it looked more like trying to fold a brown paper bag into a hopping frog.

'I *really* wanted to talk to you all about it before we begin the process, and believe me, it is a process rather than just one big chop.' Rosa added in a little laughter to break the tension, although Sarah, who was sitting in the front row between Melissa and John from IT, noticed that the good humour didn't quite make it as far as her eyes, and no one else laughed. Rosa had notes on a card. Sarah couldn't ever remember a previous meeting when Rosa had felt the need for notes.

Sarah also noticed that, besides wearing black, Rosa was making a great effort not to let her gaze linger too long on any one person in the office. There were eight of them. Not great odds. It felt like the plot of an Agatha Christie novel: *and then there were eight…*

'I also quite understand if under the circumstances people feel the need to look for other employment. We've got great skills here, and I appreciate that uncertainty is never good for morale, but please bear with us. When I know you'll know. I've been talking it over with the Hanley brothers and we're going to try our best to make this as painless as possible. Anyway, we'll be reviewing this over the next few weeks and don't worry, we'll make sure we keep everyone in the loop.'

'Or in the noose,' said Melissa, out of the side of her mouth. She crossed her eyes and did a comic hanging mime off to one side, so that Rosa couldn't see. 'I know how the bloody turkeys feel at Christmas now. It's coming but you just won't know quite when.'

Sarah looked down at her feet so she didn't giggle; giggling wouldn't have been good. At which point her mobile rang. Sarah was about to flick it onto silent when she glanced at the caller display. It read, 'School.'

The school ringing was never good either. No parent in history had ever been rung at work by their child's class teacher to be told their son or daughter had aced their spelling test. Any hope she had of avoiding Rosa's gaze vanished as Sarah got to her feet, mouthing apologies, and headed off towards the back of the office.

'Hello,' she said the moment she was out of earshot.

'Oh hello, Mrs Peterson,' said a cheery-sounding woman. 'I'm sorry to disturb you at work, but no one's picking up at home. Nothing to worry about really, but Alex says that he isn't feeling very well and I wondered if someone could pop in and collect him? He says he's feeling poorly. We've had one or two off sick this week and he does look a little pale.'

Sarah glanced up. Alex wasn't alone. Rosa, having moved on from staff cuts, was using a laptop and whiteboard to flick through a selection of cover shots for the next few editions of the magazine. Melissa was taking notes and everyone else, all of them looking a little pasty, was making the effort to look focused and enthralled, raring to go, presumably hoping that that would help deflect the axe when it fell.

Sarah hesitated before replying to the lady on the phone. 'And you say you've tried ringing home?'

'We tried there first, but as I said, no one is picking up.'

Realistically what choice did she have? 'I'll be there in ten minutes,' Sarah said; which put her right on course for the iceberg.

Up until that Monday morning Sarah had been sailing along quite nicely, blissfully happy at the helm of her unsinkable *Titanic* of a life. She had two boys, Alex, six, and Harry, eight, a lovely husband (albeit it that he was called Colin, but you can't have everything), a little house she adored in an up-and-coming part of Cambridge, and a job that she really enjoyed.

Sarah had been working for the House of Hanleys in-store magazine and their website for the best part of five years. While her official title was features editor, in truth their team was so small, with lots of people working from home, that everyone in the office did a bit of everything, so the edges were blurrier than they sounded. And generally until that morning life was going rather well – which was how Sarah felt, in fact, right up until the moment she hit the iceberg.

Sarah *had* thought that her life and what she and Colin had was pretty much rock solid. Being completely and utterly wrong about that was probably what upset Sarah the most.

*

Slipping out of the meeting Sarah hurried downstairs to the office car park and drove out into the Cambridge late-morning traffic; it was busy and slow. Pedestrians spilt off the pavement and into the road, slowing the traffic even further. She resisted the temptation to tap her fingers on the steering wheel and let her mind wander.

Never in a million years had Sarah ever imagined that she would end up marrying a man called Colin. When she had been introduced to him at a party – and up until that moment she had really quite fancied him from the other side of the room – Sarah had paused for a moment to consider whether she really wanted to get tied up with someone called Colin.

Melissa, her best friend, who had been in the kitchen at the same party finishing off the nibbles and an indecent amount of wine, said, through a handful of Bombay mix and Twiglets; 'Don't be so bloody shallow, Sarah. He's got his own teeth and hair, he's not ginger, and doesn't appear to be suffering from any contagious diseases. A name is nothing, is it, not really? He's not his name. Maybe he's got a nice middle name. Maybe you could call him that instead?'

But Colin hadn't got a nice middle name; it was Albert. Colin Albert Peterson.

But even that hadn't stopped Sarah, although maybe on reflection it should have done, because his name was *exactly* what he was. Colin had always sounded like a small, mean, picky little name to Sarah, and Colin Albert Peterson, despite his hair and teeth and lack of disease, had turned out to be a small, mean, picky little man.

Colin was in his mid-thirties and worked at the University Library. Sarah had just turned thirty, and both of them had reached that point where they didn't want to have a relationship that wasn't going somewhere. Looking back at it now, had Sarah known exactly where this one was going, she'd have probably jumped ship and waited for another one to come along. But after a few nights out, a punt on the Cam and lots of giggling, drunken sex back at her flat, Sarah ended up falling in love with Colin. It seemed like the right thing to do.

7

Maybe nobody better was coming along; maybe this was it. Nobody told her not to and nobody seemed at all surprised when they decided to get married.

Sarah gradually persuaded herself that Colin's meanness was nothing more than good old-fashioned thrift, and his pickiness purely a matter of having strong moral values and high standards. You knew the rules with Colin; surely that really ought to make life easier and simpler? Sarah hadn't been able to come up with an excuse for Colin's small-mindedness so instead chose to ignore it, and concentrate instead on ensuring that their boys' minds were broad and wide as the Atlantic Ocean, and hoped that her own generous genes would dominate.

But there are some things you can't persuade yourself to believe, or ignore, or excuse, which meant there was just no way that Sarah could have stayed with Colin after their relationship hit the iceberg. Worse still, it had changed the way she looked at their cosy little terrace house with its pretty blue door and its cheery window boxes, and the long knock-through, double-aspected, whole-length-of-the-house kitchen in the cellar that she had planned out inch by loving inch, and the loft conversion Colin has insisted on, so that he could have an office and work from home and concentrate on writing his novel. It felt like the house had betrayed her almost as much as Colin.

Up until the iceberg, the house had been her safe harbour from the world, a place where the bears and the wolves were on the outside; at least they were right up until the moment Colin let one in. Sarah wondered if that was a metaphor too far. Whether it was or not, Sarah's life changed the moment she arrived home from picking up Alex from school, walked up the path and unlocked the front door. As she stepped into the hall, Sarah spotted Ms Peony Tyler, their next-door neighbour, upstairs on the landing wearing Sarah's new birthday bathrobe, a pair of killer heels, and very little else.

The Junoesque Ms Tyler with her bottle-blonde hair and ample thighs had come trip-trapping across the landing, heading towards the bathroom. Maddeningly, the first thought that struck Sarah as she stood in the hallway, when she spotted Peony in her red patent stilettos, was that Colin was usually very strict about people not wearing shoes in the house. The second was what a stupid name Peony was; Colin has sniggered about it when she'd first moved in and had popped round to introduce herself. He said that he thought

8

she had probably made it up to make herself sound more interesting, but apparently having a stupid name and big thighs was no impediment to adultery.

And as if adultery wasn't enough Peony had been carrying Big Bunny, their youngest son Alex's all-night-long well-worn comforter, which he had had since he was smaller than the rabbit – and was making him talk in a funny very un-Big Bunny voice to Colin, who was in their bedroom and consequently out of sight. Big Bunny would never have said those kind of things in a million years; Sarah was pretty sure that Big Bunny didn't even know those kind of words until he met Ms Tyler.

What made it all the worse was that Sarah might never have known about Colin and Peony if it weren't for Alex feeling unwell. Snuggling him up in the back of the car under a blanket Sarah had promised she would tuck Alex into bed just as soon as they got home, and read him a story and bring him a bowl of homemade ice-cream. Homemade ice-cream that would make even the poorliest boy feel better.

The school had told her they'd tried the house and that no one was picking up, and Sarah could clearly see that that was true. No one had picked up their knickers or their trousers, or their shirt or that nice blue jumper they had had for Christmas nor Ms Peony Tyler's huge pink frilly bra or anything else come to that.

As storming out with a sick child in tow was not really an option, Sarah had settled Alex – who fortunately didn't appear to have noticed Ms Tyler, which later made Sarah wonder if he had seen her there before – on the sofa in the sitting room. She slipped *Finding Nemo* into the DVD player, giving the ice-cream time to soften, the people upstairs time to rearrange themselves, and Big Bunny time to come to his senses.

The first thing Sarah did after Peony made her exit in a cloud of perfume, mixed with unspoken indignation at being caught, and no shame whatsoever, was to put Big Bunny to soak in a big bowl of nice warm soapy water.

Funny how things turn out; apparently Sarah and Colin didn't have a perfect unsinkable life after all, and when it came right down to it, it was *entirely* Sarah's fault that Colin was sleeping with Peony Tyler in the first place.

As Colin explained after Peony left, since they had had the boys Sarah just didn't seem to notice he was there, no, not at all, and the cooking had gone right off and he never had nicely ironed shirts hanging all ready and waiting in his wardrobe any more, and she showed no interest in his work and was too tired for proper sex – whatever that was – and *everyone* knew how important sex and real communication were in a relationship. And there was a button missing on his best jacket, which he had pointed out repeatedly, and she had done nothing, *nothing* about it. It was the perfect example of how little Sarah cared. How could she do this to him? And he objected to the way Sarah assumed he had nothing better to do than act as unpaid childcare for her and her children. All this in a stage whisper downstairs in the kitchen while Alex ate ice-cream and watched Nemo in the sitting room.

When Sarah pointed out to Colin that they were his children too, and that she had been working all the hours God sent for years to keep them afloat financially, giving him time to write his precious book and sleep late and stay up into the wee small hours smoking Gitanes out of his office window and writing his acceptance speech for the Man Booker prize, her husband had rounded her. He said that was just *typical*. He had always known that one day she would throw it all back in his face. He'd always known she was passive-aggressive and envious and jealous of his talent and the fact that he was writing a proper book, a *real* book, not knocking out popularist advertorial drivel for the kind of people who were moronic enough to shop at Hanleys. And all that *I'm a loving wife and a wonderful mother* crap didn't fool Colin for a moment, no, not one single solitary moment because he had always been able to see right through her to her cold dark envious selfish heart.

He said that Peony was a symptom of what was wrong with their marriage not the cause, and if Sarah had any kind of sense she would be able to see that, and while he wasn't proud of what he'd done, Colin was glad it was finally all out in the open. Glad. Sarah only had herself to blame for him screwing Peony. All of which had taken Sarah a little by surprise.

Could this be the same man who the week before had told her that she was the best thing that had ever happened to him? The man who said they were true soul mates, and the very moment he sold his book he planned to whisk them all away on a luxury holiday, pay off the mortgage and buy her a sports car? Was this the same man who said she worked too hard, and that he understood and *truly* appreciated the amazing efforts Sarah was making to keep their noses above water, and that once the novel was finished and made the bestseller list and the film rights were snapped up by Harrison Ford, everything would be all right? The same man who said that he never ever took her for granted, not for one for single solitary second? Apparently it was.

It was also pretty obvious that Alex had been swinging the lead to avoid P.E., which was apparently also Sarah's fault, because half way through Colin's big speech Alex came downstairs to the kitchen with an empty bowl to demand pizza and chips and wanted to know why Big Bunny was out on the linen line, soaking wet and swinging by his ears.

Vanilla Ice-Cream

Ingredients:
   4 medium egg yolks
   2 tsp of good vanilla essence
   1 can sweetened condensed milk (about 300g)
   500ml of double cream (one large carton/tub)

Method:
Whip egg yolks with vanilla essence. Add condensed milk and then, using an electric whisk, beat well until everything is incorporated.

In a separate Pyrex bowl (or similar) whip cream until it thickens and holds soft peaks. Scrape yolk mix into cream, whisking until well incorporated. Cover with cling film and put into freezer.

After an hour remove bowl from freezer and whisk again to break up the ice crystals and keep the mixture silky smooth. Cover and return to freezer.

Whisk again after another couple of hours. An hour later whisk again and then pour into suitable container with a lid for freezing. Allow to freeze.

Remove ice-cream from freezer 10 minutes or so before serving to allow to soften slightly. (This isn't soft scoop.)

Alternatively pour the mixture into an ice-cream maker and freeze according to manufacturer's instructions.

As this recipe uses raw egg yolks it is not recommended for babies or the elderly.

Chapter Two
The Green Shoots of Recovery

In the office the next morning, given what Rosa had said and the fact people were all a bit twitchy anyway, Sarah hadn't planned to tell anyone or say anything about Colin and the buxom Ms Tyler, but it was hard to disguise big red puffy eyes, the haunted look of a woman who hadn't slept a wink, and a heart so broken that shards of it kept breaking out in big snotty miserable sobs of pain. So Sarah told Melissa all about Colin and Peony, and Alex and the ice-cream and Big Bunny, all the while feeling as if she had accidentally walked onto a film set and found herself in the leading role of a life that most certainly wasn't hers.

Melissa kept shaking her head. 'I can't believe it,' she said, handing Sarah another tissue. 'I just can't believe it. I thought you and Colin were the real deal.'

'*You* can't believe it,' sobbed Sarah. 'How do you think I feel?'

'The bastard. What did he say?'

'That it's all my fault.'

Melissa's jaw dropped. 'You mean you *made* him sleep with Peony?'

'I don't think there was a lot of sleeping going on.'

'Bloody hell.' Melissa paused and then lowered her voice. 'Are you going to stay with him?'

'Why would I? Oh, I don't know,' said Sarah. 'I think I'm in shock. None of it feels real. It's like I've walked into someone else's life.'

Melissa nodded. 'You should go home and talk. Just the two of you. While the boys are at school. There's nothing spoiling here. I mean if you're throwing him out there's nothing to talk about but if you think you can work it out...' She let the idea hang between them.

Sarah shook her head. 'All we've done is talk; we talked all night. And cried. I've done a lot of crying. What am I going to say that's any different to what I've already said, Mel? I don't understand how he could do this to us. And what if I go home and she's there?' she continued miserably. 'Jiggling all that lumpy white flesh across the landing in my dressing gown.' Her head dropped into her hands. 'God, it was awful.'

Melissa stared at her. 'Surely he wouldn't invite her round after yesterday, would he?'

'Who knows? He might. What's to stop him? I keep wondering if Peony has been popping round every day as soon as I go to work. Or maybe he goes round there. Maybe they take it in turns. You know he encouraged me to come into the office more once the boys started school; he said it would do me good to get out, said working from home wasn't always healthy. Bastard. I mean, how long has this been going on? And what if she's not the first?'

'Colin, of all people; whoever would have thought it?' Melissa said, shaking her head.

'I feel like I don't know anything about him any more. How long has he been seeing her? When did it start? Does he love her? What if he loves her, Mel? And how come I didn't notice?' Sarah wailed. 'How did I miss something like that?'

'You could always ring,' Melissa suggested helpfully. 'Let him know you're on your way.'

'What? And give them a chance to get dressed?' said Sarah. 'I don't even want to think about it.'

'So what are you going to do now?'

Sarah sighed. 'I don't know. I really don't. I don't understand how he could do this to me and the boys? Am I that awful?'

Melissa handed Sarah another tissue. 'Of course you're not. Is there anything I can do – anything? What do you want?'

'For this not to have happened, for us to be back to how we were, but that's not going to happen, is it?' said Sarah.

'No,' said Melissa, shaking her head. 'No, it's not.

*

It went on for weeks, the pain, the tears and the big aching hurt in Sarah's chest. Along with the hurt was indignation, anger, humiliation, shame, fury, a huge sense of unreality and lots of other emotions that Sarah couldn't even find names for – but whatever they were called, they were exhausting and made her head and her heart ache.

There was simply no hiding place, no respite from the intense emotions and the sleepless nights. And then there were the long earnest conversations with Colin, going on late into the night, the tears – mostly hers – and the blame, mostly hers too apparently.

Colin kept saying that sleeping with Peony had been a wake-up call for them both, as if his infidelity was some of kind of unfortunate but unavoidable accident, which he generally considered to be a good thing – and kept on about how they should start over, draw a line under it. Move on. Which sounded fine in theory, but Sarah wasn't sure she wanted to move on. Move on to what, from where? From a place where she had been happy-ish but oblivious, to a place where they pretended it hadn't happened? Or where she held up her hands and agreed that yes, it was all her fault after all?

The one time they tried to have sex, after a weepy evening and a bottle of Rioja, all Sarah could see when she closed her eyes was Peony Tyler in her stilettos, and suspected from the expression on Colin's face, his eyes screwed tight shut, that he was desperately trying to conjure up the same image. And through it all he never once said he was sorry, never once said he had stopped seeing Peony nor that it had all been a terrible mistake. Not once.

It was never going to work, and who wanted to live with something that wasn't going to work, so broken that it was barely limping along? If their marriage had been a dog they would have had it put it out of its misery.

Nonetheless Colin insisted that they went for counselling, privately, to a woman who had been recommended to him and who charged an arm and a leg. Her name was Goold, Ms Goold. During their first and only session Ms Goold steepled her long bony fingers and said, 'You have to understand, Sarah, that Colin feels as if he lost himself when he lost his job.'

Ms Goold's office was lined with books and had a Scandinavian feel to it, all dark moody panelled wood and strange orange and brown Nordic rugs. It was like being counselled on the set of *The Killing*.

'But he didn't lose his job, he jacked it in so he could write a book,' Sarah protested incredulously. At which point the counsellor had sighed and exchanged meaningful glances with Colin, and suggested that Sarah had a lot of issues that she needed to work through. Couldn't she see how emasculated poor dear Colin felt?

Not emasculated enough to stop him shagging Peony Tyler, Sarah had pointed out.

'See,' Colin snapped, like a spoilt child, waving his finger at Sarah. 'See what she's like? Judgemental, spiteful. I feel so trapped inside this marriage. It's all *so* claustrophobic. She is stifling my creativity, and what can I do if I can't write?' he whimpered.

'You could try emptying the dishwasher,' suggested Sarah. 'Or maybe whipping the Hoover round once in a while? I mean, it wouldn't hurt, would it? Worst case scenario, how about you go back to work, then maybe you wouldn't feel lost after all?'

They both stared at her.

Sarah had anger issues apparently. Too bloody right, she thought as she handed over her debit card to the stuck-up girl in reception, who enquired whether Sarah wanted to book a course of sessions. Sarah raised her eyebrows and held her gaze; the girl didn't ask again.

And then the house turned on her. When they arrived back home – Colin wasn't talking to her – for the first time Sarah noticed the peeling paintwork and the damp patch under the eves, the sagging gutter and the ill-fitting windows, which no longer meant that they had to snuggle up close to each other, but instead just let in the draughts. How could you stay in a house that had conspired against you? A house that knew all those secrets and had said nothing? Sarah lay awake all night thinking about what Ms Goold had said.

'I want a divorce,' Sarah said, as she passed Colin on the stairs the following morning as she was leaving for work.

Colin stared at her. 'What's that supposed to mean?' He was still in his dressing gown and carrying a mug of coffee. The boys were sitting waiting in the car, lunches packed, P.E. kits ready.

'I'm sure that you can work it out, Colin, and if you can't then I'm certain that Ms Goold will help you translate.'

Colin sighed. 'You see, there you go again. That's the problem, Sarah, you're just so negative about all this. You can't see what's going on here, can you? I know things are a little tricky at the moment, but you don't see the bigger picture. This isn't about Peony or what was going on between us. It's about you and me and about your attitude. I'm sure that together we can work it out. I'm certain that we can make this marriage work, Sarah, I really am,' he said.

'Up until you shagged Peony Tyler I thought it was working, *that's* the problem, Colin,' said Sarah, buttoning up her coat.

'Oh, that's it, just rub it in, why don't you?'

'I'm not rubbing it in. I'm stating a fact, Colin. And anyway after all those things you said about feeling trapped I thought you'd be relieved that it was finally all over.' Sarah picked up her handbag, keeping her tone very even and calm without a hint of emotion, although inside she was a complete mess.

Colin paled. 'You can't be serious; you can't do this. You can't mean it. Ms Goold said that we could work it out. She said that you needed to try harder.'

'I was already trying as hard as I could,' said Sarah sadly.

'But I thought—'

'You thought what?' said Sarah, finally at the end of her tether. 'You thought that you could carry on living here with me while you wrote your fucking book and screwed Peony Tyler as well? That for some reason I wouldn't mind? That I'd just keep on paying the bills and keeping house and it would all be all right? And when you got caught that somehow you could use some imagined guilt on my part to make it all my fault? Well it isn't my fault, Colin. It really truly isn't. Peony Tyler is welcome to you. You keep on about us needing a wake-up call, well, I've had mine – this is yours. I want a divorce and I'm going to put the house on the market.'

His jaw dropped. 'What? What do you mean, put the house on the market? You can't. What am I going to do?'

'Well unless you can come up with another idea we'll have to. We can't afford to live here, Colin, we both know that. We haven't been able to afford to live here since you stopped work. We've barely been scraping by, but I thought it was worth it, all the going without and the penny-pinching and dipping into our savings, because we were doing it for *us,* and that it would all come right in the end. But it didn't, did it? And to be honest I'm totally sick of it. I'm calling my solicitor this morning.'

'But where am I going to live?' he whined.

Not *I'll get a job*, not *but, what about the boys*, not even *I'm sorry*, but *where am I going to live?*

'I don't know and I don't care,' she said, the words taking her by surprise almost as much as they did Colin. 'I'll be back at six; don't forget you're supposed to be picking the boys up from school this afternoon,' Sarah added, and with that closed the door behind her.

*

In the office Melissa handed Sarah a mug of tea and the box of tissues and said, 'I've got a cousin. I think you probably met him,

Kit? A big tall guy – long arms? We used to call him Monkey Boy when we were kids. Anyway he's lovely, a bit dippy.'

'Don't think I'm not grateful, Mel,' said Sarah, blowing her nose. 'But it's probably a bit early to start dating.'

'I didn't mean as a date, you idiot, even I'm not that insensitive. No, I was thinking about somewhere for you and the boys to live when you sell your place. I know it's early days but it would be good to have something sorted out.'

Sarah nodded.

'Kit's got this fantastic rambling old house at Newnham Magna. And I know he's got a cottage he's been trying to rent for ages, because he keeps phoning my mum and telling her it would be perfect for me. Didn't we go there for party once, a long time ago – you and me and...'

Melissa stopped abruptly. Sarah could see that she had been about to say *Colin* but had managed to hold it in, which was a good thing because Sarah was sick of everything being about Colin. How could something hurt so much and not kill you?

'I could ring Kit if you like,' Melissa offered. 'See if the cottage is still empty. What do you think?'

Sarah hesitated, wondering if she really wanted to sell the house. Maybe now wasn't a good time to make any snap decisions. Maybe she should let the dust settle; or maybe she should throw Colin out, not that that would help with the state of her finances, or maybe she should wait a bit longer. Maybe she should just go round next door and punch Peony Tyler and then tell her if she wanted Colin and his small picky little mind she could bloody well have him. Maybe.

Since the iceberg and not counting their one attempt at make-up sex, Colin had been sleeping in his office on the sofa that Sarah had bought as a surprise Christmas present after he spotted it in a junk shop and said how much he loved it. It was a classic, he'd said. It was also extremely uncomfortable, which served him right.

Watching him head back upstairs in his dressing gown before she left for work, Sarah had suspected Colin would be heading off next door to Peony's the minute she'd gone. He probably wouldn't even bother getting dressed.

They couldn't go on like this. She couldn't live with him in that house any more. Maybe she should go and take a look at Kit's cottage.

In between editing an article on the perfect capsule wardrobe and the perils and joys of buying a beach hut for Hanleys in-house magazine, Sarah went online and transferred every penny she could into her personal savings account and noted that at some time during the morning Colin had updated his Facebook status from 'married' to 'it's complicated'.

'So what do you think?' asked Melissa, when they nipped into town to grab a sandwich for lunch.

Sarah stared at her and pulled a face. 'About what?' She had to get a grip and stop re-running *Colin is a bastard* movies in her head.

'About Kit and the cottage. You must remember him?' Melissa insisted. 'We went there when you still lived in that flat down by the station. Come on, Sarah? He had this big Georgian place with a terrace all along the back?'

Something was stirring deep in Sarah's memory. 'Did we get lost and I had to reverse up a lane?' she said, trying hard to remember, if only to humour Melissa.

Melissa nodded. 'Yes, that's it. This cottage of his is really cheap, and it can't be more than fifteen minutes from Cambridge, if that – and there's a fabulous village school.'

'I haven't even put the house on the market yet.'

'I know but property in Cambridge usually shifts fast – and even if it doesn't, it wouldn't hurt to look round, would it? Kit's worried that if someone doesn't live in it, it'll get vandalised or deteriorate or get overrun with field mice and bats. It's a lovely old place, bags of character. It just needs someone to live in it.'

'So why doesn't he just advertise it? It sounds like it would get snapped up.'

'I know, I've said that, but that's not really Kit's style. He's frightened of getting people he hates in there. He'd prefer to let it to someone he knows or a friend of a friend.'

'And you know all this *because*?'

'Because he really wants me to live in it and keeps phoning up my mum to tell her that it would be ideal for me.'

'And you don't want to?'

'No, of course not, first of all he's my cousin and it just seems like a creepy thing to do – and I'm practically living with Josh, and I don't want Kit talking to my mother about me or him. She thinks Kit's sweet, but the man is such a gossip. I just don't want him telling her

19

things about me. And anyway I hate owls, and bats, and the country and all that creepy crawly squawky in the night stuff.'

'And you think I don't?' asked Sarah.

Melissa nodded. 'Oh, come on. You're a natural for the country life, and the boys will love it. You could at least go and look. Try it out for size. See what you think. It would give you something to think about even if you don't take it. Show Colin that you mean business.' Melissa paused. 'I still can't believe he blames you for him sleeping with someone else.'

And before she knew it, Sarah was sobbing again, in the middle of the street on the way to buy a sandwich for heaven's sake. She sniffed and pulled a wad of tissues out of her handbag. All the sobbing was getting on her nerves; God alone knew what it was doing to her friend.

'I'll ring Kit now,' said Melissa, rootling around for her phone in her handbag.

Sarah shook her head. 'I'm not sure. I don't know. The house might take months to sell.'

Melissa rang anyway.

It was May, which in a nutshell meant asparagus and weddings in Hanleys in-store magazine. They were running a double-page spread of recipes, along with a feature on local growers. And the rest of the magazine was basically a wall-to-wall feature on the perfect wedding day, to coincide with their big national in-store promotion. Hanleys could sell you the dream right up to and including the dress, the champagne and the cake, even the honeymoon.

Miserably, Sarah glanced up at the images from this month's magazine that lined the walls in the office reception area. There wasn't a single picture of asparagus but there were a lot of very happy-looking brides. It was weddings all the way. Sarah had written most of the copy and chosen the pictures. She had cooed on about wedded bliss, crystal accents and romantic floral table centres, about sharing the best day of your life with the man of your dreams.

Directly opposite her desk was this month's cover, an informal shot of the bride and groom laughing at their reception, with the shout line 'Let Hanleys help deliver your very own happy ever after'. Sarah hadn't noticed it until now but the groom looked a lot like

Colin and the bride bore more than a passing resemblance to Big Bunny. It was almost more than she could bear.

*

The house was barely on the market a week before they had an offer at the asking price.

*

Green Shoots Oven-Baked Risotto

Serves 4 as a main course

Ingredients:
6oz (175g) risotto rice
3oz (75g) butter
1 onion, peeled and finely chopped
1 small glass (3oz or 75ml) of white wine
1pt (500ml) vegetable or chicken stock
1 bundle of asparagus, approx. 6oz (175g) – choose a bundle with similar diameter stems. Cut into 1-inch (25mm) lengths
3oz (75g) frozen peas
1 bunch spring onions, trimmed and chopped
4oz (100g) Pecorino cheese (you can use Parmesan or even a crisp very mature Cheddar at a push), grated finely
1 bunch of chives, washed and chopped (scissors work really well)
Salt and black pepper

Medium-sized ovenproof dish, baking tray

Method:
Heat oven to 150C, 300F or gas mark 2

Melt butter in a saucepan, add chopped onion and cook very gently for 5–7 minutes until soft and golden (don't brown).

Add the rice to the saucepan, stirring gently until all the grains are coated in butter.
Add white wine and stock, bring to a simmer and then tip the whole lot very gently into the ovenproof dish (I find it easier to handle if

21

you stand the dish on a baking tray to make it easier to lift in and out of the oven).

Add a good pinch of salt and freshly ground pepper.

Stir and then slide the dish on its baking tray into the centre of the oven.

Cook uncovered for 20 minutes.

Remove risotto from the oven, stir in the chopped asparagus, the spring onions and two heaped tbsp of Pecorino cheese.

Stir the rice gently to distribute all the goodies.

Slide back into the oven, uncovered, for a further 12 minutes.

Take out of the oven and add frozen peas, stir gently and return to oven for another 3 or 4 minutes till the peas are cooked but not wrinkly.

Remove the dish from the oven and sprinkle with chopped chives, gently stir through the rice.

Serve straight away with the remainder of the grated Pecorino, some crispy bread and a glass or two of the remaining white wine.

Chapter Three
Comfort Food

Never ever go to see a house in May. Going to see a house in May is the most terrible mistake. In May the sun is finally out of hiding after the long grey days of late winter and brings with it the full flush of spring and the whisper of high summer to come. Life shows real promise in May, even if your heart is broken. Things are bursting out, the bluebells, and climbers and creepers are climbing and creeping and swelling out from their lush fat green buds.

In May, with the first real heat of the sun on your back and all that rampant possibility, you don't notice windows that don't shut, baths that don't empty, boilers that don't boil, and doors with gaps under them that are so far off the ground that, come November, snow will blow in and pile up on your rugs and frost-blast your ankles. What you notice instead is the apple tree in blossom at the far end of the garden with its rope swing, and the brook babbling away beyond it, shallow and clear as gin, with gravel rills that promise hours of summer fun and paddling and don't give a hint of damp walls or the threat of flooding to come.

In May, what Sarah saw when they pulled up outside the cottage in Melissa's car, with the boys in the back, was all that and the trees in new leaf and the honeysuckle hedges and the lead lights, framed by climbing roses, the sleepy dormer windows tucked up under the sloping eaves, the lush green lawn, the old roses and the daisies, and all of it a million miles away emotionally from Colin and the house in Cambridge.

It looked like heaven. As Sarah got out of the car she heard birdsong and imagined waking under a fluffy white duvet in her big brass bed, in a sunlit room with a sloping ceiling, feeling safe and strong and mended. Woken not by a broken heart, a crippling sense of hurt and white-hot fury, but by the sounds of the stream busy bubbling by, and the dawn chorus, and knowing that life could get better after all. Just the very idea of it made her feel like a weight had been lifted off her shoulders.

It was practically a done deal before Sarah had even opened the little rustic gate and wandered up the garden path. The boys trailed in behind her, and as the cottage was empty, ran off to explore the garden, whooping and laughing across the unkempt grass, looking for all the world like a shot from one of Hanleys healthy lifestyle promotions. Within minutes Harry and Alex had found the stream.

'Can we go in for a paddle?' asked Harry, peering into the water.

Sarah was about to say no when Melissa piped up, 'They'll be fine. It's not very deep along this bit, right down to the ford and the footbridge. We used to play in it when we were kids. Just stay where we can see you, all right?'

The boys nodded and moments later were busy peeling off their shoes and socks and paddling into the chilly gravelly shallows.

'Mum, look, look, there are fish,' yelled Harry, jumping up and down in delight.

'Be very careful,' shouted Sarah.

She put a hand to her brow to shade her eyes and took a long slow look round. 'It's a bit out of the way.'

Melissa laughed. 'Bus stop at the end of the lane; you're fifteen minutes' drive out of Cambridge, tops. Stop trying to talk yourself out of it, Sarah. It's perfect and you know it is. Trees, garden, chocolate-box cottage. What's not to like?'

'I don't think we could get all our furniture in.'

'What you've got left after the great divorce divvie up, you mean?' said Melissa.

Sarah stared at her. 'God, I hadn't thought about that, I'll have to talk to Colin about what he wants,' she said miserably, thinking about all the things in her house that she loved. There was the pine tallboy and the linen chest that she had hand-stripped in the garden when they first moved in, and the big Edwardian brass bed she had bought in a house clearance sale, the kitchen table, the six mismatched chairs she'd rescued from a skip, scrubbed and lovingly re-stained and recovered; her fridge, her chopping block, the little dressing table she had found at a flea market, that the man hadn't got room for on his van and had sold her for a tenner. They were only *things*, but they were her things. Surely Colin wouldn't want them?

As if reading Sarah's thoughts Melissa slipped an arm through hers. 'My advice is just take the things you really love and can't live without and leave Colin the rest. Oh, and take photographs to prove it. I don't know why but men always accuse you of taking all the good stuff and some hideous family heirloom that you wouldn't give shed room to. Trust me, I've been there.'

'What was it?' asked Sarah, conversationally.

'His great-uncle Victor's writing desk. Bloody great thing, pug ugly. Weighed a ton.' She paused. 'Mind you, I got three hundred quid for it.'

Twenty minutes late, which was to prove a sign of things to come, Kit rolled up in his battered green Discovery.

As soon as she saw him Sarah knew that she definitely hadn't met Kit before, despite what Melissa said, and having most certainly been to his party with Colin. She was certain because if she *had* met Kit before she would have remembered him. Kit Roseberry was probably the closest thing to unforgettable that Sarah had ever come across.

He was very tall, very handsome and had shoulders that would make most grown women purr with pleasure – even a heartbroken woman who was worried about who was going to get custody of her furniture.

Kit had thick dark wavy hair brushed back off a nicely made face, and with just enough wrinkles around his eyes to make him look outdoorsy and good-humoured. He was muscular with long legs and was dressed in jeans and a cream open-necked collarless shirt that emphasised his tan and revealed enough of his hairy chest to make the curious want to see more, but the *real* clincher was that, despite his size and rugged appearance, there was something in Kit's big puppy-like brown eyes that made you want to take him home and take care of him.

Sarah tried hard not to stare. She could only think that maybe she and Colin had been to the party when they were first going out together, when they only had eyes for each other, when they were falling in love. Annoyingly she felt her bottom lip trembling and stifled a sob as Kit loped across the grass towards them.

'Hi,' he said. 'Sorry, I'm a bit late.' A black Labrador and a springer spaniel followed him across the lawn.

Melissa sighed. 'Hello, Kit, I thought you'd forgotten.'

'Nice to see you again too, sweetie,' he said, bending over to kiss Melissa on both cheeks, before turning his attention to Sarah. 'Hi, I'm Kit.' He extended a hand. 'I'm really sorry I'm late. I got held up. Anyway I've got the keys here if you want to take a look around inside.'

He waited for the boys to dry their feet on the grass and told them they could catch the fish if they lived there and that there was a tree

25

house in the woods that he had grown out of if they ever felt the need for a den, and then they all followed him up to the cottage.

Kit unlocked the front door and stood to one side to let the women in. He had to stoop to avoid banging his head on the lintel. It was really hard, even with a broken heart, for Sarah not to fantasise about what it might be like to be swept up in those big strong arms and carried across the threshold.

She closed her eyes and made an effort to clear her mind, concentrating instead on how potentially tricky it would be to get her Smeg fridge in through the front door. This was really not the moment for lusting after strange men, however tall and handsome, but perhaps it proved that Colin was right after all, and that they really weren't happy.

Meanwhile Melissa and the boys were off and looking around.

'Are you okay?' asked Kit.

Sarah nodded and followed him from room to room while he gave her the grand tour, not that there was that much to see, but what there was she liked. A lot. Downstairs there was a largish sitting room, with a window seat and an inglenook fireplace with a high hearth and a wood burner set into it. Across the hallway, which was home to the stairs, was a square kitchen the same size as the sitting room with a range, and beyond that was a tiny utility room, and toilet. Upstairs there was one big bedroom, two smaller ones, a tiny box room and bathroom. It might not be big but it was beautiful and looked idyllic and inviting – but then again it was May.

While the grown-ups talked about things like rent and council tax and tenancy agreements, the dogs, Jet and Meg, played chase in the garden with Alex and Harry, while Sarah watched them.

As if reading her mind, Kit said, 'The boys will love it here. It's a great place to grow up. The local school is really good. I don't mind if they want pets and there's room for a pony if you want one. We've got a couple of stables up at the house going begging. You can have the cottage for as long as it suits you.' He smiled warmly. 'It would be great to have a family in here again and Mel told me that you're a really good person.'

Sarah made an effort not to cry; Kit made an effort not to notice.

'There is some work that needs doing on the cottage but we can get that sorted out. You'll probably need to give me a list and nag me a bit.' He paused, leaving Sarah space to say something.

Sarah took a deep breath. 'I'll take it,' she said, all the while imagining that any second now she would wake up and find that the last few weeks had all been a terrible dream.

'Really?' said Melissa in surprise. 'Don't you want time to think about it?'

'That's great. When can you move in?' asked Kit before she had a chance to reply.

'Next weekend,' said Sarah confidently.

'Can we have a dog?' asked Harry, running in with Kit's two hounds hard on his heels.

'Maybe,' said Kit, before Sarah could say no.

*

'I can just rent the cottage for a few months,' said Sarah, as they took another walk around the garden after Kit had left. 'It's cheap enough and I'll have to move out sooner or later. The house is in the process of being sold. Maybe it's the stepping stone I need. I could take it for the summer. The boys would love it. It would be like a holiday. Just till I find somewhere permanent. It'll give me a breathing space and somewhere to let the dust settle.'

Melissa stuffed her hands into the pockets of her jacket. 'Are you sure?'

'The people who want the house are cash buyers; they want to be in as soon as possible.'

Melissa didn't reply, which was unusual.

'I'll need to organise a van and some muscle.'

'Don't you think you ought to talk to your solicitor first?' asked Melissa.

'I've got an appointment tomorrow. And anyway, this was your idea.'

'I know, but I didn't think you'd just up and say yes like that. It's not like you. You're always so sensible. I thought you'd go away and think about it, mull it over.'

Sarah's shoulders slumped. 'I know but I've got to do something. I can't just wait for something to happen, I need to be the one to make it happen. If I don't then Colin will think it's okay to carry on like we are, and we can't go on like this. We can't. The cottage is lovely and you're right, it will be great for the boys.'

'And what about school?'

'I was thinking I'd keep them where they are for the time being, to minimise the disruption. I'll drive them in and drop them off. And I can do most of my work from home; that was what was in my original contract. I was only really coming in to the office because Colin thought it would do me good to get out of the house.' Sarah shook head. 'And a lot of good it did me. How could I have been so stupid? I need to talk to Rosa about it, but I'm sure it will be okay. Aren't you? And then I can move schools in September if we decide to stay. I'll talk to their class teacher about after-school club. Lots of their friends go, they've been wanting to go for ages—'

'If you're sure,' said Melissa.

'It'll be fine,' Sarah said, with a confidence she didn't quite feel.

When Sarah got home – she had texted Colin to say that she would be late – he had left a note propped up on the kitchen table saying how hurt and how very, *very* sad he was that it had come to this, and how he thought it was best if he went to stay with friends for a while, until things were sorted out, because he couldn't bear her constant accusations, that look on her face and her trying to make it seem like it was all his fault. Colin was certain she would understand. Oh, and the estate agent had rung but he had been far too upset to talk to him. Sarah turned the note over in her fingers, and then rang him.

'Colin, I've found a cottage to rent,' she said before he had a chance to say anything. 'We need to talk about the furniture and—'

'Anything you have to say to me I'd rather you said it through my solicitor.'

'You want to pay him to talk about the furniture?'

At the far end of the line she heard Colin sigh.

*

'Are we going to live in the cottage with the man with the dogs?' asked Alex, as she dished up their supper.

'Yes,' said Sarah. 'But not with the man and the dogs, honey; it's just that Kit is the man who owns the cottage. We'll be living there on our own.'

'That's good,' said Alex. 'Because I don't think Daddy would like it if the other man was there.'

'Probably not,' thought Sarah, sliding a poached egg onto Alex's toast.

How to Cook the Perfect Poached Egg

Ingredients:

Eggs (use the freshest you can)
2 tsp of vinegar

Method:

Heat water in a frying pan until fine bubbles just start to form on the bottom of the pan.

Add vinegar to water.

Crack the eggs into a cup one at a time, and getting it as close to the water as you can, drop each egg into the water.

With a spoon ease the white close to the yolk to make a tidy shape and help the whole thing stay together.

Allow to simmer gently for a minute.
Turn off heat and allow the eggs to sit in the water for up to 10 minutes.

Using a slotted spoon remove the eggs. Drain well.
Serve with lots of hot buttered toast

Chapter Four
The First Supper

Over the next few days Sarah expected Colin to call her; she expected him to tell her where he was and when he would be back. She thought he might ring to apologise, to say how very, very sorry he was for behaving so badly and how much he loved her and how the very last thing he wanted was to lose her and the house. When he didn't, Sarah left a message on his phone to let him know what was going on, rang the estate agent back, went to see her solicitor, talked to the boys, booked a man with a van, and a handyman, and began to sort out the things she wanted to take with her to the cottage.

When Colin finally rang bright and early on Saturday morning, Sarah was in the kitchen with Melissa, putting the last few things, the kettle and mugs, teabags, milk and coffee, into the last box from the kitchen and when she saw the number on the caller display let it go to voicemail. By then it was far too late. The Titanic when it went, went down fast.

'Will Daddy come and see us?' asked Alex, carrying a box of toys out to the van.

'You'll see lots of him. I promise. I'll bring you into town to see him and he'll pick you up after school some days, just like now,' said Sarah, injecting her voice with a cheery upbeat tone and hoping it was true. According to the message he had left on her phone, Colin was apparently away, although Sarah wasn't sure exactly what that meant.

Alex stopped to consider his mother's answer. 'Will Daddy still be living at our old house?'

'No, darling, he won't. We've sold this house, so he'll be moving too.'

'So someone else is going to have my bedroom?'

'Probably.'

Harry went sailing past with a box of his own. 'They're getting divorced, and then we'll get a new daddy.'

Alex's eyes widened in horror. 'But I like the one I've got,' he said.

Sarah smiled. 'Of course you do, darling, and so you should. And he will always be your daddy and always love you. And we're not getting another one, Harry.'

Harry skipped past on his way back to get another load. 'Tom Ferguson's old dad bought him a quad bike when his mum and dad got divorced, so Tom's new dad took them all to Disneyland,' he said knowledgeably. 'In America.'

Alex looked horrified. 'We haven't got to go to America, have we?' he whispered, as a single tear rolled down his cheek.

Sarah could barely speak in case her heart broke right there in front of him. 'Of course we haven't, sweetie. We're just going to be a little drive away at the cottage. You liked the cottage, remember. And you can come and see your daddy lots.'

Alex looked up at her. 'You promise?'

Sarah nodded. 'I promise.'

Once the man with the van had left with the furniture and all her worldly goods, Sarah took a last look around the house, walking slowly from room to room, straightening the curtains, checking the cupboards, while the boys waited for her in the car. Even though she had left a lot of the furniture the place felt hollow and dead, which was pretty much how Sarah felt.

'Are you going to cry?' asked Melissa.

Taken by surprise Sarah turned round. 'Oh, I didn't hear you there.'

Melissa smiled and offered her a small box. 'I brought plenty of tissues.'

Sarah shook her head. 'I'm not sure I've got any tears left.'

Melissa hugged her. 'It's going to be fine. Come on. Let's get going.'

Sarah walked round one more time, trailing her fingers over pieces of furniture she had seen every day for years and now would probably never see again. Melissa touched her arm. 'I'll go and keep an eye on the boys.'

When she finally locked the front door, Sarah glanced across to Peony Tyler's house and wondered, fleetingly, if Colin was inside watching them. The idea came from nowhere and for a moment took her breath away and then, just in case he really was there, she made the effort to paint on a happy face and picking up her bag headed down the path towards the car with a spring in her step, and as she did, there was a part of her that really, really hoped he was watching.

'See you at the cottage,' said Melissa, heading for her car as Sarah arrived at the kerb. She nodded and followed Melissa out into the traffic. They caught up with the van after a couple of miles and she and Melissa drove in convoy out to Newnham Magna.

It seemed strange that her whole life could be packed into one measly van. Despite it being May, it turned chilly by mid-afternoon, and once they had unloaded everything from the van and the cars, Melissa lit the fire in the sitting room and made up the beds for Sarah and the boys, while Sarah set to emptying the boxes and putting things away in the kitchen.

The handyman turned up at three, so by late afternoon the pictures were up, the rugs were down, the TV in, the sofas arranged around the stove in the sitting room, cushions were plumped, the table and chairs settled in the kitchen, the cooker was wired in, the washing machine all neatly plumbed in, in the utility room, and the cottage was beginning to look, if not feel, like home. It had been a long and very busy day.

Kit had arrived after six with a bottle of wine – just as Sarah was sliding a heavy terracotta dish out of the oven and onto the farmhouse table, which looked just about perfect in the middle of the cottage kitchen.

'That smells amazing,' Kit said, as he knocked and then walked in, uninvited, through the back door. The dogs trailed in behind him and made themselves at home on the rugs by the range.

'Oh, hi,' said Sarah. 'Come in. I'm afraid the place is still a bit of a state.'

'Not at all. It looks fantastic,' he said. 'I would have been round earlier to give you a hand but I'd got a meeting in London.' Even though he was speaking to Sarah his attention was firmly fixed on the table and their meal.

Steam rose up from the dish carrying rich smells of supper with it. Kit leaned over to breathe it in. 'Oh, wow,' he said with a grin. 'Melissa didn't tell me that you could cook. And you've been so busy,' he said, glancing round appreciatively. 'It looks like you've been here for months. You've made it really cosy in here.'

Sarah felt herself redden.

But he was right. The cupboards were full, the clock and her big blackboard were up on the wall, hung from the hooks that were already there, and there were rag rugs down on the flagstone floor. It did look good and it felt good too.

Sarah smiled and backhanded a stray tendril of hair off her face. 'Thanks, it feels like I'm running on fumes at the moment. We're just about to eat. Melissa is in the sitting room with the boys if you want to go through.'

'No, I'm fine just here,' said Kit with a grin, handing her the bottle of wine. 'I thought I'd nip down and bring you something to celebrate with. A little housewarming present.'

'Thank you,' said Sarah.

Melissa appeared in the doorway carrying a log basket. 'I thought I heard your voice. Classic Kit: turning up too late to help with the heavy lifting but here in time for the food. You want to fill this up?' She held the basket out towards him.

'I will in a minute. I was just admiring supper. How do you make it?' he asked Sarah, while producing a corkscrew from his pocket.

Melissa stood the basket by the door and laughed. 'Go on, tell him, Sarah. He loves food, don't you, Kit? Anything is better than shifting logs.'

'It's easy,' said Sarah. 'You just slice up a whole chistorra de Pamplona into a big pan—'

He pulled a face. 'Which is what, exactly?'

'A sort of chorizo, it comes in a long horseshoe shape and then…' She stopped. Kit was staring down at the golden brown crust and breathing deeply.

'It smells wonderful.'

How could Sarah possibly resist? 'Do you want to stay and eat with us?' she said.

'I thought you'd never ask,' Kit replied. 'Have you unpacked the wine glasses yet?'

'Over there in the cupboard by the door,' Melissa said, rolling her eyes.

'Good show,' said Kit, slipping off his jacket.

'But you can't eat till you've got the logs in. Sarah can sort the wine out, can't you? And I've got to be making a move,' said Melissa, taking her cardigan from the back of one of the chairs. 'Josh will wonder where the hell I've got to. I'll call you first thing tomorrow, Sarah. Let me know if you need anything.'

'But I thought you were staying for supper?' protested Sarah in surprise, pointing towards the dish. 'There's plenty. I made loads.'

Melissa winked. 'I know, but five's a crowd,' she said, and with that she was gone.

Gnocchi and Spinach Bake

Serves 4-6

Ingredients:

1 chistorra de Pamplona cut into ½–1-inch slices

2 cloves of garlic, finely chopped

400g can of chopped plum tomatoes

300g fresh spinach

500g gnocchi cooked and drained as per manufacturer's instructions

1 buffalo mozzarella

Salt and pepper to taste (optional)

Method:

Heat oven to 180C, 350F, gas mark 4.

In a large pan – a wok is ideal – gently dry-fry the sliced chistorra and garlic over a medium heat, allowing the oil to seep out. Cook for around 3–5 minutes without browning.

Add the can of chopped tomatoes. Gradually add spinach, a handful at a time, allowing it to wilt before adding another handful. Stir between handfuls.

Cover and simmer for a few minutes on a low heat, stirring occasionally. Allow to reduce and thicken a little.

Take off heat and gently fold in the cooked gnocchi.

Adjust seasoning. (Sometimes I add a grind of pepper but the chorizo adds most required seasoning.)

Pour into a large ovenproof dish.

Cut buffalo mozzarella into slices and then tear into chunks. Dot the top of the dish with mozzarella.

Bake for around 30–40 minutes until the top is golden brown.

Serve piping hot.

This is *fabulous* reheated in a frying pan the next day, served with eggs and bacon.

Chapter Five
Newts and Bacon

There are moments in almost every life when the things that are going on around you don't feel quite real. Sometimes the feeling lasts for just a few seconds, other times for minutes. Sometimes a day. Sarah felt that way the whole summer long, as May and the Whitsun school holidays slipped seamlessly into June, and the cottage and the boys and her life slowly blossomed. The cottage felt like a sanctuary, a safe haven where the days were long and the walks were sunny and every day felt like a holiday.

It began the very first morning after they moved in. Sarah was woken up by the sun streaming in through the dormer windows in her bedroom, and the sounds of the birdsong and the boys laughing and talking, already up and awake and apparently playing outside in the garden.

The garden. Sarah sat bolt upright in bed and then, full of fear, she leapt out of bed and ran to the window, wondering how it was she had slept so long, and why the boys hadn't woken her and what Colin – the all-seeing, all-knowing fantasy Colin who cared about such things and wouldn't dream of sleeping with his neighbours – would think of her first attempt at single parenting. How the hell had they got into the garden on their own without her hearing them? She peered outside.

It was the most perfect blue-sky-dappled-sunlight kind of a morning. Out in the garden Alex and Harry, who were still in their pyjamas, were standing on the side of the riverbank with Kit. All three of them had shrimping nets and jam jars. All three of them were laughing.

As Sarah watched, Harry held up his jam jar and then peered at it with a giant magnifying glass that could only have come from Kit, and pointed to something in the water, which had everyone laughing even more. The dogs were there too, wagging and woofing and happily bumbling in and out of the water, carrying sticks and adding to the general jollity.

Hastily, Sarah dragged on a dressing gown over her pyjamas and headed downstairs. The kitchen was still littered with the remains of supper, not to mention the second bottle of wine she had opened when the boys had gone to bed, when Kit had lingered over the dishes to listen to the story of Colin, Peony and Big Bunny. Sarah winced.

At the back door she stopped long enough to check the clock and pull on a pair of wellies – the only outdoor shoes in sight – and hurried out across the garden. It was already getting warm, mist was rising from the dew-soaked lawn, and there was a smell of new-mown grass in the air.

'What on earth do you think you are doing?' she said to Kit. 'They're supposed to be inside asleep in bed.'

'Morning,' said Kit, grinning as he pushed the hair back off his face. 'I brought you a net and a jar too, if you want one,' he added, swooping down to retrieve them from amongst the well-trodden grass. 'Here we are.' He held them out towards her. 'The boys had first pick I'm afraid. The handle on this one is a bit tricky. Be fine with a bit of tape. Have you got any tape?'

Sarah pointedly ignored the gifts. 'Have you got any idea what time it is?' she snapped.

'I told you she was grumpy in the morning,' said Harry, his gaze still fixed on the contents of his glass jar.

'I found the nets in the shed and I thought you and the boys might like them,' said Kit, as if she hadn't spoken.

'And what? You were just passing and thought you'd drop them off?'

'Yes – I...' He stopped, when he caught sight of her expression.

'It's seven o'clock on a Sunday morning, Kit.'

'He threw stones up at our window,' said Harry. 'You know, like they do in the films.'

Sarah glared at Kit, who at least had the good grace to look uncomfortable. 'I thought you might like a bit of a lie-in, after yesterday,' he said.

'Have you any idea just how long it takes to make a child understand that they're not supposed to go anywhere with strangers?' Sarah demanded. 'To explain to them that someone being nice and giving you things doesn't necessarily make them a good person?'

'Ah,' said Kit. 'Yes, gosh. I'm sorry about that. I didn't think. Sorry.' He glanced at the boys. 'I didn't think.'

Sarah pulled herself up to her full height and folded her arms across her chest.

Kit flinched.

'It was just that it was too good a morning to be in bed,' he said. 'I was planning on walking the dogs down to the river and I thought I'd come by and see if you were up. And anyway,' Kit continued, though running out of bluster, 'we were only in the garden, we didn't go anywhere.'

The boys both looked up at Sarah, wearing can-we-keep- him faces.

Sarah raised her eyebrows in what she hoped was the look of a grown-up who wasn't in the mood for any more nonsense.

'Kit was telling us about school,' said Alex. 'It's just over there.' He pointed. 'Behind the trees.'

'We can go through the side gate and down the path alongside the cottage, then across the little bridge and the park to get there, and not have to go on the road at all, and it only takes five minutes,' said Harry.

'*And* they have after-school club there,' added Alex.

'And Kit used to go there when he was little, and Mrs...' Harry hesitated and wrinkled up his nose in a show of concentration. 'Mrs Somebody who does for Kit could come and look after us, and pick us up from school if you're working. What is it she does again, Kit?'

'You seem to have covered a lot of territory while you've been here,' said Sarah to Kit, and then turned towards Harry and Alex. 'We've already talked about this, you two. You're both staying where you are for the time being. At least until we decide whereabouts we're going to live. You can't just chop and change schools. All right? Now go inside and get dressed. I'll be in, in a minute.'

'But we want to stay here,' protested Harry. 'Kit said that we can stay at the cottage for just as long as we like.'

'And he said we could have a puppy,' said Alex.

'Now,' said Sarah, pointing towards the back door.

The boys sloped off, muttering.

Kit shifted his weight uneasily from foot to foot. 'I'm so sorry, you're right. I didn't think.'

'I can tell. And I know you mean well, but we don't know you,' Sarah said, gathering up the fishing nets and propping them up against the garden wall.

'Please don't do it again. I need to know where they are, what they're doing and who they are with; especially now that I'm on my own. And the boys are staying at their old school. Their father can pick them up when I can't and while I don't mind you—'

Something caught her eye. Sarah stopped talking and looked up at Kit, who was busy extricating something wrapped in white paper from the pocket of his Barbour jacket.

'What on earth are you doing?' she demanded.

'Have you got any bread?' he asked.

'Yes, thank you. Why?'

'Is it white sliced?'

'No.'

'Well, I suppose you can't have everything. I wasn't sure how you were fixed, what with just moving in and everything, so I thought I'd bring us some breakfast,' Kit said, slapping the flaccid white parcel into her hand. 'As a thank you for supper. It's dry cured bacon,' he continued. 'From the butcher in the village; he's very good. They do the most amazing sausages there too. You should try them some time, tell him I sent you. I get all my meat from there. Bacon and sausages are his specialities. And I've got some tomatoes here somewhere.' Kit frisked himself with some vigour. 'You know you could always have some chickens if you wanted to, although you'd need to build a decent run to keep the foxes out. I've got a chap who could build you one if you like. I was thinking bacon sandwiches?'

'You're inviting yourself for breakfast?' Sarah asked incredulously.

'I did bring the bacon.'

Sarah looked at the paper-wrapped bundle in her hand. 'In case you hadn't noticed, Kit, we've only just moved in. And I've got a lot to do today,' she said. 'Including clearing up the kitchen from last night.'

'Okay, well, don't worry, in that case, I won't stay too long. I'll just eat and go,' Kit said cheerfully. 'I wouldn't want to get in your way. They say breakfast is the most important meal of the day, don't they? I don't know about you but I'm starving.'

Sarah stared at him.

He grinned. 'Do you have any brown sauce?'

'No,' Sarah said, turning on her heel.

'Shame,' Kit said, following close behind. 'I'll bring you a bottle round next time I'm this way. Now, is there anything you want me to do or would you prefer I just stayed out of the way while you're cooking?'

The Ultimate Bacon Sandwich

For each sandwich:
    2–3 rashers of your favourite bacon
    2 slices of bread (it has to be said that thick white sliced works just as well as any other)
    Ripe tomato (enough to cover one slice of the bread), very thinly sliced
    Good mayonnaise
    Freshly ground black pepper

Method
Grill bacon to your preferred interpretation of 'done'.

On a small baking tray or ovenproof plate arrange tomato slices, sprinkle with a little pepper, slide under grill towards end of bacon cooking time so they are cooked, but not to a pulp. Tomatoes may be cooked in the microwave if preferred.

While bacon and tomatoes are cooking, toast bread until golden brown. Spread both slices with mayonnaise.

Arrange tomatoes on one slice, add a little more pepper.

Top with piping hot bacon and second slice of toast. Cut into two (or four).

Serve with a napkin and a mug of tea or coffee.

Chapter Six
All in a flap…jack

'What do you expect me to do with all the furniture you left behind?' snapped Colin.

'What?' said Sarah.

'All the things you left behind when you did your moonlight flit. What am I supposed to do with it?'

It was late Friday afternoon in a café a few minutes' walk from her office, and Sarah had been out of the house and in the cottage for almost a week. With Rosa's blessing she had gone back to working from home for most of the week, the trade-off being she went in on Monday mornings for the team meeting and all day on Friday. She was taking time to adjust. Life felt busy, very busy.

This was meant to be a civilised meeting on neutral ground between her and Colin. Their first since she had moved out. The first of what he hoped would be many, Colin had said, in the text he'd sent her saying he wanted to talk.

Calmly, he'd said, a chance to clear the air and to see if they couldn't sort things out, and for some reason, which was now completely beyond her, Sarah had agreed to meet him while the boys were at after-school club. She knew by Colin's expression that it was a mistake even before she sat down. It was far too soon for either of them to even think about being civilised. She had popped out so they could meet up and had felt Rosa's eyes on her back every step of the way as she headed towards the door.

Colin looked tired. He was hateful when he was tired. His hair was snaggled up into a cowlick on one side, which made him look as if he had just woken up, and his shirt had a button missing.

'It was hardly a moonlight flit,' said Sarah evenly, sliding her tray onto the table and arranging her coffee and flapjack, keeping her voice as calm as she could manage. 'You knew where we were going and when and why. And you could have been there, Colin. We talked about this. I texted you, sent you an email and my solicitor wrote to you. You could have been there and decided what you wanted to keep and what could go. The man with the van was more than willing to drop the rest off at the Salvation Army—'

'After he'd picked through it.'

41

Sarah said nothing.

'After he had taken all the best stuff. And you're late,' Colin continued.

'Three minutes,' said Sarah. 'I'm working.'

'Oh, that's right, *me and my precious job*,' he mimicked. 'Three minutes, three hours. It makes no difference. You're still late.' Colin tore open a brace of sugar sachets and dumped them into his cup. 'And besides I couldn't have coped, watching you leave. It would have been too much. Better for me to stay away rather than see my whole life being ripped apart. Torn to shreds.'

A lady on a nearby table glanced in their direction.

Sarah sighed. The last week had been exhausting, what with the unpacking, trying to get the boys into some kind of a routine, while sorting everything out so she could work from home; the last thing she needed was any of Colin's histrionics.

Calmly she said, 'Your solicitor told me that you'd gone on holiday.'

'I rang you. I know you were there.'

'If you like I can arrange for the man to come and collect what you don't want, or you could put some of it in storage. Or sell it, or give it away.'

'Oh, that's it, leave me to sort it all out.'

'So what do you want? I'm busy; I've nipped out of work. I've still got a lot to do.'

A heavy silence descended. Sarah sighed. The truth was she really hadn't got time for any of this. This little sidebar was biting into her office time. She had work to do. A lot of work to do. Straightening her shoulders, Sarah said, 'Colin, please, we need to move this along.'

Was that a little flash of triumph in his expression?

'Have you had any luck with finding a flat yet?' she asked.

'No.'

'The estate agents have said that the buyers would like to complete as soon as possible.' What Sarah didn't tell Colin was that, what with the rent, and the mortgage, council tax, extra petrol and the after-school clubs for the boys, running the cottage and the house was stretching a budget that was already so thin you could read a newspaper through it, to breaking point.

'I'm hoping it will all be signed, sealed and delivered soon. Six to eight weeks, they've said.'

'Oh well, don't mind me,' he grumbled and then paused. 'Actually I don't care how long it takes. I won't be there. I'm going to stay with friends until everything gets sorted out.'

'Peony?' ventured Sarah.

'Oh, that's it, just jump straight in there, why don't you? *No*, as it happens, *not* Peony. We're both agreed that what we've been experiencing is a transitional relationship; neither of us are ready to commit to...' He paused as if feeling around for the right word.

'Anything more than a casual shag?' suggested Sarah.

Colin's face reddened furiously. 'Oh, that's it, cheapen it, why don't you? And actually it's none of your bloody business what I'm doing or with whom.'

'It is if you're taking the boys there,' said Sarah.

Colin stirred his tea. Sarah closed her eyes, trying to keep calm, trying hard to not to get annoyed.

'All right. I suppose you have a point,' he said, though she could hear it pained him to admit it. 'I've moved in with Elliot, temporarily,' he said after a moment or two more.

'Elliot?'

'Yes, he's an old friend of Ms Goold's. I think he might have been one of her clients at one time. He teaches piano. Old money. Private income, trust fund I think. He's a Buddhist. Ms Goold says Elliot has a healing spirit and that he understands the creative mind. Elliot doesn't embrace the material.'

Which probably meant Colin was staying there for free, thought Sarah cynically, although she didn't say as much. Trust Colin to track down a gullible philanthropist in his hour of need.

'Ms Goold said that it was important that I moved on, and that I shouldn't be staying in the old house all alone. The vibrations there are too negative. And I've got my own room and...' Colin's voice cracked. 'My doctor says that I really don't need all this stress. I'm having these terrible, terrible headaches and palpitations.'

'I've heard Viagra can do that to you.'

He glared at her. 'My writing is suffering.'

Sarah spooned the froth on her cappuccino into her mouth. 'I thought suffering was supposed to be good for your art?'

Colin stared at her. 'I never realised how hard you've become, Sarah, you're very hard.' He leaned forward. 'I just want to sort this out in a civilised manner. I keep thinking that all this is madness. This time without you and the boys has really brought it all home to me.' He sighed and, making a great show of composing himself, folded his hands on the table. 'And I just wanted to say, Sarah, that I'm sorry. Really. Very sorry. And that I blame myself—'

Sarah, caught mid-spoonful, stared at him in astonishment. Finally Colin was *apologising*? She waited, eager to hear where this was going.

'To be perfectly honest I should have seen it coming,' Colin continued, not catching her eyes. 'Ms Goold explained to me that all this fuss and your leaving is really a cry for help. I didn't see it, Sarah, and for that I'm really, truly sorry.'

Sarah's eyes widened.

'She's helped me understand what the real underlying problems are and I can see now that you are consumed by envy for my talent and my ability – it's only natural – and obviously the opportunities that that brings someone like me. And then, of course, you saw me usurping your role, not just by me running the home but also by creating real art. I was stealing your place, archetypal woman; the creatrix. It was so obvious when she explained it all. My book is the child that you have denied yourself. She made me realise that what you really want is another baby.'

Sarah inhaled so quickly she choked. 'And you're *paying* this woman?' she spluttered.

Colin sighed. 'I should have guessed that you would be hostile, but if you could just recognise the situation for what it is, Sarah. See how far your envy has driven you to push me away, to reject me, then I really think that we can move on and heal the rift. It's not too late to put things back to how they were; it really isn't. This could be the making of us.'

Sarah leaned in closer so that her face was within inches of his. 'Colin, this is complete bollocks. I didn't push you away. I most certainly don't want another baby, I don't want things to go back to how they were and I have got better things to do with my time than sit here listening to you talking rubbish and justifying your sleeping with Peony Tyler. Now, what is it you wanted to see me about?'

His posture changed instantly. 'We really need to discuss maintenance.'

'You're going back to work?' said Sarah in surprise.

'No, of course I'm not going back to work,' he said, his amazement matching Sarah's. 'My book is my life's work, you know that. No, I just need to know what sort of allowance you're planning to give me.'

Sarah felt a rush of red heat and fury. 'What?'

'Well, I can hardly expect Peony to keep me, if I move in with her at some point in the future, can I? I've got bills to pay. Ms Goold, my yoga classes. Elliot did offer me some work doing his garden and some odd jobs around the place, but obviously I've turned that down. I mean, manual work, for goodness' sake. Anyway I'm assuming we'll split the proceeds of the house fifty-fifty once it's sold and then we'll just need to settle on how much you're going to give me. I'll need to buy a better car obviously, and then as I said there are my therapy sessions, and my gym membership – and swimming – and I'm going to be having the boys after school at least two nights a week and every other weekend. I've made a list of my expenses, they're here, somewhere.' He started to rifle through his pockets.

Sarah, who until recently had never walked out on anything in her life, found herself doing it for the second time in under a week.

'Where are you going?' Colin demanded, as she got to her feet, pocketed her flapjack and pushed herself away from the table.

'To pick up the boys.'

'But I thought you said you were at work. I thought it was my night to have them.'

Sarah swung round. 'It was, but if I'm going to pay for a baby sitter I'd prefer to get someone I trust,' she said.

Flapjacks

Ingredients:

Note: use butter for this. I've never found a margarine that works.
150g butter, plus a little bit extra for greasing
50g golden caster sugar
4 tbsp golden syrup
275g rolled oats

Method:

Preheat the oven to 190C/ 375F/ gas mark 5.

Grease and line a shallow 20cm-square tin with baking parchment or greaseproof paper.

Heat the butter, sugar and syrup in a small pan over a low heat and stir until the butter has melted. Add the rolled oats. Stir. Press the mixture into the tin and bake for 20 minutes, or until just golden at the edges.

Remove from the oven and cool for 10 minutes. With a knife cut into 10–12 portions while the flapjack is warm and still in the tin. Cool completely before turning out and cutting again with a sharp knife.

Store in an airtight tin.

Chapter Seven
That really takes the biscuit…

'You weren't very long,' said Melissa, as Sarah hurried back into the office.

'How did it go?'

'Not great,' said Sarah, slipping into her seat and smiling at Rosa who caught her eye through the window that overlooked the main office. 'And I've got to pick the boys up at six.'

'But I thought—' Melissa stopped when she caught the look on Sarah's face. 'Okay. No sweat. I heard Rose saying she was off to some sort of do this evening. She's been clock-watching since about four.'

'How do you notice all that stuff?'

'Call it a gift. I bet you a cappuccino and a cinnamon Danish that she's out of here in under ten minutes.'

They both glanced in the direction of Rosa's office.

Melissa was right; Rosa was collecting her things together and out of the door in seven. So, Sarah finished off what she was doing and then went to pick up Harry and Alex at the proper time. She was half-expecting to find Colin there as well, but he had obviously taken her at her word, and was nowhere in sight.

Both boys were tired and ratty and squabbled all the way back to the cottage. Relieved that it was Friday, Sarah couldn't find the energy to be cross with them; it had been a long, long week for everyone and they were all tired. No one protested at the idea of an early night.

Saturday morning was bright and sunny. Sarah still hadn't quite got used to waking up in the cottage. But however tired the week had left them, with the sun shining it was close to impossible to stay in bed. The boys, renewed by a good night's sleep, built a den at the bottom of the garden, while Sarah spent the day getting the cottage round and tidied, adding the finishing touches to the boys' rooms and ferrying sandwiches and drinks out to them, in their new little kingdom.

On Sunday it rained all day so they stayed in by the fire watching DVDs while Sarah altered the curtains to fit the cottage windows, and if Colin had anything else to say about babies, Ms Goold or maintenance, he kept it to himself, and Big Bunny seemed to have cleaned up his act a treat.

By Monday morning the cottage felt more like home, everyone had had plenty of sleep and Sarah felt ready for whatever came next.

Hanley's half-yearly review meeting was planned for Wednesday, so Sarah spent most of Monday and Tuesday preparing her presentation and getting the rest of her work up to date. It didn't matter how many reviews she went to, it always felt like mid-term exams.

On the big day Sarah got up extra early to double-check her notes and make sure she had time to do her hair and makeup and get the boys to school in good time. It was a big meeting, and everyone was going to be there. It was the day they looked at how the year had gone so far, at the magazine and online. They looked at what had worked and what hadn't and talked about what was in the pipeline for the next six months. Given the state of the business and the threat of cuts, the consensus was that everyone who was anyone, and anyone who wasn't, was going to pitch up to try and get a handle on what was going on.

By the time Sarah got there the conference room was knee-deep in big guns and their minions, including Magda Holmes from Harts and Holmes, the owner and executive producer of a lifestyle programme on satellite TV, who had worked hand in glove with Hanleys for as long as Sarah had been employed there – and probably a lot longer.

Despite the recession it seemed that Harts and Holmes were still doing well, profits were up, viewing figures were solid and focus groups thought they had just about got it right. Though, as Magda said earnestly, during her state of the business address, while it was good news no one was foolish enough to rest on their laurels. Everyone should be out there, looking for the next big thing, while trying hard to retain their core customers.

If Magda was cautiously upbeat Hanleys weren't, and were feeling the pinch. There had been a lot of talk during the morning about belt-tightening and slimming down to fighting weight and cutting out the deadwood, every euphemism they could come up with which avoided anyone having to say sacking people, but despite it all the general tone was still cautiously optimistic.

Two chaps from marketing and sales came in to give them all a rousing speech on the strides they'd taken to improve the company's online presence and increase exports, which was just before they discovered that their usual company lunch had been cut back to sandwiches and cake, but there was lots of talk about the blitz spirit, ensuring the customer was getting value for money, raising their profile globally, and upmarket thrift, pedalling advice on how to have a good time with Hanleys through tougher times without having to feel like you were going without.

Just as they were finishing up the item before Sarah was meant to make her presentation, the receptionist slipped into the room, doing the whole excuse me, take no notice of me, I'm invisible thing that stopped the meeting dead in its tracks.

'Sarah?' she said in a stage whisper when she finally picked her way around the table. 'There's a phone call for you. From home. They said it was urgent. Your mobile is off. Someone called Kit?'

Sarah stared at her. It took a split second for her mind to run riot and create a scenario involving Colin, blind drunk, with Peony, half-naked, taking the boys out of school and dropping them off at an empty house in a fit of pique, followed by a sudden proliferation of fire, sharp knives and other assorted peril.

Sarah felt her colour drain. 'Did he say what he wanted?'

The girl shook her head. 'No, I'm sorry. He just said he was phoning from your cottage.'

Rosa pulled a what's-going-on-face; Sarah mouthed an apology. Charlie Green, from the sales and marketing department, who had been in the midst of his summing-up, turned to glare at her, while at the far end of the table Melissa, who had been taking notes, mouthed, 'Everything okay?'

'Are the boys all right?' whispered Sarah to the receptionist.

'He didn't say.'

Eyebrows were being raised around the table; Sarah was on her feet now and making I'm sorry gestures as she threaded her way towards the door.

'Everything all right, Sarah?' asked Mr Hanley junior, who was chairing the meeting.

'I'm not sure; I'm most awfully sorry,' she said.

'Don't apologise, my dear,' Mr Hanley was saying. 'Actually I was just thinking we could all do with a bit of a break before we move on to the rest of the presentations. Is that all right with everyone else?'

There was a murmur of assent and a gathering of papers. Charlie Green sat down, while Mr Hanley eased himself gingerly to his feet and shuffled off towards the tea and biscuits. He was junior only by dint of his position in the family hierarchy and had to be seventy-five if he was a day. Sarah meanwhile hurried out into the corridor and ran down towards reception, snatching the phone up off the desk.

'Kit? What's the matter?' she asked anxiously.

'Sarah. Thank God they managed to track you down. I need you,' he replied. 'Desperately.'

'What?' blustered Sarah. 'What do you mean? Are the boys all right?'

'Yes. Well, at least I think so,' Kit said, sounding slightly bemused.

'What do you mean, you think so? You're in my house, Kit. I thought something had happened to the boys.'

'This isn't about the boys, it's about me,' said Kit, sounding wounded.

'What?'

'Please,' Kit pleaded. 'I really need to talk to you.'

'This had better be good. You just dragged me out of an important meeting.'

'I did?'

'You did.'

The truth was that since they had moved into the cottage Sarah had seen Kit almost every day, sometimes face to face, sometimes just in passing. He drove up the lane past the cottage at least half a dozen times every day on his way back and forth to the estate and the hall and twice since she'd been living there he had popped round when she was dishing up supper and she had invited him to stay, but this was not what she had expected at all.

What could be so important that he had to phone her at work? Her mind lurched between Kit a) having developed a gigantic and unstoppable crush (flattering but unlikely as all she ever seemed to do was tell him off), b) him changing his mind about the cottage and evicting them (shades of Dickens, the fickle nature of the landed gentry and a bubbling anxiety Sarah had about her and the boys' future) and c) Kit driving past and seeing the place on fire (a possibility; Sarah had been busy and preoccupied that morning; had she switched the grill off before she left for work?).

'Ah,' said Kit. 'Sorry about that.'

'What are you doing in my house?' she demanded.

'I thought you might be here.'

'I'm at work, Kit.'

'Well, I know that now, don't I? But you told me you were going to work from home a lot of the time.'

'And today I'm in the office. At a very important meeting.'

'So you said. Your phone is switched off, you know.'

'Because I'm in a really important meeting. Didn't you notice that my car wasn't there and the whole place was locked up?'

'Yes, of course I did. And I knocked first,' he said defensively. 'And then when you didn't answer I started to worry that something might have happened. Then I remembered that there's a spare key in the gutter by the back door, above the little window. But don't worry, I'll put it back. I'll show you when you get—'

'So you let yourself into my house?'

'Yes,' he began. 'I was a bit concerned.'

'You can't just go letting yourself into someone else's house, Kit.'

'I was worried.'

Sarah said nothing, which always worked on the boys.

'No, I suppose not. You're right. I'm really sorry,' he said after a moment or two. 'But I'm desperate.'

'I might have been in the bath or anything,' said Sarah, making a mental note to get the locks changed as soon as she could arrange it. 'And if it's nothing important, if you excuse me, I really do have to go.'

'I listened and I couldn't hear anything.'

Sarah sighed. 'Okay, well, never mind that now. What is the emergency? What are you so desperate about?'

'Ah yes, well, the thing is I'm having this dinner party—'

'What?'

'On Friday. Well, I'm hoping it'll be on Friday.'

'You rang me at work to invite me to a dinner party?' she said, trying hard to keep her voice down despite her outrage. The receptionist was fiddling about with her computer, pretending not to listen and fooling no one.

There was a weighted silence and then Kit said, 'Err, well no, not exactly. I was wondering if you'd cook it for me.'

Sarah was so stunned she didn't know what to say, so Kit, presumably taking her silence for agreement, pressed on. 'It'll be for about six, seven, maybe eight people at the most. I'll pay you, obviously, although I'm a bit strapped for cash at the moment. I was thinking maybe we could work something out with the rent? Please say you'll do it, Sarah, only I owe so many people a meal, and you're such a good cook. You could do that thing you did with the spicy sausage and those potato ball things. Or anything else – I don't mind – anything – really...' His voice faded away.

'You rang me up to ask if I'd cook dinner for you?' she said.

'Well yes, if you can't do it then obviously I'll have to call it off, so I wanted to be absolutely certain before I firm up the invites.'

'Kit, I'm at work. I'm busy—'

'Exactly, which was why I called round. I was thinking maybe just the two courses, something simple and a really good cheese board or maybe fruit – nothing too fussy, something easy. What do you think? Have you got any thoughts?'

Any thoughts that Sarah was currently having were unrepeatable.

'I think,' she said slowly, after a second or two, 'that I should get back to my meeting and you should get out of my house, and get back to doing whatever it is you do all day. We can discuss this when I get home and don't ever, ever ring me at work again, Kit. Or ever let yourself into my house. Is that clear?'

'Oh perfectly,' said Kit. 'So does that mean that you'll do it, then?'

Sarah hung up on him. The man was totally unbelievable. She tidied her hair and made a show of composing herself – un-bloody-believable – although as she pulled herself up to her full height and headed back into the meeting, she found herself thinking about what she might cook.

She had got just the thing; which was how it all started.

*

Back in the meeting everyone was still working their way through the coffee and biscuits. Sarah had barely closed the door behind her before Magda Holmes made a beeline for her. Barely five foot in her stockinged feet though considerably taller in her Louboutins, it was tricky to work out exactly how old Magda might be, but not at all tricky to see that she was magnificently maintained. Madga had the heart of a barracuda and an expression that, long, long before the advent of Botox, gave absolutely nothing away.

'Sarah, how lovely to see you, darling. Everything okay?' She nodded towards the door that Sarah had just come through.

'Fine, thank you, Magda.'

'Good, good, I'm glad I've caught you. I was really hoping to pick your brains.'

Sarah waited; it seemed she was in big demand from people wanting something.

'I was wondering if you could suggest somewhere that we could use for the photo shoot for our Harts and Holmes Best of East Anglian Food Guide?'

Sarah thought for a moment. 'What about one of your farmers? I imagine they'd be queuing up to have their farms featured?'

'They are and that's the problem. Caused a bit of a furore last time out. Entirely my husband Guy's fault and all terribly unseemly. Sorted now, but I really don't want to go there again.' Magda pulled a face. 'Anyway it's a bit last year, darling. I want something evocative, timeless. Obviously there'll be a decent fee. I thought perhaps you might know of somewhere.'

Sarah nodded, thinking about what Kit had just said about being strapped for cash.

'Funnily enough I might be able to help,' she said. 'I've just moved into a cottage in the grounds of a country house in Newnham Magna. It's Georgian, and all a bit ramshackle and overgrown. It's in the middle of a country estate; there's a stream, outbuildings. Very picturesque.'

Magda was nodding. Sarah could see she had piqued the woman's interest. 'Sounds wonderful, darling. Anyone else used it?'

'Not as far as I know,' said Sarah.

'Certainly worth a look then. Have you got a contact number?'

Sarah nodded. 'I'll write it down for you,' she said. 'You'll like my landlord.'

'Really?' said Magda with a sly grin.

'Really,' said Sarah.

'I'll ring him this afternoon,' said Magda.

Melting Moments Biscuits

Makes around 20–24 biscuits

Ingredients:
   180g unsalted butter
   60g icing sugar, sifted
   60g custard powder or cornflour (if using cornflour add a tsp of
vanilla essence to the butter when mixing)
   1 tsp baking powder
   180g plain flour
   2 or 3 glacé cherries, washed and cut into small pieces

Method:

Preheat oven to 180°C. Line two baking trays with baking
parchment.

Cream the butter for 2 minutes in an electric mixer. Add in the icing
sugar and custard powder and mix until combined.

Sift the baking powder and flour together then add to the dough and
mix well.

Divide dough into 20–24 small balls.
Place balls on lined baking tray, leaving plenty of room between each.

Prick each ball once with a fork, and add a fleck of glacé cherry to the
top of each.

Bake biscuits for 12–16 minutes or until light golden (they are still
slightly soft when taken from the oven and crisp up as they cool).
Watch carefully in the last few minutes as the edges can brown.

Remove from oven and leave to cool in the baking trays for 5
minutes and then transfer to a wire rack to cool completely. (A fish
slice helps.)

These are fabulous sandwiched together with buttercream and jam.

Chapter Eight
Dinner is Served

'You have to let me see the kitchen, Kit,' protested Sarah, trying to push her way past him. 'You can't expect me to cook in a kitchen that I've never seen. I need to know what the cooker is like, is it gas, electricity? And what sort of cooking equipment you've got. If you haven't got everything I need I can always bring some bit and pieces up from the cottage.'

'That would be good,' said Kit.

Sarah looked up him. 'Yes, but I still need to know what to bring.'

It was late Wednesday afternoon and while the boys played outside on the lawn, Sarah and Kit were in Roseberry Hall. The hallway where they were presently standing was untidy in a boyish bohemian way. It was filled with too many coats, boots, saddles, riding hats, umbrella stands, fishing rods, old mirrors and lamps. Standing at the foot of the impressive curving staircase was a stuffed bear in a straw hat; the creature had one huge paw resting nonchalantly on the newel post. The table of the hallstand was littered with shells, feathers, interesting stones and vintage bottles. Set into one wall was a huge fireplace, with a great ramshackle stack of logs piled higgledy-piggledy in the hearth. An old-fashioned butcher's bike was propped up under the stairs, which reached up into a vast galleried landing hung with the portraits of Kit's ancestors. A string of dusty tinsel hung round each of the picture frames.

'I hadn't actually thought about where you were going to cook dinner,' Kit was saying, still obstinately blocking her way.

Sarah stared up at him. 'What?'

'It hadn't occurred to me that you'd want to cook it here.'

'Where on earth did you think I'd cook it?' Sarah said, in amazement.

'Your place,' he replied, in a tone that implied that that was the obvious answer.

'You want me to cook your dinner at my house?'

'Well, yes. It might be better,' said Kit. 'Under the circumstances.'

Sarah ducked under his arm and pushing open the kitchen door slipped inside.

She found herself in a huge, square, high room, with a row of old-fashioned clothes-airers slung between the light fittings across the ceiling. A long battered refectory table, surrounded by an odd mismatched collection of chairs, dominated the centre. On one side of the room was a door that opened up into some sort of garden area, and there was a large sash window complete with window seat and shutters. From the window you could look out into the tangled jungle that once upon a time had probably been the kitchen garden or a laundry yard and which now grew wild.

Set into the adjacent wall was a deep fireplace in which sat an elderly Aga, flanked by two battered campaign chairs, and two dog baskets in which Kit's dogs were sleeping. Arranged around the remaining walls were an assortment of wooden cabinets painted duck-egg blue and cream, a huge wooden dresser decked out with oddments of crockery, found treasures, old bottles, and a stuffed squirrel, and finally, in one corner, tucked out of the way, was an old-fashioned electric stove, that looked as if it harked back to the fifties or possibly even earlier. The stove had bowlegs and was coated in chipped, butter-yellow enamel and would have looked right at home in a rural life museum.

'So,' said Kit. 'What do you think?'

Sarah wasn't altogether sure. 'It's a bit basic,' she began, heading for the cooker. 'Presumably this works?' She reached up to switch the oven on at the mains, but Kit was ahead of her.

'Whoa there, I wouldn't do that if I were you,' he said, knocking her hand away. 'Last time I switched it on it gave me a bit of a shock. I think there might be something wrong with the wiring. And anyway it always sets the smoke alarm off.'

'How on earth do you manage to cook?' Sarah asked, glancing round the enormous room.

Kit shrugged. 'Mostly ding cuisine. I've got a microwave in the laundry room,' he said cheerily.

'Good job,' said Sarah, bobbing down to take a look inside the grill. The pan was wedged in at an odd angle. After some wriggling and levering and nervous looks from Kit, she finally managed to prise it free. It was lined with tin foil, or at least it was probably tin foil; it was hard to tell under the covering of crispy black lava, the curly burnt things, the rancid puddles of fat and grey-green mould.

Kit smiled at her, sheepishly. 'I don't use it that often,' he said by way of explanation.

'You don't say,' said Sarah.

'Do you want me to give it a bit of a rinse?'

'I don't think that's going to help.'

Sarah forced open the oven door. Inside, nestled inside a roasting tray, were what appeared to be a mouse nest and a very battered pair of trainers. 'I think you're right, it would probably be better if I cooked at my place.'

Kit nodded. 'Good plan.'

Sarah got up. 'Does the Aga work?'

'Oh yes, I usually warm my trousers up on it and I sometimes put my boots in the bottom in the winter.'

Sarah raised her eyebrows.

'Oh, you mean to cook in?' he said. 'To be honest I'm not sure. I can't remember the last time anyone actually cooked with it.'

'Then you'd better get it switched it on, hadn't you? I haven't got all day.'

'I thought you said you'd cook at your place.'

'I was thinking I could use it to keep the food hot and warm the plates.'

'It takes a while to warm up.'

'Now,' snapped Sarah.

'What's your daily lady called?'

'Mrs Oates,' said Kit, peering into the innards of the Aga. 'She's a gem.'

Sarah nodded. She'd have to be to take all this on, she thought grimly.

While Kit fiddled with the stove Sarah glanced round; the kitchen was lovely in its own quirky way. It had a faded sepia olde-worlde quality to it. Mrs Oates was obviously just about keeping on top of the grime, but only just, nothing matched, nothing fitted, nothing was level or square. The huge old sink could have doubled as a bath, and was supported by a pile of breezeblocks at one end. The flagstone floors rolled and dipped, and from where she was standing, Sarah could see that the table legs had been wedged up with slivers of wood and folded Christmas cards to keep the whole thing level, and at some stage the sash window had dropped a little at the top and never been closed. A tentative finger of ivy had managed to find its way inside and now climbed unhindered up towards the ceiling.

'There we are,' said Kit triumphantly. 'Shouldn't be too long now before it heats up. Takes a bit of a while to settle down but it's fine really.'

Sarah looked at the ancient stove wondering exactly what constituted fine in Kit's book.

'Do you think that the Aga will get hot enough to keep the food warm till you're ready to eat?'

'Oh yes, I'm sure it will,' Kit said, with remarkable confidence. 'And help yourself to anything else you need.' He lifted a hand to encompass the battered kitchen, while Sarah followed the gesture with her eyes, considering what else that might be.

*

Come Friday evening Sarah was back in Kit's kitchen. The guests had already arrived and were gathered round the fire pit outside on the terrace with a tray of olives, tiny sweet stuffed peppers and bread sticks, to bridge the gap till suppertime. Even with the kitchen door firmly closed she could hear them talking and hooting with laughter. For a man who claimed to be cash-strapped Kit was very generous with the wine.

More bottles were busy cooling in the fridge alongside a carton of double cream and the summer pudding Sarah had made for dessert. The main course – a summer fish pie – was finishing off in Kit's aging Aga; everything was more or less ready. Sarah wiped her hands on her apron and took stock of what there was left to do. There was some crusty bread to cut up and put in a basket, a green salad to put together. She stretched; it wasn't every day she was asked to cook for so many people.

As Sarah worked through her mental check list something caught her eye out in the garden, and for the briefest of instants she thought it was one of the boys outside playing. She was about to call out, when she remembered with a start that they were staying with Colin for the weekend. The realisation stopped her in her tracks.

The phone had been ringing when Sarah got back to the cottage on Wednesday afternoon after her recce of Kit's kitchen and – because she was expecting to hear from Melissa how the half-yearly meeting had gone down – she had picked it up without thinking.

'Ah,' Colin had said, as if she had taken him by surprise. It was the first time they had spoken since meeting in the café on Friday, so Sarah was naturally a little wary.

'If this is about babies or maintenance,' she began.

'I've just spoken to my solicitor,' Colin had said, briskly. 'This is ridiculous, but I suppose we really should start off as we mean to go on. He suggests that I ought to have the boys for some of the time, you know, over the weekends and holidays and things. He suggested that we spend alternate weekends with them. So I was thinking I could pick them up after school on Friday and they could come and stay with me for the weekend.' Nothing about the way he said it indicated that Colin was happy with the idea.

Whatever was going on between them Sarah had no intention of using the boys as leverage. 'Okay, well, that sounds like a good idea,' she said cautiously. 'They've missed you.'

'Whose fault it that?' he snapped. 'It wasn't me who broke the family up.'

Sarah fought the temptation to bite back; it would only encourage him to launch into the wake-up call speech that he had fine-tuned over the last few weeks.

When she didn't rise to the bait, Colin explained that Elliot, his new landlord, was very happy for the boys to stay, and Colin thought he should have them, after all why should she have them all the time. They were his children too, he said.

'That's fine,' Sarah said, carefully.

He would pick them up after school on Friday and bring them back on Sunday around three. Did she need to write this down? he added in a snide voice.

So when Sarah dropped the boys off at school that morning she had left them with a change of clothes, their pyjamas, tooth brushes and Big Bunny, all packed into a rucksack, and had then hurried off to work. She had been so busy all day and since she'd been back to the cottage that it hadn't really hit home that she was on her own.

Sarah backhanded away an unexpected tear. It felt strange and unsettling not to have the two of them around or factored in to what she was doing. For years her days had been framed by sleepy mornings and breakfasts together, dropping the boys off and picking them up, by teatimes, and baths and bedtime stories. It had been so long since Sarah had had any real time to herself that she had forgotten what it felt like to be without responsibilities.

While she had been busy working it was fine but what on earth would it be like to go back to the empty cottage, knowing that Harry and Alex weren't going to be coming back till Sunday afternoon? What was she going to do?

Sarah sniffed away another flurry of tears, pulled out a tissue and blew her nose; this wouldn't do. She made an effort to concentrate, took a deep breath, tidied her hair, washed her hands, and took a long look round the kitchen while collecting her thoughts. Crying wouldn't make it better and she was worried that once she started she might not be able to stop.

It was first time since she had left Colin that Sarah felt any sense of panic; it was like delayed shock, and threatened to bubble up and drown her. Up until now there had been too much to do, what with work, and unpacking, and arranging and rearranging things, reassuring the boys and sorting out their new life, and now suddenly here they were. This was it. This was what their lives were going to be like from now on. The realisation was like a splash of ice-cold water.

Beneath the threat of tears was a whole tsunami of sadness, the grief of losing her marriage and her home and the whole of her unsinkable life. She felt betrayed and angry and hurt right through to a big red raw core. Sarah closed her eyes. Now was not the moment, it really wasn't – she needed to focus on Kit's dinner party.

She took another deep breath and waited for the waves of panic to pass. It would be all right, it would, it really would, she told herself in the voice she usually reserved for the boys when they were having a bad dream.

Sarah hadn't thought much about what her future might hold, and now as it loomed up ahead, dwarfing her, blocking out the light, she felt faint. From outside she heard a whoop of manic laughter and the sound of a glass breaking. It was enough to break her train of thought and stop her spinning away. This was her new life; all she had to do was take it one day, one dinner party at a time. The panic slowly ebbed away, her pulse slowed, the tears passed.

It was going to be all right. It was.

Sarah turned her attention back to cooking and Kit's dinner party. After she had written the kitchen off as a dead loss, they'd taken a long hard look at the dining room. It was a grand panelled affair which would need a month to clean, clear and sort it before he could have a dinner party in there, and so Sarah suggested that they eat in the kitchen. Rather than turn on the main light and reveal the grubby, battered fixtures and fittings, Sarah had had Kit and Mrs Oates round up some table lamps from the rest of the house, which she had strategically placed on the cupboards and on the dresser so that the whole room was bathed in a soft golden glow.

Given carte blanche to pillage the kitchen Sarah had gone through every drawer and cupboard and found a big cut-glass bowl under the sink, which (having put it through her dishwasher) she'd filled with flowers picked from the garden, and stood it in the centre of the battered refectory table, surrounding it with tea lights and candles in all sorts of little pots and jars. Now they were lit the candle flames reflected and flickered in the faceted glass.

In the back of the pantry she'd found a stack of mismatched crockery and complemented it with truly beautiful, very long-stemmed wine glasses from a box on a shelf in the utility room. With a little work and a lot of improvisation the table looked really welcoming and elegant in a quirky way.

For a moment Sarah glanced out of the window wondering what the boys were up to, wondering if they missed her, all the while trying to ignore the ache of sadness in her chest.

'Oh, thank God you're here,' said Kit, breaking into her thoughts as he opened the kitchen door just a crack and slipped through. He pressed the door tight closed behind him and made a beeline for the fridge.

'I was beginning to get a bit worried in case you weren't going to show up and I'd have to phone for a takeaway. I'll just grab a couple more bottles of wine. I told them I had to come and stir something. Those olives aren't going to hold them for much longer. They're starving. How long before we can eat?'

'Another ten minutes,' said Sarah.

Kit nodded. 'Righty-oh. Smells fabulous.' He paused. 'Can you just talk me through it again?'

'No, Kit, I can't, and I've still got things to do. And if anyone asks for any recipes just say they're a state secret. All right?'

He nodded and then took a hasty look around. 'The table looks nice. Thank you for doing all this and for not getting flustered when I bumped up the numbers, Sarah. It means a lot to me. Oh, and you know that woman you told me about, Magda Holmes? The TV bod?'

Sarah nodded cautiously.

'Well, she rang me last night. I meant to tell you, she and her husband are the two extras. They seem charming, and we've been getting on like a house on fire. She seems very impressed with the house. She's coming back for a bit of a recce next week.' Kit paused and then grinned. 'I reckon she's going to go for having her photo shoot here. I was wondering if maybe you could maybe cook for—'

'No. Don't ask,' Sarah said sternly, folding a pile of cotton napkins that she had brought up from the cottage, and laying one onto the side plate alongside each place setting. 'This isn't going to be a regular thing, Kit. Do you understand?'

'Oh, of course,' he said, not that Sarah believed him. She could see his mind working overtime, but before he could say anything else there came the sound of footsteps in the hallway.

'Kit, where are you?' called a woman's voice from somewhere beyond the kitchen door. 'Are you in there?'

'Just coming,' Kit called, making for the door, and then to Sarah added, 'I've got to go. Ready in ten minutes?'

Sarah nodded. 'And then I'll be off.'

He paused, a wine bottle in one hand and a second tucked up under his arm. 'You don't want to stop and help me dish up?'

Her expression was answer enough.

'I'll take that as a no then,' he laughed. 'You know, this was a really good idea. And it's so easy. We really should do it again some time. I mean, what does it take?'

Before Sarah could tell him, the kitchen door swung open and a woman popped her head round it. 'Oh, there you are,' she said. 'I wondered where you'd got to.' The woman's hair was awry and her face flushed. It took a second or two for Sarah to realise that it was Magda Holmes.

'Oh, hello, Magda,' said Kit, before Sarah could speak. He practically leapt across the room to block her progress and her view. 'I thought I told you to stay out on the terrace.'

'I know you did, but it's getting a bit chilly out there, darling, even with the fire. And I was just wondering where you were? And how long before we eat?' she continued, trying her best to peer around him. 'I'm starving. And is there just a drop more of that wine?' She wiggled her glass at him.

'Of course there is. I'm just bringing it out now.'

'And how's the food coming along?' she asked.

'It's absolutely fine. One of my bombproof recipes. Another ten minutes and we can eat. It's all under control. I just needed to check nothing was burning.'

'And was it?' she purred.

'No, not at all. It's doing just fine. Come on, off you go, can you take the wine out to the others? I'll be there in just a minute.'

'Fabulous,' said Magda, allowing herself to be guided back out into the hallway. 'It smells really good, I'm ravenous. I had no idea you could cook, Kit.'

He laughed. 'There's a lot about me that you don't know, Magda, I'm a man of many talents.'

'So I can see,' she murmured. 'Impressive.' Magda's tone was flirtatious and overly familiar for someone who Kit had just met. Gently but firmly he shooed her out of the kitchen.

The second they were alone Kit swung round and whispered, 'What's the thing in the fridge in the bowl with a brick on top of it?'

'Summer pudding. And why on earth did you tell Magda you were cooking dinner?'

'Oh, I told everybody,' said Kit. 'I didn't think it would hurt. And everyone seems really impressed. I've already told them it's nothing fancy – just a little something I'd thrown together.' Kit acted out the speech with a little flourish.

Sarah looked heavenwards.

'Anyway, tell me about the summer pudding,' he said.

Sarah laughed and shook her head. 'Okay, you take the brick off and the side plate, unpeel the cling film, put the big blue plate on top of it and then tip the whole thing upside down. The pudding will just slide out onto the plate.'

Kit looked sceptical. 'Really?'

Sarah nodded. 'Yes, and it will look amazing. Just peel off the cling film, be careful and it should just come away. There's a little jug of extra juice in the fridge as well, so if there are any white bits on the pudding you can just pour some juice over the patches. There is some extra fruit in there too, and I'd just spoon it out and arrange it around the bottom. Got it?'

Kit nodded. 'Uhuh, and I serve that with the cream?'

'Yes, now go away. I've got the salad to finish off and the bread to warm in the Aga. The main course you can just put onto the table and let people help themselves. Okay?'

Kit puffed out his cheeks. 'Right, full steam ahead then.' He grinned. 'Sarah, I won't forget this, you know that, don't you? I owe you. Big time. You're a real star'. He blew her a kiss. As he reached the door Kit paused and glanced back. 'I've been thinking. Do you think you could manage lunch on Sunday for six?'

He was out of the door just before the screwed-up napkin hit the doorframe.

Summer Fish Pie

Serves 4–6

Ingredients:

For the pie:

> 250ml vegetable or fish stock (stock cubes are fine)
> 100g undyed smoked haddock
> 250g salmon
> 250g pollock fillets/firm white fish fillets
> 150g raw or cooked prawns
> 75g frozen peas, defrosted
> 1 small bunch parsley, chopped
> 150ml white wine
> 100ml double cream
> 1 heaped tbsp cornflour

For the topping:

> 1kg new potatoes; cut large ones in half so they are all same size
> 2 tbsp olive oil
> 1 small bunch spring onions, roughly chopped
> 70g cheddar, grated
> 1 bunch chives, chopped

White pepper

Method:

Put ovenproof dish into a preheated oven (200C /gas mark 6).

Boil the potatoes in salted water until tender (10–15 mins). Drain well before returning to the pan with the olive oil, chopped spring onions and half the cheese and the chives. Crush lightly with a fork or potato masher. Set aside while you make the sauce.

Heat the stock in a small pan. Pour the wine and cream into the pan and simmer to reduce a little. Mix the cornflour to a paste with 1 tbsp of the sauce; pour into the rest of the sauce, whisking to ensure there are no lumps. Simmer gently until thickened. Leave to cool a little, adjust seasoning (remember smoked haddock can be quite salty – I usually just add pepper at this stage).

Next remove any bones and skin from the raw fish. Cut the pollock, salmon and smoked haddock into chunky bite-sized pieces. Layer with the prawns and peas in a deep ovenproof dish.

Pour sauce over the fish. Using raw fish makes it a much more succulent and chunkier pie.

Spoon the crushed potato mixture over the fish. Sprinkle on the remaining cheese and chives.

Cook for 35–40mins until the topping is golden and filling bubbling.

Serve piping hot with green salad and chunky bread to mop up the sauce.

Summer Pudding

Serves 8

Ingredients:

4oz (225g) strawberries

8oz (225 g) redcurrants

4oz (110g) blackcurrants

1lb (450g) raspberries

5oz (150g) golden caster sugar

7–8 thick slices of good white bread from a large loaf, cut so that they are around ½-inch thick (crusts removed)

1½ pt (850ml) pudding basin, lightly buttered

Cling film

This recipe works well with any berries. You can substitute chopped fresh apricots, plums, peaches or nectarines but whatever combination you choose make sure you have a good proportion of dark berries to colour the juice.

Method:

Wash fruit and dry on kitchen paper.

Remove leaves from strawberries and slice or if small cut in half.

Set strawberries to one side.

Strip redcurrants and blackcurrants from stems by holding the stem firmly then sliding stem between tines of a fork and pulling the fork down gently but firmly. Discard stem.

Check raspberries and discard any that are mildewed.

Carefully line pudding basin with cling film, allowing a generous overhang at the top. It's easier to use two pieces and overlap them by about 6 inches rather than try to work one sheet around the curves of the bowl.

Put sugar and 3 tbsp water into a large pan.

Heat gently until all the sugar dissolves. Stir occasionally.

Bring to a boil for 1 min. Add all the fruit (except for the strawberries).

Cook for 3 mins over a low heat, stirring very gently 2–3 times.

The fruit should have softened, but remain reasonably intact and be surrounded by dark red juice.
Drain the fruit well and save the juice.
Set fruit aside.
Taste the juice. If it is too sweet add a little lemon juice.
Allow fruit and juice to cool.

Dip the slices one at a time into the juice (just for a second or two) and neatly line the basin, beginning at the bottom.
Cut the bread to shape as you work.
Overlap the slices to get a nice seal and press the pieces firmly together.
Don't worry if the slices are not totally covered with juice as you will be adding more juice later.
Use offcuts of bread to fill any holes. You're aiming for a totally lined bowl, with no gaps.

When the basin is lined carefully spoon in the fruit, adding the sliced strawberries a few at time so they are evenly spread through the rest of the filling.
Fill the basin right to the top.

Carefully spoon the juice over the fruit, saving around 2/3rds of a cup for later.
Save any spare fruit for garnish.

With remaining bread cover the whole of the top of the basin, cutting off any overhanging bits.

When the top is covered fold the overhanging cling film over the bread.
Place a large saucer or tea plate over the cling film and then add a weight –
tins work well.

Chill in the fridge for at least 6 hours or overnight.

To serve, remove tea plate, unpeel the cling film, put a serving plate upside-down on top of the bowl and flip over. Slide bowl off and carefully remove the cling film.

Use the leftover juice to colour any patches that haven't soaked up the juices.

Serve with leftover juice, extra berries and cream or good vanilla ice-cream.

Chapter Nine
If life gives you lemons…

Sarah trudged back to her car for the short trip down the drive to the cottage. She was carrying the box full of the things she'd needed to finish off Kit's dinner party. She fumbled for her car keys, struggling to open the door. The sounds of the guests followed her on the breeze. She could smell wood smoke and hear the tinkle of laughter, and glasses and people having fun. It stirred up a sad lonely feeling in her heart. So this was what life was going to be like now she was on her own.

It was early days yet, cautioned a kinder, gentler, less judgemental voice in her head. She just needed to give herself time to heal and sort out a routine, plan things to look forward to. And she had made an extra fish pie and summer pudding so there was something delicious to eat when she got home. Sarah climbed into the car and backhanded a tear away.

Back at the cottage Sarah made her way inside and, pushing open the kitchen door, slid the box onto the kitchen table, turned on the lamps and took a long hard look around her new home.

Although it wasn't exactly chaotic there were still empty bowls and dishes stacked by the sink, empty wrappers and oddments by her chopping block. It looked like she had missed a party, and despite the smell of supper cooking, the cottage felt horribly empty.

Turning on the radio to cover the silence, she tidied up, poured herself a glass of wine and then took the dish of fish pie out of the oven. As she put it on the kitchen table she realised that she had made enough for four. It was the final straw. Sarah sat down at the table and burst into tears.

*

The following morning, Saturday, Sarah was woken early by the summer sunlight streaming in through the dormer windows of her bedroom. They framed a great slab of clear blue sky. Against all the odds Sarah had slept like a log and woke feeling refreshed. It took a second or two for her to register exactly where she was, and that she had the house to herself.

The sun was insistent and horribly cheery. Sarah screwed up her eyes, put her head under the duvet, and made a concerted effort to ignore the morning, but the sun was having none of it. She could feel it creeping across the bed, so eventually, when she couldn't stand its prodding any more, Sarah got up, went downstairs and made a pot of tea, all the time thinking about what she ought to do with the weekend that stretched ahead of her like a forced march.

Feeling sorry for herself wasn't going to do her any good at all, so instead she had a shower, pulled on some old clothes, threw open all the doors and windows, and cleaned the cottage from top to bottom.

It was ironic really, given how many times over the years since the boys had been born that she had longed for a lie-in, and a few more child-free hours to do things without any interruption, that now she had them, all she felt was lost and lonely, and she struggled not to spend the time counting down the hours till the boys got back, while trying to convince herself that in the end it would all work out for the best.

Fortunately hard labour and summer sunshine were the perfect antidotes to loneliness and the blues. Sarah found two old terracotta chimney pots in the lean-to shed at the back of the cottage, along with a stack of flowerpots, a couple of hanging baskets and half a bag of compost, which was inspiration enough for her to drive over to the garden centre and buy trays of bright cheap and cheerful annuals, and spend what remained of the day digging and weeding and generally working herself into exhaustion.

When Kit dropped by with a bunch of flowers in the afternoon her mood had lifted. Her landlord on the other hand seemed the worse for wear, not unlike the flowers, which looked as if he had bought them from a garage forecourt.

'Do you want me to stick them in some water?' he asked, holding them out towards her, as she lugged a tray of petunias across the garden.

Sarah eyed the bouquet speculatively. 'It would probably be kinder just to put them straight into the compost bin,' she said. 'Did they make you pay for those? If so you were robbed.'

At least Kit had the decency to look embarrassed. 'Sorry,' he said. 'It was all they had. And it's the thought that counts and all that. I just wanted to say thank you for everything last night.'

Sarah relented. 'It's fine. It was fun. Did they enjoy it?'

'Oh God, yes. It was fabulous. There wasn't a scrap left and Magda took the last of the summer pudding home with her.'

Sarah smiled. 'Good. I'm glad.'

'About Sunday lunch tomorrow,' he said, while watching Sarah tease a plant out of its little pot to put into one of the hanging baskets she was working on.

'No,' said Sarah, holding up a hand to stop him.

He grinned. 'Was my thought exactly. I was going to say how about we do it next weekend instead? It'll give us both a bit of time to recover.'

Sarah straightened up and stretched her back. 'And I'm going to do this because?'

'Because I showed Magda round last night after we'd eaten and she wants to use the apple barn and the kitchen garden and the dove cote for her photo shoot and she is going to pay me in cold hard cash.'

'And that means what exactly?'

'That I can pay you for doing the cooking.'

Sarah stared at him. 'You told me you were going to pay me anyway. Didn't you?'

'Oh. Ah well, yes, of course, I was,' Kit blustered. 'But this way I can actually give you the money and not just knock it off your rent. So, how about next Sunday? There'll only be six of us.'

Sarah raised her eyebrows; her gaze didn't falter.

Kit wriggled miserably. 'Oh go on, Sarah, please say you'll do it,' he said. 'Cold hard cash and I promise never to buy you flowers again. Not ever, cross my heart.'

Sarah laughed. 'Okay,' she said, 'but just this once, all right? And then that's it. No more. Do you understand?'

He nodded. 'I'll leave the flowers here, shall I?'

Sarah nodded and watched him slope off back towards the Discovery. As he was about to clamber in, Kit turned. 'I've got some troughs up at the house. Would you like me to bring them down for you?'

Sarah stared at him. 'You want me to feed your guests from troughs?' she said incredulously.

'No, I was just thinking that they'd looked really nice planted up with flowers.'

Sarah smiled. 'That would be lovely, thanks.'

71

And then he was gone and Sarah turned her mind back to the plants and getting through her first weekend alone.

*

On Sunday afternoon Colin came to drop off the boys. For some reason he sat outside in the car, staring fixedly ahead. He pipped the horn to attract Sarah's attention when he first pulled up, and then pipped again just as she opened the door, presumably in case she hadn't heard him the first time. He didn't let Harry or Alex out until Sarah was alongside the car.

'I didn't want to let them go on their own just in case they got lost or wandered off, you can't be too careful,' Colin said, before she had a chance to speak. He was parked right next to the garden gate, so close that Sarah could barely open it. Wandering off wasn't much of an option.

The two boys bundled and tumbled out of the back as soon as she opened the door, barely hugging her before they skipped up the garden path and into the cottage. They smelt unfamiliar. Alex had Harry's tee shirt and no one had brushed their hair.

'And I haven't washed their school clothes,' Colin added, turning round to drag the boys' bag off the back seat.

Sarah nodded. She had already decided, given how pleased she was to see her sons back, to be nice, and hope that Colin felt the same and that he would leave without launching into a conversation about how all this was her fault and asking if she had any idea how much he was suffering, although when Sarah took a long hard look at him it was quite obvious that he was.

Colin looked old, unwashed and unkempt, and his sweater – one that she couldn't remember seeing before – had a nasty, greasy, dried-eggy stain down the front of it that did nothing to help the impression that without her, he was letting himself go. For a moment Sarah was torn between pity and the realisation that she had no idea what it was she had seen in him all those years ago. Looking at his face it was blindingly obvious exactly what kind of man Colin was.

He had a thin angry mouth and a miserable peevish expression, which she knew wasn't just about how things were between them now, but what he saw as a lifetime of personal slights, grievances and humiliations. His whole body announced that he thought life owed him, and owed him big – and that at the moment, Sarah owed him most of all.

'I think Alex has got head lice,' he said, stuffing a stray pair of pyjama bottoms into the bag. 'And it's high time he got out of the habit of sleeping with that damned rabbit. *Where's Big-Bunny, I need Big Bunny,*' he whined in a sharp impression of Alex's little-boy voice. 'It's ridiculous for a boy of his age.'

Still Sarah didn't bite, although it was getting harder with every word. She knew from years of living with him that Colin was trying a scattergun approach, hoping that something he said would hit home and hurt and that she would retaliate and then they'd be off. Except that she wasn't planning on playing that game again; not now, not ever again if she could possibly help it.

'Thanks for bringing them back,' she said, taking the bag as he passed it through the window. She kept her tone neutral and made a point of not catching his eye.

Colin sniffed and nodded towards the cottage. 'Looks like you fell on your feet, Little Miss Happy, roses round the door and your hanging baskets; living your happy-ever-after life in your little cute country cottage. Makes me wonder if you didn't have this planned all along.'

Sarah made the effort to keep her expression blank, turned and walked back towards the cottage. 'And we really need to talk about money,' he shouted after her. Sarah kept on walking, although the temptation was to turn round and see just how much of the boys' weekend bag she could stuff down his miserable throat.

What stopped her was the revelation that actually Colin was right. Not that she had planned it, obviously, no one could have planned for Ms Peony Tyler, but Sarah couldn't remember a time in the last few years when she had felt so at ease with her life or so relaxed – lonely weekends apart. *Little Miss Happy*? Against all the odds Sarah smiled.

As Colin was about to pull away Kit drove up behind him in his Discovery. Sarah turned to watch as Colin slowed down, and her landlord jumped out.

'Hi, I brought you those troughs I was telling you about,' Kit said, apparently oblivious to Colin still crawling along the verge in his car.

'That's great. Do you need a hand to unload them?' asked Sarah.

'No, you're fine,' he said. 'Where would you like them?'

'I was thinking maybe under the windows either side of the front door might be nice.'

Kit nodded. 'Yeah, you're right. Oh, and I've got a couple of bags of compost you can have. I'm not using them, although you'll probably need more, and you might want to put some slow-release fertiliser in with it.'

Sarah nodded. 'That's brilliant, thank you.'

'My pleasure,' said Kit. 'And if you need any more plants there's a chap in the village; he lives in one of the bungalows opposite the church, sells them from his back gate, Fred Tullet. We've always got our plants from him.'

In the lane Colin was finally pulling away from the verge, but not before Sarah saw the expression on his face. He didn't look at all happy, his lips pressed tight shut in a peevish angry line. And wickedly and unbidden, but with no malice at all, Sarah's smile widened out a notch or two.

'I'll put the kettle on,' she said to Kit, who was busy opening the tailgate. 'Do you want a slice of cake?'

'Has the pope got a balcony?' he asked, grinning.

Sarah headed inside and realised as she did that actually Colin had been spot on; she was already beginning to love the cottage and their new life without him. It wasn't just a shelter from the storm that her life had become, it was a new life and one that, given time, she would be happy to grown in to, and that the grief and sense of loss would come and go and eventually fade.

Since they'd moved in Sarah and the boys were all getting up earlier, woken by the sound of birdsong and sunshine; their days began with breakfast in the kitchen, with the back door open to let in the view of the tangled summer garden, the air heavy with the smell of roses and lavender and just a hint of the honeysuckle that really came into its own in the evening. Working from home three days a week meant that Sarah had time to enjoy more of it, and it was hard to put into words just how lovely it was for the boys to have the garden and the stream and the run of the estate. Yes, there was no denying that the weekend had been lonely, but watching Colin drive away she knew that she would adjust and get used to it, she really, really would.

Colin and Peony and the house in Cambridge that she had loved so very much already felt like something in an almost distant past.

Sarah walked inside, dropped the boys' dirty clothes by the washing machine, plugged in the kettle and was surprised to find herself humming cheerily, while at the front of the house Kit arranged the troughs, helped by Alex and Harry who had gone outside the minute Colin had driven away.

Sarah took the cake tin out of the pantry. She had done the right thing, she really had, now all she had to work out was what happened next.

'Tea up,' she called, sliding plates and mugs onto the table, and was rewarded by the sounds of feet.

After Kit had gone Sarah set about planting up the troughs. Kit had been right; she was going to need more compost and more plants if she was going to fill them all.

'Do you fancy a trip down into the village?' she asked the boys who, having eaten a lot of cake and crisps, were playing in the garden.

'Can we walk?' asked Harry. 'We can cut across by the stream. Me and Alex can take our nets and a bucket. Kit said there are trout down the bottom end.'

'Not really. I need to get some more plants from a man Kit told me about. I'm not sure what he's got, but if they come in trays like the other ones I bought, we won't be able to carry them back if we're walking.'

Harry nodded. 'Are you going to get married to Kit?' he asked thoughtfully, as Sarah went in to grab her handbag and lock up. He seemed to have grown up a lot over the last couple of weeks.

'No, of course not. What makes you say that?'

'Dad said.'

Sarah smiled and stroked her fingers through Harry's curly hair. 'No, honey. Kit's very kind, and he is our friend, Harry, you know that, but that doesn't mean we're getting married. All we are doing is renting the cottage from him.'

Harry considered his reply for a second or two. 'Yes, but Dad said, you see, next thing you know they'll be shacking up together. Doesn't that mean getting married?'

Sarah shook her head, silently cursing Colin, and wondering who he had been talking to; she just hoped that it wasn't the boys.

'No, no, it doesn't, Harry. You can help me plant the flowers when we get back if you like. Come on, let's go and get in the car.'

'What's a trout?' asked Alex.

Fred Tullet was selling all sorts of plants from a little roadside stall on the green, right opposite to the church, like Kit had said. In his garden behind his bungalow he had a greenhouse packed with annuals and houseplants, and alongside it was a big gravelled area filled with all sorts of cottage garden perennials and shrubs, potted up, labelled and ready to go.

Sarah didn't know where to start. Fred's garden was a little treasure trove, and the plants were just perfect for the cottage. She only wished she'd found it before going to the garden centre, and had gone on Saturday without the boys, who didn't see shopping for plants as any kind of a treat.

'Can we go home?' whined Alex, as Sarah sorted through the pots.

'I won't be long,' she said. 'I promise.'

'Can we have an ice-cream?'

'They don't do ice-cream here. You can have some as soon as we get home.'

'I'm bored and I'm hot *and* my legs ache,' Alex sighed, as he slumped down onto the path. Sarah was about to tell him to get up when she realised how pale he looked and for the first time noticed the bags under his eyes. 'Are you okay?'

'I want to go home,' he whinged.

'Are you tired?'

He nodded again. 'A bit, me and Harry stayed up and watched films with Daddy's friend. And he taught us how to meditate, and I fell asleep and then the next day we went down the pub. And Peony said we could have just as many fizzy drinks as we wanted and—' At which point Harry appeared.

'I'll look after him while you choose your plants,' he said, coming over all big-brotherly and man of the house, and hauling Alex to his feet, looking for all the world as if he was about to frog march him back to the car. Sarah was about to say something about late nights and fizzy drinks, and then realised that there was no point; Alex and Harry were powerless here. They couldn't decide where they went or what they ate or what time they went to bed. She needed to have a word with Colin.

Closing her mouth, Sarah said, 'You both look tired. Why don't you go and sit in the car? How about when we get finished here, we go home and have some supper and a bath and then I'll read you a story and everyone has an early night?'

'Sounds like a great idea to me,' said a man's voice.

Sarah jumped, dropping one of the pots she had been holding, and turning, stared up into the face of a tall blond man, dressed in shorts and tee shirt, who was clutching two pots of foxgloves and another of lupins. He set his plants down and picked hers up, scooping up the spilt compost.

'I'm so sorry, I didn't mean to make you jump,' he said with a grin. 'It's just that it's been a long day. The idea of a hot bath and an early night is heaven.'

He looked as if he had been out in the garden too. Along with the shorts he was wearing Cat boots, with thick socks folded down over the tops, and had a smear of compost across one cheek. His long legs were tanned and muscular. Sarah looked away, realising with a start that she was staring.

She managed a smile as she took the flowerpot from him. 'Thanks, but actually I was talking to the boys.'

He nodded. 'I guessed.'

He had blue eyes framed by a network of laughter lines and a tan that suggested he spent a lot of time outdoors. Something about him lit a tiny, long-dead spark deep inside her. Sarah made the effort to get a grip. She recognised the feeling and felt herself blush; *she fancied him*. She was so stunned that she almost said it aloud.

Fortunately the man seemed more concerned by the selection of plants she'd got arranged in a tumble around her feet. 'Why don't you let me give you a hand with those. Fred's got some boxes round behind the greenhouse. Do you want me to go and grab you a couple?'

'No, no, that's fine, thanks, I don't want to put you to any trouble,' said Sarah, aware that he was eyeing up her too, and the sensation was far from unpleasant, although she could feel her colour rising even more, and wished she had taken the trouble to do her hair before coming out. Her oversized tee shirt and cut-offs weren't exactly flattering and her hair was pulled up and back in a scrunchie – all except for the hot sweaty bits that had escaped and she suspected were currently glued to the side of her face.

'I insist. I'm helping Fred get the place tidied up,' he said. 'It'll be good to get rid of some of them. He can't bear to throw anything away. Hang on, I'll just nip and get you a couple.'

'Do you work here?' asked Sarah, before she could stop herself.

He grinned. 'No, or at least, not really. I'm starting a new job in a few weeks' time and I said I'd help Fred in the meanwhile. And to be honest I quite like working outside.'

'Are you local?' she heard herself saying as he was about to turn back towards the greenhouse. God, what must she sound like?

Alex tugged her arm. 'Stranger danger,' he hissed out of the corner of his mouth. Sarah stared down at him.

Harry nodded. 'We don't know him, Mum,' he whispered. 'You're not supposed to talk to him.' Sarah smiled as the penny dropped. Both boys scowled at her.

'I'm buying a house up on the Becks,' the man said, oblivious.

Sarah nodded as if she knew what that meant. Maybe the boys were right. What sort of man flirts with a woman with two children? And where had her fancying gene been hiding itself all these years?

'How about you?'

Sarah smiled, not wanting to be specific. 'I've just rented a cottage in the village.'

Damn, she thought, she should have said we.

Just then an elderly man appeared from the back door of the bungalow carrying a large cardboard box. 'Here you go, Miss. Thought you'd like this,' he said. 'I saw you struggling. Now have you found everything you want?'

'I think so, thank you. You've got some lovely plants here.'

The old man grinned. 'Nice of you to say so, old varieties most of them. I like the traditional cottage garden flowers. Anything special you're looking for?'

Sarah shook her head. 'No, not really,' she said. 'Just browsing for anything that catches my eye. But I'm sure I'll be back now that I've found you. I've got some troughs to fill up and I'm thinking maybe I could sort out the flowerbeds now I know where to get the right plants.'

The old man nodded. 'Well, if you need any help, I'm always happy to give advice. You local, are you?'

Sarah was about to answer when the blond man returned with a couple of plastic trays, and thinking about what the boys had said, she decided not to go into any more detail.

Seeing Fred, the man smiled. 'Ah, pipped at the post again.'

'You know me, I'm a sucker for a fine-looking woman,' said Fred, with a wink.

The man laughed while Sarah felt her colour rise. 'I know when I'm beaten, Fred,' he said. 'I'll go and get the compost bins sorted.' He turned to Sarah. 'Nice to meet you.' And with that he headed back up the path.

Fred looked at her collection of plants. 'Right you are, now if that's everything I'll add them up and then me and your boys'll help you load them into the car, won't we, lads? You gardeners too, are you?' he asked Harry and Alex, as he boxed everything up. The boys started to chat to him as he explained what to do with each plant and where to plant it and gave them both a little packet of sunflower seeds to experiment with when they got home.

'You'll need a cane or stake when they get really tall. Get your daddy to find you one.'

'Our daddy doesn't live with us any more,' said Alex, in a voice that made him sound like a Dickens orphan.

Sarah stared at him hoping to will him into silence but instead Fred smiled and said, 'Well, in that case if you can't find a cane or a stake you come back here and I'll find you one. All right?'

Alex nodded.

Sarah thanked him and a few minutes later they were all packed up and ready to go. As she was about to drive away she looked up the garden path towards the greenhouse. The blond man was there and he was looking in her direction. Catching her eye, he waved, which made her stomach do that odd flippy thing.

'I want a wee,' whined Alex.

'And I want a drink,' said Harry, which focused Sarah's mind on things other than her newly rediscovered libido.

'And more cake,' said Alex.

Canadian Lemon Loaf

Ingredients:

One-third cup of soft butter
1 cup of white sugar
2 eggs
1½ cups of self-raising flour
1 tsp baking powder
dash salt
½ cup of milk
grated rind of a lemon
To decorate: a third of a cup of sugar and juice of the lemon

Method:

Preheat oven to 350 Fahrenheit

Put butter in mixing bowl, mix thoroughly (use an electric beater), slowly add sugar, keep beating.

Meanwhile in a second bowl mix (by hand) the flour, salt and baking powder. Then grate the lemon rind into the 'flour' bowl. Mix.

Back to the electric mixer bowl. Add the eggs one at a time and mix well. Add the milk a little at a time, alternating this with a little flour, add each in turn, finishing off with the last of the flour, all the while beating slowly. Mix well.

Pour into a well-greased loaf tin and bake at 350 degrees for about 45–50 minutes. Test by sticking a long pin or skewer into it. If mixture sticks, give it another 5 minutes.

When loaf is baked, take from oven and while still warm, with a toothpick or skewer make some holes and pour the following mixture over it: one third cup of sugar mixed with juice of lemon.

Let cool before trying to remove from pan.

Chapter Ten
...make lemonade

Now that Sarah was working from home three days a week, Melissa often caught the bus and came over to work with her at the cottage; so on Thursday a few weeks later, the two of them were working from Sarah's kitchen table, Wi-Fi going flat out, as between them they mocked up the Hanleys bumper Christmas special edition of the magazine. The content they wrote for the magazine was always a minimum of three months ahead of publication date, but the stories and features for some dates and events were in place months before they were needed.

Getting big chunks of Christmas sorted by the end of June was an absolute must if they were to have everything done before the rush started. Working from Sarah's cottage had been Melissa's idea; after all, who didn't need a field trip once in a while? And according to Melissa, morale in the office was low.

'You'll see for yourself when you come in tomorrow. It's like a morgue in there at the moment.'

Sarah nodded absently. 'Seemed all right to me. I was in for the Monday meeting, remember? Everyone seemed okay then.'

Melissa rolled her eyes. 'That was before Mike in technical support went; he said he was going before he got the old heave-ho,' she said, cramming another biscuit into her mouth. 'Cleared his desk out and off he went, said it was better to jump than be pushed. I'm going to miss him. It feels like the fickle finger of fate creeping round the office.'

Melissa mimed a claw-like finger and then, giving a big theatrical sigh, closed her laptop. 'It is just me or are all these bloody reindeer getting on your nerves as well? It's strappy-top and suntan-lotion weather outside and I'm here advising the Hanley hoards on the great deals we've got on silk- and cashmere-mix thermals and last-minute gifts for those tricky people in your life.'

Melissa sat back and stretched. 'How last-minute can you get about Christmas in June, for heaven's sake? How's it going over there?'

Sarah glanced up. 'Oh, okay. I'm just thinking about the fickle finger of fate, and about maybe moving the boys to the village school in September and about what to cook for lunch for six – three courses, two vegans and a Buddhist – on Sunday, for your bloody cousin.'

Melissa laughed. 'I was thinking more along the lines of copy for the Christmas special. I need two paragraphs on why tartan pyjamas are the perfect Christmas gift.'

'Oh, sorry,' said Sarah, reddening furiously. 'You mean about work. It's just that this cooking lark is taking over. So far I've done a Sunday lunch, a dinner party, two picnics and some sort of cold buffet business lunch thing for him. Although this time I have said right, that's it, no more. Surely he can't owe anyone else food? So, what does Kit do as soon as I tell him the catering service is finished? Starts sending me emails about people he'd like to invite and how am I fixed for catering a midsummer party, a Halloween bonfire, and a thanksgiving dinner for some American friends, that's not to mention the fact he's already booked me for Christmas.'

'I knew you'd fit right in here,' Melissa pointed out. 'I hope Kit's paying you well.'

'Not yet, but he will be very soon, thanks to Magda Holmes.'

'The wicked witch of the East?' said Melissa in surprise.

'The very same. I told you she was looking for somewhere to do a photo-shoot for their Best of East Anglian Food Guide and she's going to do it here, didn't I?'

Melissa nodded.

'Well, they're here next week, I think. And she's paying him.'

'And what, you're going to do the catering for it?'

'Good God, no. The plan is that Magda's going to pay Kit and then Kit will pay me.'

'Sounds like a perfect arrangement. You know, it feels like you've always lived here.'

Sarah laughed. 'You mean in amongst the owls and stuff, and your lunatic relatives?'

'Something like that.'

Sarah glanced around the interior of the kitchen, thinking about how much her life had changed over the last few weeks.

'So, tartan pyjamas?' she said, turning her attention back to her laptop.

Melissa groaned. 'Oh no, don't.'

'Do you want some lemonade?' Sarah asked, getting to her feet.

Melissa nodded. 'Anything has got to be better than bed socks and hats with antlers.'

Sarah took two glasses off the dresser, her mind on what to cook for lunch on Sunday, and reached for the lemonade as she opened the fridge door. Maybe couscous and aubergines? Or stuffed peppers or—

'Aren't you going to get that?' asked Melissa.

The sound of her voice made Sarah jump. She snapped back to the here and now with a jolt and stared at her friend in total surprise. Close by the phone was ringing.

'I could get it if you want,' suggested Melissa, making no effort to move.

'No, thank you, I'll get it,' said Sarah, sliding the jug onto the table and checking the caller display. It was Colin. 'You need to add fizzy water to that,' she said. 'It's in the fridge.'

It was tempting to let the machine take the call but from her experience over the last few weeks Sarah knew that he would only ring her back, calling over and over and over until she finally relented. Picking up the receiver she headed upstairs to her tiny office in the box room.

'I just wanted to let you know that I'm moving in with Peony,' Colin said, without any preamble. 'Probably over the weekend. I need you to explain to the boys. I mean I'm sure they'll be fine with it. After all, I think it's time we all moved on, and they know Peony. All that chanting is getting on my nerves and Elliot seems to think that I ought to be doing something around the house.' Colin's tone was mocking. 'Doing something; like working on my book isn't enough. Apparently I need something physical to ground me and to learn to actively embrace what it means to share a space. For God's sake, the man is barking mad. It's only because he wants his garden done, and he's got a dishwasher. I honestly can't see his problem with me leaving my washing up in the sink. And there are only so many lectures on being at one with the universe that a man can take. Anyway, it makes more sense if I'm next door so that I can keep an eye on the house till the sale goes through.'

Sarah said nothing and instead had a vivid picture of Colin wandering round to greet their prospective buyers in nothing but his dressing gown, hair awry, scratching himself; if that didn't lose them the sale nothing would. The idea of his being with Peony oddly left her almost completely indifferent.

'Any idea when the money will be through?' he was asking.

'The solicitors said about another couple of weeks; they are waiting for some searches or something,' said Sarah. 'Last time I rang they told me everything should be complete by the middle of July.'

'What's to search? This is just taking too long.'

'These things take time. The people who've bought it are as eager to get in as we are to sell it. It shouldn't be long now.'

Colin sighed. 'So you keeping saying. You told me that there was no chain, the couple who want it are living in a rented house and it would be a cash sale.'

'And as far as I know nothing's changed.'

'Probably drug dealers, or money laundering,' sighed Colin. 'What kind of people have that kind of money just sitting round?'

'People who've already sold their house,' suggested Sarah, not that Colin was listening. He was back onto the downside of living with Buddhists who cared about tidiness, personal space, and foot odour.

Through the little window in the box room Sarah could hear birdsong and the whisper of the wind in the leaves of trees. The sounds led her gaze out over the rolling parkland that surrounded Roseberry Hall and the cottage. From the box-room window she could make out Kit walking across the field towards the cottage. He appeared to be deep in conversation with Magda Holmes, who was looking up at him with undisguised delight.

As they got to the stile that led into the lane, Sarah watched as Magda clambered up onto the step, grabbed hold of Kit and – pulling him down towards her – kissed him. Hard. Kit pulled away as if he had been scalded and then after a moment or two looked as if he might have relented at which point she kissed him again. As the two of them parted, Magda was smiling like the cat that had the cream, and then they carried on walking up the lane back towards Roseberry Hall.

Stunned, Sarah stared at the two of them.

Colin meanwhile was still talking. 'Anyway it'll all be over soon and I'm damned if I'm paying to have his precious rug cleaned. I was thinking maybe I should ring the buyers and see what the hold-up is.'

Sarah looked heavenwards. 'God give me strength,' she muttered under her breath. 'There isn't any hold-up. This is how long it takes. It's not anything they're doing. Please don't ring them.'

'Why not?'

'Because we can't afford to lose this sale.'

Colin paused. 'So you say. And by the way your solicitor hasn't replied to my last letter. I want you to ring him.'

Sarah sighed and closed her eyes. 'Can we talk about this later, Colin? I'm working at the moment.' Working and also thinking: Magda and Kit? Maybe she had been seeing things.

'Oh and I'm not working, is that what you're saying?' growled Colin.

'No,' Sarah began. 'I want to talk to you about the bo—'

She was going to say boys, but before she could, Colin snapped, 'I'll ring you another time, when you're calmer. Peony finds it terribly hard when you keep ringing me up and upsetting me.' And with that he hung up.

'I don't bloody well ring you,' said Sarah to the open burring line and then took a deep breath. Eventually all this stuff with Colin would be behind her and there was part of her that couldn't wait.

'You okay up there?' shouted Melissa.

'Fine,' called Sarah.

'In that case get yourself down here and help me sort through these bloody reindeer.'

Lemonade Cordial

Ingredients:

8 lemons, plus more for cutting into slices as a garnish if desired

12 ozs Sugar or 340grm of golden or ordinary granulated sugar or honey

(this can be adjusted to taste)

500 mls or 1 pint water

Fizzy or still water to dilute to taste

Method:

Wash lemons thoroughly.

Roll lemons firmly on a hard surface until they become soft. This will make them easier to juice.

Carefully remove the zest from 3 lemons.

In a pan over medium heat, add the sugar, the lemon zest and 500ml (1pt) of water.

Simmer gently for about 5 minutes or until sugar has dissolved and the mixture has a light yellow colour. **Do not boil**.

Remove from heat and allow to cool.

Squeeze the juice from all the lemons.

Strain the lemon juice into a jug.

Strain the sugar mixture into the jug, stir.

Fill chilled glasses with ice and pour in a little of the lemonade cordial.

Top up with still or fizzy water to taste.

Garnish each glass with sliced lemons and a sprig of mint.

Serve.

Store any unused cordial in the refrigerator.

Chapter Eleven
When life goes a bit bananas

Later that afternoon Sarah dropped Melissa back at office and then went to pick the boys up from school. She had barely pulled into the drive of the cottage when Kit drove up behind her in the Discovery and hurried over to intercept her.

'Where's the fire?' she asked.

'What?' Kit looked even more befuddled than usual.

'It's just an expression,' said Sarah. 'If someone looks as if they're in a hurry and a bit anxious.'

'Oh right. I'm both of those. We need to talk,' he said as the boys bundled inside with their P.E. kits and book bags. 'I've got a problem, well, not so much a problem, more of a job.'

Sarah shooed the boys into the house. 'I'll be in in a minute,' she called after them, and turned her attention back to her landlord. 'Kit, I'm not really with you and I have to get the boys something to eat. Anyway I thought you were the idle rich. Don't you already have a job managing the estate, shooting things and oppressing the poor?'

Kit looked appalled. 'Good God, no. I'm useless at all that sort of thing, just like Daddy. My mother and the trustees sorted it all out so that other people manage the estate and I get an allowance. No, this is much, much worse. Magda wants me to work for her.'

Sarah stopped mid-stride. 'Magda? You mean Magda Holmes?'

Kit nodded. 'She came over to see me today.'

Sarah didn't let him know that she had seen them together, instead she nodded.

'Magda's got this plan,' said Kit, sounding miserable.

'What sort of plan?' asked Sarah cautiously, sensing that Kit was about to drop a bombshell.

'Can we talk about this inside?' he said, glancing over his shoulder.

'Of course we can. Although I'm sure no one can overhear us.'

'Oh, it's not that,' said Kit. 'It's just that I'm starving.'

A few minutes later tucked up at the kitchen table with a mug of tea and a big slice of cake, Kit said, 'Magda wants me to do a cookery thing for her TV show.'

Sarah stared at him. 'Are you completely mad, Kit? You can't cook.'

Kit shifted his weight uncomfortably. 'Well, I know that and you know that,' he said. 'The thing is Magda wants to take you out to lunch and talk about it.'

'Me?'

He nodded.

'Oh okay, I see. So she knows that it's me who is actually doing the cooking for you?' asked Sarah.

'Not exactly, and I'd rather we kept it that way,' he said, looking increasingly sheepish.

'You're going to have to tell her sooner or later if you're going to do a show for her, Kit, or are you hoping that I will?'

'No, please don't say anything,' said Kit.

Sarah stared at him. 'Are you serious?'

'I know it's a big ask but to be perfectly honest I need the money, Sarah. The trustees and Mummy keep me on a very tight rein and treat me like some sort of overgrown child that needs taking care of and who can't be trusted.'

Sarah raised her eyebrows. 'I wonder why that is?' she said. The sarcasm was entirely lost on him.

'This is the first thing I've ever done in my entire life that's truly mine,' he said.

'But it's not yours,' Sarah said gently. 'It's mine.'

'Not the cooking, maybe, but the presenting would be.'

'Presenting?'

He nodded enthusiastically. 'We did some filming while they were doing the photo shoot. It went really well and was huge fun. Anyway Magda likes my style. She said so. This is my big chance. Please, Sarah, don't tell her. I just want to do this for myself. Please, say that you'll help me.'

'Magda really ought to know,' Sarah said.

'No, she didn't,' he said. 'Please. Look, it's just one segment on her show. Just fifteen minutes.'

Who could possibly resist?

'So what do you want me to do?' sighed Sarah.

Kit smiled. 'Just the cooking,' he said, taking a bite out of the cake. 'Oh, and if you could work out the menus and all that sort of stuff, that would be great. You know this cake is very good – maybe we can get in on the show.'

Which was why, the following week, Sarah and Magda Holmes were in Cambridge having lunch in a smart little restaurant at a table on a balcony that overlooked the Cam.

'Darling, I'm so glad you could come. I can't thank you enough for introducing me to Kit. What a gem he's turned out to be,' purred Magda, guiding the morsel of dessert that clung to the corner of her mouth between her generously re-plumped lips with the tip of a perfectly manicured pinkie. Magda paused. 'And he's very cute, don't you think?'

Magda had done the inviting, leaving Sarah to make the arrangements. The restaurant was within walking distance of Sarah's office, the food there was always good, the staff were lovely and on a sunny day, sitting out on the balcony, there were few places in Cambridge that could beat it.

When Sarah remained silent, Magda laughed, leaning in a little closer and patting her hand. 'Oh come, darling. Don't tell me you haven't noticed? Or has what's his name put you off men for life? Let me tell you, sweetie, husbands come and husbands go but the possibility of a little off-piste lust is a joy forever. You need to get back in the saddle, get back out there. Plenty more fish in the sea.

'Kit's told me how much he loves having you and the boys living in the cottage, in fact if I think he might have a bit of a crush,' Magda paused, eyes gimlet-sharp, 'I might get just a teensy-weensy bit jealous, you know.'

She paused again; it didn't take a genius to see that she was fishing. She watched Sarah carefully, gauging her reaction, and when there was none, Magda continued, 'I presume that Kit has told you about the TV pilot we've got planned, hasn't he? We're going to be going with a short segment to begin with that we can slot into our show Harts and Holmes – like a little show reel. A show within a show.'

Sarah nodded. 'He did mention it. I thought you said that Guy was going to be here today?'. Guy, the long-suffering and extremely charming Mr Holmes.

'At a pig farm, darling; he's obsessed with them. They're doing a blind sausage tasting with some boy scouts and the local vicar. Not really my kind of thing at all, if I'm honest. He sends his love but I'm sure neither of us will miss him, will we?' said Magda. 'Not when we've so many other things to talk about.'

'What exactly are we here to talk about?' asked Sarah. So far throughout lunch Magda had pointedly avoided talking about anything very much at all.

'Oh, I like someone who cuts to the chase,' Magda said. 'What I really wanted was to say a little thank you in person for putting me in touch with Kit. And you were so right about Roseberry Hall. The walled garden was absolutely perfect for the photo shoot for the new Harts and Holmes book. That whole rural rambling vibe – perfect, perfect, perfect and I love what you're doing with it for the magazine. Rosa let me have a little peek at the feature you've been working on. And you know Kit was the most perfect host. You should have seen the buffet lunch he did when I went to talk to him about my ideas for the show.' Magda leaned in a little closer.

So that was who the business lunch had been for, thought Sarah, as the other woman continued, 'We've got plans for Kit, I mean big plans – we're really excited, Sarah. You should see the menu Kit's come up with for his first slot on the show. It's wonderful – very simple, but striking, really accessible and bang on trend. I'm telling you, the man is a genius, pure genuis. I think we might be looking at the next big thing.'

Sarah stared at her, feeling her stomach tighten. 'Kit told me that he was just going to do a little feature in one show. Ten minutes, tops.' Although she obviously didn't mention it, it had taken her ages to come up with something Kit could actually manage to put together without ruining it.

Magda waved the words away. 'I know, that's right, it's just that I don't want to frighten him off. Take it one step at a time; but between you and me we've got a lot of ideas, plans. I'm just buzzing with the possibilities. I'm already putting feelers out to people at the BBC, Sky, Channel Four. As far as I'm concerned with Kit the sky is the limit.'

Sarah stared at her. 'Are you serious?' she whispered.

'Oh gosh, yes. Has Kit never cooked for you, darling?' Magda said. 'Because if he hasn't you should go down on bended knees and beg him to. It makes you wonder where someone like him has been hiding all this time, and why I hadn't heard of him before.'

As she spoke Magda toyed with her fork. 'Actually I'm thinking that you should seriously consider getting Kit to write for the magazine. Prime the pump; get his face out there, start to build him an audience.'

'Right,' Sarah began, trying to sound casual, turning her attention to the remnants of her dessert.

'Really. I'm telling you. You should. He's a natural. I mean really. We're already talking to people about a book deal.'

'You are?' asked Sarah.

'Obviously, if we can get a tie-in. I really think it might be good for the magazine if you got him on board early,' Magda continued. 'Rather than just doing a feature, get him to write you a few things, maybe a regular column. What do you think?' she pressed.

Sarah was feeling increasingly panicked and realised that she was not altogether sure what she was being asked. The problem was that Kit's entanglement with Magda was her fault. If she hadn't needed the money then she would never have suggested getting Kit to let Magda use the house for the photos and none of this would be happening.

Sarah stared nervously at Magda Holmes, who smiled wolfishly.

Why the hell couldn't Kit have told Magda the truth? He had put her in an impossible position.

Across the table Magda was still speaking. 'Guy and I have been discussing several options. If the pilot goes well we're going to go all guns blazing to get Kit onto prime-time mainstream – what do you think? As I said I've been talking to people already. We're thinking cross- platform. I've got someone working on a mock- up for a website, and then there's a book and I was thinking maybe a DVD.'

Magda mimed a spotlight with two perfectly manicured hands. 'A Year at Roseberry Hall. Christmas at Roseberry Hall. Kit's Perfect Picnics – the possibilities are just endless. What I was thinking was – well, let me get straight to it, Sarah. There are two or three things. First of all I want you to think about helping write Kit's book. I'm not sure how well he can write and you've got already got a track record with the magazine, writing for our target market. And I think we really need something more than just recipes, we need something about his life, his values, his whole ethos. We need to showcase Kit as a person, as a man, as much as his cooking.' Magda paused.

When Sarah didn't reply Magda sighed. 'I'm offering you a job, Sarah.'

Sarah was about to say that she already had a job when she saw something else in Magda's expression and felt the words drying in her mouth.

'But—' Sarah began.

Magda raised her eyebrows, which was no mean feat with all that Botox, and then she mimed having her throat cut.

'Me?' gasped Sarah, feeling her own throat constricting.

'Not just you, poppet. The whole department; redundant,' said Magda, sotto voce, glancing over her shoulder to ensure that no one else could hear what she was saying. 'Although you're not to breathe a single word, you understand. Not one word. Rosa will kill me if she knew that I'd told you.' She laughed, apparently totally unaware of the impact of what she was saying. 'The whole thing is being wound up after Christmas and going to be put out to freelancers. But I'm sure you'll be all right, sweetie. I mean Rosa loves your stuff, and this thing with Kit can't do you any harm, can it? There'll be an overall editor, obviously, and someone in admin, but everything else will be outsourced. It had to come. Let's face it, the whole thing was a bit of a dinosaur.'

Sarah felt as if someone was sitting on her chest.

Completely oblivious Magda pulled out her smart phone and scrolled through the pages till she reached the screen she was looking for, dipping into the notes as she spoke. 'Right, so as I said, what I'm thinking is that we need to get a glimpse of the man behind the façade, his approach, his ethics.'

'The whole department,' Sarah murmured, still in shock.

Magda nodded. 'That's what Rosa said, now about Kit…'

Sarah wasn't altogether sure if she wanted to talk about Kit, but Magda pressed on. 'He was telling me about how committed he is to ethically sourced food, buying local produce, and to the environment.'

Sarah stared at her. 'What? I'm sorry?'

'Kit, he was telling me about how concerned he is about the environment. We need to get that across.'

'We are talking about Kit here, aren't we?' said Sarah.

She didn't like to point out that this was the man whose of idea of saving the planet was eating ready meals straight out of the microwave, in the little plastic dish, to save on the washing up.

Magda breezed on. 'Anyway I've already talked to Kit about it and he seems to think you're just the person for the job. He's going to be big, Sarah. He's going to be a household name. What do you think?'

'I'm not sure. Kit always strikes me as being quite a private person, really quite – quite, er…shy,' blustered Sarah, playing for time, trying to process all the things Magda had told her.

'Oh, come on. You're joking, aren't you?' Magda said. 'He doesn't strike me as being at all shy. No, not at all. He was absolutely fabulous when we did the food guide photo shoot at the hall. He's a natural. We did a piece to camera with him during the show. Caught him off guard, better than any screen test, and he was fabulous. I can't tell you how much the camera loves him. And you have to admit he is very good-looking. I rather like that whole little-boy-lost thing he does, those eyes, that devil-may-care approach to life. And I'm sure a lot of our viewers will feel the same – that and his approach to cooking.'

'You've seen him cook?' asked Sarah.

'Obviously,' said Magda.

Sarah tried very hard to keep her expression neutral, knowing damn well Magda was lying. 'And what did you think of his kitchen?'

Magda's eyes narrowed. 'I'm sorry?'

'The kitchen. His kitchen; didn't you think that it might not be quite up to scratch? A bit basic?' Sarah stared pointedly at Magda, who looked away. 'Actually, Magda, in my opinion, it's more bush tucker than basic.'

Magda laughed. 'Really? Is it? Well, maybe you're right. Yes, well, clearly you are. Surely that's half the charm of the place. If Kit can produce amazing food there then surely any of us can manage it anywhere. Anyway let me get to my second point – oh, hang on – that's my phone.'

She looked relieved to take the call.

Sarah turned to watch the river flowing by, studded with ducks and cut by the punts as they made their way up and downstream. Redundant – the word hung over her like a great storm cloud. What the hell was she going to do? Maybe she should take Magda up on her offer and write a cookbook starring Kit.

Sarah glanced across at the other woman. Harts and Holmes had had a cosy little arrangement with the owners of Hanleys for as long as anyone could remember. It was tricky to pin down exactly where the arrangement had originated and what it consisted of, but Sarah – and to be fair most of the rest of the staff – had always assumed that at some point in the distant past Madga had to have slept with one of the Hanley brothers or possibly both of them.

At some time, long before Sarah had joined Hanleys, Magda had made in-house training films for the company, and at some point branched out, and moved up into making lifestyle magazine programmes for satellite TV. Ever since Sarah had worked at Hanleys one part of Magda's show was always featured in the magazine, pushing some must-have gadget or a holiday or the next big thing in beauty, home or garden, which Hanleys would stock via a mutually run website and shift the stuff by the lorry-load.

Across the table Magda snapped her phone shut, dropped it into her handbag and without so much as a pause carried on speaking.

'The other thing I wanted to discuss,' she said, her voice lowering to a conspiratorial whisper, 'is if there is anyone I should know about?'

'I'm sorry?' Sarah was totally bemused now. 'I'm not with you? Do you mean another production company?'

Magda laughed. 'No, not another company. No.' She paused for a moment or two. 'Actually maybe you're right, maybe it is that he is just very private about his personal life. He is very secretive.'

'Who, Kit?' Sarah stared at her. 'In what way?'

'Oh, come on, Sarah, there's no need to be coy with me. He's a good-looking guy. You live there, for heaven's sake, you must see all the comings and goings. Has he got a girlfriend, a wife, maybe an ex-wife?'

'Oh, I see what you mean. No, as far as I know Kit's single.'

'And not gay?'

'Not as far as I know,' said Sarah. 'He's had girlfriends in the past, I think – he never really talks about that kind of thing.'

'And you're not, you know?' Magda tipped her head suggestively. 'You and him. I mean it wouldn't be the first time, lord of the manor up at the big house, lonely single woman all on your own in that little cottage.'

'Good God, no,' said Sarah quickly. 'No. He's not my type at all.'

Sarah didn't add when she saw Kit it was more like having another child around the place than a potential boyfriend, and that he spent a lot of his supposedly secretive deeply private time playing football in

94

her garden, fishing stuff out of the stream with the boys or drinking tea and eating cake in her kitchen.

'Good, in that case what I'm about to suggest won't tread on anyone's toes then, will it? I've been talking this over with my team and what we've been thinking is what we want to go with is a traditional family vibe, children on the lawn eating tea and sandwiches with the crusts cut off, and great slabs of cake, family and friends gathered round the table looking up lovingly while Daddy carves the Sunday roast. Family on a beach picnic, walking through the woods to a campfire barbeque.'

'With Kit? Are you serious?'

Magda nodded enthusiastically. 'That whole old-fashioned traditional family thing really sells. We've done surveys. That whole retro Fair Isle sweater, homespun, cake-baking thing.'

'And you're telling me this because?'

Magda smiled and tipped her head towards Sarah. 'Because besides needing a ghostwriter, Kit needs a family, darling. A wife, maybe a couple of kids.'

There was a moment's pause and then Sarah shook her head. 'Oh, no,' she said, as the penny dropped and she realised that this was what lunch invitation had really been about. 'No, no way, Magda.' She held up her hands to ward off the suggestion. 'You can count me out. There is no way in hell I'm going to pretend to be Kit's wife. No, no and no.'

'Oh, come on, just hear me out, darling. It would only be an on-air thing obviously, and we'd pay you a retainer on top of anything we get for the book. You and the boys. And we'd never actually say that he's your husband, just imply it – the magic of television. You know what it's like. People join up the dots for themselves.'

Sarah shook her head and said nothing, trying to imagine what Colin would say if he saw her playing happy families on TV with another man. God, it didn't bear thinking about.

Magda paused as if considering how much to tell her and then she sighed. 'All right. I'll put my cards on the table, Sarah. I'll be spending quite a lot of time with Kit over the next few months, working up this new project, creating the brand, to get a genuine feel for it. This is a big deal for a company like ours, we've never done anything like this before and we want to get it right. But you know what men can be like. Guy frets about every little thing. He's concerned about how much time I'm spending with Kit as it is, and when this takes off – to be honest I have no idea how long I'm going to have to devote to Kit to get this project off the ground, nor how Guy is going to take me being around a tall, red-blooded, good-looking, younger man. I mean it's all absolutely innocent, and if Guy thought that Kit was happily married…' She let the idea hang in the air between them.

Things were falling neatly into place. Sarah had no doubt that she was being manipulated by a real pro. The news of the magazine folding, the promise of work, all those little prying questions, but most of all Guy not being at lunch with them. Sarah shook her head. 'Magda, it's never going to work. Guy knows me, remember? He's seen me at Hanleys and I've worked with him on all sorts of the features for the magazine for the last five years.'

'Yes, I realise that, but everyone knows you left your husband and it wouldn't be the first time a woman has run away with a tall, good-looking man who lives in a great big house.' Magda smiled with all the warmth of a basking shark 'So what do you think?'

'I don't have to think about it. It's completely crazy.'

Magda waved the waiter over to bring her the bill and carried on as if Sarah hadn't said a word. 'So, I want you to think about it. We need someone to write the book with Kit, and provide him with a family and to be honest I'd like to work with someone I know and trust and who I know will turn in a good job, but you're not the only fish in the sea, poppet. I just wanted to give you first bite of the cherry. I thought you might be needing the work. Maybe you should think it over? Oh, and one more thing, we'll be needing someone to road-test Kit's recipes.

'We've already got a home economist on the show but frankly we know she'll get it right and adjust anything that needs to be adjusted, so what we really want is a plain Jane Bloggs in her cottage kitchen to try it out, someone ordinary, and you fit the bill to a tee, and you're so convenient. Kit said that you'd be perfect. What do you think? How about I email the recipes over to you and you can see how you get on with them?'

Sarah, open-mouthed, couldn't think of a single thing to say.

Banana Bread

Ingredients:
- 3 ripe bananas (the riper the better)
- 2oz brazil nuts (chopped)
- 2oz dried apricots (chopped – I often cut mine up with kitchen scissors)
- 8oz wholewheat flour
- 6oz sugar
- 2 eggs
- 2 tsp baking powder

Method:

Preheat oven gas mark 3 (170C)
Mash bananas, add beaten eggs, sugar, baking powder, nuts, and apricots, then mix together and slowly add the flour.
Grease a 1lb loaf tin and bake for one hour.

This tastes fine without the nuts and you can replace the apricots with dried cranberries or any other dried fruit you have about.
An excellent way to use up over-ripe bananas!

Delicious served warm and spread with butter.

Chapter Twelve
All Change

Knowing the fate of the staff at the magazine was horrible, and carrying the secret on her own was almost unbearable. It hung around her like a horrible dull grey headache that refused to be shaken. There was no way she could say anything, but then again as her best friend, how could she not warn Melissa? Although from experience Sarah knew that if she told her then by the end of the day everyone else in the office would know. So she said nothing and made plans; so many that in the end her brain was spinning with plans and ideas, along with icy cold shock.

If Sarah needed to go freelance and if she would be totally working from home it made more sense to move the boys to the village school. Magda's offer rumbled around inside her head. Writing the recipe book would be one thing, but being Kit's stand-in wife and family was a complete non-starter. Sarah rang the school as soon as she got home, and arranged an appointment to meet the head teacher and to take a look round.

'Let's go into my office,' said Mrs Howling, the head teacher, to Sarah as they completed their tour. 'So, what do you think?'

'The school is amazing. I'm sure the boys would love it here,' Sarah said, glancing out onto the playing field where they were currently joining in an after- school game of rounders with some of the other local children from the village. 'And I really like the idea of them walking to school and being part of the village.'

Mrs Howling nodded. ' 'I can understand that. We try and combine a solid academic approach with good pastoral care, and I'm lucky in having some wonderful staff and our numbers are on the up. Please do take a seat. Would you like some tea?'

'Yes please.'

Mrs Howling plugged in the kettle. ' So, you've moved onto the Roseberry estate?' She said conversationally, as she took two mugs from a cupboard.

Sarah nodded. 'We moved in in May.'

'I'm envious. It's a lovely spot. Kit and his family have always been very supportive of what we do here at the school. We often take the children onto the estate for natural science lessons. There are so many lovely trees and ponds, and he lets us use the big lawn at the front of the house for school fetes.' She smiled. 'Anyway we would be absolutely delighted to have the boys here at Hallswood. We have places for both of them in September and as you've seen we run lots of after-school and holiday activities, which I gather from both Harry and Alex are very much part of the attraction.'

Sarah laughed. 'Yes, that is true and I have to say Kit has done a great job on the advertising front. I didn't want to move the boys until I was sure we would be staying. But it seems silly for me to drive to and from Cambridge when you are just five minutes' walk away.'

And come Christmas she would have no reason to drive in, Sarah thought grimly.

Mrs Howling nodded. 'Well, I'm very glad that they'll be joining us. Very sensible. I've got some forms here for you to fill in, although one thing I should perhaps mention before we go any further is that I'm retiring at the end of term. We'll be having a new head teacher from September.'

'Oh, that's a shame,' said Sarah, before she could stop herself.

Mrs Howling smiled. 'Don't worry. Our new head is absolutely wonderful. We're very lucky to have him joining the school. We worked together on lots of projects over the years and share the same vision of what constitutes good education. He was the deputy head here for several years and I suppose I saw him as my natural successor to be honest, then he moved away to get married and take up a headship there. Anyway the good news is he's back and he'll be here from September. Right, now let's have some tea.'

Sarah glanced out of the window.

Harry took a thoughtful swing at the ball and managed to hit it clean and true, sending it up high into the late-afternoon sunshine. There was much cheering from his team as he started to run. It felt like an omen.

When Sarah got home there was an email from Rosa in her inbox along with another from Magda, one inviting her to an extraordinary meeting at the office, one with a list of recipes and veiled pressure about making up her mind, along with a suggested fee for the whole package, writer, tester and imaginary wife. Sarah sat for a long while thinking about the replies.

Chapter Thirteen
For starters

'Right,' said Sarah. 'So before you cut the haloumi into slices you need to make sure that you've got all the ingredients ready and that you've got the grill on. Okay?'

Kit, who was standing on the other side of the long kitchen table, staring down at the array of food, bowls, pans and knives in front of him, nodded. But Sarah wasn't convinced he was listening.

'It's simple,' Sarah continued. 'You'll be absolutely fine. I've written the recipe on the blackboard. Here.' She pointed. 'All you've got to do is follow the instructions and do exactly what it says. Everything is numbered; you can't go wrong; number one, haloumi, number two, lemons. Just try and make it sound like you know what you're doing. And be careful with the knife. It's sharp.'

Kit ran his fingers through his hair, wearing an expression that made him look as if he was about to perform open-heart surgery.

'You'll need to wash them again now.'

'What?'

Sarah pointed towards his hands. 'Your hands, you need to wash them again. You can't do that thing you do with you hair and then touch the food.'

'Right, okay, can't we just pretend?' he asked. 'After all, there's only you and me and the chances are the dogs are going to end up eating it anyway.'

'I'm just saying.'

'Right.' Kit poured himself a glass of wine. 'You want one?' he asked, looking around for a second glass.

'No, and neither do you. Come on, we've got to get this nailed, Kit. I've got to go and pick the boys up from school in half an hour. Come on,' she snapped.

Even given all the faffing about Sarah could see exactly why Magda might think Kit would be perfect for her TV show. She could just see Magda imagining Kit in some stylish open-plan kitchen, knocking up something simple and delicious for supper while they shared a bottle of Pinot Grigio. That lazy grin, those big capable hands, the way he tipped his head to one side when he was with you, making it seem that of all the voices in the room it was only yours he was listening to. The problem was that looking perfect wasn't going to be anywhere near enough. Kit had to cook, and the more she tried to sort out the cooking the more obvious it became that he couldn't – not at all. Lord only knows how he had survived this long.

'So – you're good to go?' pressed Sarah.

Kit nodded again and did a sort of limbering-up shimmy and shoulder roll, not unlike the kind of thing you'd see on the rugby pitch.

'Right, that's good. Let's just run through it then, nice and slow, and see how we get on,' she said. 'And no need to worry if you mess anything up; not that you're going to, but if you do I've got plenty more ingredients. Okay, in your own time – whenever you're ready. Off you go.'

Anxiously Kit's eyes tracked left and right along the kitchen table.

'From the left, Kit,' prompted Sarah.

He swallowed hard and looked up at her. 'Is that your left or my left?'

She took a deep breath.

'Okay okay,' he said, holding up a hand before she could speak. 'Don't tell me, don't tell me. I can do this. I can. What is this stuff called again?'

'Haloumi.'

'Uhuh – right. And haloumi is what, exactly?'

'Cheese.'

'It doesn't look much like cheese to me.'

'Well, it is, you'll just have to trust me on that.'

'Okey-dokey,' said Kit. 'And you can get it where?'

'Supermarkets, delicatessens, specialist shops—'

'So, pretty much everywhere, then?'

'More or less.'

'Okay, so off we go then,' Kit said. He paused for a long moment, staring at the blackboard that Sarah had propped up on one of the kitchen chairs, and where she had written the recipe, then painted on his heart-melting needy man-cub smile and began to speak.

'Hi, my name is Kit Roseberry and it's great to have your company. I've always really enjoyed cooking.' He paused and let the grin widen out a fraction. 'Actually, that's not true, what I love most about cooking isn't actually the cooking, it's the eating – but one thing kind of naturally leads to the other. So, over the next few weeks

I'm going to be sharing some of my favourite recipes with you here on Harts and Holmes.'

His voice was lush and deep, ex-public school with lots of good humour, a hint of flirtation and a nice measure of vulnerability. Ms Harts and Holmes was right on the money about Kit. When it came to wanting someone to keep you company in the kitchen every week, Kit Roseberry was going to be very hard to resist.

'I love having friends round for long lazy supper parties with plenty of wine and great conversation, and those Sunday lunches with the family and evenings curled up in front of the fire with supper on a tray with the kids.'

'Whoa there,' said Sarah, holding up hand to break the flow. 'What family and kids?'

Kit looked bemused. 'You and your boys of course, my lot are all too old and too mad to use. I got an email about it this morning. Didn't you get it? I think Magda copied you in.' Kit pulled a crumpled sheet of paper out of his back pocket, scanned the text and handed it to her. 'Yup, here we are, blah blah blah family vibe, blah blah blah, Sarah and the boys.'

Sarah snatched the email out of his hand. 'Bloody Magda,' she exclaimed. 'This is outrageous. I haven't agreed to this, Kit – she is making assumptions.'

Kit looked crestfallen. 'Really? Oh, that's a shame. I was looking forward to it. I didn't think you'd mind. Magda said it made me more saleable. And if it takes off we'll get to do some cool stuff, picnics, days at the beach. Big Christmas thing. It's been ages since I've had a proper family Christmas.'

Sarah sighed. It felt like she was kicking Tiny Tim. 'No,' she said, although she could feel her resolve wavering.

'Couldn't we just pretend?' he pleaded. 'Just for this one. Just to keep Magda happy. Please?'

Bloody Magda; Sarah guessed that this was what she had in mind when she sent Kit the email.

'All right then, but just for this little segment and then no more, all right? Do you understand?'

Kit nodded, took a breath and then started again.

'I love having friends round for long lazy supper parties with plenty of wine and great conversation, and those Sunday lunches with the family and evenings curled up in front of the fire with supper on a tray with kids.'

Sarah had to admit that he was good.

'You know the kind of thing,' Kit continued. 'Where the food is easy and you don't have to worry about getting it right because it always works. Those are exactly the kind of recipes I'm planning to share with you. We're going to start with one of my all-time favourites.' Kit smiled broadly. 'It's something really simple that just takes a few minutes to prepare.'

He slid the haloumi across the board and picked up the knife, looking as if he knew exactly what he was doing. Maybe this wasn't going to be as bad as Sarah thought after all.

'It looks amazing, tastes great and really is incredibly easy to make. This dish works as a starter, although I sometimes rustle it up to have with a salad or maybe some freshly baked bread or even just chopped up and stirred into couscous at lunchtime.'

Sarah nodded; so far he'd remembered everything she had told him.

Kit grabbed a breath and stared down at the chopping board as if he was seeing it for the first time. He set the knife down and turned to look at her, his shoulders suddenly slumping forward.

'You know actually, Sarah, I don't think I can do this. I really can't. The talking is fine, but all this chopping and cooking lark. It's complete madness. Why did I say I'd do it?'

'Because you need the money and because Magda Holmes told me over lunch you were a natural and that you've got real talent.'

'Maybe Magda wasn't talking about the cookery,' he said with a sly wink.

Sarah rolled her eyes. 'For God's sake, Kit, get on with it, will you? Just do what I told you. This is your own fault. Why on earth didn't you tell Magda that you couldn't cook, and that it wasn't you who whipped up that fabulous supper she kept raving on about?' Sarah paused. Kit said nothing.

'Or that little lunch à deux— or the amazing buffet lunch you managed to rustle up. She went on and on about it to me, Kit. Why did you let her think you'd cooked them? You could have said something. How hard would it have been?'

Kit shifted his weight and picked at a fingernail. 'I know, I know. I didn't mean to. She was impressed and all bright-eyed and bushy-tailed and telling me how wonderful I was and it just kind of happened.'

Sarah waited.

'I didn't think it would do any harm. That first evening she just assumed that I'd cooked supper, and then we had another bottle of wine and she said that in her experience with men—'

'Which appears to be varied and extensive,' Sarah observed.

'I didn't say that,' Kit protested. 'She just said that in her experience men who love food and wine are always good in bed. She said that she liked her men to have a healthy appetite.'

'Did you ask if that included her husband?'

Kit flinched as if Sarah had slapped him. 'Don't, I think Guy had passed out in the corner by then,' he said. 'And I'm not someone who plays around with married women, you know that. Magda was completely straight with me from the get-go. She told me before any of this started that she was married, but their marriage is a sham. They're only staying together for the sake of the business. Separate lives, separate beds, separate interests, that's what she said.'

'And you believed her?' Sarah raised her eyebrows, thinking about what Magda had said about Guy worrying about how much time she was planning to spend with Kit. 'I wonder if anyone has told Mr Holmes that?'

Kit ignored her. 'Magda says that a man with a passion for food has a passion for life.'

'Oh, please. And what does she say about a man who gets his tenant to do all the work for him and then passes it off as his own home cooking?'

Kit looked uncomfortable. 'The conversation never came up. It didn't occur to me in a million years that she would offer me a bloody job.'

'You could have turned it down, Kit, and it's not a job, is it. It's a cookery programme. On TV. You could have told her when she suggested it that you can't cook. What would it have taken?'

'I know, I know, I could have done, but...' He held up his hands in surrender. 'I didn't. Okay? Magda thinks I'm fabulous, Sarah. She said she'd never met anyone like me. She said that my red onion and goat's cheese tartlets were the best thing she had ever tasted and that she wanted to show me off, to share me with the nation. She said she could make me rich, make me a household name. I was flattered, Sarah.'

'You were drunk.'

'I just got carried away in the moment. How could I possibly tell her that someone else had cooked them? How could I let her down?' he protested.

'It's a cheese tart, Kit, not the secret to world peace,' Sarah said with a sigh.

'Anyway it's no big thing.'

Sarah wondered if he was talking to himself as he eyed up the haloumi, squaring it up to it, like it might up and bite him. 'Like we said, I've only signed up to do this little feature thing. Ten minutes – that's all. And you've already sorted out the menu and I'll get the hang of this. I will, I promise, really. How hard can it be?' There was a slight hint of desperation in his voice, not much but enough if you knew where to look.

'Okay. Let's get back to the job in hand, shall we? What are you going to do with haloumi?' said Sarah, tapping the blackboard.

Kit paused and puffed out his lips. 'Fuck knows,' he said after a short pause. 'I can't believe people eat this. Up until about half an hour ago if you'd asked me what haloumi was, I'd have sworn blind it was an island in the South Pacific, certainly not whatever that is.' He waved the knife at the wet rubbery white block on the chopping board. 'It doesn't even look like cheese; it looks like something you clean the windows with. It even squeaks.'

Sarah sighed.

'So what am I going to do with it?' he asked after a moment or two.

'You're going to cut it into slices around quarter of an inch thick and arrange them on the pan under the preheated grill along with some lemon wedges then grill them for two or three minutes till the haloumi and the lemon wedges are golden brown. Then you're going to turn them over and cook the other side –and while you're grilling those you're going to cook some sugar snap peas in a little unsalted butter, a drop of olive oil and a splash of water, just for two or three minutes, keeping them moving and keeping the crunch. You can try one to test if they're cooked – and then when they're more or less ready, you stir in a little finely chopped mint, and let that heat through and flavour the juices.'

Kit nodded again, although Sarah guessed he was still trying to humour her.

'When it's done you're going to put a slice of grilled haloumi onto a warm plate, pile some of the sugar snaps peas on top, add a good squeeze of lemon, trickle a little minty butter over it and serve with the grilled lemon garnish and maybe some hot pitta bread; simple. Two slices of haloumi per serving.' Sarah paused.

Kit didn't move.

'Is that grill actually on, Kit? You did clean the oven out and get it fixed, didn't you? You told me you would, Kit. We can't do this otherwise.'

He glanced across at her. 'I didn't think we were going to be doing it for real.'

'Oh, for goodness' sake, Kit. Are they planning to film you here?'

He shrugged. 'I suppose so. I don't know.'

'What do you mean, you don't know? Give me strength. Surely Magda must have said something to you about it.'

'I didn't ask. I just assumed that Magda would sort all that sort of thing out. Don't they bring their own stuff with them?'

'Their own cooker?'

'Well, I don't know, do I?' Kit peered suspiciously at the haloumi. 'I'm guessing that this isn't so great in a sarnie with a spot of Branston?'

'I don't know, I've never tried it,' said Sarah grimly. 'We can always fry it if we can get the top plate on the Aga hot enough.'

Kit looked sceptical. 'I'm not sure I've got that much time,' he said. 'How about I knock us up a bacon sandwich instead? I don't know about you but I'm totally famished,' he continued, heading for the pantry, reappearing seconds later with half a loaf of thick white sliced, which he slid onto the table, before hunkering down to rootle around in the back of the fridge.

'How are you going cook the bacon if the cooker is still broken and the Aga's off?' asked Sarah.

'I'll usually whack it on a plate and stick it in the microwave in the utility room. I suppose I could always bring that in here for the show. Oh, and I've got a camping stove in one of the barns, two rings – still in its box, I think. Do you want brown sauce on your sandwich?'

'Yes, why not,' sighed Sarah, admitting defeat. She pulled out a chair and sat down, settling in to watch him work. 'You're going to have to come clean, Kit. You're never going to be able to cook for the TV show on that cooker or the Aga, you do know that, don't you?'

'I don't see why not, you do it,' said Kit.

As he spoke he was carefully arranging the slices of bread in a row on the kitchen table and doodling his initials onto them with the brown sauce, before using a spoon to spread it. When he was done, he stepped back to admire his handiwork and licked the spoon thoughtfully.

'Actually you've cooked some amazing food here. If it hadn't been for you, you know I wouldn't have got this job in the first place.'

'So you're telling me it's my fault?' Sarah demanded. She had to admit that that was exactly how it felt.

'No, no, not at all. I'm just saying that you've cooked some amazing food here.'

'But that's just the point, Kit. I haven't. I've never cooked here. Never. I always cook it all down at the cottage, bring it up here and stick it in the Aga to keep warm,' said Sarah.

'Really? Maybe we just could do that.' He grinned. 'There we are. Sorted.'

'It barely gets above lukewarm some days—'

'Maybe if I got it serviced?'

'You mean like you got the cooker fixed?' asked Sarah, raising her eyebrows.

'I don't see why we couldn't do it my way. You could cook it and I could just whip open the Aga door and say, "Ta-rah, and here's one I made earlier".' He mimed a flourish.

'Just tell Magda the truth, Kit. Maybe they could find you a job presenting on the show. You said it was the talking you like best.'

His expression changed to something more serious. 'It's not that easy; I can't tell her that.'

'What do you mean, you can't? What's so tricky about telling her it was a mistake? Magda really likes you, I'm sure you can work something out.'

'I've already spent the money.'

Sarah stared at him. 'What?'

'The money Magda gave me. When she told me how much they were planning to pay me I asked for a bit of sub, you know, to tide me over, so I'm kind of committed now really.'

'How much of a sub?'

'Pretty much all of it. She didn't seem to mind.'

'Kit, you are such a moron.' Sarah glanced around. 'Bloody hell. You're going to have to talk to her. You can't cook here. The place is a tip. Have you spent all of the money?'

He looked uncomfortable. 'Quite a bit of it. Why?'

'I was wondering if you'd got enough left over to buy a cooker and some decent kitchen equipment.'

'Er, probably not,' said Kit.

'Kit, you're a total disaster. Okay, you need to phone her and say you've got a problem with the cooker; Magda has actually taken a look round in here, hasn't she?'

Kit shifted his weight and looked uncomfortable. 'Yes and no,' he said.

'Which means what exactly?'

'Yes, she's been in here when we had supper and she was a wee bit tipsy and then the only other time, no, she wasn't really looking around, and she certainly wasn't that interested in the oven.' He paused. 'We hadn't got very long.' He reddened and stared down at the space where the slices of bread were so neatly arranged. 'We had other things on our minds.'

Sarah followed his gaze back to the end of the kitchen table. 'Oh, my God, please tell me you've wiped it down since then.'

*

Grilled Haloumi and Sugar Snap Peas
Serves 4 as a starter, 2 as a supper dish

Ingredients:
250g haloumi
1 large lemon
1 tbsp olive oil
1 knob unsalted butter
Approx. 1 tbsp water
180g sugar snap peas
Generous tsp of freshly chopped mint

Method:
Cut lemon into 6 wedges, longways.

Cut haloumi into ¼-inch thick slices and place, along with 4 lemon wedges, under a preheated medium-hot grill. Retain two lemon wedges.

Grill haloumi and lemon wedges for 2–3 minutes on each side, or until golden brown.

While haloumi and lemon are cooking, heat oil, water, and butter in small pan over a medium heat. When mixture is bubbling add sugar snap peas. Cook for 3–4 minutes, shaking pan frequently, so the sugar snaps are sautéed but retain their snap.

Add chopped mint to pan. Cook for further minute. Take off heat, while you:

Arrange haloumi slices on a warm plate.

Pile sugar snaps peas onto each slice, spoon over some of the juices from the pan.

Squeeze lemon juice from retained wedges over each slice, garnish with grilled lemon wedges.

Serve with warm pitta bread.

Chapter Fourteen
Going Going…

'Ah, I'm so glad I caught you,' said Rosa casually, appearing from her office just as Sarah pulled on her jacket. Sarah was about to head home the following Monday afternoon, and had no sense that Rosa's appearance in the corridor was in any way an accident.

Sarah's plans involved fetching the boys from school and, on the way home, picking up some more plants from the man by the church. An hour or so in the garden in the sunshine would be the perfect antidote to putting the Hanleys Christmas special to bed after it had been signed off at the Monday meeting.

Rosa's plans quite obviously involved something different. 'Really nice work on the Christmas magazine,' she said conversationally.

Sarah smiled. 'Thank you.'

Neither of them moved. Sarah wondered if this was how a rabbit felt when it was caught in the headlights.

'And you got my email about the meeting on Friday?' asked Rosa.

Sarah nodded. 'Yes, thank you.'

Rosa's expression didn't change. 'Good, good. I wondered if you'd got five minutes?'

There was no point saying no, Rosa wasn't the kind of woman who took no for an answer.

Melissa, who was still sitting at her desk, looked up as Rosa guided Sarah into her office. Sarah saw the look of panic on her friend's face and tried very hard not to let it shake her.

'Come on in and have a seat, Sarah,' Rosa said warmly as she closed the door behind them. So far, so good.

Sarah sat down while Rosa fiddled about with the orchids she kept on a side table by her desk. 'I keep meaning to ask how things are going,' she said taking a plant mister from one of the cupboards.

'Going?' echoed Sarah, watching as a cloud of moisture settled on the plants. Rosa was very careful not to catch her eye, not a good sign.

'Yes, you know, going back to working from home after all this time, and the move and – and all that.'

All that being Colin and the boys and the mess of selling up a house and pulling a family apart, presumably, thought Sarah.

'Fine,' she said. 'Bit of an upheaval but we're getting there.' She was pretty certain that her private life was not the reason for Rosa getting her into her office.

'Good, and have things have settled down with er, with er…'

'Colin. Kind of, we're sorting things out. You know how these things are.' She had no intention of sharing any of the gory details with her boss.

'Not easy,' said Rosa, without a shred of emotion.

Sarah wasn't altogether sure what Rosa's domestic arrangements were, since she never brought a partner, husband, wife or lover to any of the magazine functions and the only thing she had in her office that showed the slightest signs of life were her orchids.

Sarah nodded, wondering when the woman was going to get to the point.

'Magda came to see me,' Rosa said, tweaking off a tiny curled dried leaf. 'She told me that you're thinking of leaving us.'

Sarah nearly choked. 'That isn't true—' she began, but Rosa was ahead of her and held up a hand.

'Don't worry. I quite understand and to be perfectly honest in your shoes I'd be doing the same thing. We'll be sad to lose you, of course – and to be honest I would have rather heard it from you, but I understand that you wanted to be sure of the situation before burning your bridges. Nice to have a job to go to—'

Sarah took a deep breath. 'Actually Magda is making all sorts of assumptions and she hasn't offered me a job, she offered me some work,' she said, measuring every word. 'If I was planning on leaving then I would have come and told you – and yes, I am considering Magda's offer but it's not that straightforward.' Sarah couldn't help wondering if Magda had mentioned the whole imaginary wife part of the job description.

Rosa leaned a little closer and lowered her voice. 'She told you about what's happening here at Hanleys, didn't she?'

The words jammed up in Sarah's throat and she wondered for a moment if it was worth pretending that she didn't know. In the moment of silence Rosa sat down and, knitting her long fingers together, leaned forward to rest her elbows on the desk.

'I admire your discretion, Sarah, but I know what Magda's like when she wants something. She wouldn't be able to keep it to herself if she thought it might persuade you – and it's a great lever, isn't it? Knowing you'll be out of a job in six months?'

Sarah reddened and then nodded. 'She did tell me, but I haven't said anything to anyone and I haven't accepted her offer.'

'Yet?' suggested Rosa.

'I feel like she is steamrollering me and there is more to it than just writing.'

Rosa laughed. 'There always is with Magda, but more often than not what Magda wants Magda gets. We're going to be shedding people before Christmas and I'd be happy for you to be amongst them if that's what you want. We can work out a redundancy package. And I'm sure Magda's already told you we'll be using freelancers in the New Year and given you understand how we work here at Hanleys I'm really hoping you'll be amongst them.' Rosa paused. 'Magda seems very keen for you to be working with her on this new project of hers.'

Sarah nodded, wondering exactly how much she had told her.

'Anyway, it all sounds very exciting. Magda has always had an eye for the main chance. There's no need to worry about the details now, but it would be helpful if once you know when you're leaving you let me know.'

Rosa had said when, not if, Sarah realised.

'Have you got any idea yet?' continued Rosa.

Sarah stared at her; it felt like she was walking into a bad dream.

'No, no, I haven't,' Sarah said, shaking her head.

Rosa smiled in a way that suggested their meeting was over.

'Well, when you do, just let me know. We'll be sad to see you go but then we'll be sad to see everyone go. At least this project with Magda will give you a cushion and she seems very enthusiastic. Who knows, it might be the start of a whole new career.'

Feeling slightly giddy Sarah got to her feet. As she was about to pick up her bag, Rosa said, 'Obviously I'd appreciate if we kept all this to ourselves for the time being.'

Sarah nodded; fat chance, everyone and his wife in the office had seen her being guided into Rosa's inner sanctum, and even as she thought it Sarah saw Melissa walking past Rosa's office window, making a beeline for the outer door, presumably hoping to pick off Sarah on the way out.

She wasn't wrong. As Sarah headed for the lift Melissa appeared from the Ladies toilet – fooling no one, as she had clearly been lying in wait.

'Well?' Melissa said, hurrying to catch up with her friend. 'What did she want? Are you okay? Do you want to go for a coffee? Did she sack you? I've got tissues.'

'I'm fine.'

'Really. I thought she got you in there to give you the old heave-ho.' Melissa mimed as she spoke. 'And if you've got it then I'm bound to be the next to go. Or maybe they'll keep me on as I'm a minion? What do you think?'

What was she supposed to say? Melissa was in step with Sarah now. Sarah was trying hard to think of a reply. Melissa was her best friend; she had to say something and in the end there was only some shade of the truth. 'Magda has offered me some work. To write a cookbook. For Kit. And she wants me to do a column for the magazine too because there is no way he's going to be able to do it. And she wants me to pretend to be his wife.'

Melissa stopped dead in her tracks. 'What?'

'She wants him to write a recipe book. And I'm going to be doing that bit. But the wife thing...'

Melissa stared at her. 'You're taking the mickey. What did Rosa really say to you?'

The lift pinged to announce its arrival and the doors opened. Sarah hesitated. It was such a dilemma. If the situations were reversed Melissa would have rung her the minute she got back from lunch with Magda and would even now be giving her a word by word rerun of what Rosa had said. Melissa would have told everybody, but she would have told Sarah first.

'Well?' Melissa pressed.

'She offered me redundancy if I wanted to take Magda up on her offer.'

'You were serious about Magda?' Melissa's eyes widened.

Sarah nodded.

'And you said?'

'That I'd let her know.'

'Magda or Rosa?'

'Both.'

Melissa slid into the lift alongside her. 'Right, so what does that mean?' She screwed up her face, now deep in thought.

'I don't know,' said Sarah. 'I really don't.'

Driving home with the boys chattering away in the back Sarah turned the options over and over in her mind. In a nutshell she could hang on at Hanleys and try to pick up some freelance work from them after Christmas or take Magda up on her offer and Rosa was right, it might take off, in which case there would be more work and she would be a fool not to at least give it a try.

Fred, the plant man, was pleased to see her. 'How are the others coming along?' he asked, as she got out of the car. 'Get them all planted up, did you?'

Sarah nodded. 'They look lovely, that's why we've come back for some more.'

'And we planted our sunflower seeds,' said Alex.

'And I water them,' said Harry seriously. 'Every day.'

'Good man,' said Fred. 'So how can we help you today, young lady?'

Sarah smiled; it was a while since anyone had considered her young. 'I'm not really sure what I want. I thought I'd have a look round and see if anything catches my eye.'

Fred nodded. 'Good plan. You know where everything is.'

The three of them trailed in through the gate behind him.

'Is it all right to give the lads an ice-cream?' asked Fred. 'And I've got some toys my grandson left if they wanted something to do while you're browsing. They could sit up at the table on the patio or play on the grass if you want. You can keep an eye while you're looking round.'

'Are you sure you don't mind?' said Sarah.

Fred laughed. 'Course not. Longer you take looking the more you spend.'

Sarah grinned. 'Sounds like a plan.'

At which point the man she had seen the last time she had been there appeared, wheeling an enormous old-fashioned wooden wheelbarrow full of terracotta pots. 'Not bribing you, is he?' said the man, with a smile.

He was wearing cut-off jeans and a blue chambray shirt with the cuffs rolled back and he looked hot in every sense of the word. Sarah made the effort not to stare at his muscular arms or tanned legs or the way the sun had lightened his hair.

'Probably,' she managed to say. 'But at least this way I get to look at the plants in peace.'

'He's such an old shark,' said the man affectionately. 'Ice-cream for the boys and you'll be spending an extra tenner thinking what a nice man he is.'

Sarah laughed.

'Do you want any pots?' asked Fred. 'His nibs here says they're cluttering up the place. We're going to put them out the front and see if we can't sell them off. They're vintage apparently.'

'Like their owner,' said the man, with a wink.

Sarah realised that a part of her had hoped that Fred's good-looking helper would be there; she just hadn't realised quite how much. The wink had made her blush, but if he saw it he said nothing.

'Actually I wouldn't mind a few pots,' she said hastily.

'Help yourself, my love,' said Fred. 'Take as many as you like. Pound a piece for the big ones, fifty pence for the small ones. Those ones in the box are brand new.'

'I'm off home, Fred, okay?' said the man.

The old man nodded. 'Thanks for your help. You coming back tomorrow?'

'Depends on the weather. I'm hoping to get some work done at my place if I can,' the man was saying.

Fred meanwhile was picking up a flyer he had weighed down on the bench he was using for wrapping and packing. 'Here we are, my dear,' he said, handing it to her. 'You might want to come and give us a little look over the weekend. Saturday we've got the church fete, there'll be lots of stalls, hog roast, live music, dancing and me and him'll be up there on the school field selling plants.'

'And pots,' laughed the man. 'If we don't have a mad rush and sell the five hundred or so Fred's got stashed behind his shed in the meantime.'

'Take no notice of him, he's only jealous and we'll have plants in all them pots,' said Fred.

Enjoying the good-humoured banter Sarah took the flyer and nodded. 'Thank you. Sounds like fun.' The man was smiling at her, her colour deepened. 'The boys would like that.'

'Bring your husband along,' said Fred slyly. Talk about a leading statement, thought Sarah.

'I'm in the process of getting a divorce,' she said lightly.

'Ah,' said Fred, nodding his head. 'Shame. Anyway I'd better go and get them lads the ice-cream.'

'My name's Shaun, by the way,' the other man said as Fred vanished into the house, and she sensed in him the same slight awkwardness that she was feeling, as if they were both a little surprised to find themselves there, grinning like teenagers at each other, over a pile of old flowerpots.

'Sarah,' said Sarah, holding out her hand, and for a moment as their palms touched she felt a peculiar little electric charge run through her, so real that it took all her time not to snatch her hand away in surprise. Sarah told herself was totally ridiculous and completely mad; things don't happen like that, except in story books, and her life was just about as far from a story book and happy-every-afters as you could get.

The moment was shattered by the boys running across the lawn to find the toys Fred had promised them.

'Hope to see you there, then,' said Shaun. 'I'm afraid I've got to go and I need to get this lot shifted before I do.'

Sarah nodded. 'Okay. See you there, then.' And then he was gone, and as soon as he headed off across towards the sheds Sarah convinced herself that she had imagined it.

*

The following day, Sarah and Melissa were busy working in Sarah's kitchen. The back door was wide open, and spread all over the table were piles of paper, brochures and various flyers, all weighed down by jars, cans and bottles.

Now that the Christmas issue of the magazine was all put to bed, despite the heatwave going on just outside the door, inside it was all about New Year's resolutions, diets and getting your skin through the harsh rigours of winter.

Amongst the pile of papers were samples of moisturiser, lip balm and various potions that promised an inner glow and repair from the icy blast, all brought over from the office by Melissa, together with photos, price lists, reviews and the mock-up of a money-off coupon that was destined to be dropped into the article that Sarah had just finished.

Melissa, Sarah guessed, was really hoping that there was more dirt to be dished, more news to be had, and besides that there was always something interesting to eat at the cottage, something you couldn't guarantee in the office. They were finishing off a lunch of homemade mushroom soup and little bread rolls that Sarah had baked in Fred Tullet's flowerpots.

'So what's with the flowerpot bread?' asked Melissa.

'Just something a bit different. What do you think?'

'Nice idea,' Melissa said, buttering the remains of her roll. 'And they're delicious. I love homemade bread.'

Coincidentally Sarah was sorting out the photos for a piece on how to shed those Christmas pounds, with the help of a book that wasn't even off the presses yet.

Melissa leaned across the table and helped herself to another bread roll. 'So is this for Kit's cookery book?' she said, nodding towards the remains of lunch. They had been talking about Magda's offer on and off all morning, or rather Melissa had. 'I really think you should just do it. When does the filming start?'

'Next week, according to Kit, although I haven't heard anything official from Magda yet.'

'Maybe she's waiting for you to sign up.'

Sarah nodded. 'Maybe she is.'

'Maybe she'll offer you more money.'

Sarah laughed. 'I don't think so; what she offered was pretty generous as it is.'

'There you go then. What's stopping you? You've got to do it.' Melissa paused. 'Maybe you could do both?'

Sarah considered. 'I'm not sure. I suppose I could talk to her about it. And this is just a pilot, it might not take off.'

'Well, I was thinking you might be able to get me a job. I don't mind ghosting recipes.'

'I'm fine with the writing, it's the fake family thing that's bugging me.'

'Oh, come on. Anyone who knows you, knows that you and Kit aren't a couple, and no one else matters really, and if the money is good you should grab it with both hands. Although that Magda's got a big mouth, fancy telling Rosa. It puts you in a difficult position, doesn't it?'

And not just with Rosa, thought Sarah, miserably. She still hadn't spilt the beans about the office closing.

As if reading her mind, Melissa said, 'I'd go for it, because if you ask me I reckon we're all doomed at Hanleys. If I got a chance like that I'd grab it with both hands.' She tore off a lump of the bread and used it to mop up the remains of her soup. 'This is fabulous. You should definitely put this in his book.'

At which point there was a knock on the front door.

'Expecting someone, are we?' asked Melissa with a sly grin. 'Your imaginary husband, maybe?'

Sarah laughed. 'No, and if you mean Kit then he always comes round to the back door and walks straight in. I keep expecting to find him in here one morning making himself breakfast.'

'That's imaginary husbands for you.' Melissa grinned. 'And it sounds like you're getting mighty chummy, you two.'

'He is, I'm not,' said Sarah, getting to her feet. 'A little too chummy for my liking.'

Sarah opened the front door. Standing on the doorstep was tall plump sweaty man clutching a clipboard. 'Delivery for Mr Roseberry?' he said, with just a hint of desperation.

'I'm afraid not, you've got the wrong address. You want the hall,' said Sarah helpfully, pointing towards the gates and the driveway that led up through the estate. 'It's not far; maybe quarter of a mile, if that. Big house, you can't miss it.'

The man sniffed and dabbed at his face with a large handkerchief. 'I know where it is, Missus. I've been up there, round the front, round the back. We can't make anybody hear.'

'So you thought you'd deliver whatever it is here instead?' she asked.

The man's eyes narrowed. 'No, there was a note on the back door.' He handed it to Sarah. It read, 'Gone swimming. If you want anything talk to Sarah, in the cottage down the lane.'

'Bloody cheek,' said Sarah.

'Do you know him?' asked the man.

'Sadly yes,' said Sarah.

'We thought you might have a key or something.'

Sarah nodded. Although she didn't like to mention it, usually Kit left the kitchen door unlocked. 'What is it you've got to deliver? Do you want to just leave it here with me?'

'Best you come and look,' said the man. 'I'm not getting it out just for the fun of it.'

Which was why a few minutes later, while Melissa stayed at the cottage, Sarah found herself up at the hall watching two men and a pallet trolley wheeling a top-of-the-line Smeg duel-fuel cooking range into the kitchen, which would nicely complement the great stack of cooking equipment that was piled up on the kitchen table. There was a free-standing chopping block, storage jars, sieves and colanders, wooden spoons, whisks, bowls and pans and a fabulous selection of kitchen knives. For someone like Sarah, who loved to cook, it felt like she had died and gone to heaven. There was a part of her though that was slightly concerned about what it was that Kit had had to sell or promise to get so many beautiful things.

The dual-fuel range was superb; obviously Kit had taken what she said to heart, thought Sarah. It took the men a while to whip out the old cooker and make a start on installing the new one. Behind it they fixed a stainless steel splashback and a cooker hood, and were almost finished and ready to fire it up when Kit strolled in.

He was dressed in shorts and a tee shirt, all tan and teeth, with damp hair combed back off his face. The dogs ambled in behind him.

'Wow, that looks fabulous,' he said with a cheery grin. 'Did Sarah make you some tea?'

The men nodded and, maybe sensing a storm brewing, turned their attention back to the cooker.

Sarah glared at Kit and hissed, 'Why didn't you tell me you'd left that note on your door? I'm not your bloody PA, you know.'

'Aye up,' said one of the cooker fitters, in a stage whisper. 'Trouble in paradise.'

Sarah swung round to give him a look to match the one that she'd just given Kit.

'I know, I'm sorry, I meant to call in and ask you, but I was running late,' said Kit. As he spoke his gaze wandered across the piles of kitchen equipment. 'It was all a bit spur of the moment. Nouska and Vivien invited me over for a dip in their pool, to repay me for Sunday lunch the other week. Which was fabulous by the way. I would have stayed longer but the dogs kept leaping into the pool and then wandering off into the house. Made a bit of a mess. Cream sofas, white carpet. I told Nouska to send me the cleaning bill.' He paused, working his way around the kitchen. 'Do you think we're going to have room for all this stuff?'

Sarah nodded. 'You will. Once you've cleared all the crap out. When I went looking for serving dishes I found three pairs of wellies and a bag of knitting in one of the kitchen cupboards. And I think there is something dead in the one under the sink.'

Kit looked momentarily chastened, but it wasn't a look meant to last. 'So what do you think then?' he asked, waving a hand to encompass the contents of the table and the new cooker. 'Will it do? I think there's some sort of kitchen bench thing coming too.'

Sarah nodded. 'Frankly I'm amazed, Kit—'

'Does that mean you approve?'

'Yes, of course I do. But I thought you told me you hadn't got much of the money left that Magda gave you?' Sarah picked up one of the pans from the stack and glanced at the base. 'This is about as good as it gets. I can't imagine you knowing what to choose – I would have helped, you know. What did you do, just go round the shop and look for the things with the highest price tag?'

'Oh no,' said Kit, casually picking up one of the bowls. 'I didn't get them. Magda got them for me.'

Sarah stopped in her tracks. 'Magda?'

'Yes, you know? Magda Holmes?'

'I know exactly who Magda is, Kit. I introduced you, remember? We're supposed to be working together.'

Kit nodded. 'Well, I rang her, like you said, about the cooker, and she said that you'd mentioned that my kitchen maybe wasn't quite up to scratch and I said I had to agree with you, and I was worried that the cooker was a bit iffy and she said not to worry.'

Sarah waited; there just had to be a punch line.

'What?' Kit said, looking at her vacantly. 'What was I supposed to say? I agreed with you. Then Magda said it would be fine and to leave it with her. And then she said, "So what else do you think you need?" And I just said how about everything and Magda said, "I like your style, sweetie. As long as we're able to push it on the show, then I think we can get away it." And then all this stuff started showing up and then she rang me last night to say that Hanleys were happy to give me a cooker.'

'This isn't just a cooker, Kit, it's a work of art,' Sarah said, looking at it lovingly.

'Oh good, she said they really wanted me to have it. All I've got to do is go in store and do a couple of cookery demonstrations, maybe a talk. And then a weekend here with some other people. A house party – I think that's what she said.' He paused. 'She's working on a schedule. You know that woman is a real powerhouse, and if I'd known getting stuff was this easy I'd have done it years ago. Once it's all set up in here they're coming out to do another photo shoot. For the book that I'm writing? How's it coming along by the way?'

Sarah stared at him. 'Are you serious?'

He nodded.

'Okay, let me put it another way, Kit. Are you totally and utterly mad?' she said.

'What do you mean?'

'Kit, I can't hold your hand while you're doing demonstrations. This is crazy,' she hissed, trying to keep her voice down, well aware that the delivery men were hanging on every word.

'Was I asking you to?' he snapped, glancing past her towards the man with the spanner.

'No, no you weren't,' she conceded.

'But you will, won't you?' he added in a stage whisper. 'She said she wants me to go on the road. Makes me sound a bit like the Rolling Stones.'

'I can't, Kit, and neither can you. At the moment I've still got a job, and the boys to look after if you hadn't already noticed. This is too much. It's gone too far. You need to talk to Magda about taking it slowly – at least until you've got the hang of things.'

'Oh, come on, Sarah, I'm not a complete idiot. I'm sure it won't take me long to get a grasp of the basics, how hard can it be? It's not like it's rocket science.'

As he spoke, Kit padded across the kitchen, opened up the door to a brand new fridge, took out an open tin of baked beans, took a tablespoon from the draining board and started to eat them straight out of the can.

Sarah shook her head; maybe for Kit it was rocket science.

*

Real Cream of Mushroom Soup

Serves 2

Ingredients:
4 tbs butter
8oz mushrooms (field mushrooms and open mushrooms have a better flavour than button mushrooms)
1 tsp salt
1 medium onion, chopped
1 pint of chicken or vegetable stock
1/8 tsp ground nutmeg
250ml double cream
Salt and pepper
Chopped parsley for garnish

Method:
Clean mushrooms with piece of kitchen roll and chop roughly.

Gently fry onions without colouring in the butter till they are soft – stirring frequently. Stir in chopped mushrooms and fry for a minute or two. Add a pinch of salt and a little pepper.

Add stock, bring to the boil and simmer for around 10 minutes. Remove from heat.

Pour the double cream into a blender or liquidiser and add soup. Whizz for 30 seconds or so. Return soup to pan and bring back to the simmer (don't let it boil). Adjust seasoning. Pour into two bowls, sprinkle with nutmeg and parsley. Serve.

If you haven't got a liquidiser, take pan off heat and add cream, using hand blender to liquidise.

If you don't want to liquidise the soup you might want to cut your mushrooms and onions more neatly.

Flowerpot Bread

Ingredients:
1lb strong white bread flour or your favourite bread flour
2 tsp sugar
1½ tsp salt
½oz. fresh yeast or 2 tsp dried yeast
½pt lukewarm water

Optional Extras

2oz poppy seeds
2oz mixed seeds
2oz pumpkin seeds
2oz chopped walnuts
2oz grated cheese
2oz chopped olives
2 garlic cloves, peeled and crushed
2 tablespoons mixed herbs
2 tablespoons chopped chives
½onion, peeled and grated
2 tbsp sun-dried tomatoes, drained and finely chopped

Preparing your flowerpot
You'll need:
vegetable oil
lard
butter

Directions:
Before using your flowerpots they need seasoning. Take two to six traditional earthenware/terracotta flowerpots (3 to 6 inches in size). Wash thoroughly and grease them inside and outside, with lard, butter or oil. Use *new* flowerpots.

Put directly onto shelves in a preheated oven at 190C; 375F, gas mark 5, for 25–30 minutes, with a baking tray under the shelf to catch any drips. Switch off oven. Open oven door and allow to cool in the oven or remove and stand on cooling rack.

Repeat the process two or three times to create a good seasoning and non-stick surface to your flowerpots.

Before using them to bake with, line the base with greaseproof paper or baking parchment.

Method:
If you are using dried yeast, dissolve one teaspoon of sugar in the warm water then add the dried yeast. Leave until frothy (about ten minutes). If you are using fresh yeast, blend it into the warm water.

In a large mixing bowl put flour, salt and sugar. Add any of the smaller extras you wish to use at this stage.

Add the yeast liquid to the dry ingredients and mix to a soft sticky dough.

Turn the dough onto a floured work surface and knead the dough by folding towards you, then pushing down and away from you with the heel of your hand. Give the dough a quarter turn and repeat the action. Knead until smooth, satiny and no longer sticky. This takes around 10 minutes. If you are using larger extras add them at the end of the kneading process. Stretch the dough out on the work surface, scatter your extras on the surface and knead briefly to spread them through the mix.

Arrange your flowerpots on a baking tray. Cut the dough into evenly sized pieces and place in the prepared and well oiled/buttered flowerpots. Glaze top of dough with milk or salted water and sprinkle with mixed seeds.

Place each pot inside a large oiled polythene bag, leave in a warm place until the dough doubles in size (around an hour).

Remove the polythene bags and bake pots on the middle shelf of a hot oven at 230C (450F) or gas mark 8 for 10 to 30 minutes, depending on the size of your flowerpots, or until the bread is nicely browned and sounds hollow when tapped.

Remove the bread from the flowerpots and allow to cool on a wire rack.
Once they are cool you can slip them back into the flowerpots to serve.

Alternatively if you are using a breadmaker follow the manufacturer's instructions, remove when mixed and allow to rise in flowerpots as before.

Chapter Fifteen
Something Fishy

'Right, now what I want, Kit, darling,' said Magda, 'is for you to just hold it there while we get the lighting right. And it would be nice to get a few stills of Kit with the fish. Anyone? Who's got the stills camera?' She swung round to glare at one of the crew who was busy on a stepladder, desperately trying to clamp a lamp onto the side of the kitchen dresser. 'Simon, sweetie, can you get it sorted out?'

Kit, meanwhile, was standing behind the brand new workbench smiling and holding up the fish that Magda had presented him with when she arrived. He smiled at it as if it was a new toy. It didn't smile back. Apparently a friend had dropped a couple off for her that morning, fresh, line-caught sea bass from the Wash.

Up on the ladder Simon growled something about dodgy wiring and woodworm and how he couldn't do everything at once.

'Okay, okay. I'll tell you what, how about we all take five. I'm dying for a cup of something. How about you, Kit, darling? Tea? You're doing brilliantly,' Magda purred. 'Just pop the fish back in the fridge and we'll get the kettle on. You're not phased by the fish, are you? I thought it was perfect. Locally caught sea bass, fresh from the sea. What's not to like? And this is just a trial run, guerilla cooking, I rather like that. We could maybe do a segment down on the beach at some time. Shellfish and seeing what people have caught and then cooking it there and then.'

Kit nodded, although Sarah could see the panic in his eyes. Sarah and Kit had been through the things for his segment for Magda's programme ten, maybe fifteen times over the last few days. He had even got to the point where he was pretty much convinced that haloumi really was cheese. Springing a fish on him was totally unfair. As was the fact that Magda was directing the shoot. She could barely keep her hands off him and it was putting everyone off, including Kit.

It was Wednesday morning and they were in Kit's kitchen along with the film crew from Harts and Holmes and a stylist and lord only knows who else. It was a big room but it felt packed and if it was hot outside it was hotter still under the lights they had set up to film with. A girl came into shot, mopped Kit's brow, and relieved him of the fish, although Sarah suspected it was probably sheer terror rather than the heat that was making him sweat.

It had been an eventful few days.

On Friday morning a mournful Rosa had announced that staff would be shed up until Christmas, and that she saw only a skeleton staff remaining into the New Year. She would be sad to see them go. She really, really would.

In the silence that followed you could almost hear the tumbleweeds rolling through the office. Her uplifting endnote, which involved enhanced redundancy payments, fuelled by the Hanley brothers' innate sense of fair play and the promise of freelance work, was scant compensation.

As soon as Rosa had gone back to her orchids Sarah had emailed Magda and accepted her offer, as long as she could combine it with working on the magazine until the redundancy package could be sorted out.

She had barely pressed send when an email appeared in her inbox from Colin. It was brief. 'All settled. Would like boys for the weekend. Colin.'

Ever since she had known him Colin treated email as if it was a telegram; she often wondered if he thought he was paying per word and was always surprised not to see 'stop' inserted at the end of each sentence.

Other than a single call from his solicitors to check on the progress of the house sale, she hadn't heard from him since the one and only time he had had the boys for the weekend. Presumably all settled meant that he was tucked up with Peony. Sarah couldn't help wondering what Peony thought of him now that he was there all the time.

Sarah had been planning to take Harry and Alex to the village fete over the weekend, but it would be nice to have a break and have a weekend to herself, and her solicitor had already advised her to cooperate with Colin over the children, and all of a sudden a weekend by herself sounded like a great idea. She emailed him back.

'Fine. Please could you come and pick the boys up from the cottage this evening, so I have a chance to send some play clothes with them?'

He had to have been hovering by the computer waiting for her message, because she'd barely pressed send before his reply snapped back:

'Would prefer you to drop them off. And can you make sure they've eaten? Colin.'

Sarah shook her head. Bloody cheek, she thought, and decided to let him wait for a reply. Since Colin's announcement that he planned to move in with Peony, Sarah had very carefully and tactfully explained to Harry and Alex that Daddy had a new girlfriend, and had been slightly perturbed that neither of them seemed to find it that strange, nor had they asked any questions, which backed up Sarah's theory that they already knew all about Peony.

'Are they going to get married?' Harry had asked.

'I don't know,' said Sarah truthfully.

'Only if they are, I'm not wearing any funny clothes, okay, Mum?' he said, sounding very serious.

Sarah waited; there was bound to be more. Alex was nodding in agreement, so obviously funny clothes and weddings had been a hot topic at some time or other.

'They made James King in my class wear a kilt and a frilly shirt when his dad got married.'

Alex nodded. 'I don't even know what a kilt is,' he said anxiously.

Sarah smiled. 'Don't worry, if Dad does get married again then I'll make sure you don't have to wear funny clothes.'

Reassured, Harry had gone back to his colouring. Alex said, 'What is a kilt, Mum?'

'It's like a skirt but for boys,' said Harry without looking up. 'And you don't wear pants.'

Alex's eyes widened.

*

It felt very odd driving back to the old house, and even worse parking in the road outside and seeing the curtains that she'd left up at the windows to try and convince burglars that there was someone still living there. It was worse still when she opened the car door to let the boys out and realised it wouldn't be her path they would run down. She was just unfastening Alex's seat belt when Colin scurried out of Peony's house, and opened the front gate.

He smiled at the boys and waved them into the little front garden. 'If you just want to wait there,' he said, 'we'll all go in together.'

Sarah went to the boot to get the boys' backpacks. Colin looked extremely uncomfortable and kept glancing over his shoulder back towards the house. 'Next time you drop the boys off, would you mind waiting in the car?' he asked.

Sarah stared at him. 'What?'

'Peony finds it unsettling.'

'Unsettling?' Sarah said, feeling a little flare of annoyance rising in her stomach.

'Yes. I'm sure you can see it from her point of view.'

It was all Sarah could do not to slap him. 'And what point of view would that be?' she said, in an undertone so that the boys couldn't hear. 'The point of view of a woman who was sleeping with my husband right under my nose, and can't face me? And I'm supposed to be the one staying in the car? I haven't done anything to be ashamed of, Colin, so I'm going to be getting out of the car whenever I like, and going wherever I like. Is that clear? I'm sure you can see it from my point of view.' She mimicked his tone. 'And if it worries you that much next time come and pick them up yourself.'

Colin stared at her. 'What on earth has happened to you, Sarah? You never used to be like this; you're so negative.' His tone was patronising.

Sarah handed him the boys' backpacks. 'I woke up,' she said, looking Colin straight in the eye, 'and when I did everything had changed.'

He flinched. 'Come along, boys,' he said quickly, and turning away, guided them into Peony Tyler's house.

On Saturday morning, instead of feeling blue or lonely or even angry, Sarah had got up early and, settling herself at the kitchen table with a pot of tea, worked on some ideas for Kit's recipe book, then she cleaned the house, watered the hanging baskets, and had a long lazy bath and generally enjoyed the time off.

And then there was the fete.

In an ideal world Sarah would have liked to have gone with the boys, but they weren't there and besides, no one would mind if she went on her own, or even notice come to that. As Sarah thumbed through the clothes rail in her wardrobe she smiled to herself; who was she trying to kid?

One of the main reasons she was going was because Shaun was likely to be there. The fact that her fancying gene was still alive and well had come as a nice surprise. She had no idea where it had been hiding all these years but it was reassuring to know that marriage and children – mostly marriage – hadn't killed it off, she thought grimly, pulling out a print dress and holding it up against herself and checking the mirror. What did you wear to a village fete where you wanted to look wonderful but not look as if you were trying too hard?

*

'Sarah? Sarah?' Sarah, shaken out of her reverie, looked up. totally bemused.

'What? What is it?' she said.

'They're going start filming in few minutes,' whispered Kit, 'and they're going to want me to deal with the fish.'

Sarah took a moment or two to get her bearings. 'The fish?' she said.

'Yes, you know, the fish, the sea bass,' Kit hissed. 'I can't cook fish. I've never cooked fish that wasn't finger-shaped. I don't know how to cook fish. This is a fucking disaster. You were right, this is total madness. I'm going to have to tell Magda.' He raked his hands back through his hair, although before she could speak he said, 'I know, I know, I need to wash them now. So tell me what I've got to do with the fish.'

'I thought you were going to tell Magda you couldn't do it.'

'Yes, I was for a second there and then I thought about you needing a job and the boys starving and all money I've already spent that she is just bound to want back; so, tell me all about the fish.'

'First of all you need to gut it as soon after it's caught as possible, and then you can fillet it, or eat it whole, head on or head off,' Sarah began. 'I don't think those have been gutted. Although they should be all right, Magda said they were caught last night. Okay, so first of all you'll need to gut it and descale it.'

Kit looked at her and gagged. 'Gut it?' He swallowed.

Sarah nodded. 'It's not hard. You'll be fine. Look, I'll do one of them to show you how to do it and you can do the other one while they film you. It's easy, and we won't fillet them.'

Kit nodded. 'And what about cooking them?'

'Sea bass are fabulous and they don't need much messing with – you need a lemon and some olive oil, garlic, salt and pepper, and we've got all those.'

He nodded. 'Right, so…'

'So, come on,' she said. 'Let me show you. Go and get me one of the fish.'

He did as he was told and followed her over to the butler sink, where Sarah took out a chopping board and a knife and grabbed some newspaper from the box near the back door.

'I won't ask you what that's for,' Kit said miserably, staring down at the newspaper. 'It's going to get messy, isn't it?'

'No, just man up, Kit,' said Sarah firmly, keeping an eye on the film crew who had taken themselves outside into the kitchen garden to drink tea and eat biscuits. 'First of all you rinse the fish and you put it on the newspaper, then take a knife and using the blunt side just scrape it up and down a few times to take off any scales. Okay?'

Kit nodded.

'Then rinse it off and do the other side, then…' She leaned across and took a pair of kitchen scissors from the pot of tools on the counter – a pot that she had brought up from the cottage and was gradually filling with duplicates of her favourite ones. 'And then you cut off the fins; can you see it's got spines in the fins? Watch those.'

Kit nodded again, watching anxiously.

'Okay, then you slide the knife into the belly of the fish on the underside and cut from the tail to the gills. And then simply pull out the insides – take it all out. It's best if you use your fingers, you can scrub any bits that won't shift with a bit of salt on your finger. There we are, now just wrap all that up in the paper and get rid of it, and then rinse the fish inside and out under the tap. You want to leave a nice clean empty space, which you could stuff with some slices of onion or lemon.'

Kit waved at the neat paper parcel of fish innards. 'And if you didn't want to do all that?'

'The fishmonger will usually do it for you. You don't usually get sea bass with all the innards still inside. Then, if you want to, you can take the head off; cut it off behind the gills. You can use a knife, a cleaver or poultry shears. It's really simple.' She set the fish down on the board. 'Use firm even pressure, cut here – and down.'

The bone gave a meaty crunch. Kit flinched. Sarah slid the head to one side. Kit eyed it speculatively; the fish head returned the compliment.

'You can use it to make stock if you want to,' said Sarah. Kit didn't seem impressed. 'And once you've done just give it another really good rinse and wash your hands – if they smell a bit fishy you scrub them with a bit of lemon.' She set the clean fish back down on the block. 'All sorted and ready to go.'

'Couldn't you do them for me?' Kit asked.

At which point Magda reappeared. 'No, no, we'd really like you to do it on film, Kit. People should eat more fish and I want them to see how very simple it is,' she said. 'And look, that one's done. Had you thought about how you are going to cook them?'

Sarah saw the panic on Kit's face. 'Actually we were just talking about that,' she said. 'Kit was telling me about this really simple way of doing them, weren't you, Kit?'

Kit nodded mechanically. 'That's right.'

'Oh good,' said Magda, looking interested. 'We like simple.' Her expression suggested that she was expecting more.

'And we were just debating whether we'd got all the ingredients,' said Sarah cheerfully. 'No point if we haven't.'

Magda didn't move.

'We'll just go and look in the pantry; come on, Kit,' said Sarah. 'We won't be a minute.' Kit didn't need any further encouragement. He practically ran to catch her.

A few minutes later and he was back at the kitchen bench, with the spotlights back on, hands washed, nose shine powdered away, stripy apron on, and with the second sea bass lying on the chopping block in front of him, which the stylist had tarted up with a bunch of parsley and a wire basket of lemons.

Kit smiled up at the camera and then pulled some newspaper over to the block. 'A friend of mine brought me a couple of these little beauties last night. Sea bass has a lovely flavour and personally I don't think they need too much doing to them, particularly when they're as fresh as these. If you're buying fresh fish always check them before taking them home – they should have bright eyes, the flesh should be firm and there shouldn't be much of a smell beyond the smell of the sea.

'So we're going to be doing a very simple recipe.' He slid the fish onto the newspaper. 'Okay, so I like to use newspaper,' he went on cheerily. 'Keeps everything nice and contained and then we can just roll it all up and throw it away when we've done. First of all we're going to descale the fish. And you can see how I'm using the back of the knife here. Just to get rid of all those scales. Nobody wants to find those on your plate or in your mouth, and I'm going to rinse it off and then turn it over...'

So far, so good, thought Sarah as she watched Kit going through the motions. Magda was right, he was a natural in front of the camera.

'Once we've rinsed off the scales, we're going to snip off these fins.' The camera crew moved in closer to catch the action.

'Do watch out for any spines. I prefer to use kitchen scissors as they're easier to handle, get in nice and close – and snip – and there we go. Next we have to...' Kit paused and took a breath. It was getting hot under the lights. Sarah could see his throat working.

'Next we have to gut the fish. Now there's really no need to be daunted by this,' he said with at least an air of confidence. 'And if you're buying fish usually your fishmonger will have already done it for you.'

Around him the camera crew were moving in even tighter for the close-up. Beads of sweat were breaking out on Kit's top lip.

He took a deep breath. The fish glistened, silver and inviting under the lights. 'Make sure your hands are dry and if you're worried about it slipping then just use some kitchen roll round your fingers like this – then take a sharp knife and open the fish up,' Kit said, swallowing hard, and as the camera focused in on his hands he slipped the knife in, drawing it along the fish's pale creamy-white belly.

'And then,' Kit began as the cavity widened and the innards began to slither out onto the newspaper; under the lights the smell of fish guts filled the air. Kit took one long breath and then turning, still clutching the knife, his eyes wide with panic, ran to the sink and threw up.

'And cut,' said Magda.

Sarah ran over to the sink. 'Fish allergy,' she said in answer to the look on the faces of the crew.

Kit heaved again.

'Why didn't someone tell me?' demanded Magda.

Sarah turned on the tap and poured Kit a glass of water. 'He didn't want to disappoint you, and it's nothing serious,' she said quickly. 'And he'll be fine now. Won't you, Kit?'

Kit nodded miserably. 'Just fine,' he said.

Over in the corner, Simon, who was watching the playback on a tiny video screen, said, 'We've got plenty of prep footage, we can just cut and fade out the sound track when he started throwing up in the sink.'

'Way to go, Simon,' said Kit with a valiant sniff as he drew the back of his hand across his mouth.

They were all done and dusted by early afternoon; the crew ate the fish and all the rest of the food Kit had managed to rustle up, while the star of the show disappeared off into the house.

Simple Sea Bass

Ingredients:
2 medium sea bass (1 per person, cleaned and scaled)
4 garlic cloves, crushed
2 tbsp good olive oil
1 tbsp Italian seasoning or 1tbs fresh parsley leaves
2 tsp fresh coarsely ground black pepper
1 tsp sea salt
1 lemon cut into wedges for garnish
1/3 cup white wine (optional)

Method:
Preheat oven to 220C/450F

In a small dish, mix the garlic, olive oil, salt, and black pepper.

Place fish in a shallow glass or ceramic baking dish.

Rub fish with oil mixture.

Pour wine over fish.

Bake the fish, uncovered, for 15 minutes. Sprinkle with parsley or Italian seasoning and continue to bake for 5 more minutes (or until the thickest part of the fish flakes easily).

Drizzle remaining pan juices over fish and garnish with lemon wedges.

Chapter Sixteen
Dating

While the crew were packing away, Sarah took the time to go through her ideas for Kit's book with Magda, who nodded absentmindedly, her eyes wandering off towards the kitchen door.

'Do you think I ought to go and see if Kit's all right?' Magda said, just as Sarah was asking whether she thought the book ought to be broken up into seasons or maybe into sections for starters, main courses and desserts?

'I'm sure he'll be just fine,' said Sarah, wondering exactly how much notice Magda had been taking of what she had been saying.

'You seem very close, you two.'

'Well, we're good friends if that's what you mean,' said Sarah, packing her notes and sketches away. Now was obviously not the moment.

'Not anything more?' pressed Magda.

'No,' Sarah laughed, sliding her notebook back into her bag. 'And I thought we'd already had this conversation, Magda. He's my landlord and if we film the rest of the things you've got planned, then he's my imaginary husband, but no romance in real life – not so much as a smidgen. All right?'

'Right,' said Magda. 'And I'm determined we will be filming the rest of it, I've been talking to Guy about it and I really think we should go with it so we have something truly impressive to show the mainstream broadcasters. And if not, it's not as if it'll be wasted, we'll just use it ourselves. I'm working up a schedule, and sorting out the tour days. Has Kit talked to you about the tour?'

Sarah nodded. 'Yes, but I've already told him that I can't go, not with the boys.'

Magda narrowed her eyes. 'Was anyone asking you to?'

'No, no, of course not,' Sarah said hastily, 'I just thought—'

But Magda was ahead of her. 'No, don't worry, Kit will be just fine with me. I think he was hoping you would feed the dogs. I was thinking we could start off in Cambridge, have a bit of a trial run and also, I've been thinking that while the weather is good we should sort out some sort of house party here. I know it's quite short notice but it will be wonderful as a marketing tool and we could use local people so I can't see that it would be a problem.'

Sarah made a concerted effort not to protest or panic.

Magda nodded. 'We've got the crew, you see. And I'm just thinking tea party. Nothing tricky. As we're going with the traditional vintage village feel it would chime beautifully and besides locals won't want a fee, probably be grateful. And then in the summer holidays we could do picnics on the beach. I'll talk it over with Kit.'

At which point Sarah's mobile phone pinged to announce an incoming text message. 'I'm so sorry,' she began, 'I thought I'd switched it off.'

Magda waved the words away. 'Not a problem and actually if you wanted to check it feel free, I really should check mine. Guy's having some sort of crisis.' She rolled her eyes. 'Although to be honest that man is always having a crisis.'

Sarah pulled the phone out of her pocket and glancing at the screen felt her colour rising. Magda was very obviously watching her every move. 'Who is it?' she said. 'Is it Kit?'

Sarah shook her head. 'No, actually it's someone I met at the weekend.'

Magda raised her eyebrows. 'So you took my advice and got back up there on the horse. Good girl.'

Sarah felt her colour deepen. 'Not exactly, no. It's a bit too soon really,' she said, as she opened the text.

'Never too soon in my book, darling,' said Magda, taking out her own phone. 'Do you know if Kit has a mobile? He's very vague about things like that. I was thinking of getting him an iPhone as a little present, what do you think?'

Sarah glanced down at the screen and read: 'Hi, great to see you on Saturday, maybe we could get together for supper some time? Best wishes, Shaun.'

Sarah felt her heart do that little pittery-pattery-thump thing.

'Not bad news, I hope,' asked Magda drily.

'No, no, he's asked me out,' Sarah said, before she could stop herself.

'When did you say that you met him?'

'Saturday.'

Magda pulled a face. 'And he can't find the time to text you till Wednesday? I'd delete that one, darling. Throw him back.'

'He told me that he was going to be away for a few days, off the grid.'

'Phuh,' said Magda. 'No one is off the grid these days unless they want to be. So, what are you going to say?'

Sarah looked at her. 'I don't know.'

'Well, the first thing is don't reply to him straight away, make him wait.' Magda rolled her eyes. 'Wednesday, for God's sake.'

Sarah glanced down at the phone.

The last time anyone had asked her out was when she had first met Colin; it was a man from work called Mac who she had fancied for months, and then when he finally plucked up courage to ask her, she had to tell him that she would love to have gone but that she was seeing someone. God, how many years ago was that? Fleetingly, Sarah wondered what had happened to Mac, and what might have happened if she'd said yes and left Colin for dust.

'How long should I make him wait?' Sarah asked in a small voice.

Magda sighed. 'Well, if it was me, darling, I'd just tell him to sling his hook, but if you're keen and he's gorgeous, then I think probably this evening would be plenty soon enough.'

Sarah stared her. 'So, not now then?'

'No, most certainly not now,' said Magda. She took the phone out of Sarah's hand and read the message. 'Nice, is he?'

Sarah nodded.

'Good-looking?'

She nodded again, wondering as she did what on earth had possessed her to get Magda on side as her romance coach.

'So go on then,' said Magda, handing the phone back. 'How did you meet him?'

'I was buying plants,' Sarah began. 'He's a gardener.'

Magda did a so-so gesture with her hand, mirrored by the expression on her face. 'Good with their hands, nice body on him if he's under forty, all right for fun, sweetie, but I'd chuck him back once you've done with him.'

Sarah stared at her.

'I'm serious, last thing you want now is a proper relationship, not after being married. No, what you want now is a bit of fun. Anyway,' said Magda. 'Let's have the juicy details.'

'There aren't any really. I bought some plants from the man he's helping out in the village and they invited me to the village fete.'

'Oh, my God, that is so sweet, darling, and so quaint. So, local, is he?'

Sarah nodded.

'How very convenient,' said Magda. She glanced down at her phone and scrolled through the screens with her thumb.

'You don't really want to all know this,' said Sarah, self consciously, gathering her things together. 'If we're done here I think I'll be heading home. I've got some things I need to do before I go to pick up the boys.'

'No, I do, go on. Please,' said Magda, gesturing for her to continue. 'I'm interested, really. I'm all ears.' She might be saying the words but it didn't take a genius to work out that in reality Magda was just waiting, hoping that Kit might reappear, yet Sarah found herself telling her anyway.

'It was at the fete,' she said. 'They invited me last time I went to buy plants—'

'So you said,' said Magda.

Saturday afternoon had been really warm with barely a cloud in the sky. After a lot of thought Sarah had decided on wearing skinny pedal-pusher jeans with a fitted blue and white checked shirt, arty earrings, and sandals with a little wedge heel that made her legs look great, but which meant she wouldn't sink into the grass on the playing field, and so by the time she wandered down to the village, she looked sun-kissed and slim and as if she had just thrown the outfit on and *not* spent two hours plucking her eyebrows, shaving her legs, ironing her shirt and applying her makeup so that she looked naturally outdoorsy and radiant – the hardest look of all to get right.

The main road into the village was closed to traffic at the crossroads, with big diversion signs up, but there was a steady stream of people on foot heading into the village centre, and every building, cottage and house around the green seemed to be decked out with a mass of bunting and streamers. There was music playing over a tannoy and the smell of barbecuing in the air.

Outside the village pub were row after row of tables and chairs that spilt down over the verge and into the road, which had been blocked off with barrels of flowers and flags. The tables were filled with people enjoying a pint and lunch in the warm summer sunshine, and although the fete was technically on the playing field, stalls had spread out all along the roadside. Some people had bric-a-brac tables and game stalls in their front gardens, while around the churchyard there was a treasure hunt going on. Sarah really wished now that she had brought the boys with her; they would have loved it.

She took her time wandering down towards the main field, checking out the roadside stalls, treating herself to a homemade smoothie, buying some fudge and a game for the boys, and trying on a hat at the nearly new stall by the old post office.

'Suits you,' said a familiar voice. Sarah swung round.

'Oh Kit. Hi, how are you? This is great, isn't it? Why didn't you tell me about the fete?'

He shrugged. 'Didn't I? Surely I told you?'

She shook her head. 'Not a word.'

'Slipped my mind, I guess. All this cookery thing. I'm complete rubbish, aren't I? The hat looks good. You're okay for filming on Wednesday?'

'More or less. We can run through the menu again tomorrow if you'd like to.'

Kit nodded. 'Good idea. Look, I've got to go.' He looked around. 'Where are the boys?'

'They're with their dad this weekend.'

'Oh, that's a shame; they'd have liked the stalls. Anyway I hope you have a good time,' he said, glancing back towards the crowd that had gathered in the playing field. He seemed completely preoccupied.

'Are you okay?' asked Sarah.

'Yes, it's just that I was meant to be meeting someone.'

'Here?'

'No, I've got to go. I'm late as it is. I'll see you tomorrow.' And with that he bent down and kissed her on the cheek. 'Buy the hat,' he said, over his shoulder as he hurried away, striding back towards the hall. Sarah watched him go, wondering what the problem was. Kit wasn't often ruffled by real life. She put the hat on again and took another look in the mirror, wondering if he was right. Maybe she should buy it.

This time the sound that broke her concentration was a wolf whistle. Sarah turned, half-expecting Kit to have come back, but instead it was Fred Tullet, the plant man. 'Looking good there, my lovely,' he said with a grin. 'Suits you.'

He was carrying a big plastic tray of plants.

She smiled. 'You think?'

'Oh yes. Ideal for a day like this. Keep the sun off.'

'Do you need a hand with those?' she asked, nodding towards the plants.

He shook his head. 'No, you're fine, my love, I can manage. I'm just pleased to see you've shown up. I'll tell Shaun that I've seen you.'

Sarah felt uncomfortable under the old man's amused gaze. He leaned in a little closer. 'He had exactly that same look in his eye when I mentioned you. I reckon it must be something going round. Drop by the stall when you've got a minute. He needs cheering up. Right up the end we are, by the horse chestnuts. Can't miss us, I've got a lot of hanging baskets round the stall. Looks lovely and I've told people they can't take them till the end of the day.' He paused. 'Shaun said he wondered if you might drop by.'

Sarah nodded dumbly; he had been talking about her, thinking about her? She tried not to make any kind of whooping sounds. She felt almost exactly the same as she had back when she was fourteen, she just tried not to show it.

'I'd get that hat,' Fred said, heading for the playing field. 'Suits you.'

Sarah gave the lady the money and tried to carry on browsing, but her mind wasn't really on the crafts, the homemade jam and pickles or the hand-knitted tea cosies; instead she found herself heading for the field, wondering whether it would have been more sensible to have walked to the stall with Fred, chatting casually. As it was, she felt as if she was walking across the grass in a spotlight, despite the crowd, because as she stepped in through the gate to the field she saw Shaun, and knew damn well he had seen her.

He'd grinned as she walked up towards him, and she had grinned right back and then, after that, she couldn't really remember what they had said except that it sound awkward and a bit silly, and that she had laughed a bit too loud and he had gone red and offered to come and help her with her garden, and then Fred said that he could cope all right on his own, if Shaun wanted to go and grab a cup of tea, and they had gone together. There had been a second as they headed across the grass that the back of their hands touched and they had both laughed self-consciously and Sarah wondered if he would hold hers or whether she should reach for his and then the moment was lost.

Lots of people seemed to know him and said hello, and looked her up and down.

And then they had sat in a marquee and had tea and cake and he teased her about her hat and they talked about her plans for the garden, and he said his life was complicated at the moment and that he had to go away for a few days and sort things out, and then maybe when he came back she might like to go out for a drink or supper or a walk or something. And Sarah said she would love to, and that her life was complicated too, so she understood and that funny feeling of excitement and desire arced between them, and she was relieved because however complicated Shaun's life was and even if she never ever saw him again it really didn't matter, because sitting in the soft light of the marquee in her hat, eating cake and drinking tea, Sarah suddenly knew with absolute certainty that everything would be all right, and that there was life after Colin.

After a while Shaun said that he really ought to go back to the stall and help Fred, and Sarah nodded and thanked him for the tea and cake, and said she wanted to go and look round the rest of the stalls, and then Shaun had asked for her number and she gave it to him, and he borrowed the girl behind the counter's pen and wrote it on the back of his hand.

But that wasn't what Sarah told Madga. Sarah told Magda an edited version, mentioning that she had seen him a couple of times in the village and bumped into him at the village fete, and he had asked for her number and that he was tall and blond and good-looking and Magda nodded her approval.

'Sounds scrummy, sweetie, but don't be too eager. Men prefer a challenge.'

At which point Kit, now showered, and dressed down in a battered tee shirt, ripped-knee jeans and sandals, reappeared through the kitchen door, clutching a can of beer.

'Thank f—' he began, on seeing Sarah still there, but before he could complete the sentence Magda was on her feet and closing in fast.

'Ah, there you are, sweetie,' she said. 'I was hoping to catch you.'

Kit jumped, eyes widening in what looked like horror. Not wanting to get caught in the crossfire Sarah shouldered her bag;

obviously Magda had a *do-as-I-say-not-as-I-do* policy when it came to men.

Easy Summer Pickle

Ingredients:

500g courgettes
3 shallots
salt

For the pickling liquid:

500ml cider vinegar
140g golden caster sugar
1 tsp mustard powder
1 tsp mustard seeds
1 tsp celery seeds
½ dried chilli (crumbled up)
1 tsp ground turmeric

Method

Draw a fork down from top to bottom on the outside of each courgette to make 'stripy skins'. Go all the way round each courgette. Slice very thinly (using a sharp knife, the slicing blade of a food processor or a mandolin).

Finely chop shallots.

Place the courgettes and shallots into a glass bowl and sprinkle with salt.

Cover with cold water, stir to dissolve the salt and leave for 1 hr.

Drain the courgettes very thoroughly and pat dry using kitchen roll or a clean tea towel.

Meanwhile put all the remaining ingredients into a pan and bring them to a gentle simmer. Simmer for 3 mins, making sure the sugar has dissolved.

Set aside to cool until the liquid is still warm but not hot. Add the courgettes to the pickling liquid and stir.

Spoon the mixture into 2 x 500ml sterilised jars
Seal the jars and leave for a few days in the fridge to mature.
Kept chilled, this pickle will keep for a couple of months.

How to sterilise glass jars:
Wash them in hot, soapy water, then dry in an oven heated to 170C/150C fan/gas mark 3 for at least 10 minutes. Always put your pickles, jams and chutneys into jars while the jars are still warm.

Alternatively you can sterilise glass jars in the microwave; wash well in the normal way, rinse, but leave them 'wet'. Pop them into the microwave for about a minute, use while still warm.

Remember not to stand warm or hot jars on a cold surface as the thermal shock may crack them

Chapter Seventeen
If music be the food of love

Sarah decided to ignore Magda's advice and texted Shaun as soon as she got back to the cottage.

'Supper sounds lovely,' she wrote, and then tucked the phone back in her bag, just in case watching it, waiting for a reply, jinxed her luck. Tea, that was the answer. Sarah had barely had the chance to fill the kettle before the phone rang, and she had to scrabble through the contents of her bag to find it.

'Hi,' said Shaun. 'Thanks for getting back to me so quickly.'

'Was it too quick?' asked Sarah, before she could stop herself.

'No, I don't think so. Why?'

'I was wondering if I should be playing hard to get.'

Shaun laughed. 'Oh, okay; how about we take that as read? Where do you fancy going?'

Sarah pulled a face. 'I don't know really. Pathetic, isn't it?'

'No, no, of course not.' He paused as if thinking or maybe he was waiting for Sarah to come up with a suggestion.

'It's just that it's years since I've been out on a date,' she said.

'Me too,' he said, and Sarah could hear that he was smiling. 'So, is there anywhere you fancy going?'

'The pictures? A meal – er,' she said, floundering and feeling hot and flustered. 'Can I phone a friend?'

Shaun laughed again. 'If you want.'

'And I'll have to get a baby sitter.'

'But you do want to go?' said Shaun.

'Yes.'

'Okay, that's a relief. How about Friday?'

'Sounds great, if I can get someone to babysit the boys,' said Sarah, thinking that maybe Melissa might be free.

'Okay. And you don't mind where you go?

'No, well, within reason.'

'Do you like music?'

'Yes.'

'What sort?'

Sarah laughed. 'That's a big question. All sorts, although not weird all over the place jazz, but most other stuff.'

'Only there's a band playing in a pub in the city that I've been wanting to see for ages; they're sort of a folksy, rocky kind of a thing. Really good though. So I was thinking that maybe we could eat first – and...' Shaun stopped. 'Sorry. I'm a bit nervous. Am I being too pushy? We could always do something else if you want to?'

'No, no, it's fine. How about you choose this time and then next time I'll pick somewhere, when I've had more chance to think about it.'

'There's going to be a next time?' he said.

'Well, hopefully,' said Sarah. 'Maybe.'

'Okay, maybe. Maybe is good.' Shaun paused and let out a long breath. She wondered just how long he had been working up the courage to text her. 'So...'

'So,' said Sarah. The silence between them settled down into something slightly more intimate and less fraught. 'So, I'll ring my friend to see if she can babysit on Friday and then I'll get back to you.'

'Great,' he said.

'What time?'

Shaun made a thinking noise and then said, 'Is seven thirty okay? It'll give us time to eat.'

'Seven thirty is just fine.'

'And would you like to meet in town or I could come and pick you up if you like?'

Sarah hesitated; the truth was however nice Shaun seemed, she didn't really know him, so she said, 'How about we meet in town, this time?'

'Okay. Have you got somewhere in mind?'

Sarah chuckled. 'It's been a while since I've done this. It's more complicated than I remember.'

'Me too.' She could hear the warmth in Shaun's voice. 'How about if we meet outside the Round Church, seven thirty, Friday. Do you know where that is?'

'Yes, I do. Okay, so, seven thirty, Friday, the Round Church,' she repeated. 'If I can get a sitter.'

'Brilliant.' Shaun sounded relieved. 'Now, what was complicated about that?'

Sarah laughed. 'Nothing,' she said. 'And everything. I'll ring you when I've sorted the boys out.'

'Look forward to it,' he said. 'Bye. And thank you.'

'Thank you?' she said, with a question in her voice.

'For saying yes.' And with that he hung up.

Sarah stood for a long time holding the phone and staring out of the kitchen window, rerunning the whole text and conversation thing in her mind. She'd been asked out on a date. A date. A proper date. Sarah found it hard to suppress a grin. By a man she fancied. Just like that. After all these years. Bloody hell.

After a few more minutes she rang Melissa, who answered on the second ring.

'Thank God you rang,' Melissa said, in a voice barely above a whisper. 'It's like a morgue in here this afternoon. Val's gone,' she hissed before Sarah could speak.

'Val? You mean the country show, gardening and rural affairs lady? Worked from home a lot of the time? Always wore a Barbour or one of those green padded gilet things?' asked Sarah.

'The very same,' said Melissa. 'Gone.'

'I haven't seen her for ages,' said Sarah.

'Well, you won't be seeing her at all from now on. She came in at lunchtime to tell Rosa and the rest of us that she's got a job editing some green, pony, gardening, self-sufficiency, goaty thing; apparently she'll be covering the work she's got on here until the end of the month and then pouf, gone. How the hell are we going to keep the magazine running if all the bloody staff leaves before Christmas? We can't cover it all. I'm not wading around in the mud at weekends for anyone unless it's at Glastonbury.'

'Has Rosa asked you to?'

'No, but I'm just saying. Have you got any idea when you're going?'

'Not yet. Rosa said that HR will be in touch, and meanwhile as long as I cover what needs doing on the magazine I can work with Magda.'

Melissa snorted. 'Talking of Magda, how did the filming go?'

'Okay. Well, maybe not okay – actually it was a bit of a disaster.' At which point Sarah told her about the fish and then, while Melissa was still laughing, edged the conversation round to Shaun and Friday night. 'What I really rang for was because I need a favour.'

'So what's new?' Melissa said, still chuckling. 'What do you want this time?'

148

'I've got a date,' Sarah said, totally unable to keep the glee out of her voice.

'What? Really?' Melissa sounded genuinely surprised. 'Wow, that's fabulous. Oh no, don't tell me, it's not Kit, is it?'

'No, of course it's not Kit. No, it's the gardener I was telling you about. Shaun. Anyway, I just wondered if you could come over and babysit the boys this Friday? Josh could come as well and we can get some DVDs in, and I'll leave you loads of food, and – why aren't you jumping in and saying yes, Mel?'

There was a moment's pause and then Melissa said, 'You know I'd love to but I can't this Friday, Josh and me are going up to the Dales for the weekend to meet his parents.'

'God, that sounds serious,' said Sarah. Oddly she wasn't that disappointed or surprised that Melissa couldn't come over; there was still a part of her that thought being asked out was a figment of her imagination.

'That's what I thought, but Josh seems keen. You could always ask Colin.'

'No,' said Sarah emphatically. 'I'm not asking Colin, and besides he had them all last weekend.'

Although she didn't say anything the boys had been very subdued when they arrived back on Sunday evening, and Sarah still hadn't got to the bottom of exactly what had happened. Expecting them to go back so soon seemed cruel, not that she could bring herself to ask her husband.

'Okay, how about Kit?' suggested Melissa. 'I'm sure he wouldn't mind, and let's be honest he owes you big time. You know he even rang my mum and told her about the TV show. I didn't have the heart to tell her the truth. And besides the boys love him and you're not going to be out all night, are you?'

'No, of course not,' said Sarah, slightly thrown by the idea.

'There you are then, ask Kit.'

Sarah rang him as soon as she got off the phone from Melissa.

'Is Magda still there?' she asked.

'No, thankfully she had to go to some meeting. Did you want to speak to her?'

'No, I just didn't want to interrupt anything.'

Kit sniffed. 'Well you haven't.'

'I was wondering if you might be able to babysit for me on Friday.'

'Oh, that would be great,' he said. 'Would it be okay if they came up here? I've got an Xbox and the Wii and—'

'They can't play games that involve killing or maiming or car theft, okay?' said Sarah, in the same voice she used for Harry and Alex. Maybe this wasn't such a great idea after all.

'No, of course not,' said Kit, sounding horrified that she even suggested it. 'I've got one with hopping frogs and then there's this basket and a net – oh, and I've got a DVD with penguins, and lots of books – do they like books?'

'Whoa,' said Sarah, laughing. 'I'm only going to be three hours or so, Kit.'

'Oh.' Kit sounded crestfallen. 'It's just that I've been wanting to read my Winnie the Pooh books to someone for year, and I've got a boxed set of all the Narnia books and—'

'Maybe there'll be another time.'

'And the Borrowers,' sighed Kit. 'I always loved the Borrowers.'

Sarah smiled. 'If you're sure you don't mind?'

'Of course not. It'll be fun.'

'I'll make sure they've eaten. If I could drop them off at about quarter to seven?'

'I was thinking maybe five,' said Kit.

'Five? We usually don't get home till at least six,' laughed Sarah.

'Six, then,' said Kit cheerily. 'We can take the dogs for a walk and get fish and chips from the van in the village. I usually have fish and chips on Friday, and that would give you time to get ready.'

'Are you serious?' asked Sarah incredulously.

'Of course I'm serious. It would be brilliant. I haven't got anyone to play the frog game with and although I love the house sometimes it can feel a bit empty all on my own.'

Unexpectedly Sarah felt a lump in her throat. 'If you're sure it's no trouble?'

'No, I'd love to.'

Which was why on Friday evening, straight after work, Sarah dropped the boys off at Kit's house, waved them goodbye and then went to the cottage to get ready for her date.

All day at work, despite the heavy atmosphere in the office and a general air of doom, Sarah had found herself singing quietly under her breath and thinking about what to wear, aided and abetted by Melissa. They had speculated on where Shaun might take her and what they might eat and how it might go and whether or not she had far too many expectations. And how nice Shaun seemed and how good-looking, and how Sarah couldn't believe that he had asked her out. And then full circle back to what to wear.

Actually she had been thinking about what to wear since she'd texted Shaun after talking to Kit on Wednesday.

'See you Friday,' she'd written.

'Looking forward to it,' he had texted back seconds later, almost as if he was waiting to hear from her.

So, on Friday evening after she dropped the boys off at the hall, Sarah sped through her check list as she peeled off her office clothes and dropped them into the linen basket in the bathroom: quick shower, wash hair, get dry, pull on flowery print dress that she had ironed the night before that said feminine, with a good figure, but wasn't too revealing, but was fitted, was sleeveless and looked great with the soft blue cardigan that she had left hanging alongside it. The colour brought out the blue in her eyes, Melissa said. She planned to team the outfit with a big straw bag, strappy sandals and take a little linen jacket with her, just in case she got cold later.

The plan was to drive into Cambridge and park in the office car park, which meant that she was just a few minutes' walk from the Round Church. Sarah had given Kit her mobile number in case of accidents and emergencies and so, at just after twenty-five past seven, Sarah was striding down the street with the Round Church in sight, feeling fabulous. She was excited and really looking forward to see Shaun again. Just as she got to the church her phone beeped to announce an incoming text message; she'd told Kit to ring so it couldn't be him. She wondered if it might be Colin.

Sarah pulled her phone out of her bag. The message was from Shaun and read: 'I'm so sorry, something's come up, I am running late. I've booked a table at Nico's – the Italian place on Bridge Street. Can we meet there? And please order. I won't be long. So sorry. Looking forward to seeing you soon, Shaun x.'

Although she was a bit disappointed, these things happened, and at least Shaun had had the good manners to let her know. Dropping the phone back into her bag Sarah looked up the street towards Magdalene bridge, which was lined with chic restaurants, pubs and cafés. The truth was – bearing in mind she'd not eaten since lunchtime – that she was famished, and in some ways it would be nicer to meet inside rather than on a street corner, so she headed for Nico's. As she got to the door Sarah realised she had no idea what name the table was booked in. The good news was that as it was relatively early the place was almost empty so Sarah had no trouble getting a table. Shaun could sort the reservation out when he got there.

'Would you like something to drink?' asked the waitress, once Sarah was settled in a corner table with a good view of the door.

'Yes, please, could I have some fizzy water. I'm waiting for a friend.'

The woman nodded. 'Righty-oh; would you like me to bring you a little tray of something to nibble on while you wait?'

'That would be great,' said Sarah, as she slipped her jacket over the back of the chair. 'I'm starving.'

The woman laughed. 'We like starving people in here. Shall I just bring you some antipasti, or would you like the menu? Maybe some bread?'

'Antipasti and some bread sounds great,' Sarah said, while her stomach growled its approval.

*

'So, would you like some coffee with your dessert?' Sarah's waitress asked, as she stood alongside Sarah's table, pencil hovering over her pad.

Sarah, pressing the napkin to her lips, nodded. 'Yes, please. A cappuccino?'

'Chocolate on that?'

'Yes, please.'

It was well after nine. The restaurant had filled up and started to empty out again in the bright, noisy tidal flow of Friday-night socialising. Sarah glanced towards the door as a couple came in, the man guiding the girl he was with by the arm. They were laughing and chatting.

The odd thing was that despite Shaun's no-show, Sarah wasn't really that disappointed. It felt strangely liberating to be out, even if she was on her own. She had waited as long as she could before ordering but in the end thought what the hell, if she was going to be stood up then at least she wasn't going to do it hungry.

The food was superb and the waitress had brought Sarah a newspaper so that she had something to do rather than just stare at the door, and actually against all the odds she was having a good time, albeit alone.

'Are you sure I can't get you a glass of wine or maybe a Baileys or something to go with your coffee?' asked the waitress.

'No, unfortunately I've got to drive home,' said Sarah.

'Shame, I'll just get that coffee for you.'

At which point for some reason Sarah glanced up and saw Shaun peering in the window, one hand cupped around the side of his face so he could see inside. When he spotted her, she waved and he hurried in. The waitress watching the exchange intercepted him on his way across the floor.

'You want a coffee?' she asked.

Shaun did a double take and then nodded. 'That would be good, thank you.'

'You'd better have a good excuse,' the woman said. Shaun winced and headed over to Sarah's table.

He pulled out a chair. 'Do you mind if I join you or would you just like to slap me now?'

'Sit down,' she said. 'I'll wait till we're on our own, I don't want to make a scene.'.

'I am so, so sorry, Sarah. God, what a way to start.' He glanced around the table. 'Have you eaten?'

She nodded towards the remains of her dessert. 'For future reference they do a really good tiramisu here.'

Shaun shook his head. 'I was going to text you again but I just had no idea how long I was going to be and – I'm not usually like this.'

'But it's complicated?' Sarah raised her eyebrows.

He nodded, as the waitress reappeared with two coffees.

'How was your dinner?' he asked.

'Quiet,' Sarah said, not letting him off the hook. And then she smiled. The waitress was still there, hanging around close by.

'You want me to bring you a pudding?' she said. 'You might want to share it, get yourself back into her good books?'

Shaun shook his head. 'Coffee will be just fine, thank you. And I think I've got a way to go to make it up yet.'

The waitress nodded. 'You most certainly have,' and then she winked at Sarah and headed back towards the kitchen.

Shaun jiffled his chair in closer.

'So?' said Sarah, tipping her head to one side, opening the way for his explanation.

'So,' said Shaun. 'I'm half way through a divorce and there are lots of other things going on too – well, it's tough and messy.'

Sarah nodded. 'I know how that feels.'

He nodded. 'Sorry, yes, of course you do, and to be honest it's the very last thing I want to talk about.' He smiled. 'I was really looking forward to meeting you tonight. I feel like I've blown it already.'

Sarah took a sip of coffee, noticing how tired he looked and how nice his eyes were. 'You need to work at it, that's for certain.'

'I plan to. How about we finish our coffee and head for the pub? I reckon that the band should be on by now, and next time I promise I won't be late. Cross my heart.'

'I'll hold you to that,' said Sarah, as Shaun waved the waitress back and insisted on paying for Sarah's meal and left a healthy tip, and then they walked over the river towards the pub. Sarah wasn't altogether sure exactly how to play it. She was a bit upset at being made to wait but real life was like that sometimes, and Shaun seemed genuinely upset about keeping her waiting. And he was cute. But even so it was tricky to know quite how to pick up the pieces of the evening.

'Would you like me to be angry with you?' asked Sarah.

'If it helps.'

'It won't and I'm not angry, I'm just pleased that you're here. I was looking forward to seeing you too.'

He nodded. 'Me too. Okay, so how about we start again. From here. This minute.'

'Fair enough.'

'So was the food good?' asked Shaun. 'I've been planning to eat there since it opened.'

'Not bad, maybe we could go there another time – and I do understand about being held up, but you could have texted me and said you didn't know how long you were going to be. I would have been fine with that—'

'You're right.' He nodded. 'I just wasn't sure what to do. And I didn't want you to go. I thought perhaps if I said I didn't know how long I was going to be you might just go home.'

They were ambling down the road, side by side. If they knew each other better they would probably be holding hands, thought Sarah. She wasn't taking an awful lot of notice of where they were going, but as they turned a corner, Shaun stopped and said, 'What is that noise?'

Sarah looked up and listened; there was horrible shrieking screeching thumping banging sound coming up from somewhere ahead of them, and it occurred to them both at around the same time that it was coming from the pub they were heading towards.

'Oh no,' said Shaun, stopping dead in his tracks. His face was a picture.

Sarah couldn't help laughing. 'Is that the band you've been desperate to see?'

Shaun shook his head. 'I bloody well hope not. That can't be them, surely?' He turned round. 'God, what a disaster. I really don't know what to say, Sarah. I'm so sorry.'

'Don't be sorry,' laughed Sarah. 'You never know, this lot might be their warm-up act.'

Shaun laughed. 'I admire your optimism. If they are, we'll probably have the place to ourselves. Let's take a look, shall we?'

Sarah nodded.

Outside the pub on a chalk board was the name of the band that were playing, something involving death, sex and bodily fluids, above another sign that announced the cancellation of the band that Shaun had been hoping to see.

'Right,' he said, with a hint of desperation in his voice. 'Let's get away from this racket. I'll tell you what,' he said, checking his watch. 'How about we go to the late screening at the cinema in the Grafton Centre? We can make it if we hurry. It'll probably be an adventure film or something or we could just go and have a quiet drink somewhere instead, if you like? What do you think?'

Behind them somewhere deep inside the bowels of the pub the band came to a noisy cymbal-clashing screaming climax and in the instant of silence that followed Shaun's phone began to ring.

'Bugger,' he sighed, obviously torn between answering it and ignoring it. 'I'm so sorry. I thought I'd switched it off.'

Sarah could see his discomfort. She touched his arm. 'Take the call. I'm fine, really. It's been a long week and to be honest I'm dog-tired. I think I'm going to head home.'

'Let me at least walk you back to the car?' he said. The phone rang on.

She smiled. 'It's okay. I'll be fine, honestly. Take your call.'

'Can I call you?' he asked.

Sarah smiled and nodded. 'Of course you can.' And with that she turned on her heel and made her way back towards the office car park. When she glanced over her shoulder Shaun was still outside the pub, walking up and down, the phone clamped to his ear.

Sarah sighed; it was such a shame that the evening hadn't worked out as they'd planned, but maybe it was a sign, maybe she wasn't ready, after all it was early days, and from the way Shaun was talking animatedly into the phone maybe he wasn't ready either.

Just as Sarah reached Magdalene bridge there was a great clap of thunder, and almost at once it began to rain. Hard. Sarah pulled on her jacket, turned up the collar and quickened her step as the drops got bigger and bigger. But by the time she got to the car park she was soaked to the skin.

Taking out her car keys she tried to open the little side gate alongside the barrier with her office pass. The card slipped down through the reader, but the gate didn't open. She did it again; nothing happened. Sarah wiped it on her sleeve and swiped it again – nothing – and then she looked more closely at the barrier. Usually there was a row of red lights on it to warn you it was closed, but tonight there was nothing, so it had fused or had been switched off or maybe the storm had taken it out. Sarah stared into the locked yard. She could see her car but she couldn't get to it, and even if she clambered over the barrier there was no way to get it out. Overhead there was another huge clap of thunder and the rain turned into a torrent.

Sarah looked up into the heavens. Bloody marvellous. The perfect end to a perfect evening. She walked up towards the taxi rank, the rain squelching out of the front of her sandals, the lining dying her toes blue, or maybe it was the cold. There was a queue.

Tiramisu

Ingredients:

568ml pot double cream
250g tub mascarpone
75ml Marsala, rum or brandy
5 tbsp golden caster sugar
300ml strong coffee, made with 2 tbsp coffee granules and 300ml boiling water
1–2 packs sponge fingers
25g chunk dark chocolate
2 tsp cocoa powder
1tsp vanilla essence

Method:
In a large bowl whisk the mascarpone, double cream, caster sugar and vanilla essence in a bowl until it has the consistency of thick cream.

Mix around the coffee with spirit of your choice and allow to cool (taste and adjust strength). Pour in a small flat dish (this dish is just used for dipping).

Dip the sponge fingers quickly into the liquid in the small flat dish and then arrange a layer in your serving dish. (Dip one side in the liquid for a second or two then the other. Don't leave them too long –you don't want your sponge to be too soggy.)

Spoon half of the mascarpone mix over the sponge fingers.

Using a coarse grater, grate a layer of chocolate over the mascarpone mix.

Repeat process, ending with a layer of the mascarpone, so that you have 2 layers of sponge fingers and 2 layers of the mascarpone mix.

Cover with cling film and chill overnight in fridge.

Before serving, sieve cocoa powder over the top and then finish by grating the remaining chocolate.

Will keep for up to two days in the fridge.

Chapter Eighteen
Coming Home

The taxi driver made her sit on a black polythene bag in the back, but he did at least turn up the heater to boil and make sympathetic noises as they headed out of the city centre towards Newnham Magna. Sarah had intended to get him to drop her off at the hall, but when the taxi swung into the lane, she could see that every light in the cottage was on, and Kit's Discovery was parked up by the gate. Feeling a great wave of panic, Sarah paid, got out and ran up to the door, which swung open just as she reached it.

'Hello,' said Kit.

'Is everything all right?' she gasped.

Kit looked her up and down. 'I reckon it should be me asking. What the hell happened to you?'

Sarah shrugged. 'I'm fine.'

'You don't look fine to me, come on in and get yourself dry. The boys were getting tired so I thought I'd bring them home rather than disturb them once you got back, although I have to say you're here a lot earlier than I expected.'

'Me too,' said Sarah, shucking off her wet jacket. She could feel the tension easing out of her shoulders. She peered round the door into the sitting room. The wood burner was lit, the lamps too and Kit's dogs lay curled up in the hearth. A book lay open over the arm of the chair and there was music playing. The rain lashing at the windows oddly just made it feel all the cosier. Looking round, Sarah realised what a relief it was to be back home. The thought took her by surprise too: *home*. Sometime over the last few weeks the cottage had moved seamlessly from being just a place to live to being their home, and it felt really good to be back.

'The boys?' she began.

Kit looked upstairs towards the bedrooms. 'Are both safely tucked up in bed. Faces washed, teeth brushed, PJs on. We read some Paddington Bear. They seemed to like it. I think Alex is hoping he can have marmalade sandwiches for breakfast.'

Sarah looked at Kit and unexpectedly felt her eyes welling up with tears.

'Tea?' Kit asked, oblivious. 'We've eaten all the cake. Apparently there are some biscuits somewhere but I'm damned if I can find them.' He headed for the kitchen. 'So,' he said, without looking back. 'How was it?'

'So, so,' said Sarah, easing off her sandals with her toes. Her feet were bright blue.

'So, so?' he repeated.

'Okay, so not great.'

He nodded. 'Nice chap, though?'

'Can we not talk about it?' asked Sarah.

'Of course,' said Kit, casually. 'Not if you don't want to.'

'I don't. I'm just going to go upstairs and change out of these wet things. Do you mind making the tea?'

'No, as long as you tell me where the biscuits are?'

But Sarah was already half way up the stairs. She grabbed a towel from the airing cupboard and in the quiet confines of her bedroom peeled off her sodden clothes. She was wet right through to her carefully chosen underwear, her skin lard white, blotching and cover in goose pimples. Attractive, she thought grimly. She towelled her hair dry and pulled on a pair of jogging bottoms, a big comfy sweater and her slippers. It hadn't been Shaun's fault that the evening had been a disaster – well at least, not all of it, and she didn't blame him, but she felt deflated and a bit weepy. Sarah sniffed and looked in the mirror. Her hair was a mess, her makeup all gone, she looked tired, cold and fed up, which just about summed it up.

Downstairs, Kit had brought a tray through from the kitchen to the sitting room: on it was a teapot, along with two mugs and a little jug. Sarah sat down by the fire and warmed her hands. The two dogs looked up to check nothing exciting was going on and when they were sure slipped back into snoring, dream-filled sleep.

'So the boys behaved themselves?' asked Sarah, steering any planned questions away from her date, at the same time as pushing a stray log further onto the fire with the poker.

Kit nodded. 'They were really good. We had a great time and Harry thrashed me at the frog game. Oh, and I got a phone call from Magda. She wants to know if we can do her tea party next weekend?'

'Her tea party?'

'You know, for the programme, out on the terrace, checked table cloths, little cucumber sandwiches and Victoria sponge, lemonade and that sort of thing. A new twist on an old idea.'

Sarah stared at him. 'Are you serious?'

He nodded. 'I said yes, you didn't mind, did you? Magda said that she'd talked to you about it, and she's going to invite some people from the village, the vicar, and Mrs Alliott who breeds Labradors in Church Lane, the old postmistress, Mrs Howling from the school, that sort of thing.'

'I don't mind but there's an awful lot to sort out and I'm not sure people will be able to come at such short notice.'

'Well, apparently they will – everyone she's asked so far has said yes. I think it's the idea of being on the telly. You know what Magda's like, doesn't take no for an answer and she's promised to get them some publicity and prizes for the annual Christmas Raffle, and—'

'That's months away.'

'I know but she seemed very certain she wouldn't have any problems, and apparently she hasn't.'

'How many is this tea supposed to be for?'

'Oh, I don't know. I didn't ask. A dozen? I'll ring her back tomorrow and check on the numbers. Oh, and what's his name rang.'

'What's his name?'

Kit nodded. 'Sorry, I'm not very good on names. The man you were married to.'

'Colin?'

Kit nodded. 'That's it, Colin. He rang.'

Sarah looked heavenwards. That was all she needed. 'Did he say what he wanted?'

Kit shook his head. 'No. Actually he rang twice. I think the first time he thought that it was a wrong number. A man picking the phone up and everything.'

'And the second time?'

'He said, "Is Sarah there?" And I told him that you were out, and that he could ring you tomorrow if he liked, or did he want me to get you to ring him, but probably not when you got back in because it might be late. He was quite rude and then he wanted to know where the boys were and I said—'

Sarah found herself hanging on Kit's every word.

'And I said that they were with the baby sitter, because I didn't think he sounded the kind of man who would approve of me looking after them, and then he wanted to know what I was doing in your house. To be honest I'd sort of painted myself into a corner by then, so I said it was none of his business and that we were friends and he said, "Oh really", and then he hung up.'

Sarah opened her mouth to say something, but then realised that there was nothing really that she could say.

'Tea?' asked Kit, indicating the pot on the tray.

Sarah nodded. Kit bent down to pour it and handed her a mug. Floating on the top of the tea were half a dozen little pink fluffy blobs.

'What on earth are those?' Sarah said in astonishment.

'Marshmallows, I bought them for the boys,' said Kit, taking a sip from his mug. 'You looked so cold and fed up. I couldn't find the hot chocolate so I thought I'd put them in your tea instead. What do you think?'

Sarah looked across at him to see if he was serious. She guessed from his expression that he that was.

'Tell you what,' said Sarah, getting to her feet. 'Are there any more?'

Kit nodded. 'Loads. They're on the kitchen table.'

'How about I make us some hot chocolate and find the biscuits?'

He nodded. 'Sounds perfect. And if you like I could read you some Paddington Bear?'

How could she possibly resist?

Homemade Hot Chocolate

Ingredients:

300ml milk
225ml single cream
2oz dark chocolate, coarsely grated
2oz milk chocolate, coarsely grated
½ tbsp golden caster sugar
1 tsp pure vanilla extract
1 tsp instant coffee (optional)

1 tsp cocoa powder

Method:

Heat the milk and cream in a saucepan on medium heat to just below the simmering point.

Remove the pan from the heat and add the chocolate.

Stir until the chocolate has melted, add the sugar, vanilla extract, and coffee (if desired) and whisk vigorously until frothy.

Reheat gently, pour into two mugs.

Sieve cocoa onto top.

Serve immediately.

Optional extras: canned 'squirty' cream, marshmallows, extra grated chocolate.

Chapter Nineteen
Recipe for disaster

After Kit went home, Sarah lay in bed, snuggled up under the duvet listening to the pitter-pattering of the falling rain on the cottage roof and dripping from the eaves. She was thinking about Shaun, and Colin and the boys, and Kit, and the trials of working for Magda, and how to go about writing a cookery book and how long it might be before Hanleys sorted out her redundancy package, and when the money for the house might come through, and whether she would need to water the hanging baskets despite the rain, and what had become of the robe that Peony Tyler had been wearing the day she had discovered the woman with Colin; Sarah had really loved that robe. In fact she was doing everything except sleeping, so she wasn't at all phased when her mobile pinged to announce the arrival of a message around midnight.

She rolled over to retrieve her phone from the bedside table. The message was from Shaun and read, 'Hope you got home safe and sound. You looked fabulous tonight. I was looking forward to spending some time with you. I hadn't planned on the whole evening being a disaster from beginning to end. I wondered if you fancied trying again?'

Sarah sat up and switched on her bedside light. 'And risk pestilence, plague, and maybe a swarm of locusts?'

'You're awake?'

'My brain won't switch off.'

'I'm sorry about this evening.'

'Me too.'

'So do you want to try again?'

Sarah grinned. It felt very odd and strangely intimate to be texting by lamplight. 'Why not?'

'Okay. This time you can choose where we go.'

'Lol. No pressure then. Let me think about it.'

'Don't think too long.'

'I won't. How disastrous do you want it to be?'

'Don't,' he texted. She could almost hear him laughing.

'Maybe next weekend?' she typed.

'That would be great, but I've got a couple of things on. Can I let you know when I'm free later in the week?'

'Sure. Me too,' said Sarah. 'Just let me know. And I'll think of somewhere.'

And with that it seemed like their conversation had come to a natural end. 'Night, night. Sweet dreams,' Shaun texted.

'And you too,' Sarah typed.

An instant later he replied with three kisses, which made Sarah smile, and with that she closed her phone and turned out the light. She was asleep in seconds.

*

'Fold means turning the mixture over very gently with a metal tablespoon or a spatula,' said Sarah in despair, as Kit butchered the sponge mixture in the bowl on the workbench in his newly revamped kitchen. It was the following morning and the boys were playing outside in the kitchen garden while Sarah was trying to show Kit some of the basic techniques involved in baking.

Kit dipped his finger into the bowl and licked it thoughtfully. 'It tastes all right to me.'

'The whole point is that we're trying to keep the air in the mixture by sieving the flour and then very gently incorporating it into the rest of the mixture, not beating it to death.'

'It'll be all right. Oh, did you see the new dishwasher they put in, in the utility room? I've been washing everything. Me and the boys tried it out last night. It'll do ornaments and I did those glass lamp shades that were in the pantry – rubbish at shoes though.'

Sarah stared at him.

'Okay, so where are we?' he said, staring into the bowl.

'Up the creek without a paddle if you don't concentrate, Kit. Do you want to do the tea party next weekend?'

He nodded.

'Right, then, you have to concentrate.'

From outside Sarah could hear the boys whooping with delight, a stark contrast to the atmosphere in the kitchen. 'You need to concentrate and make more effort,' she said.

Kit dipped a finger into the mixture again. 'They used to say the same thing to me at school.'

'What is it the boys are doing out there?' Sarah asked, putting her notes down and going outside to take a look. In the corner of the ramshackle overgrown garden was a brand new wooden fort complete with ladder, slide, monkey bars, a trapdoor and little windows with shutters. Alongside it was a huge sand pit and all the toys a boy could ever need to enjoy it.

Sarah stared at them. 'Where on earth did those come from?'

'Magda. She had them delivered and two men came and put them up yesterday. It's all about ambience apparently, happy families, cheery children,' said Kit, still busy with the spoon. 'I think there's a swing and a seesaw coming as well. I'm going to have someone come in and do the garden.'

'Kit, this really has got to stop,' said Sarah. 'You realise that Magda is buying you, don't you? By accepting all this stuff you must know that at some point she is going to call in the favour.'

Kit stared at her with what looked like an expression of genuine surprise. 'Do you think so?'

'For goodness' sake, Kit, I know so. All this kitchen equipment, a dishwasher, that stuff for the kids, you've sold your soul – you do understand that, don't you?'

'Oh,' said Kit. 'Right.' He had another spoonful.

Sarah stood for a moment or two watching the boys playing contently in amongst the overgrown grass and old fruit trees. Kit came over and stood alongside her. 'You know that Colin's girlfriend locked Big Bunny in the cupboard last weekend, don't you? All weekend.'

Sarah looked up at him; his tone was altogether more measured, Kit the boy receding, as they watched Alex carefully turning out the latest in a long line of perfectly formed sandcastles, his face a blissful mask of concentration, his curly hair tipped gold by the summer sun, his efforts being overseen by the battered toy rabbit.

'She told him that only babies have toys like Big Bunny and that if he kept crying she would throw Big Bunny on the bonfire, with all the rest of the rubbish from next door that his daddy was burning.'

Sarah stared at Kit, feeling tears of fury and hurt prickle up behind her eyes.

'And she told him that if he sucked his thumb it would rot and drop off and then they would have to cut his hand off.'

The breath felt as if it was being squashed out of Sarah's chest. 'She said that to Alex? How could she? How dare she? Are you serious?'

166

Kit nodded. 'And when Harry said that she couldn't do that and that she should leave Alex alone, Colin came in and told Harry off for being rude to whatever her name is.'

Sarah felt the tears were about to fall. 'Oh no. Oh Kit, no wonder they were so quiet when they came home. I knew something had happened but they wouldn't tell me what it was. Why on earth would she do that? Why on earth would anyone do that?'

'Because she is a fat evil witch,' said Kit, dipping the spoon back into the bowl of sponge mixture. 'Or at least that is what Harry said, and I'm inclined to agree with him.'

'What am I going to do?' said Sarah anxiously, thinking aloud more than really asking a question.

'Well, there's no point talking to Colin, he's obviously all loved up and smitten and can't see the bitch for trees, and the woman—'

'Peony—'

Kit raised his eyebrows. 'Really? Presumably her parents hated her on sight, right from the get-go, giving her a name like that – you can't talk to her because she's obviously a child-hating sadist, which just leaves you with the sensible option.'

'Which is? Not let them go?'

'No, talk to the boys, explain that obviously Big Bunny is wasted on Peony who can't be trusted with him, so he'll be much safer left at home with you so that she can't get her miserable rabbit-strangling hands on him.'

'And what should I say about the thumb-sucking?'

'Tell Alex not to put his thumb in his mouth while she's around. Used to work with my nannies.' Kit paused. 'And hope your stupid bloody husband comes to his senses and gets shot of her as soon as possible. She even pulled the "no child of mine would do that" line on them apparently. Presumably she hasn't got any children?'

'Why didn't they tell me?' said Sarah, staring at the boys playing so happily out in Kit's garden.

'Because they didn't want to upset you. They might be little but they understand a lot more than you think, and they're protective of both of you.'

'They're too little to have to cope with all this,' said Sarah, the words catching like shards of glass in her throat.

'So, what? You're planning to forgive and forget and go back to Colin, are you?'

'No. God no.' Sarah shook her head. 'I can't.'

'No, exactly. So you have to do the best you can with what you've got; I think kids can cope as long as they know that some things don't change: that you're always there for them, and that they have a framework, routine, and understand that you love them; that the core things are still there, and it will sort itself out. It'll just take time.'

Sarah stared up at him. He didn't seem at all like the Kit she knew, which made her wonder just how much of his childishness was an act.

So,' said Kit, peering down into the bowl he was holding. 'Back to the sponge – do you think we can salvage it?' He tipped it towards her.

Sarah looked inside; there was barely any mixture left.

'Let's start again, shall we?' she said. 'I've got a foolproof all-in-one recipe in my notebook. We'll work up slowly to folding.'

They were both back in the kitchen and waiting for Kit's first sponge to come out of the oven when the phone rang. It was Magda, and because they were still busy weighing out the ingredients for a batch of scones, Kit put it onto speakerphone. 'Hello, Magda,' he said, adding more butter to the mound already in the pan on the scales.

'Kit, darling. Busy?' she purred.

'I'm in the kitchen, whipping up a sponge and a batch of scones.'

'I might have guessed. How wonderful. I just wanted to confirm that we'll be there to film on Friday and over weekend.'

'Saturday and Sunday?' asked Kit. He had already sieved the flour. It looked like Christmas had come early to Roseberry Hall.

'Probably. I thought we could shoot the preparations and baking on Friday and then we'll have the tea party on Saturday afternoon – everyone has RSVP-ed already – and then anything we've missed we can do again on Sunday morning. What do you say?'

'Sounds fine to me,' said Kit, smiling at Sarah, who rolled her eyes and nodded. He had flour on his nose and a bow wave of it wiped through his hair. 'Will you be wanting the boys?'

'Boys?'

'Sarah's boys.'

'Oh yes, obviously, although maybe just for the tea party.' Magda paused. 'They'll add to the whole family feel.'

Sarah felt uncomfortable being privy to this exchange and Magda not knowing that she was there.

'And I've been thinking,' Magda continued. 'It's going to be rather a long way to trek backwards and forwards to your place every day.'

Kit nodded and made a noise of agreement.

'And I'm really hoping that we can make an early start. You know, you walking the dogs through the morning mist on the estate, coming home and making a hearty home-cooked breakfast. So I was wondering if—'

'If you can all stay over?' said Kit, pre-empting her, and making it sound as if he was genuinely delighted. 'That would be great. How many of there are you? Will it be the same people who came last time?'

He had obviously completely wrong-footed Magda, who started to back-pedal. 'What? No, I wasn't thinking about everyone staying. I mean I don't want to put you to too much trouble and there is a pub in the village that—'

'Oh no,' said Kit, 'it'll be no trouble at all. It'll be fun. How many people do you think there will be? I'll have Mrs Oates, my daily lady, make up the beds. It's not like I haven't got the room here. We can all muck in. It'll be fun, just like scout camp.'

There was silence from the other end of the line; Sarah suspected that what Magda had in mind was something altogether more intimate and not like scout camp at all.

'Right,' said Magda, although she sounded far from convinced. 'I'll tell you what, darling, how about I email you the schedule, and I'll see who wants to stay up at the hall, and who would rather do the travelling, or maybe stay in the pub?'

'Friday night is fish and chip night, and we could light the fire pit,' said Kit cheerfully, apparently thinking aloud. 'Oh, it'll be great. We could play charades. Does anyone play the guitar?'

'No, no, I don't think they do,' sighed Magda.

Sarah suppressed a grin and went back to weighing out the rest of the butter.

*

'Can't we stay here and play?' whinged Harry, as he swung from the monkey bars on the fort's walkway. All the cooking done, Sarah was ready to head back to the cottage.

'No, we can't. We have to go home and have some lunch. Come on.'

The boys trailed behind her into the kitchen, dragging their feet. 'We could eat here, Kit wouldn't mind, would you, Kit? He's a really good cook, he's going to be on TV,' said Harry earnestly.

Sarah said nothing.

'They could stay if they want, if you've got things to get on with.'

Sarah raised an eyebrow. 'And what were you thinking of having for lunch?'

Kit looked at the scones they'd just got out of the oven and the cake cooling on a rack near the sink. 'And I've got Haribo for afters,' he said cheerfully.

'No,' said Sarah firmly. 'It's a shame we didn't do the quiches today.'

'We could do them now,' said Kit, all eager beaver. 'I've got eggs.'

Sarah shook her head. 'No, we can't. What you need to do is clean the kitchen.'

He stared at her as if she was barking mad. 'It's fine,' he said without so much as glancing round.

'No, it's not. It needs to be pristine. If they're going to film in here you need to scrub all that whatever-it-is off the top of the stove and wipe the paw prints off the fridge door.'

'You think?' Kit frowned. 'Maybe I should get Mrs O to do a few more hours while the filming is going on. Buff the place up a bit before they get here.'

'Good idea,' said Sarah, picking up her bag and shooing the boys out of the back door as they said their goodbyes and thanks. 'We'll do pastry next time.'

Kit nodded. 'Excellent,' he said. 'What are you having for lunch?'

'A sandwich.'

He looked crestfallen. 'You could have that here.'

'Kit, I have to go home, there are things I have to do.'

The boys were about as enthusiastic as their host.

Back at the cottage the postman had been. There was a letter from Sarah's solicitors waiting for her on the mat, telling her that the end was finally in sight and that if everything went to plan the sale of the house should be completed and the money in the bank by Friday lunchtime.

There were just three lines, including Dear Sarah, to inform her that one phase of her life was most definitely over. Along with it was a letter from Hanleys setting out the details of her redundancy package – twice the statutory rate, along with their deepest and most sincere regret, an agreement to let her name her own leaving date, and an invitation to submit freelance work in the new year. Sarah stood both letters up on the kitchen table where she could see them. Between them they represented the end of an era.

As she made sandwiches for lunch she couldn't help thinking about how her life had been turned upside down over the last few weeks; she thought about how she had found the Cambridge house, the job she loved, her marriage, all her plans and all those hopes – all gone, swept away in no time at all. The end of all the things she had thought of as the unchanging truths at the centre of her life. Sarah backhanded a tear away. She ought to ring Colin and let him know about the house, which made her think about Peony and the boys and Big Bunny. She really needed to talk to him about that too.

Once the boys had finished lunch and settled down with cars and dumper trucks out on the lawn, Sarah rang Colin's number. There were lots of things they needed to talk about.

'I would prefer that you didn't ring here,' he said by way of greeting.

'I need to be able to contact you, Colin. I thought you'd like to know that the house sale should be completed on Friday. And the money should be in the bank on Friday.'

'And not before time,' he said.

'And I'm being made redundant.'

It was the first time Sarah had mentioned it to Colin, not wanting to say anything until it was official or give him another stick to beat her with.

'Oh, very clever,' he sneered.

'Sorry?'

'I suppose you think that means you won't have to pay me maintenance, don't you?'

'Colin, my solicitor has already said that as I've got the children and you won't be contributing to their upkeep and I don't earn that much, you won't be entitled to—'

'That's what my solicitor said but as I pointed out to him, this is not about entitlement, Sarah. This is about what is morally right.'

'I'm going to be unemployed.'

'And your point is what, exactly?' he pressed.

'You'd take money that I need for the boys?'

'Don't be so melodramatic. You'll get another job, you know you will. And I have to eat. I have to live – and there's my book to consider.'

Sarah was speechless with fury. Colin was incredible.

'I won't be paying you any maintenance, Colin, and that's the end of it.'

Colin sniffed. 'It seems unreasonable.'

'And I'm going to write a book,' she said. Colin didn't need to know that it was a recipe book.

He sniffed. 'Oh, very funny.'

'And next weekend?' she said, trying to stay calm, looking for the moment to bring up Peony, Alex and Big Bunny.

'What about it?'

'If we're having a weekend each then it will be your turn to have the boys next weekend. I've got something organised for Saturday, so If you'd like to have them on Friday evening and bring them back Saturday morning or if you like, I could bring them over to you on Saturday evening and you could bring them back on Sunday as usual.'

Colin sniffed again. Sarah waited, wondering what spanner he was planning to throw in the works this time.

'Yes, about that,' he said after a moment or two. Sarah could hear something strange in his voice. 'To be honest I was quite concerned when they came over last weekend. They were very disruptive and rude. I was planning to ring you and have a chat to you about it. Harry in particular has become very, very cheeky. He was incredibly rude to Peony – and after she had invited them to stay with us as well. I think it might be better for all concerned if I just had them for the day. On Sunday. Peony is going on to see her family.'

Sarah took a breath, thinking about what Kit had said about Big Bunny and the cupboard; this was the moment. 'What happened?'

Colin coughed. 'I've said before that it doesn't do to baby them.'

'Meaning what exactly?' Sarah pressed, keeping her tone reasonable.

'Alex was making a fuss about nothing and Harry snapped at Peony, which is really totally unacceptable. She is very sensitive to that kind of thing.' His voice lowered to a whisper. 'He said she was a fat witch. She's terribly sensitive about her weight; apparently it's her glands.'

'Maybe he was protecting his little brother.'

'Protecting him? From what?'

'From Peony,' said Sarah evenly.

'Don't be so ridiculous, why on earth would Alex need protecting from Peony?'

'People have very different ideas about how children should be treated,' Sarah began, carefully edging her way forward. She needed Colin to talk, and to hear what she had to say, not hang up on her.

'Oh, you're talking about the nonsense with that damned rabbit, aren't you? Storm in a teacup.'

'She threatened to burn him, Colin. I don't think that's nonsense.'

'It was a joke. And it's not a him, Sarah. It's an it; it's just a toy, for God's sake.'

'Not as far as Alex is concerned.'

'There you go again, babying him. Well, I agree with her,' said Colin. 'Alex is too old to be carting that scabby rabbit everywhere he goes.'

'He finds it a comfort, you know that; he'll let go of it when he's ready, but at the moment because everything has changed Alex needs Big Bunny more than ever.'

'And whose fault is that, exactly?' Colin snarled.

Sarah made a concerted effort not to bite back; it was so tempting to give Colin a mouthful and hang up, but she knew that that would only make things worse. For all his miserable mean ways she wanted the boys to have a relationship with their father, and the boys would have to go there again. 'They've been very unsettled and quiet since they came home.'

'Oh, and that's my fault, is it?' he said.

'No, I'm not saying that. Peony's not used to children.'

'You've spoilt them.'

Sarah looked heavenwards. Time to make a tactical withdrawal. 'Anyway if you'd like to have them on Sunday, that would be fine.'

'And what about the money for the house? Fifty, fifty, that's what we agreed?'

'I'll talk to my solicitor, you should have it next week.' She didn't say that her solicitor had suggested that they try to persuade Colin to settle for less. It wasn't worth the aggravation.

By the time she put the phone down Sarah was trembling with a mixture of fury, frustration and sadness.

When the phone rang a moment or two later it was all Sarah could do not to pick it up and swear into the receiver, but she was glad she took a second or two to compose herself before speaking – particularly as it wasn't Colin ringing back for another go at her, but Magda.

'Hello, darling, I'm sorry to disturb you at the weekend. I do hope that you don't mind,' Magda said, without a shred of sincerity. 'But I wondered if Kit had talked to you about filming next week.'

'He has.'

'Good, good, I was just checking to make sure that you're all right about it all. I'll email you a schedule, obviously. For the filming?'

'I'm fine, Magda, thank you.'

'And how are the boys?'

'Fine, thank you.'

Which was exactly the same moment that a long shadow fell across the kitchen table and Sarah looked up to see Kit standing in the open doorway.

'Okay, Magda,' said Sarah, with extra emphasis on her name, beckoning him in.

Kit shook his head violently and pressed a finger to his lips. 'I'm not here,' he mouthed.

'Good,' said Magda. 'We won't actually be filming the boys per se, we just want them there to add to the ambience. On Saturday. You know the kind of thing,' Magda continued. 'We really want to make this a feel-good show, warm, accessible. I know we're discussed this before, Sarah, but I want to make sure that you understand how important that aspect of it is.'

Sarah waited, confident that eventually they would get round to the real reason Magda had called. Kit pulled out a chair and sat down.

'Kit has insisted that I stay over,' she continued, casually. 'At the hall. I've booked the crew into the local pub, after all we can't have everyone roughing it, but Kit really wants me there.' She laughed lightly.

'Kit wants you to stay with him at the hall?' said Sarah, staring directly at him.

Across the table Kit's eyes widened. Sarah held a finger to her lips and said nothing, certainly not letting on that she had been privy to the conversation Magda had had with Kit earlier.

'Anyway the thing is…' Sarah could hear Magda's discomfort. 'I was explaining my plans for the shoot to Guy, and he said that he'd like to pop down over the weekend, to see how things are coming along. I can understand the logic, we're putting an awful lot into this project, and it's all on my say-so. I'm not sure that he can see what the attraction is; but he trusts my judgement on things like this. Anyway we want him to see what brand Roseberry will look like, you know, get a feel for the whole thing. The whole package.'

'The whole package?' Sarah repeated.

'Yes, you know, happily families, sun-kissed young couple walking around the garden with the boys, hand in hand, arms round each other when their guests arrive, bit of a peck on the cheek, you know the kind of thing.' It sounded as if Magda might be speaking through gritted teeth.

'Are you talking about me and Kit?' said Sarah, incredulously.

'Who do you think I meant? Of course I mean you and Kit,' Magda snapped. 'And I want it to look authentic.'

'Authentic. For Guy?' Sarah said, even more incredulously.

'No, not for Guy. Of course not for Guy. For the show,' Magda growled.

'No,' said Sarah. Across the table Kit was watching her anxiously. 'What?'

'No, Magda, I don't mind being around while you film. I don't even mind you implying that Kit and I are a couple, by…' Sarah paused, trying to come up with a solution and seeing one slap bang there in her own kitchen. 'I don't know, maybe Kit sitting one end of the table and me sitting at the other, but I'm most certainly not walking hand in hand with him and I'm not cuddling, kissing or in any other way canoodling with him. Okay? Does Kit know about this?'

'Not yet. I was planning to mention it to him just now, but when I rang I just said "Hello, have you got time to talk?" and we seemed to get cut off,' said Magda. 'I think there might be a fault on the line and his mobile keeps going to voicemail. It's just about the whole vintage, those were the days look,' said Magda with a slight tinge of desperation in her voice. 'I'll email you the schedule. Kit told me that he would send you the recipes direct. Although I need a copy so I can think about how we'll shoot it. Just have a little think about the couple thing, Sarah. I mean, it's only acting, darling. For the sake of the show.' And with that Magda hung up.

Sarah looked across at Kit.

'She wants more of me than I'm prepared to offer,' he said, primly.

Sarah nodded; she felt much the same way too.

'And she lied,' said Kit. 'She told me that her marriage was a sham.'

Sarah plugged in the kettle.

'She told me that they were only together for the sake of the business. And I believed her, Sarah. I really did. And then just after you left Guy rang me to ask how it was all going, telling me how proud he was of Magda. Apparently he just happened to press redial. He loves her, he said. Like teenagers the two of them, he said. He's taking her to New York for a romantic weekend, shopping, the theatre, for their wedding anniversary and then, when they get back, he's having a new car delivered. A new bloody car, Sarah. With a big red bow and everything. Does that sound like a sham to you? Does it?' Kit said, sounding increasingly desperate.

'And then he told me he'd be dropping in over the weekend to see how his Baby-bunny-boo's new project is coming along. Baby-bunny-boo? Have you ever met anyone less Baby-bunny-boo in your whole bloody life than Magda?' Kit's head dropped into his hands. 'God, what have I done? The woman is all over me like a bad suit. Oh, and then Guy said, did I know he was a black belt in – in something that sounds extremely painful. He knows, Sarah. He knows and he is going to kill me.'

'No, he's not. Guy's lovely.'

'You're not having sex with his wife.'

Sarah raised her eyebrows.

'Twice,' said Kit, in answer to the unspoken question. 'The first time she got me drunk and the second time she jumped me in the kitchen, and she's been hankering after going for the hat trick ever since. The woman is an animal. A complete animal.'

Sarah eyebrows were raised so far now that they'd soon be on top of her head. She held up a hand to stem the flow, there was only so much detail she felt able to handle, but Kit was on a roll.

'She is an attractive woman. And I won't deny it; I was flattered. Very flattered. And then when she started to talk about getting me on TV, making me a household name. Making me some real money, instead of my allowance. We had champagne.' He shook his head again. 'Actually I was mad. Mad, mad, mad.'

'So you're sleeping your way to the top?'

Kit's face went bright crimson. 'What am I going to do, Sarah? Let's face it, Magda is not the sort of woman who takes no for an answer. She sent me a text.' He started to rootle through his pockets and handed her his brand new iPhone.

Before Sarah could read the message, Kit said, 'Apparently all the crew are planning to stay in the pub next weekend but she said she is very happy to accept my invitation. Very happy. I'm going to have to barricade myself in my bedroom to keep her off, Sarah. And then what if Guy turns up, and comes over all black belt and irate husband, and kills me? God, and just when I've got a job and money and everything. She won't make the pilot if I don't sleep with her, will she? Don't answer that. I know she won't. You should see the look in her eyes, Sarah. I feel like a bacon sandwich at a station buffet. What am I going to do? You have to help me.'

Sarah stared at him. 'I do?'

He nodded. 'My future depends on it. Your future depends on it. Our future depends on it. Think of the children.'

'Kit, you need to get a grip; you're being melodramatic. You have to face up to it and tell her that you don't think it'll work. Tell her – tell her anything.'

'What if she pulls out of the cookery deal? What if she takes the dishwasher away?'

'I don't think she will, Kit, because she's right about you being bankable and the kind of man that women want in their kitchen; between us we've got what it takes. You've got the look.'

'And you've got the talent, don't tell me,' he said. 'And chances are now I'll have the heave-ho to go with it.'

'Once your segment has aired on Harts and Holmes, if Magda doesn't want you then maybe someone else will. You've got something to show people—'

'But I can't cook,' whined Kit.

'For goodness' sake, man up,' Sarah said. 'You're not telling me anything I don't already know, Kit. All you have to do is say that you don't think it's appropriate for you to have a relationship.'

He stared at her. 'We're not having a relationship. Magda's having one all on her own, with me. I just thought it was a bit of fun and now I've sold my soul. To Bunny-baby-bloody-boo.'

'I don't think it's your soul she's after,' said Sarah.

*

After Kit had gone home Sarah checked her own phone; there was a message from Shaun. 'Hope you're having a better Saturday.'

'Lol,' she typed back. 'Are you working with Fred today?'

'No. Have you decided where we're going next weekend?'

'Are you free Sunday?'

'I am.'

'Okay, then how about we go into town, have some lunch and go to the pictures – simple.'

'Sounds perfect. Any idea what's on?'

'Nope – but it'll be easy. Let's pick something funny, made for children, or full of big explosions and car chases.'

'You're on,' Shaun said. 'I could pick you up.'

Which made Sarah realise with a terrible heart-stopping lurch that her car was still in Cambridge. She stared out of the window at the parking space and wondered how the hell she had forgotten. 'Fine,' she texted. 'Got to go.'

She picked up the phone and rang Kit; there was no answer and she didn't fancy tracking him down on foot, so she rang Melissa's mobile, remembering as she did that Melissa was in the Lakes or the Dales or wherever it was that Josh hailed from. Damn. She was about to hang up when Melissa answered.

'You're a dark horse,' said Melissa, before Sarah could get a word in. 'Have a good time, did we?'

'Not exactly. Sorry, I didn't mean to disturb you. I was going to ask if you could do me a favour and then I remembered you were away this weekend.'

'Well, your luck's in, kiddo. We didn't go in the end. Josh's mum and dad have got some sort of bug and didn't want us to get it. So, what is it, and what's the bribe?'

'I'll cook you lunch next week.'

Melissa laughed. 'I'd rather have all the gory details of your date. I saw your car in the car park this morning when I went into town. Bad girl. I didn't want to ring just in case you were busy.'

If only, thought Sarah grimly.

Idiot-proof Sponge

Ingredients:
6oz (175g) self-raising flour
1 heaped tsp baking powder
3 large eggs
6oz (175g) butter (at room temperature)
6oz (175g) caster sugar
1 tsp good vanilla essence
1 tbsp strawberry jam or lemon curd for filling

Method:
Pre-heat oven to 170C, gas mark 3, 325F

Lightly grease two 8" diameter x 1½-inch deep (20 x 4cm) cake tins. Line each with a circle of lightly greased baking parchment.

Sieve the flour and baking powder together into a large mixing bowl.

Break 3 large eggs into the flour, add the caster sugar and room-temperature butter and the vanilla essence.

With an electric hand whisk, beat the ingredients together until you have a smooth, well-combined mixture (which as long as the butter is nice and soft should take you around a minute). If you haven't got an electric whisk you can use a wooden spoon, but it will obviously take a little longer.

Divide the sponge mixture equally between the two cake tins. Smooth the surface lightly with a palette knife.

Place them on the centre shelf in a preheated oven and bake for 30–35 minutes.

Don't open the oven door until 30 minutes have passed!
To test if they are cooked, very lightly touch the centre of each sponge with your finger. If it leaves no impression and springs back, the sponge is cooked.

Take sponges from the oven and allow them to rest for 5 minutes. Turn them out onto a cooling rack and carefully peel off the baking parchment.
Leave the sponge to get completely cold before you add the filling.

Chapter Twenty
Cleaning Up

Sarah made her apologies to Rosa for not being able to get in for the office meeting at Hanleys the following Friday morning. Instead she and Kit's daily, Mrs Oates, were up at Roseberry Hall, finishing off what had been a week of scrubbing worktops, floors and walls, trying very hard to beat a silk purse out of a sow's ear.

Shooting a longer episode for Harts and Holmes meant that the film crew wanted to see more of the house and of Kit's life, and Magda was extremely keen to start collecting some stock footage to use if they needed to pad out other episodes in the future – which meant cleaning, a lot of cleaning, not to mention sorting out the food for the crew while they were working at the hall.

'Shame they can't do like they do in films, you know, that computer-generated stuff when they have dinosaurs and talking toys and all that sort of thing,' said Mrs Oates, pouring yet another bucket of grey soapy water down the sink.

Sarah nodded. 'I don't think they do grime,' she said, backhanding a strand of hair off her face.

'Pity, that,' said Mrs Oates. 'I keep telling Kit that this place is too much for one person to look after, and for one person to live in come to that. Rolling around in here on his own like a ball-bearing in a barrel. I tried to get him to move into your cottage when the last people moved out, but his mother wouldn't hear of it.'

'What's his mother like?' asked Sarah, putting the stuffed squirrel back on the dresser alongside the other bizarre treasures that Kit had collected over the years.

'Cold,' said Mrs Oates. 'We don't see her very often. I don't think I'm talking out of turn here when I say she's quite flinty. Very attractive, but not what you'd call warm. His father was a lovely, gentle man, a bit soft like Kit. He needed someone to keep it all together and Lady Jane was perfect for that, but she's not my idea of a mother. She told Kit he had to live in the hall or she would cut off his allowance. What sort of a way is that to treat your children?'

The sink gurgled ominously. Mrs Oates beaded it with an unsympathetic glance. 'I've got the plunger,' she said over her shoulder, making it sound like a threat. 'I keep telling Kit that them drains need sorting out, and the electrics and the roof. The trustees should get the work done for him, poor little scrap living here all on his own.'

Sarah smiled; Mrs Oates was talking about Kit as if he was a little lost boy in a hovel, not a grown man camped out in a grand old mansion.

'Maybe when he gets a TV deal,' suggested Sarah.

'Be a good thing all round, I'd say. Long as you're here to sort it all out for him. He's a lovely lad, and I'd like to see him settled down, you know. This place needs a woman's touch.'

Sarah nodded and got back to the cleaning, wondering as she did if maybe that was what Magda had in mind. Lady Magda of Roseberry. The idea hung like a dark cloud; surely Magda saw Kit as a fling, not as a long-term prospect? It was a worrying thought.

Between working on the menu for Kit's village tea party, finishing off the outstanding work for Hanleys magazine, helping Kit get to grips with the cooking, and buying and preparing all the ingredients, tins, pans, bowls and tools, Sarah, ably assisted by Mrs Oates, had been working up at the hall on and off all week, and as a result the whole place was brighter, cleaner and had a definite air of life about it. Sarah, on the other hand, was exhausted.

'What time do you reckon they're going to be here?' asked Mrs Oates, strangling a damp cloth into submission.

'According to the schedule Magda sent me, half past ten,' said Sarah, putting the last large glass bauble back on the dresser shelf. 'I want to make sure everything is ready for lunch. I was thinking we could put the food in the dining room to keep cool, and so that no one accidentally eats anything that is supposed to be in the programme.'

Mrs Oates nodded. 'Sounds like a good idea to me. Quite exciting, isn't it?'

Sarah laughed. 'And exhausting. I was thinking it might be an idea if we put the tea and coffee making things in there too, so they don't make a mess in here?'

Mrs Oates nodded. 'Don't worry, I've got it under control. I'll do a tray and sort out the food just as soon as I'm done in here. And then I'll be back in time to help with lunch.' At which point she checked her watch. 'It's nearly ten now. Don't you think you ought to go and get yourself spruced up?'

182

Sarah glanced down at her grubby tee shirt and jeans. She had only meant to pop up and finish off the dresser, but as with everything at the hall it was on such a grand scale that it always took far longer than she planned. 'You're right. I'll nip home and get changed. Have you seen Kit around anywhere?'

Mrs Oates shook her head. 'Not a sign since before you arrived. Hang on, though, you can't run away and leave me to let them in if you're both off somewhere.'

Sarah nodded. 'No, you're right. He can't have gone far. I'll go and see if I can find him.'

She headed off into the depths of the house, looking into the downstairs rooms. Between them they had dusted, swept, polished, rearranged and in the case of one room, repainted it, so that the rooms Kit planned to let the crew use looked less unkempt and had a more boho chic vibe. Lots of the rooms had been mothballed under dust sheets so it had been nice to uncover things and hunt out treasures to dress the rooms that they would use for filming.

Mrs Oates's husband, Stan, had come up in his tractor and mowed the lawns and some men from Hanleys had delivered a long trestle table and set it up on the terrace, along with benches and a striped canopy intended for the giant tea party on Saturday afternoon. Sarah had invited Melissa to come over and help and it felt like they were more or less ready.

Sarah had spoken with Shaun every day by text. He said he was away getting things sorted out. Although she didn't press him too much about what those things might be, nor how long they might take, she realised as the days passed that she really looked forward to hearing from him. A couple of lines of warm jokey text could bring a smile to her face however busy she was.

'Kit?' Sarah called into the cavernous hall. 'Kit, are you there?'

She listened hard for a reply. Somewhere off in the distance she could hear banging, and tried to work out where the sound was coming from, playing a game of warmer and colder all on her own, finally following the noise upstairs and across the landing, through a set of double doors and then down a long, badly lit corridor.

'Kit? Is that you?' she shouted.

At the far end of the corridor a familiar face appeared around one of the doors. 'Yes,' Kit said, somewhat unnecessarily.

'What on earth are you doing? Magda and the film crew will be here any minute, I need to go and get changed and someone needs to be here to greet them.'

'Really?'

'Yes, really.'

Kit had a curl of wood shavings in his hair. 'Because actually I'm a bit busy at the moment.'

'Doing what?'

'I'm fitting locks on some of the bedroom doors, and a few bolts.'

'Doors?' said Sarah.

Kit nodded. 'I thought if I locked more than one then it might put her off the scent.'

Sarah sighed. 'How many have you done?'

'Four so far, and I've nearly finished this one, so that'll be five and then I was thinking I might go and sleep in the east wing. I've got a bed roll and some emergency rations.'

'Is that the one where the roof leaks?'

Kit nodded. 'Yes, but only in some of the rooms, and she'll never think of looking for me there,' he said earnestly.

'And which is your room?' said Sarah, looking back along the corridor towards the main part of the house through the double doors.

He stared at her, expression unreadable.

'What?' Sarah asked.

'I'm not sure that I should tell you, just in case you accidentally let it slip or in case she bribes you or worse.'

'Oh, for goodness' sake, Kit, what is Magda going to do? Waterboard me?'

Kit opened his mouth to reply, but Sarah held up her hand to silence him.

'No,' she said. 'I don't want to know. God forbid that it's me who unleashes Magda on you.'

'The woman is like a bloody Rottweiler. She keeps texting me, you know, all hours of the night and day,' said Kit miserably, pulling out his iPhone from his back pocket. 'I think she must have a dedicated phone just for me.'

'Have you told her that you think having a relationship while you are working together is a bad idea?'

Kit nodded. 'She told me she thought it was close to perfect. Look at this,' he said, holding the phone out towards her. '"I can't wait to see you. I want to have you all to myself, love and kisses M", and, "I'm not sure how I'll be able to keep my hands off you, kiss, kiss".' He looked up. 'I mean, what is the woman like? And what if Guy sees them? The woman is unstoppable.'

At which point the text alert on Sarah's phone went off.

'Oh, my God, see? She's texting you now,' groaned Kit.

'No, she's not,' said Sarah, opening the message. It was from Shaun. The text read: 'On my way home now, are we still on for Sunday?'

She smiled. When she looked up Kit was peering at her. 'Don't tell me; it's the rainy date, isn't it?' he said.

'None of your business.'

'I can see it on your face.'

'And what does my face say, Kit?'

'It says that even though your date was a total disaster you still really like him and you're going to give him a second chance.'

Sarah nodded. 'Very perceptive. And what do you think my face says now?' She raised her eyebrows and tipped her head to one side.

Kit stared at her for a moment or two and then shook his head. 'No, no, I'm not getting it. Oh, I know – are you hungry?'

'No, this face says you need to get your arse in gear and get yourself downstairs just in case the film crew show up, while I go down to the cottage and get changed into something with less of your kitchen floor on it.'

'I'm meant to get all that from a look?' Kit frowned and then looked her up and down. 'I think you look all right, actually. Kind of casual and comfortable.'

'Now,' said Sarah, pointing back towards the stairs.

Kit did as he was told.

Back at the cottage Sarah grabbed a quick shower and slipped into a summer dress and sandals, brushing her hair off her face and adding a touch of mascara and lipstick before hurrying back up to the hall. Another text came in as she was half way up the drive. It was from Melissa. 'If you need me today as well as tomorrow just ring; people are practically throwing themselves out of windows here. Am

185

thinking I might get my hair done for tomorrow, for my screen debut.'

Sarah laughed, and stuffed the phone back into her pocket.

The crew's Mercedes van, assorted cars and Magda's silver Audi were parked in the driveway when Sarah got to the house. The back doors of the van were both open and the crew were busy ferrying bits of equipment in through the ornate front doors and into the hall.

Seeing them all there, Sarah made a decision to slip round the back and go in through the kitchen door before anyone spotted her, but she had barely had the thought before Kit came running down the front steps and said, in a loud voice, 'Sarah, darling, there you are. I wondered where on earth you'd got to. I was just saying I thought you'd nipped upstairs to fetch something.' Before Sarah could reply he swooped in to embrace her and as he did, whispered, 'Guy's pitched up – absolutely charming, doesn't look like a murderer, but who can tell? And Magda looks like she's been sucking lemons. Or worse.' And then in a louder voice he said, 'I was worried we were going to have to start without you. Come on, darling, everyone's here except for you.'

As he turned Kit took hold of her hand. Sarah glared at him and tried to pull her hand out of his, which only made him tighten his grip. He glanced at her, his expression desperate. Sarah sighed and finally let him lead her up the steps and into the house, where Magda and Guy appeared to be in the middle of some sort of tense standoff.

'Ah, there you are,' said Kit with impressive joviality. 'Magda, Guy, I think you both know Sarah?' As he spoke he pulled her close and wrapped his arm clumsily around her shoulders. 'My partner, Sarah.'

Magda looked relieved, while Guy did a double-take and then Sarah, seizing the initiative, and keen to get out of the clinch, smiled and stepped towards him. 'Yes, of course we know each other, don't we, Guy? We've worked together on several projects for Hanleys. Lovely to see you again. How are you?'

'Fine. I didn't realise...' He looked first at Kit and then back at Sarah. 'I heard that you'd split up with your husband, but I didn't realise that you and Kit were an item.'

Sarah suspected it was Magda who had to have told him; Guy didn't strike her as the kind of man who would normally be interested in other people's love lives.

'I tried to tell you, but you didn't want to listen,' said Magda, confirming Sarah's suspicions. 'But it's all water under the bridge now,' she snapped, apparently unhappy at being sidelined even when it covered her scheming. 'We really need to be getting on.'

But it was obviously working. 'So you two are a couple now?' said Guy.

Kit nodded. 'Oh yes. Sarah is just wonderful. I am so lucky to have found her.'

'And where did you two meet?' he continued.

Sarah felt a flurry of panic and glanced at Kit who simply smiled and said, 'Why don't you tell him, darling.'

'Through friends,' Sarah lied.

'Yes,' said Kit. 'Lovely friends. They thought we would be just perfect for each other and they were right, weren't they, pumpkin?'

Pumpkin? Sarah glared at him.

Guy visibly relaxed. Sarah sighed. It looked like she was playing into everyone's hands.

'I'm a very lucky man,' said Kit, to no one in particular, going all gooey-eyed.

Sarah resisted the temptation to elbow him sharply in the ribs, and instead said, 'So are we ready to start filming?'

'No, not yet,' said Guy. 'The crew need a while to set up in the kitchen. Tell you what, while Magda and Kit get all the boring stuff sorted out why don't you take me on a tour of the house? Looks a fascinating place, it must be fabulous living somewhere as handsome as this. So much history. Amazing architecture, bloody nightmare to heat, I bet – who was the architect?'

Sarah was about to say that she didn't live there when she felt two pairs of beady eyes fixing on her, and Kit said hastily, 'A chap call Kaufman, there's a painting of him over the fireplace in the billiard room, alongside Vesper, who was the chap who designed the park. We've still got all the drawings and plans in the library if you're interested in taking a look, haven't we, darling?'

Sarah glared at him.

'Fascinating. So how about you give me the grand tour?' said Guy, still smiling at Sarah.

'That would be lovely,' she said, thinking fast. 'But to be honest, I'm no expert. I've barely scratched the surface since I've been here. Kit's the man for that. I'm sure he'd be only too happy to show you

187

later on, and besides I promised him I'd help get everything ready, didn't I, Kit?'

'Oh yes, yes, she did,' Kit agreed.

Guy laughed. 'Okay, maybe we could all take a look later? I'm genuinely interested.'

'Oh yes,' said Kit with more confidence. 'Later would be fine. Wouldn't it, darling?'

It took Sarah a moment or two to realise that Kit meant her.

Chapter Twenty-One
Keeping Everyone Sweet

'And there we are, it couldn't be simpler,' said Kit, with a flourish, sliding the mould off the dessert. 'Looks amazing and is a fabulous showy dish with no tears. Sarah, darling, can you just pass me those extra strawberries and then come and have a spoonful and see what you think?'

Sarah, who had been standing out of shot, cue cards in hand in case Kit got in a muddle, gritted her teeth. All morning it had been Sarah, darling this, and Sarah, sweetheart that. It was all getting a bit jarring. Although Sarah assumed from the look on Magda's face that most of Kit's words of endearment were going to end up on the cutting-room floor.

'And cut,' said Magda crisply, clapping her hands. 'Can we just take it from when you plate it up, Kit, and say, "And there we are, it couldn't be simpler"? I don't really think we need Sarah in this one, do you?'

Sarah was almost as pleased about that as Magda obviously was.

'And can we make sure we've got the close-up?' continued Magda to the cameraman, waving him closer as the crew set up for the retake. 'Then I thought once we'd done that we could maybe break for lunch?' She swung round to Kit. 'I'm assuming that that's okay, sweetie?'

'Oh yes, fine,' said Kit cheerily. 'I'm starving.'

Magda laughed. 'That's good. What have we got? Have you got something special for us for lunch?'

Kit looked panic-stricken. 'Have I?' he said, glancing round. 'I don't—'

But Sarah was ahead of him. 'We thought that you might like to eat on the terrace. Just something simple, bread, cheese and pickles. Mrs Oates has got everything set up in the dining room.'

'She has?' said Kit, wide-eyed. 'That's brilliant.'

Guy laughed. 'Looks like you got yourself a little treasure there, Kit. You want to hang on to her. Doesn't he, Magda?' He slid an arm around his wife's shoulders and squeezed her tight up against him. 'When you find your perfect woman it pays to grab her and hang on tight. Perfect woman, perfect partnership – isn't that right, Magda?'

Magda's eyes narrowed as she wriggled free of his embrace. 'I'm working, Guy,' she said.

'Sorry, Pusscat, of course you are,' said Guy. 'I was thinking, Kit, Magda said that you'd invited her to stay over. I was just wondering whether the invitation extended to me too?'

'Well yes, of course,' said Kit, a little too quickly. 'I just assumed you'd be too busy. We wouldn't mind at all, would we, darling? It would be a pleasure.'

Sarah glanced up at him; was he totally mad? And then she caught sight of the stunned look in Magda's eyes, and it was almost worth it. 'Of course,' Sarah said.

Magda's mouth snapped tight shut. 'That's very kind,' she managed. 'But I thought that you told me you were snowed under with work, Guy? Isn't that what you said? And we really don't want to inconvenience anyone, do we? What about your work?'

'Oh, it can wait,' said Guy. 'And if they've made a bed up for you I'm sure I can squeeze in beside you.'

Magda looked horrified. At which point Simon, from the film crew, who had been sorting out the camera positions, called her over and announced that they were good to go for the retake.

'Just a minute, we won't be long,' said Sarah, slipping her arm through Kit's and guiding him out into the kitchen garden. 'Kit and I need to have a little catch-up.'

Kit, although he looked bemused, had the good grace to keep his trap shut and follow her outside.

'Are you completely nuts?' Sarah whispered the second they were out through the door. 'Guy thinking that we're a couple is one thing. But inviting him to stay? He thinks that we live together. You realise that this means I'm going to have to sleep with you now.'

Kit reddened. 'Really? I – I – I wasn't expecting that,' he blustered. 'I'm not sure what to say.'

Sarah sighed. 'I don't mean for real, you numpty, but at the very least I'll have to go into the same room as you when we go up to bed, and what about the boys?'

'That's a pity. What about the boys?'

'Well, they can hardly stay in the cottage on their own, can they?' growled Sarah.

'Oh, I see what you mean, no, of course not. I'm sure we can sort something out. I'll have a word with Mrs Oates, get her to make up the beds in the nursery. It would be an adventure for them, a proper sleepover. And I could read to them some more. Or – hang on, I know. I have a plan.'

Sarah looked sceptical.

'Kit?'

They both swung round. Magda was standing framed in the doorway.

She glared at Sarah. 'What on earth do you think you're doing?'

'Me?' asked Sarah.

'Yes, you – elbowing your way into every shot. Inviting Guy to stay. You knew that wasn't what Kit and I had in mind.'

'I didn't invite him,' protested Sarah. 'He invited himself.'

But Magda was on a roll. 'You knew that Kit and I were planning this weekend so that we could have time together. And after I've arranged all this work for you.'

Sarah felt her jaw drop, but Kit for once was quick off the mark in her defence. 'Magda, I invited Guy, not Sarah and we can still—'

'Still what?' snapped Magda. 'We certainly won't get any time to ourselves. I thought that was the idea. I thought that is what you wanted. You and me, I thought you wanted some time alone.'

'To discuss the show?' suggested Kit.

Magda sighed and went back inside.

'Wait,' Kit called after her. 'I'll have Mrs Oates show you both up to your room over lunch.'

Magda looked back over her shoulder and shook her head in apparent disgust.

As soon as they reshot the end sequence for Kit's dessert, filming finished for the morning and everyone headed to the dining room for lunch. Magda was tight-lipped and quite obviously furious with the turn of events. Guy seemed oblivious to the tension in the air and ate like a horse, and Sarah spent lunchtime wondering how she was going to explain camping out at Kit's to the boys without them giving the game away.

At one fifteen her phone beeped. She pulled it out wondering if it might be Shaun but instead it was from her solicitor. The house was sold, the money in the bank. One phase of her life had just ended.

Kit came over. 'Lover boy all right, is he?'

Sarah handed him her phone. Kit smiled, put his arm around her and kissed her gently on the top of the head. This time she didn't pull away or resist. Her eyes filled up with tears.

'Oh, Sarah,' Kit said, and she knew the affection was genuine as he hugged her tighter still. 'I think we should have champagne.'

Sarah looked at him. 'Are you serious?'

He nodded. 'New beginnings. Come on. I'll need a hand with the glasses.' And with that he broke out the bubbly and some ice-cold beers for those with a thirst, which was undoubtedly a huge mistake but it made the next few hours go with a swing, although by late afternoon everyone was flagging. Everyone that is except for Sarah, who had had the good sense not to have more than a token sip of champagne, and drove into Cambridge to pick up the boys.

When she got back Kit was there outside the cottage waiting for her. 'I've worked it out,' he said, as she was busy unstrapping her sons from the car and shooing them upstairs to get changed.

'I thought you were supposed to be up at the house filming, Kit? Or are they all curled up in the dining room sleeping it off?'

'No, they're having another tea break. Magda wants to do some background shots, you know, you and me and the boys around the estate.'

Sarah stared at him. 'Are you serious?'

'And then we're all going to have tea up at the hall. As it's Friday I suggested we have fish and chips. Save me from cooking.'

Sarah raised her eyebrows. 'Fish and chips?'

Kit nodded. 'Yes, from the village. Fish and chips and mushy peas and curry sauce. And I've asked Mrs O to sort out the bedrooms for us.' He sounded quite excited. 'We're going to be using Mummy and Daddy's old room.'

Sarah stared at him. 'For what, Kit?'

'Oh, oh, I see what you mean. Daddy used to snore so they had two rooms with a dressing room between. We called it Mummy and Daddy's room but it's actually two rooms. I've got Mrs Oates making it up now. You can have one room and the boys can share the other one.'

'And what about you?'

'I've got my own room,' he said, sounding offended.

'No, what I mean is if we have to go to bed through the same door?'

'Oh, I see what you mean. No, you don't have to worry about that. I can get to my room, no trouble at all. I used to do it all the time when I was little. I hated thunder.'

Sarah nodded as if this made sense.

'Nanny and Mummy used to tell me off for being such a wimp, but my father always understood. I'd creep downstairs and spend the night with him if things got a bit rough. I quite liked his snoring; rather reassuring to have him there beside me honking and snorting away like a great steam engine.'

'I'll be up in a little while,' said Sarah. From upstairs she could hear the boys giggling and playing. 'I need to sort Alex and Harry out.'

'Of course,' said Kit. 'Hang on. Do you think they could arrive up at the hall in their uniform? I mean it would look more normal.'

Sarah nodded. 'Okay. I'll see you there.'

*

'So,' said Sarah, putting the boys back into their discarded school clothes. 'We're all going to go up to Kit's house.'

'Why have we got to get dressed in our school clothes though?'

'It's for the film Kit is making about cookery.'

Harry nodded. 'And he wants to make a film of us in our school uniform?'

'No, but we're going to pretend you're arriving home from school.'

'We don't need to pretend that,' said Alex.

'Mum means at Kit's house, don't you?'

Sarah nodded. 'That's right. And then we're going to stay the night there.'

'Cool,' said Harry.

'Really?' said Sarah in surprise.

Harry nodded. 'Kit's got some really good toys.'

'Soldiers and a fort,' said Alex. 'Not just computers.'

'And aeroplanes. Are we going to sleep in the nursery?' asked Harry.

'I don't think so. Right, so you need to get back into your school clothes. And while you do that I'll get a set of play clothes, tooth brushes, PJs, slippers and dressing gowns and put them in your backpacks.'

Alex made a strange little noise.

'And Big Bunny,' said Sarah.

He sighed with relief.

'Are we going to live there for good?' asked Harry.

'No, just for tonight.'

'I'd like to live there,' said Alex.

'Come on, let's get going. Kit said we could have fish and chips.'

They clambered back into the car and Sarah drove up to the hall. Kit was waiting on the doorstep, with the film crew in attendance, recording their arrival home for posterity.

'How about you go upstairs and get changed, and then we'll go for a walk,' said Kit cheerily, at which point Sarah followed the boys – who seemed to know their way – upstairs to the nursery, which was bright and airy on the top floor with three small beds in a cosy room off the main playroom. The main playroom was set up with train sets and forts and soldiers and a table with a jigsaw puzzle half-completed in its centre. There were shelves full of children's books, under one window was a rocking horse, and under another a little sand pit, the sand dry and concreted into solid lumps.

'Can we sleep here, Mum?' asked Harry.

'Can I have the bed by the window?' asked Alex.

'I don't think so. I think we're going to have a room downstairs.'

Alex pulled a face and headed for the bedroom, tucking Big Bunny under the faded counterpane, before slipping off his school uniform.

Without any more prompting the boys changed into their play clothes, each putting their things on a different bed, and then went back downstairs.

The rest of the afternoon was like something from the pages of an Enid Blyton story. Kit, Sarah and the boys walked in the park, trailed by the film crew. Alex and Harry had a fine old time playing with Kit in the stream and then they headed back to the house tempted by the lure of fish and chips and one final piece to camera where Kit said, 'I love cooking but to be honest on Friday night after a long week in the kitchen a trip to our local chippie is bliss and something we all look forward to. And that's where we're headed now…'

'And cut,' said Magda.

As soon as Simon and Magda had made sure they'd got what they needed, Guy sent one of the crew down to the chip shop and everyone ate out on the terrace in a mass of paper, vinegar, salt and sauce. When they had finished the boys ran down onto the lawn to play.

'What a great place for kids to grow up,' said Guy, having polished off his pie, saveloy and chips.

'It's brilliant here,' said Harry, over one shoulder, catching the conversation as he swung out on a tyre swing that hung under an ancient cedar of Lebanon growing in the lawn. No mention of not living in the house, no mention of the cottage, nothing, just two very happy small boys, a warm summer evening, and a feeling that all was well with the world.

Having eaten, the crew departed for the pub around half past six, leaving just Sarah, Kit, Magda, Guy and the boys out on the terrace. They talked about the house, the show, the plans for the following day, and time slipped by unnoticed, until Sarah decided that the boys should go to bed.

'Would now be a good time to take the grand tour?' asked Guy, finishing off a glass of prosecco that Kit had assured him was the perfect accompaniment to pie and chips.

Kit nodded. 'Certainly. Do you want to come too, Magda, Sarah?'

Magda sniffed. 'I'd love to but presumably Sarah's already seen it, given that she lives here?'

There was an icy edge to her voice. Sarah glanced at Kit. 'Actually I think I should take the boys upstairs and get them ready for bed.'

Kit nodded. 'Good plan. Tell you what, Guy, why don't Sarah and I get the lads settled and then we'll come down and show you around. I've got another bottle in the fridge, how about I bring that out so you've something to while away the time?'

Guy nodded. 'Sounds like a plan to me. And thank you for inviting us to stay, very kind, and it's a fabulous, fabulous setting for the show. I can absolutely see why it caught Magda's eye.'

Magda said nothing.

Sarah went to fetch the boys, still playing on the lawn with a football. 'Do we have to go?' whined Alex.

'No, we don't have to go; we're going in and you're going to stay, remember?' said Sarah quietly.

'In the nursery?' asked Alex.

Sarah decided not to reply. She could see he was tired after a week at school and the excitement of the filming and having tea with Kit.

He slipped his thumb into his mouth and leaned up against her. 'Please, Mummy,' he said.

'Come on, old chap,' said Kit, who had followed her across the lawn. He lifted Alex up onto his hip. 'Let's get you upstairs. You look shattered.'

'Can we stay in the nursery?' said Alex.

'We'll see, you need to have a bath and get your pyjamas on first.'

'How will I hear them if they're not with me,' asked Sarah.

'There's a back stairs. I'll show you. Come on.'

Sarah dutifully followed Kit back into the house, trying to make it look as if she knew where she was going. Upstairs on the third floor, the nursery was quiet and still. The boys headed for the bathroom. It seemed as Mrs Oates had anticipated the boys' wishes by leaving enormous white fluffy towels out for them, all hung over an old-fashioned towel heater.

The enamel bathtub which stood in the centre of the bathroom was easily big enough for both boys, and once it was filled with water, Kit brought in a supply of ducks, boats and enough bubbles to ensure that everyone had a fine time. If he was tired before he went into the bath Alex was on the verge of sleep by the time he was lifted out and towelled dry.

The beds in the nursery bedroom were child-sized, each with a little reading light on the wall above and a little painted bedside cabinet alongside, and Sarah could easily understand why the boys wanted to sleep there.

'Three,' she said.

Kit nodded. 'One for me and the others were for my sisters, Enis and Elizabeth. They're both older than me. Enis is in New Zealand married to a sheep farmer and Elizabeth is in America married to an oil baron. We always talk at Christmas, exchange cards, birthdays, that sort of thing but they've got their own lives now. I still miss them.'

'I really don't think they should sleep up here, Kit. They're miles from anywhere.'

'It will be fine. Promise. We'll only be downstairs on the floor below,' said Kit, pointing to a door. 'You can just come up Nanny's stairs if they wake up in the night. And they can leave a light on.'

'Please, please, please let us,' begged Harry and Alex in unison. Sarah glanced at the third child-sized bed – if it had been bigger she would have suggested sleeping up there with them herself.

'And I'll be sleeping downstairs?'

Kit nodded. 'Within earshot. Really. I'll show you.'

'Please, Mum,' said Harry. 'We'll be good.'

So between them, Sarah and Kit made up the nursery beds from the crisp white bed linen stacked in the airing cupboard, and then Sarah tucked the boys in while Kit went off in search of the story book he loved most. By the time Kit got back, Alex was already asleep and Sarah was sitting in the lamplight with Harry looking at the book he had brought home from school, his eyelids by now heavy and drooping.

'Too late,' said Kit, holding the book out towards her.

'I think so,' said Sarah quietly, and then to Harry said, 'Come on, darling, snuggle down.' He didn't protest. Sarah kissed him goodnight and turned off the lamp.

'I really don't like the idea of them being up here all on their own,' she said. 'Maybe I should stay.'

'They'll be just fine. I promise,' Kit said, opening the door he had shown her earlier and indicating that she should follow him. The door led out onto a landing, which in turn led to a narrow staircase that came out on the floor below in a long well-lit passageway. It was obvious from the lack of adornment that this corridor was meant for the servants.

'Where I am going to be sleeping?' asked Sarah.

'Just here,' said Kit, crossing the narrow hallway in a single stride. 'This is the service door into my parents' bathroom and dressing room. You can prop it open if you like so you can hear the boys.' He beckoned her inside. Beyond the door was the most amazingly luxurious bathroom with a huge cast-iron bath, black and gold tiles and ornate gold bathroom fittings Through a door to the left of the bathroom was a bedroom that could have come straight out of the pages of Hello magazine.

The room was completely decorated from floor to ceiling in pink and cream; one wall was dominated by the enormous four-poster bed, which sat on top of a dais, the whole edifice draped in heavy pink satin curtains and dressed with throws and ruffled pillows and bolsters.

Under one window was a raspberry pink chaise longue, alongside which was a sweetheart dressing table. There were bow-fronted ivory-painted wardrobes in the alcoves that flanked the fireplace, the distinctive design echoed by matching tallboys and bedside cabinets. Each side of the hearth was a pink armchair with ivory satin cushions. On the dressing table was a silver brush and mirror set along with a whole row of crystal pots, bottles and jars. Each window was dressed with complex floor-to-ceiling swag and pleat curtains, over an ivory-coloured roller blind. It was a bedroom fit for a Disney princess.

'What do you think?' said Kit eagerly. 'Will it be all right for you? Daddy had it done for Mummy. I think she had seen it in a magazine and said that she liked it, and he had the designers come and remake it here for her.'

Sarah stared at it. 'And did she like it?'

Kit sighed. 'I don't know really. She was spending a lot of time in London by then.'

Sarah decided to change the subject. 'And what is your room like?' she said, pointing towards the open door on the far side of the room

'Oh, that's not my room. It's Daddy's. You can take a look if you like. The whole point about this is that we can come in through the door out on the main landing into Mummy's room, and then you can sleep in the pink room and I can slip out through servants' door and go to my room. Magda and Guy will be none the wiser.'

Sarah couldn't resist opening the door into Kit's father room. In contrast to the palatial room next door it was a tiny but much cosier space with wooden panelling and a small double bed pushed up against the wall, with a little chest of drawers alongside it, topped by a radio and reading lamps. The walls were lined to waist height with bookshelves, all bar one corner where there was a battered wardrobe and washstand. It looked more like a student's room than something befitting a lord of the manor.

'Come and look at this,' said Kit. He caught hold of Sarah's hand and practically dragged her over to the window seat. From the huge window Sarah took in the breathtaking view out over the parkland and the stream, through the woodland leading down to what looked like a folly in the middle distance.

Being so close to Kit felt odd and slightly unsettling. 'We should be getting back to Magda and Guy,' said Sarah. 'We've been gone ages.'

'Oh, they'll be fine. Let's just stay up here a while longer,' he said. 'The sun goes down over the tower. When my father remodelled the rooms for Mummy he kept the view. He said she could have everything else.' Kit paused. 'I suppose you could say that she got it.'

Sarah felt her heart aching for him, at which moment her phone beeped to announce a text.

'Ah, that'll be lover boy,' said Kit, getting to his feet. 'Best not keep him waiting. I'll be downstairs with our guests. Stay as long as you want. No one will disturb you.'

'I can't really come down with you and leave the boys,' said Sarah, glancing towards the open door. 'The terrace is miles away. What if they wake up?'

Kit grinned. 'It's not all dark ages here you know,' he said, and reaching into his jacket, pulled out a baby alarm and – having switched it on – handed it to Sarah. 'There you are. You might want to fiddle with the volume a bit. I've tried it out. You'll be able hear them snoring from the terrace and from one end of the house to the other. Fabulous range.'

Sarah turned up the volume switch and an instant later heard the soft rhythmic breathing of her precious boys.

'There you go.' Kit grinned. 'See you downstairs.'

Cheat's Strawberry and Vanilla Gateau

Take two ready-made sponge flan rings and, using the base of a spring-form tin as a template, cut out a disc from the centre of each. Discard the rest.

Whip a carton of double cream with a little caster sugar (to taste), and a tsp vanilla and a shot of Drambuie (or similar) until it is stiff, and then fold in a small carton of ready-made luxury custard.

Place one sponge disc in the bottom of the spring-form tin.

Take some large strawberries, cut off the green end, and cut in half lengthways. Line the ring with the strawberries, cut side against the metal.

Spoon the cream and custard mixture in the centre of the ring and spread gently to the edges.

Smooth out then place the second sponge disc on the top.

Chill for a while then remove the tin by first warming around the edges with a hot cloth.

Dust the top with icing sugar, and using a metal skewer heated over a gas flame, quickly score a diamond pattern into the sugar. (Optional!)

Decorate with mixed berries and mint leaves.

Chapter Twenty-Two
Stormy weather

When Kit was gone Sarah turned her attention back to her phone. Shaun's text read: 'Hi, I'm back – finally – and I was wondering if you maybe fancied coming out for a drink?'

Sarah's fingers worked over the keys: 'I'd love to but I'm staying overnight with a friend tonight, and the boys are already sound asleep in bed. I'm really looking forward to Sunday.'

'Me too. I was thinking we should pack a picnic, hire a punt.'

'After last time? Are you serious?' Sarah texted back. 'Let's stick to lunch and a film.'

'Lol,' he typed. 'Maybe you're right.'

Sarah could hear the muffled voices of Kit, Magda and Guy outside on the terrace. She really ought to join them.

'I have to go. See you Sunday,' Sarah typed, added a kiss and then, shoving her phone in her pocket, hurried downstairs.

'Ah, there you are, my dear,' said Guy as Sarah appeared. 'Just in time to help us with the guided tour.'

'And to show me where our room is,' grumbled Magda.

Sarah glanced at Kit. 'I thought Mrs Oates showed you earlier?' she said.

Magda nodded. 'She did, but the place is like a rabbit warren. We'll be lucky if we ever find it again. Or find our way out, come to that.'

Kit laughed and patted Sarah on the bottom. 'Sarah was like that when you first moved in, weren't you, darling?'

Sarah glared at him. 'I still am,' she said.

Kit got to his feet. 'Come on. We'll start with the library,' he said. 'It's my favourite room in the whole house.'

Sarah smiled. 'If you'll excuse me, I think I'll go upstairs with the boys, if you don't mind.'

'Very cosy,' sniped Magda, as she turned to go back inside. Sarah pretended not to hear.

'Oh, come on,' said Kit. 'Come with us. The boys will be fine. And it'll be nice to show Guy and Magda round together.' He took hold of her hand. 'Let's start with the library. It was originally built by my great-great – actually I'm not sure how many greats it goes back, but it's the oldest part of the house and the rest was remodelled around it. So, the Georgian part is all rather new,' he laughed, as waved for Guy and Magda to follow him. 'Do bring the prosecco and the nibbles; we're going to need sustenance.'

Guy smiled. 'My pleasure.'

It took them nearly two hours to do the full tour, stopping here and there to admire and explore the finer points of the grand old house, the massive library – which ranged up over two floors and was topped by a great glass dome – then on through the billiard room and the orangery, the grand formal dining room, the parlours and the powder rooms, the smoking and the drawing rooms, on through the suites of bedrooms.

Sarah was glad that she had made the effort to go on Kit's impromptu tour. The house was wonderful, far bigger and quirkier than she imagined, and had a touching faded grandeur. The ornate pleated, swagged curtains in the huge rooms were sun-bleached to pastel shades, in some places fragile as butterfly wings. In most rooms the magnificent carpets and rugs were threadbare, and here and there plaster peeped through the plush curling wallpaper. In all the public rooms the furniture was antique, the fabric crumbling, the lines classic, all still arranged – Sarah suspected – much as they had been the day they were first carried in by a retinue of staff, and set out around the huge fireplaces, and all now silently decaying under dark crackled portraits of Kit's illustrious ancestors.

Sarah couldn't imagine what it must be like to live in a house where it was so obvious that you were just passing through, just the latest member of a long line of Roseberrys, mere custodians of a grand old house and its contents.

Their tour was ended by their arrival at a pretty little sitting room, which overlooked the lawns, and was close enough to the small hidden staircase so that Sarah could get her bearings.

'So, there we are then,' said Kit, brightly. 'That's about it.' He busied himself around the room, switching on the lamps, and indicated that Sarah should sit on the other side of the fireplace to him.

'This is our sitting room. Cosier than the formal one,' he said. 'Anyone cold? Would you like me to light the fire?'

Guy should his head as he and Magda took up residence on a large overstuffed sofa. 'No, we're fine.'

'Only it does get a little chilly in here even on the warmest days. Doesn't it, Sarah?'

She found herself nodding, suddenly aware of how very tired she was. It had been a long day.

The furniture in the sitting room was more homely than the rest of the house but still showed signs of age and wear.

'Now, what can I get you?' asked Kit, ever the convivial host. 'Tea, coffee, more prosecco, or a beer maybe?'

'We didn't get to see your room on the tour,' said Guy conversationally to Sarah. 'Grand, is it?'

'Quite the opposite. Too untidy,' Kit said hastily, before Sarah had time to come up with an answer. 'If I'd known that you'd want the full tour we'd have tidied up, wouldn't we, darling?' He managed a laugh.

Sarah managed a smile.

'Now about that drink?'

'Have you got to traipse all the way down to the kitchen to get a drink?' Guy asked Sarah.

'It's no trouble, you get used to it,' said Kit quickly. 'Right, so what's it to be? Glass of wine for you, Sarah?' he suggested, in a voice that implied he knew what she wanted.

'No, thanks,' Sarah said, wondering when she could reasonably call a halt to the charade. She was tired and headachy and wanted nothing more than to be in bed, not playing let's pretend for the benefit of Magda and Guy. 'If you'll excuse me, I really should go and check on the boys.' She got to her feet, taking the baby alarm, before anyone could protest, and paused briefly at the door. 'Actually I've got a bit of a headache, I might stay up there.'

Kit pulled a face. 'Oh, darling, I'm so sorry. I didn't realise you weren't feeling well. Do you want me to bring you something?'

'I think it's the weather. It feels like there's a storm coming.'

Kit nodded. 'Poor thing. Are you sure you don't want anything?'

Sarah shook her head. For one terrible moment she thought Kit was going to swoop her up in his arms, but fortunately he made do with a peck on the cheek.

'Night, night, sweetheart. I won't be long,' he said. 'See you in a little while.'

Guy and Magda added their goodnights although Magda's expression was poisonous.

The moment Sarah closed the door behind her she felt the tension starting to ease out of her shoulders. Bloody man, she thought, how on earth did Kit think they were going to be able to keep this up?

Composing herself, she hurried along the corridor, through the kitchen and out to the car to get her overnight bag. Outside the evening air crackled with the promise of a coming storm. Sarah went back inside and up to the nursery to check on Harry and Alex, who were both sound asleep. Finally she headed back downstairs to the room Kit had had Mrs O make up for her. In reality she would have preferred Kit's father's room to the over-the-top flounces and pleats of his mother's room, but when in Rome...

Sarah had a quick wash in the luxurious bathroom, brushed her teeth, pulled on her pyjamas and headed for bed. Propping up the baby alarm and her phone on the bedside cabinet she slipped between the cool crisp sheets, wondering what the chances were that she would be able to get any rest in a strange bed. It was the last thought she had before sliding effortlessly into a deep dreamless sleep.

At first Sarah wasn't exactly sure what it was that had woken her nor, for the first few seconds, where she was. There was a little green light on the baby alarm, which cast an eerie glow over the bedside cabinet, letting her know the battery was still alive and well. Baby alarm? It took Sarah another moment or two to join the dots, and then she remembered, and by then the instant of waking panic had passed.

She listened, trying to find out what it was out the darkness that had disturbed her. Sarah hadn't closed the curtains so the room was softly lit by moon and starlight. She could hear the boys breathing over the radio; at least they were okay. There was a whisper of wind outside, which grew and grew, and then the rain started tip-tapping on the window and a second later the whole sky was lit up with a great crackle of summer lightning, followed moments later by the guttural growl of thunder. That was it; the storm had broken.

While neither Alex nor Harry was afraid of thunder Sarah didn't really want them waking up in the middle of a storm, in the middle of the night, in a strange house all on their own, so she clambered out of bed, picked up her dressing gown, slippers and phone and hurried through the bathroom out into the servants' hallway.

The whole house seemed to be in darkness except for a tiny nightlight that glowed bright as a star at the bottom of the back stairs, leading the way to the nursery. The thunder rolled overhead. Sarah crept up the stairs. Another nightlight glowed on the landing, guiding her towards the nursery door.

Inside everything was quiet. Moonlight picked out the toys on the windowsills, the bears and the dolls, the army of brightly painted wooden toy soldiers lined up in ranks on the table under the bay window. Quiet as a mouse, Sarah crept across the playroom floor and peered in round the bedroom door.

Alex was sound asleep in the bed by the window. He had one arm around Big Bunny and his thumb wedged firmly in his mouth. Harry was in the bed next to him, lying at full stretch, one arm flung carelessly across the pillow, and sound asleep in the far end bed, his features picked out by the lamplight, was Kit, concertina-ed up in the tiny bed, his feet peeping out from under the eiderdown, his hair a mess, eyes tightly closed. Curled up on the floor alongside him were his two elderly dogs, both snoring softly.

As the thunder rolled again Harry opened his eyes. Before Sarah could speak he put a finger to his lips and nodded towards Kit. 'Ssssh, don't wake him up,' Harry whispered. 'He took a long time to get to sleep.'

'Are you okay?' whispered Sarah.

Harry nodded and pointed towards Kit. 'He didn't want to be on his own if there was a storm. He's afraid of thunder.'

Sarah glanced across at the great lump under the bedclothes and wondered if it was one of Kit's plots to make sure the boys didn't wake up and worry at finding themselves all alone in the nursery, although it occurred to her that given what he had said earlier, maybe it might just be the truth.

'He snores a bit,' said Harry conversationally. 'But when it gets too bad I've been poking him with this.' He pulled up a toy fishing rod from beside his bed.

Sarah laughed.

'I heard that,' said a sleepy voice. Kit stirred and stretched and then very slowly unfolded himself from the tiny bed. It was something of a feat. Sarah could hear his joints cracking and complaining, until finally he clambered out and stretched. 'Hello,' he said with a grin. 'Where did you come from? I thought you were sleeping downstairs?'

Kit was wearing stripy pyjama bottoms and a tee shirt and had the hair of a startled guinea pig.

Overhead the thunder rolled again, a whiptail of wind and rain lashing against the nursery windows. Everyone jumped.

'Don't worry,' said Harry, eyes wide. 'It's only a storm.'

Forked lightning lit the room up, bright as a flare, and was followed an instant later by another great roll of thunder. One of the dogs woke and whimpered miserably.

'It'll be all right,' said Harry. 'Won't it, Mum?'

Sarah nodded. 'Of course it will. It's just weather. Come and look.'

She had barely spoken when there was another great crackle of lightning that seemed to split the sky.

Harry's eyes widened. One dog started to howl, the other to whimper and drool.

'How about I light the fire and we have some hot chocolate and watch the storm blow itself out,' said Kit brightly.

'Yes please,' said Alex, from his bed under the window. 'Can Big Bunny have some too?'

'Of course,' said Kit, shuffling out of bed. 'Sarah, you get the fire lit, I'll go and sort out the hot chocolate.'

Chapter Twenty-Three
Breakfast at Roseberry's

They all slept in the nursery, camped out in front of the fire in a great nest of blankets and pillows Kit found for them, and the bedding that the boys had taken off their bed, weathering the storm, adults, dogs and small boys together.

Sarah woke the next morning feeling remarkably refreshed, curled up with her arms around Alex, and Kit's Labrador cuddled up to her back. She blinked and rubbed her eyes, trying to work out what the time was and what had woken her. She looked round; it appeared that Kit and Harry had vanished, and there was a smell in the air. She sniffed.

'Bacon and onions,' said Alex, sitting bolt upright and suddenly wide awake.

Sarah laughed. 'I think you're right.'

'Kit said that he would make us bacon sandwiches,' said Alex, wriggling out from under her arm and the blankets. 'Come on, Mum. Do you know where my slippers are?'

Sarah shook her head, but Alex was already heading back to the nursery bedroom and moments later appeared triumphantly with both slippers and his dressing gown. He offered her his hand. 'Come on, Mum, don't just lie there, get up. Kit said that he'd make us breakfast.'

'Okay, okay,' said Sarah. 'I just need to get my dressing gown and nip to the loo.'

Alex thought for a minute and then nodded sagely. 'Me too.'

Ten minutes later they were all downstairs in the kitchen, Kit in charge of the grill, Sarah in charge of the teapot, toast and orange juice. They'd just got settled at the table when Magda appeared.

'So, this is where everyone is,' she said grimly. 'You're taking this happy families thing a bit far, aren't you, Sarah? I thought you said you weren't going to do it at all?'

Kit seemed oblivious to any tension. 'Morning, Magda, bacon butty? Or sausage sandwich? I can do you either or both.'

She shook her head. 'Just coffee for me please, darling.'

Kit pulled a face at Sarah, and mouthed the word, 'Instant?' and a questioning hand gesture. Sarah suspected that wasn't what Magda had in mind at all, and got up to plug in the all-singing all-dancing coffee machine that had been delivered as part of Magda's sweetener to Kit.

Sarah's phone, still in her dressing-gown pocket, burbled to announce an incoming message. She glanced at it surreptitiously. It was from Shaun, and read: 'Just one more day. Have you seen what a lovely morning it is out there? Be nice to go for a walk?' She smiled.

'Lover boy?' whispered Kit, without taking his attention off the sausages under the grill.

'Might be,' Sarah said quietly. 'Not that it's any of your business.'

Magda swung round. 'You're seeing someone?' she asked, her voice echoing her obvious surprise.

Sarah glared at her and then nodded towards the boys who, deeply engrossed in breakfast, seemed not to have noticed Kit's comment.

'So, is that a yes?' Magda pressed. Sarah felt her colour rising and then nodded.

'Only just,' Sarah began, but Magda grinned triumphantly.

'Oh, that's fabulous,' Magda said. 'Not the Wednesday chap? The one who texted you?'

Sarah nodded.

'Why on earth didn't you say something before? I thought you were – what I mean is that I wouldn't have been so upset with you if I'd have known you really were acting. We had already discussed the arrangement with Kit, and you said no. I thought perhaps, that maybe – maybe you'd got together for real in the meantime.' She glanced at Kit and then shook her head. 'But no, obviously not. Well, this is just perfect, Sarah. You've convinced everyone that you're all snuggled up here with Kit. I know it's put Guy at ease – about the project, you understand. I don't think he'll bother coming along next time we're filming, not with the state of the plumbing and the wind whipping in through those window frames in our room. Guy is a man who likes his creature comforts. Actually, while we're on the subject of creatures, I'm pretty sure that there was something eating something else in the wall last night, you could hear the poor thing being dragged about squeaking and scratching. But yes, very clever, Sarah. Well done. Although I wish you had told me—'

'Told you what?' said a familiar voice. Everyone looked round. Guy was standing in the doorway to the kitchen wearing a maroon silk smoking jacket over matching pyjamas.

208

'That I don't know how you use this coffee maker,' said Sarah quickly. 'I don't want to break it.'

Guy grinned. 'I'm sure you haven't,' he said, heading over to take a look at it. 'We have one of these at home. Marvellous contraption once you get the knack of them. Here, let me show you. Have you put the water in yet?'

Sarah glanced over Guy's shoulder; the boys were busy eating breakfast, while Magda was busy drooling over Kit, who wisely kept his eyes down and his attention firmly on cooking the next round of bacon and sausages. 'Sandwich?' he said to Guy.

'Don't mind if I do,' said Guy, and then to Sarah said, 'Right, it looks okay to me, all we need now is the coffee. Did you hear the storm in the night? Magda said it absolutely tipped down, not that I heard a thing. I slept like a baby, damned comfy bed. I didn't hear a peep all night. Must be all that country air.'

The convivial mood over breakfast was contagious and, as the crew rolled up, spread through the lot of them like a benign plague, even Simon seemed cheerier. Now that Magda realised Sarah wasn't really after Kit and with Guy completely convinced that she was, the producer was a changed woman. Setting up, preparation, cookery and shooting went like a dream and by lunchtime all the film they needed for the programme and the still photos of all the dishes Kit had rustled up – except for the ones of the tea party itself – were in the can.

Everyone ate out on the terrace.

'Right,' said Magda, as they were all tucking in. 'A few quick notices for this afternoon. We've asked the locals to be here between three and three thirty for makeup and a briefing, and then the plan is to shoot from four onwards while the light is good. People arriving, getting settled, you know the score. Then we're hoping to shoot the party and then maybe Kit and Sarah going down to the river with the kids, as a nice way to finish the day, that kind of thing. Everyone okay with that?'

There was a murmur of assent and much nodding. Sarah sidled up to Kit. 'I have to go home, get changed and sort the boys out for filming.'

Kit nodded. 'Okay, I think I can probably hold the fort till you get back. And thank you, I couldn't do any of this without you.' He leaned in and kissed her on the cheek. Sarah stared up at him, and for an instant as their eyes met, she thought that it was a real shame that she didn't fancy him. Kit's grin widened and Sarah felt an oddly unsettling flutter in her chest, at which point Magda practically pounced on him.

'Kit, darling,' she said. 'Do you think we could have a word?'

'Of course,' he said, turning away.

'And you too, Sarah?' Magda said.

Sarah turned. 'I'm sorry, I'm just going,' she said.

Magda stepped in closer. 'Going where?' she whispered. 'Not off to see your boyfriend, are you?' She managed to make it sound like an insult.

'No, of course not. I'm going home to get the boys some clean clothes, have a shower and get changed for the tea party.'

'Good, good,' Magda said with an emphatic nod. 'Just don't let Guy see you. Actually I'm thinking that we might need to get a stylist down to help you.'

Sarah stopped midstride. 'What?'

'Just thinking aloud, poppet, but we're selling people the dream here, and it's important we get the look right. Who knows where it might lead? A clothing range, household goods – let's face it, it's not like it hasn't been done before. But to be honest I really think you might need some help.'

Sarah decided not to rise to the bait and instead gathered up the boys from the garden and headed back to the cottage.

As she opened the back door and stepped into the cool familiar interior of her own kitchen it felt like a month since Sarah had been in the cottage, rather than the few hours she had spent up at the hall. It was such a relief to be back that she wondered if there was any way she could get out of filming. The simple answer was no, but it was tempting to try and come up with some excuse.

Sarah glanced at the clock; they had just over an hour before they had to get back to the hall. She herded Alex and Harry upstairs into the bathroom.

'Do we have to have a bath?' moaned Harry. 'We had one last night.'

'I know but today is really important for Kit and we want to look clean and smart, don't we?' she cajoled.

'Are we going to live with Kit all the time?' asked Alex, as Sarah helped him into the bubbly water.

'No, darling. We live here.'

'But I like it there. And I like Meg and Jet, the dogs. And there's lots of room.'

'Yes, but this is our house, we're just helping Kit out, now close your eyes while I wash your hair.'

Alex sighed.

Harry, who was sitting at the other end of the bathtub, slippery as a fish and playing with a plastic dinosaur, said, 'We could, you know. He wouldn't mind. He's lonely there all on his own.'

'Is Kit your boyfriend?' asked Alex.

'No, he's not,' said Sarah emphatically. 'Now stop wriggling, you don't want shampoo in your eyes, do you?'

'Only that lady wanted to know about him,' continued Alex.

'Which lady?' asked Sarah. As if she couldn't guess.

'Maggot,' said Harry, while getting his dinosaur to execute a perfect swallow dive. 'She came out when we were on the climbing frame. She said she just wanted to make sure.'

'Make sure?' said Sarah.

Harry nodded.

'She wanted to know if you were Kit's girlfriend. She had biscuits,' added Alex.

Bloody woman, thought Sarah, murderously. 'Her name is Magda, not Maggot.'

'She asked me about your proper boyfriend,' said Harry.

'Have you got a proper boyfriend?' asked Alex.

'We thought it was most probably Kit,' continued Harry. 'But we didn't tell her that.'

'No,' said Sarah gently, 'I haven't got a proper boyfriend, but I might have one day. And Kit is my friend, who just happens to be a boy.'

Harry nodded wisely. 'So you don't kiss and stuff?'

'No, we don't. Now come on, we need to get finished in here and get dressed for Kit's tea party.'

Once the boys were dry and dressed they went to play in Harry's bedroom, while Sarah climbed into the shower. She needed to have a word with Magda about the morality of bribing her children for information.

211

Just as she was towelling herself dry, Sarah heard a car pull up in the driveway and wondered if it was one of the tea-party guests arriving early or perhaps getting lost. Magda had said that as everyone she had invited was local they would know where to come, but there was always the exception. Seconds later there was the sound of a car door slamming shut and then what seemed like an instant later, the sound of the knocker clattering on the front door of the cottage.

Sarah stopped dead in her tracks and wondered if maybe it was Shaun. She hadn't had time to reply to his text. Hadn't he said he fancied going for a walk? Maybe he thought he might just drop by on the off chance. She glanced in the mirror and tried out a smile on her reflection, not that there was time to do much about her appearance beyond drag a comb through her hair.

Sarah did just that, pulled on a bathrobe and, heading across the landing, opened the tiny window that looked out over the front garden.

'Hello,' she called. There was someone, not Shaun, but a woman, standing half in, half out of the porch.

The woman knocked again, more frantically this time.

'Hello,' said Sarah. 'Up here.' The woman stepped back, looked around and then finally looked up. As their eyes met Sarah's mouth dropped open in astonishment.

'Peony?' she gasped, not quite believing who she was seeing on the doorstep. Peony Tyler, husband-stealing, robe-wearing, bunny-threatening Peony Tyler.

'Oh, thank God I've found you. Can I come in? We have to talk,' Peony said, without a shred of shame or contrition.

'I don't think we do,' said Sarah, pulling the window to.

'No, wait, please,' Peony begged.

Sarah sighed, wishing she was naturally crueller and harder and with a mean streak to fall back on.

'I've just got out of the bath,' she protested. 'And I have to be somewhere one else in—'

'Just five minutes,' sniffled Peony. 'Please, Sarah. I really do need to talk to you.'

Tightening the belt on her bathrobe Sarah made her way downstairs.

'I really haven't got time for this. What is it?' she began as she opened the front door, at which point Peony's shoulders dropped

212

and, all bluster gone, she burst into hot snotty miserable tears and let out a great long mewling wail.

'You'd better come in,' sighed Sarah, opening the door wider still.

'Sorry, sorry,' said Peony, backhanding the tears away. 'I'm so sorry. I know what you must think of me. This is crazy and there is no reason why you should talk to me of all people, but I couldn't think of anyone else who would understand.'

'Five minutes,' said Sarah, guiding Peony into the kitchen and handing her the kitchen roll. Peony sat down at the table, ripped off two sheets of paper, and blew her nose vigorously.

'I'm desperate. I just don't know what I'm going to do,' Peony whimpered.

At which point Harry sloped downstairs and peered in around the kitchen door. 'Who is it, Mum?' he whispered, and then, spotting the hunched sobbing woman at the kitchen table, said, with no apparent surprise, 'Oh hello, Peony.'

'Hello, Harry,' said Peony, between sobs.

'Harry, can you go back upstairs and help Alex get his socks and sandals on,' Sarah said. Harry pulled a face and then mouthed, 'Is she coming to Kit's tea party?' Sarah shook her head and shooed him back upstairs and then, turning to her unexpected guest, said, 'I'm sorry but the boys and I really have to leave soon. I'm working. And I need to get dressed. I'll put the kettle on. You can have a cup of tea, and then you're going to have to go.'

'That's very kind.' Peony nodded and blew her nose miserably. 'I can't go on like this,' she said.

Sarah resisted the temptation to ask why or what, when or who and instead waited until the woman had composed herself.

After a moment or two, Peony sniffed and said, 'Colin is a complete nightmare.' Something about the way she said it made it sound like an accusation, as if it was somehow Sarah's fault.

'I really had no idea. He's driving me mad,' Peony continued. 'He's taken up the guitar now, you know. He just sits around all day in his dressing gown, practising. Nothing on but his dressing gown. Half open. All day.' Peony shuddered. 'I didn't mind him for staying for a few days till he got himself sorted out. But it never occurred to me that he'd want us to move in together. I thought of Colin more as fling, not a thing, if you know what I mean. I can't help but wonder if he wanted to move in because it was convenient. When I said that it to him he got really upset, so I said if he really wanted to stay maybe he could help out with the bills or by doing something round the house to help, and do you know what he said?'

Sarah waited.

'He said that he was an artist. An artist, darling. A creative. A creative? All I can see is how much work he creates. I had no idea. I've started staying at my sister's at weekends to get away from him. And when I said I thought that it might be better if he found somewhere else to live, he said that he had given up everything to be with me, and that he had nowhere else to go and how could I be so cruel, so very, very cruel when I had destroyed his entire life. Destroyed his entire life.' She started to cry again. 'It wasn't me coming round every day with a bottle of wine asking if I wanted a glass because it was too sad drinking alone, or bringing flowers and offering to mend things and telling me how lonely he was and how you just didn't understand him.'

Sarah practically choked; oh, she understood him all right. Peony meanwhile pressed on, apparently oblivious.

'He's got no concept of what he's done to my life. He hates my friends, he hates my furniture. And hates my cats, says he's allergic.'

Sarah didn't know what to say and it would have been rude to laugh so she said nothing.

'How in God's name did you ever put up with him?' snapped Peony, swinging round to glare at her. 'You might have warned me.'

'What?' spluttered Sarah, completely taken aback.

'You could have said something. You never moaned about him over coffee, never dropped hints about what a selfish miserable self-seeking little weasel he is. I mean I came to all your parties, I dropped in for coffee and to borrow a cup of sugar. We talked when you were out in the garden. Why didn't you say something? I thought we were friends. I might have thought twice then.'

Sarah laughed. The woman had to be barking mad. 'Are you serious?' she said incredulously. 'I should have warned you not to have an affair with my husband? What planet are you on, Peony? I want you to leave—'

'But you said I could have a cup of tea,' protested Peony. The woman really was incorrigible. 'We need to talk this through. You have to help me. Can't you see that I need help here?'

'I'm sure you're right, but not the kind of help I can give you,' said Sarah, waving Peony to her feet.

'And what is that supposed to mean?'

'Peony, I don't know what you're expecting from me, but whatever it is you're not going to get it. You were the one who slept with Colin, you were the one who wanted him and you can have him, but what you can't do is come to my new home and whine about what a mistake you made, what a bad catch he is and how I should have warned you. Please go. Now.'

'But I thought you'd understand,' protested Peony. 'I thought we were friends.'

'Do I need to tell you that friends don't sleep with their friends' husbands?'

Peony pulled a face.

'I want you to leave now and please don't come back. I have to get dressed,' said Sarah, pointing towards the door.

'I could make us some tea.'

'No.'

'So what am I going to do?' Peony said, getting to her feet.

Sarah shook her head in disbelief. 'To be perfectly honest I don't care, throw him out, change the locks, marry him and live happily ever after. He's not my problem and neither are you. I truly really don't care, but don't come back here, oh, and while we're at it, don't be horrible to my children, or their toys, or threaten to burn them or cut off their thumbs. Is that perfectly clear?'

Peony had the good grace to wince. 'I'm sorry about that, Sarah. That was wrong. I realise that. It was just that—' Something about Sarah's expression must have dried the words in her mouth. 'I was cross with Colin. He just assumed I'd look after them. I mean they're his children, not mine.'

'Actually they're my children too,' Sarah growled. 'And I love them and don't expect them to be bullied or threatened by people who should know better.' She was at the front door now, holding it open, trying very hard not to lose her cool. All she really wanted was for Peony to be out of the cottage and gone.

Peony sighed. 'Thank you. I know things must be hard for you at the moment, given how much you love Colin. He told me that you wanted another baby, so I really do appreciate this,' she said, then paused. 'Actually, I think that he would take you back if you asked him.'

Speechless, Sarah bit her tongue, which just about stopped her biting Peony. As she stepped through the door Peony stopped long enough to attempt to hug Sarah, who took a hasty step back.

'I really think we should try and stay friends,' said Peony, wiping her face. 'For the boys' sake and in lots of ways we're on the same side or at least in the same boat.'

It was the final straw. The woman was clearly nuts or at best totally deluded. Sarah felt a wave of fury welling up. 'Peony, we are not on the same side and if I thought for one moment I was in the same boat as you I'd jump over the side and take my chances with the sharks. Now get out,' she snapped.

'Did you keep up with the counselling?' Peony persisted, as she stepped out into the garden, pausing to root through her handbag, apparently completely unaware of how very thin the ice was that she was skating over. 'Did Colin tell you I introduced him to Ms Goold? She's very good. I've got her number here somewhere if you'd like it. She might be able to help you. Women in denial are her speciality.'

It was all Sarah could do not to punch Peony. She slammed the door tight shut and locked it. The instant the door was closed Sarah burst into tears. Bloody woman.

But she had barely had a chance to wipe her face before there was another knock, this time on the back door. The nerve of the woman. Sarah hurried through the cottage and threw the door open. 'Will you just—' she began.

Melissa was standing on the doorstep looking like she had just stepped out of a fashion shoot for classy bird does country. 'Whoa there, Rambo, who lit your fuse?' she said.

Sarah shook her head. 'Sorry. You wouldn't believe it if I told you.'

The Perfect Sausage Sandwich

Serves 2

Ingredients:

2 nice crusty bread rolls, halved and toasted
or alternatively 4 thick slices of bread cut from a crusty loaf
6 good quality pork sausages (or veggie sausages)
1 large thinly sliced onion
1 tbsp clear runny honey
1 tbsp Dijon mustard or English mustard
A good splash of balsamic vinegar.
The sauce of your choice: piccalilli, HP, tomato, Branston, burger relish – whatever

Method:

Heat a little olive oil in a heavy frying pan and slowly cook the sausages for about 15 minutes over a medium heat, turning over occasionally. Don't prick them.

Take out and put to one side.

Into the same pan put the onions and cook until caramelised. Stir in the balsamic vinegar add the mustard and honey.

Return sausages to pan to warm through.

Put 3 sausages and a pile of onions in each sandwich. Add sauce of choice.
Serve.

Chapter Twenty-Four
Out in the Open

It was almost half past three by the time Sarah, Melissa and the boys finally made their way back up to Roseberry Hall. One of the crew was helping the last of Kit's guests to park on the driveway, while others were showing guests into the house. There seemed to be a lot more crew than had been there first thing.

'Hired help,' said Melissa knowingly. 'Like sheep dogs. You can't have Joe Public wandering off causing havoc and falling into ditches.'

Sarah took hold of Alex's hand; she was preoccupied. She couldn't quite believe that Peony had had the nerve to show up at the cottage and assume she would be welcome, let alone expect her to offer advice on Colin.

Melissa had helped to finish getting the boys ready, while Sarah dried her hair and splashed cold water on her face to try to reduce the puffiness around her eyes. It took a while. By the time she put on her makeup it had been three o'clock and she felt unsettled and ruffled and most certainly not ready to play happy families for Magda's benefit.

Then Melissa had said that the dress Sarah had picked out the day before looked frumpy, and as soon as she said it, Sarah knew she was right. She could almost hear Magda's voice beetling around inside her head talking about image and stylists and the look they were going for. Finally after much umming and ahhing and rifling through her wardrobe with Melissa at her shoulder, Sarah settled on something she'd bought for a wedding the summer before. It was a black and white column dress that with a jacket would have been too dressy, but with a soft pink cardigan and pretty sandals she hoped would be about right, and which Melissa said was perfect.

As they got to the door of the hall, Melissa gave her hair a bit of a fluff up. 'How do I look?'

'Fabulous.'

'You too,' said Melissa with a grin. 'Chin up, chuck, you're meant to be the lady of the manor, remember?'

Sarah sighed. She didn't feel very fabulous, but said, 'In that case we'd better get inside and mingle.'

In the main hallway Mrs Oates and some girls from the crew were handing out soft drinks provided by Hanleys, while the dozen or so tea party guests gathered around the signing-in table.

Magda, meanwhile, was standing by the fireplace schmoozing a man in a sports jacket and Italian designer specs, who Sarah recognised as the editor of one of the local papers. Alongside them a photographer was busy sorting out his lenses. As Sarah, Melissa and the boys came in Magda pasted on a huge smile and hurried over to greet them, opening her arms in welcome.

'There you are, Sarah, darling. I was just telling Roland here how wonderful you've been about us taking over your home. Roland, Sarah – and these are Alex and Harry, Sarah's boys, aren't they just divine? And this is...' She paused.

Melissa painted on a faux smile. 'Melissa. I'm Kit's cousin and a friend of Sarah's. I'm one of the minions at Hanleys?'

Magda made an attempt to smile, while Roland turned to greet Sarah and Melissa and offered the boys his hand. Each in turn dutifully shook it before Sarah suggested to Harry that he go and get a drink and Melissa said that she would go with them.

Roland turned his attention to Sarah. 'Delighted to meet you, Sarah. Magda has been telling me all about you and Kit. Quite a story.'

Sarah's smile froze. Her gaze fixed on Magda, who just carried on smiling. 'It's all right, sweetie, I've explained to Roland that it's all off the record, obviously,' said Magda, tapping the side of her nose.

'At the moment,' Roland chipped in, lifting his glass in a toast to Sarah. 'It would make the perfect feature for our lifestyle section. True love conquers all. Falling in love, moving into an old manor house and wanting to find a way to make it pay so you can refurbish it together, Kit's love for cookery and you seeing a way forward – it's just the kind of thing our readers love. We could do a gorgeous feature in our lifestyle section.'

'First things first,' Magda said hastily, before Sarah could protest. 'We're all really excited about today's filming. Did I mention we're negotiating a series, Roland? There's been a lot of interest.'

Sarah wasn't sure if this was the truth or whether Magda was just talking it up for Roland's benefit.

'Now let's see, who else we can introduce Roland to, Sarah. Apparently everyone knows everyone. Small villages, what can I tell you?' Magda laughed, and slipping her arm through Sarah's, guided them both towards the drinks table to join Guy and a small posse of guests, who were busy chatting to each other and to the crew.

Just as they did, Kit came jogging down the stairs, looking relaxed and tanned, and freshly washed, and all gussied up in a blue and white striped collarless shirt worn over jeans. People turned to smile and say hello. He stopped and did a big two handed wave.

'Lovely to see you all,' he said, smiling broadly. 'Thank you so much for coming, it shouldn't be too long now. People are just setting up the tables and things outside and then we can make a proper start. And I'm sure they'll have lots of things they need to tell you. I'll try and catch up with everyone.' He grinned when he saw Sarah, Melissa and the boys and, stepping down from the staircase, hurried over to meet them. 'Sorry I'm a bit late. I was waiting for the hot water to heat up.'

'Trials of an old house,' said Roland, conversationally.

'Don't apologise. We were rather hoping you were going to squire us around,' said Guy, cheerfully. Sarah couldn't help but wonder if there wasn't something extra in his apple juice. His eyes were awfully bright and he was quite flushed. Aware that Sarah was looking at him, Guy grinned. 'Good turn out.'

A little behind him Melissa rolled her eyes and mimed drinking.

'Kit,' said a plump woman in a bright blue pinafore dress, who was busy elbowing her way over towards them.

Kit smiled. 'Mrs Alliott, June, how lovely to see you. How are you? I'm so glad that you could make it. June breeds gun dogs – Meg and Jet came from her.'

'I'm just pleased to be here. Lovely of you to think of me. I wouldn't have missed it for the world,' gushed Mrs Alliott. 'They were saying that you are going to have a TV series. It's all very exciting, isn't it?' she continued, looking expectantly at the rest of the group.

'Yes it is,' Kit said.

'Aren't you going to introduce us?' Mrs Alliott turned pointedly to look at Sarah, who was standing alongside Kit.

'Yes, of course, this Magda, who is producing the TV show, Guy her husband,' said Kit.

'And partner in crime,' Guy laughed, giving the woman's hand a hearty shake although it didn't take a genius to see that Mrs Alliott wasn't interested in either of them. Her eyes were firmly fixed on Sarah.

'And you know my cousin, Melissa?'

Mrs Alliott smiled. 'Hello, dear.'

'And...' Kit began.

'Roland,' said Roland, proffering his hand. 'Cambridge Star and Recorder. I'm hoping to talk to you later.'

'And this is...' Kit hesitated for just a split second as he got to Sarah.

Guy laughed. 'No need to be so coy, Kit. Mrs Alliott, June – this is Kit's partner, Sarah.'

Mrs Alliott's eyes widened and then she beamed and grabbed Sarah's hand. 'Really? Oh, I'm so pleased to meet you, Sarah. Kit, you're such a dark horse, that's lovely; what does your mother think? I'm sure she's delighted. That really is the best news.' And with that she caught hold of Sarah and kissed her firmly on both cheeks before embracing a stunned Kit.

'I'm so glad. He's such a lovely lad,' she continued. 'It's high time that he settled down. Oh, Melissa, isn't it wonderful.' Melissa just smiled. At which point Harry and Alex reappeared with their drinks.

'Are these two yours?' she whooped. 'Oh gosh, what poppets. A ready-made family. That is just perfect. Presumably you'll be having your own children too though – son and heir and all that kind of thing. Gosh, how lovely – this is such a perfect spot to raise a family.'

'Right,' said Magda, face rigid. 'I think we should make a start, don't you? I need to check the guest list.'

'So,' said Mrs Alliott, brightly. 'Are we going to be hearing the sound of wedding bells soon, Kit, or maybe the pitter-patter of tiny feet?'. Sarah felt herself flush crimson. Melissa choked on her fruit juice.

'Oh, early days yet,' said Guy. 'They've only been together a little while. Give them a chance.'

It was Mrs Alliott's turn to redden now. 'Oh gosh, of course. I'm sorry. I'm just so excited for you both. And happy.'

Which was Roland's cue. 'Is everyone here, Magda?'

'I'm just going to go check. I think so.'

'Good, then maybe we could get a group photo before the off?'

Magda took the clipboard from one of the crew and ran her finger down the list. 'We're more or less there, still a couple short, but I

221

think we should really make a start. I mean this isn't only photo you'll be taking, is it, Roland?'

Roland glanced towards his photographer, who shook his head. 'No, no,' he said. 'We'll be for a little while yet. At least another half an hour and then I think we've got a summer hog roast at…' He turned to his photographer, who shrugged. 'I think it's somewhere out near Cambourne.'

'Why don't you join us for tea, then?' suggested Kit. 'There's plenty, isn't there, Sarah?'

'Tempting,' said Roland. 'But I'm awfully afraid that we can't. Anyway if we could get everyone into a group. Maybe on the stairs?'

Magda clapped her hands to attract everyone's attention and with a little cajoling and shepherding Roland and the photographer got everyone into formation.

'If you'd like to stand on the second step, Sarah, and if you could put your arm round her, Kit. Can we have some glasses, maybe an apron? Oh, a whisk and a bowl, that's perfect. Lovely,' Roland said, as the crew obliged with a selection of props.

The photographer stepped up, and with much flapping of hands on his part, and giggling on the part of Kit's guests, he took the first photo.

'Not bad,' the photographer said, checking the image. 'Can we just do that again. Kit, if you can get in closer to, I'm sorry, I've forgotten your wife's name.'

Kit stepped closer and slipped his arm around Sarah's shoulder. 'Sarah,' he said.

'Partner,' Sarah corrected, not that anyone was listening.

'Lovely,' said the photographer. 'Lovely, just a little closer and can you both smile?'

Sarah looked up at Kit just as he looked down at her. As their eyes met, he grinned and she felt a little unexpected flutter in the pit of her stomach. 'That's the money shot,' purred the photographer.

Kit carried on grinning and still on a downward arc, kissed her, though to be fair it wasn't so much a kiss as the briefest touch of lips. Sarah gasped. The camera flashed again. Sarah laughed and pulled away, feeling light-headed and struggling to compose herself.

'Now you can't say that wasn't fun,' said Kit.

'Behave,' she murmured, and as she did, the flash fired again, and from the corner of her eye Sarah saw someone moving. As she turned away from Kit, she spotted Shaun standing alongside Mrs Howling, the head teacher from the village school.

The moment hung, time slowed.

Sarah stared at Shaun. Shaun stared at her. His mouth fell open. Sarah felt her stomach do a back flip; Shaun looked and then looked again as if he couldn't believe what he was seeing. For one moment she was convinced he was going to turn and leave, but Mrs Howling slipped her arm through his and pulled him in tight, smiling as she lifted a hand to announce their arrival. Sarah held her breath.

'I'm so sorry we're late,' said Mrs Howling brightly. 'Entirely my fault, Shaun was there on time. Weren't you?'

'Ah, our last two guests. Would you like to come and join us?' said Magda, waving them over. 'We're just having the official photo.'

Shaun hung back and who could blame him?

'I'm sure everyone knows each other,' Magda began, but Mrs Howling was ahead of her.

'I'm Amanda Howling. I was head teacher at the local school until this summer, and this is Shaun MacMillan, who will be taking over from me in September. I'm sure several of you probably remember him.'

Headteacher? Sarah stared at Shaun and he stared straight back at her, his jaw set. As Mrs Howling spoke, Sarah tried to wriggle out of position but the photographer held up a hand. 'Can we all stay where we are.' And then, turning, he beckoned Shaun and Mrs Howling over.

'If you two would like to join the group; there would be fine.'

Sarah couldn't manage a smile as the flash fired up again. Glancing left she could feel Shaun's eyes on her.

Magda glanced down at her clipboard. 'Right, time is pressing, so let's get this show on the road, shall we, ladies and gentleman? First of all I'd like to say how delighted we are to see you all here today.'

As Magda rolled out her welcome speech, Sarah tried to keep Shaun in sight. She tried out a smile on him. His expression didn't change. Magda was still speaking.

'And I'd like to extend a very warm welcome on behalf of Kit who I know many of you know, and his partner, Sarah.'

Sarah closed her eyes and wished that the floor would open up and swallow her whole. When she opened her eyes Shaun had looked away, which made her heart sink.

Magda gave the guests a team talk about ignoring the cameras but listening to instructions, chatting normally but not too loudly, and just how much patience would be needed when they got to the filming and had to reshoot a scene. It seemed to Sarah to go on forever. Finally Magda ended by saying, 'So if you would care to follow the crew out into the garden we'll make start and I hope you all have a really lovely afternoon.'

As everyone peeled away to follow the girls wearing crew tee shirts, Sarah ran down the steps to catch up with Shaun, who was heading towards the door.

'Shaun, wait, please,' she said, calling after him.

He turned. 'Why didn't you say something? You're Kit's partner.' He glanced back towards the stairs. 'Why did you agree to go out with me?'

'It's not what it looks like,' Sarah said desperately, checking over her shoulder in case anyone was close enough to hear her. 'Please, Shaun. I can explain.'

He laughed and shook his head. 'I thought you said you were getting divorced.'

'I am.'

'It'd better be one hell of an explanation.'

'It is,' said Sarah.

'We had a date tomorrow.'

Sarah stared at him, feeling tears welling up in her eyes. 'We still do, don't we?'

'He kissed you,' Shaun pointed out.

'It wasn't really a kiss – and really, it's not what it looks like.'

'So you keep saying. It looked like a kiss from where I was standing.'

'Kit is my landlord,' said Sarah.

'And what, you're paying him in kind?'

Sarah felt her face flush crimson. 'Don't be ridiculous, of course not.'

'So what?'

'So I'm pretending to be his girlfriend for the TV programme. It's a long story but it's not complicated. Please, Shaun, you have to believe me.'

At which point Mrs Howling, who had been following the herd, reappeared. 'Oh there you are, Sarah. You know Shaun?' she said in surprise.

Shaun nodded stiffly. 'We have met.'

'Shaun will be teaching your boys next year,' said Mrs Howling cheerily.

'I thought you were helping Fred?' said Sarah, eager to have something else to talk about.

'I am…'

'Can we hurry it up, please?' called Magda, waving them along. 'We need to get outside and start the filming before the light goes.'

'Come on, Sarah,' said Kit from the doorway that led into the kitchen.

'Can we talk later?' Sarah said to Shaun.

He nodded briefly, although it didn't take a genius to work out that he wasn't very happy with the idea. Sarah caught his eye and tried out a smile. He leaned in towards her and said, 'Great second date.'

Sarah felt herself redden. 'I can explain.'

Explaining was not on the cards for a while though. There was a mass of work to do to ferry the food out of the kitchen and onto the terrace. The girls who had handed out the drinks helped serve but weren't allowed to be in shot so there were lots of takes and retakes as Kit and Sarah carried out bowls and pots and trays with cakes, and everyone ate and drank and ate and drank for take after take. Wine and beer and juice flowed; Kit hammed it up for the cameras and Sarah made an effort to keep smiling as she passed round the dishes of food that had featured in the filming the day before.

'This is fabulous,' said Melissa, glass in hand, as Sarah handed round another bowl full of salad. 'What's up, you look awful.'

'Stress,' said Sarah.

'I thought it was going really well, everyone seems to be having a whale of a time.'

Sarah nodded. If she could get Melissa on her own she could explain and her friend might be able to help or would have done if she hadn't had quite so much prosecco. 'So when are you two getting married?' she said with a giggle and in a loud voice.

'Don't,' said Sarah. 'Please.'

'Oh, come on, we'll be cousins-in-law, we could have the wedding reception here. Now that would make a good programme. Maybe I should suggest it to Magda. Maybe she'll give me a job?'

Sarah poked her sharply; she would have slapped her if the cameras hadn't been rolling.

'Ouch,' complained Melissa. 'Come on, get into the swing of it. You're supposed to be acting all lovey dovey.'

Meanwhile Shaun chatted to the people around him and smiled on cue but he looked horribly uncomfortable and Sarah wondered if he might jump ship.

Finally as the light began to fade and they were setting up a shot of Kit lighting a fire pit Sarah finally managed to ease her away over to Shaun and Mrs Howling.

'We've had the most fabulous time,' said Mrs Howling. 'Although I think Shaun is eager to get home, aren't you, Shaun? Probably tired. He was saying it's been a long week.'

He nodded, all the time holding Sarah's eye. 'Yes, I've got lots of other things to do,' he said.

'Might I have a quick word with Shaun before you go,' asked Sarah.

'Oh, of course,' said Mrs Howling. 'And you should have told me you were going out with Kit. I'm so pleased for both of you.'

Tight-lipped, Sarah nodded her thanks.

'So,' said Shaun as they edged away from the rest of the guests.

'It's not what it looks like. It's purely for the TV show,' said Sarah. 'The producer thought it would be a better selling point, you know, happy families, all that sort of stuff.'

'So you're telling me that you and Kit are not a couple?'

'No, of course not. I told you I'm in the middle of getting a divorce.'

'And you really are his tenant?'

Sarah nodded. 'I live in the cottage at the end of the drive with the boys, and this is just a job. It's all smoke and mirrors.' She moved closer still. 'I'm ghosting a cookery book for Kit. And the producer – the woman organising it all – is after him and I'm just a decoy. This way I cover her tracks.'

'And you're doing this because?'

'Because Kit is my friend, I'm getting paid to write the book and work as his assistant on the programme, and...' Sarah paused. 'I'm not really sure if I should tell you this.'

Shaun waited.

'You have to promise me that you won't tell anyone.'

Now he looked bemused. 'What is it?'

Sarah leaned in closer still and then at the last moment pulled away. 'No, I can't tell you. Not here. You just have to believe me when I say that Kit and I are friends and nothing more; it's just that at the moment he really needs me.'

Shaun nodded and something in his expression made her think that maybe he might believe her. Around them the crew were showing the guests back to their cars while others started to pack up the equipment.

'Are you ready?' Mrs Howling said to Shaun, and then to Sarah added, 'Thank you so much for inviting us. We've had the loveliest time.'

Shaun nodded. As he went to turn away, Sarah said quietly, 'I'm sorry you had to find out this way. I was going to tell you.'

'Okay,' he said.

'So are we still on for tomorrow?' Sarah could see him hesitating, and made the effort to smile. 'I'm sorry. I'd got no idea you were going to be here today. I would have told you about Kit, and all this. Why don't you come round to the cottage later? It's only at the end of the drive. The boys will be in bed by half past seven. Come round for coffee or a glass of wine or a sandwich or something. I'll explain everything.'

Finally Shaun smiled. 'Okay. Eight thirty suit you?'

Sarah nodded.

As Shaun followed Mrs Howling back towards the house Melissa came over and, eyeing him up and down, purred, 'And who was that?'

Sarah sighed. 'My date.'

Melissa stared at her. 'No? You're joking? Not Mr Son of the Soil, I'm a humble gardener with a very complicated life?'

Sarah nodded. 'The very same.'

'Bloody hell,' said Melissa. And then she thought about it. 'Bugger. Did you explain to him about Kit?'

227

Kit's Basic Quiche

Ingredients:
- 1 packet of chilled ready made shortcrust pastry
- 2 large eggs
- 4 rashers of unsmoked streaky bacon
- 1 small tub of double cream (around 250ml)
- 3 tbsp of mature cheddar, grated
- 1 heaped tbsp of grated parmesan
- 1 small bunch chives, chopped
- Salt and pepper to taste

Method:

Grease a 9-inch loose-bottomed tin.

Roll out the pastry – don't over-work or press too hard – and ease it into the baking tin. Trim away excess pastry. Leave in fridge to rest for 15 minutes.

Heat the oven to 350F, 170C, gas mark 4.

Cover the inside of the pie crust with baking parchment or tin foil and add baking beans or something like dried haricot beans so that the pastry crust can't rise during cooking. This is called baking blind. Make sure the beans cover the whole surface of the quiche base right up to the sides of the tin.

In the same oven spread the bacon out on another small baking tray and cook until crispy (7–12 minutes). Remove bacon and allow to cool.

Bake the pastry case for 20 minutes. Remove the beans and parchment. Bake for another 5 to 10 minutes until the pastry is just starting to colour. Remove from the oven and allow to cool.

Preheat oven to 180C, 375F, gas mark 5.

In a jug beat the cream and eggs together until well combined. Add salt and pepper.

Sprinkle the base of your pastry case with cheddar cheese, crunch up and add the cooked bacon and then chopped chives.

Pour the egg-and-cream mixture into the pastry case and sprinkle the grated Parmesan over the surface.

Place quiche in the centre of the oven and bake for 35–40 minutes until golden and firm in the centre.

Leave to rest for 10 minutes before serving.

Serve with salad and new potatoes.

Chapter Twenty-Five
It's Complicated...

With filming all wrapped up, the crew began heading home by seven. Alex and Harry were exhausted by the time they clambered into Sarah's car and were driven back down to the cottage. They had barely got their teeth brushed and PJs on before they were snuggled down in their beds and sparked out.

Tired or not, there had been much talk on the short drive home and during the washing and undressing about Mrs Alliott's puppies, who were looking for new homes, and whether or not Sarah and the boys might like to go over and look at them.

Once the boys were asleep Sarah went downstairs, tidied up and opened a bottle of wine. She hadn't had so much as a single glass all the time Magda and the crew had been filming, and now what she really fancied doing was sitting down, putting her feet up and relaxing. For a moment or two Sarah wondered whether it had been a mistake to invite Shaun round, but then decided it was better to explain now than wait. So she lit the lamps, closed the curtains, put on some music, put her glass down on the coffee table and curled up on the sofa, settling back amongst the cushions. She hadn't meant to close her eyes, and most certainly hadn't meant to fall asleep...

When she woke up Sarah had no idea where she was, what the time was or what was going on. She took a second or two to get her bearings and then realised that there was someone knocking at the door.

She got up slightly unsteadily, taking a second to look at her reflection in a picture hanging in the hallway before opening the door. Shaun was standing on the doorstep with a bunch of flowers that looked as if he had just picked them.

Sarah smiled. 'It's so nice to see you, come on in,' she said.

He did, wiping his feet on the mat, looking around.

'So you really do live here?'

Sarah nodded.

'These are for you,' he said, handing her the flowers.

'They're gorgeous.'

Shaun laughed. 'Fred insisted; I dropped in to see him on the way home. He said you were worth the effort.' He paused.

'The flowers are lovely. I'll put them in some water,' Sarah said.

There was an odd moment when she wasn't sure whether to show Shaun into the sitting room and make him wait, or let him follow her through into the kitchen. It had been a long time since she had had a strange man in her house.

In the end he followed her into the kitchen. 'It's a lovely place you've got here,' he said, looking around.

Sarah nodded. 'I love it and the boys do too. I rent it from Kit,' she added in case there was any doubt left in his mind.

'Your new partner?' he said, raising an eyebrow.

'About that,' Sarah said, wondering just how much more she should tell him and then realised that if she wanted to have any kind of a relationship with Shaun that she really had to explain everything.

'Why don't you sit down and I'll make you a tea or a coffee or pour you a glass of wine and I'll tell you all about it.'

He grinned. 'Sounds like a plan. You want me to put the kettle on while you do the flowers?'

'Okay.'

And so Sarah told him; she told him all about Kit and Magda and Guy and last of all she told him that Kit couldn't cook.

'Are you serious?' asked Shaun.

'Uhuh, which is why Kit recommended that Magda take me on as his assistant. And she came up with the partner thing to cover her own designs on Kit.'

They were in the sitting room now, Shaun had lit the fire while she had made them cheese on toast and she realised how comfortable she felt with him. It seemed perfectly fine that he was helping. They'd talked and laughed and talked some more in between finishing off the bottle of wine, as any remaining tension finally ebbed away. They were sitting by the fire, Sarah on a stool and Shaun on a cushion on the raised hearth, with a plate and glasses between them.

'You're not to breathe a word though,' said Sarah. 'Promise?'

Shaun nodded. 'Cross my heart.' And as he spoke he leaned in a little closer and very, very gently kissed her. Sarah's eyes widened and she felt her heart flutter.

'Ohhhh,' she said softly.

'Oh?' he repeated, eyes bright with amusement and delight. 'I thought given how what you got from Kit wasn't really a proper kiss that maybe you would like the real thing.'

231

Sarah smiled.

'Maybe I should do it again?' he said.

And so he did, and this time Shaun kissed Sarah properly. It was stunning. She couldn't remember the last time she had been kissed properly. Pulling away breathlessly, she said, 'Bloody hell.' She paused for a moment. 'Now you.'

'Now me what?'

Sarah giggled. 'I've told you all about me, now you have got to tell me about you.'

'I'm not sure there's that much to tell, and it certainly doesn't involve TV programmes, cooking or lords of the manor,' said Shaun.

Sarah waited.

After a moment or two, Shaun said, 'Okay, I got married four years ago and left Newnham Magna to go and live in Edinburgh with my wife, Naomi. She's a fabulous woman, a nurse, and she originally came from Scotland. She was always telling me how she found it hard to settle south of the border. I think we both knew that that was a bit of an excuse, but she was never really happy with her life down here, and rather naively I assumed that moving back would make things better for her. But as soon as we got settled in – even before really – I think we both knew it was a big mistake. She hated her job just as much, hated the dark. Hated me in the end, I think, and so we decided to split up.

'We'd been good friends before we got married, but we just didn't work as a couple. Anyway the split was amicable. She was planning to work overseas, find herself.' He smiled. 'I'd always been close to her parents and late last year her mum was diagnosed with cancer. Everyone was devastated, including me, which is why I've been backwards and forwards, helping, and supporting Naomi and her dad and the rest of the family out. Her mum is in a hospice at the moment; it's just a matter of time, really. Such a terrible shame. We've all put our lives on hold.'

The words dried up. His eyes were bright with unshed tears.

'I'm so sorry,' Sarah said.

Shaun nodded. 'Thank you. She is a lovely woman and everyone will miss her. Anyway Naomi and I stayed friends, and I carried on in the teaching job I had up there, and then Amanda Howling rang me and let me know that she was planning to retire this summer and suggested I apply, and so the long and short of it is, here I am.'

'Working for Fred?'

Shaun nodded. 'When I knew I was coming back, and given that Naomi's mum was so unwell, I decided to hand my notice in and take some time off; get a house sorted out here, be free to head back north of the border when needs be.'

'Which is why your life is complicated?' asked Sarah gently.

He laughed. 'I think you may trump me when it comes to complicated. I'm not the one with an imaginary boyfriend.'

Sarah smiled, and was glad he understood that she really was telling the truth about Kit. Shaun was very close, his eyes bright with desire and good humour, and Sarah was wondering if he might kiss her again, as a consolation prize for having the most complications, when someone started hammering on the front door. Sarah jumped so violently that she knocked a plate off the hearth.

'Oh, my God, who on earth can that be at this time of night?' she exclaimed, clambering to her feet. It felt like she had been caught red-handed, up to no good. Self-consciously, Sarah ran a hand over her hair and tidied her clothes. It was almost midnight, but whoever it was, was determined not to be ignored and kept on knocking.

Shaun was on his feet. 'Let me get it,' he said, heading for the hallway.

Sarah smiled to herself, touched by his chivalry.

Whoever it was thumped again, harder this time. Shaun pulled the door open, obscuring whoever was outside from Sarah.

'Who the fuck are you?' said a familiar voice.

'Colin?' gasped Sarah, in total amazement, stepping around Shaun.

'You have to let me in,' snapped Colin.

'Hang on a minute,' said Shaun, as Colin was about to push his way inside. Shaun looked at Sarah, bemused. 'Do you have to let him?' he said in a very calm and reasonable voice, totally at odds with Colin's tone and expression.

'No, not really. I certainly don't want him in here,' said Sarah, surprised by how much she meant it.

'So, who is he?'

Colin glared at him. 'This is ridiculous, Sarah. Just let me in, will you. I need to come inside.'

'Well, at the moment he's my husband, but very soon he'll be my ex-husband and no, I don't want him in here and I don't want him to wake the boys,' said Sarah.

Shaun nodded. 'Fair enough. You definitely win the prize for complications.' And then turning to Colin said, in a very reasonable voice, 'Do you mind keeping your voice down.'

From the look on Colin's face Sarah thought there was a fair chance he might explode with sheer fury. In the light cast by the open doorway she could see his face getting redder and redder.

Shaun, shaking his head, continued to speak to Sarah. 'How do you manage to keep it all together?'

Sarah laughed. 'With some difficulty.'

'Will you stop ignoring me, and just let me in,' growled Colin, stamping his foot like a petulant child. 'It's bloody freezing out here.'

Sarah turned, still not sure whether she really wanted him in the cottage. 'What it is you want? Why are you here?' she asked, taking the time to get a better look at him. Colin was wearing a green padded jacket over well-worn jogging bottoms and flip-flops. Not his usual style at all.

'This is all your fault,' he said, miserably.

'My fault?'

'Yes, your fault. Entirely your fault. Peony has thrown me out and I've got nowhere else to go.'

Sarah stared at him. 'How can that possibly be my fault?'

'She said she came to see you this afternoon. Although to be perfectly honest I've got no idea why.'

Sarah nodded. 'Because she was unhappy with you gatescrashing her life, Colin.'

'She wasn't unhappy until you poisoned her mind against me. Anyway she said you told her to throw me out and change the locks.'

Sarah felt her colour drain. 'As a parting shot, after I asked her to leave. I didn't think she'd do it. I told her what you and she did had got nothing to do with me, that she should do what she liked.'

'You told her to change the locks and throw me out.'

'As a throwaway remark.'

'Well, she took you at your bloody word, Sarah. I'd just got out of the bath and Peony said, "Can you pop down the off licence and get a bottle of that special red we like,'. So I grabbed the first things to hand, got in the car and went.'

'Really?' said Sarah, incredulously. She couldn't remember the last time Colin had run an errand for her, and most certainly not in the middle of the night.

Colin at least had the good grace to look uncomfortable. 'Peony had sort of hinted that when I got back we could drink it in bed,' he said, without meeting Sarah's gaze. 'And so I jumped in the car and drove half way across bloody town on a promise, and then when I came back I couldn't get in. I couldn't even get the key in the Yale. She had had the locks changed. Changed, for fuck's sake. I'm assuming she must have organised it when I was in the bath. And she must have paid extra to get a locksmith out at this time of night – probably some sort of emergency service – anyway he had to have been waiting at the end of the street or something. So I rang the doorbell and hammered on the windows and she refused to let me back in. She told me what you'd said. In the end the people in the house the other side threatened to call the police if I didn't go away.'

'And so you came here?' said Sarah.

'Where else was I supposed to go?' Colin demanded, as if coming round to his almost ex-wife's house was the most reasonable thing in the world. 'You wanted to ruin my new life, didn't you? Admit it. Now let me in.'

'I'm afraid you can't come in,' said Shaun pleasantly. 'Have you got some friends you could ring?'

'I haven't got any friends,' said Colin.

'A hotel then?'

'I'm not going to stay in a hotel. And who the hell are you anyway?' said Colin, screwing up his eyes against the light.

'I'm a friend of Sarah's,' Shaun said.

'Oh really.' Colin gave a smirk that left no doubt what he really thought.

'Me too,' said another voice from out of the darkness. Colin swung round.

'Kit?' gasped Sarah in astonishment, as he stepped into the pool of light created by the front door. 'What on earth are you doing here?'

'I just got back from the pub and saw the lights on.' He grinned at Shaun and extended a hand. 'Well, well, well, so you're the mystery man,' he said. 'Nice to see you again; I wondered who it was that Sarah was seeing.'

Shaun smiled. 'And there was me thinking it was you.'

Both men laughed.

'Sarah's explained?'

Shaun nodded. 'Yes, although I'm not sure I believe her.'

Sarah looked at the two of them.

'You know each other?'

Before either of them could speak Colin looked from face to face. 'I don't know what's going on here, but it's midnight. I've been thrown out of my house because of Sarah. I've got nowhere to go, I don't think it's unreasonable to expect for her to put me up. We are still married after all, so if you could just step to one side, gentlemen. I'm exhausted and need some sleep. I've just about had enough for one day.'

Sarah stared at him; Colin looked tired and grubby and as if he was about to burst into tears. The truth was that for all they had been through, and however badly Colin had behaved, she did feel sorry for him, and for a moment she felt her resolve wavering.

It was Kit who said, 'I'm terribly sorry, old chap, but that's not going to happen. You can hardly stay here when Shaun's staying, now can you? Three's a crowd and all that,' Kit continued, in a voice that suggested Colin's position was non-negotiable.

Colin's eyes widened; Sarah made the effort to keep her expression neutral and Shaun, raising his eyebrows, said, 'Exactly,' quite obviously following Kit's lead. 'You're lucky we weren't already in bed.'

Colin looked as if he was about to snap off a reply and then his shoulders slumped. 'This is all your fault,' he said to Sarah, petulantly. 'Now I've got nowhere to go and I'm supposed to be having the boys tomorrow.'

'Tell you what,' said Kit cheerily. 'Why don't you come up and spend the night at the hall? Just one night, mind you. You can get yourself sorted out tomorrow. If you leave your car here I'll give you a lift up in the Discovery.'

'I suppose it's better than nothing,' Colin said and then turned to Sarah. 'I'll be back first thing tomorrow.'

This time it was Shaun who leapt into the void. 'Actually Sarah and I had planned to get off early as you were having the boys. We were going to drop them with you on the way.'

At another time Colin would have protested or said that Sarah would just have to change her plans, but he sighed and admitted defeat.

'I was going to take them swimming,' he said miserably.

'Well, don't worry, old chap, you still can,' said Kit brightly. 'I can lend you some trunks and a towel.'

Colin looked first at Kit and then at Shaun. Finally he sighed and they watched him turn on his heel and amble miserably back towards the lane and Kit's Discovery.

Sarah looked up at Kit. 'Are you mad?' she whispered, as her almost ex-husband vanished into the gloom.

Kit shook his head. 'No, he doesn't know it yet, but he's doing me a favour. Magda's waiting in the Discovery. Guy and the film crew all went home hours ago, but not her. I've been putting off coming back home as long as I dare. Colin showing up is close to perfect.'

Sarah raised her eyebrows. 'For you maybe.'

Kit grinned. 'See you tomorrow. I'll let you two love birds get off to bed.' He lifted a hand in farewell and winked at Sarah.

Sarah reddened furiously. Shaun smiled and bade Kit goodnight before closing the door behind him. 'There you are,' he said. 'We have carte blanche from your imaginary husband.' And with that he kissed her.

Sarah pulled away from him, eyes wide. 'I'm not sure that—' she began.

Shaun laughed. 'Don't look so worried. I'll wait till they've gone and then I'll head home.' He paused, eyes bright with mischief. 'Unless of course you wanted me to stay?'

'No,' said Sarah hastily, and then thinking that might sound rude, although even as she thought it, that struck her as crazy, added, 'I mean, not that I don't like you but – but – it's too soon…'

Shaun held up a hand. 'It's okay, I'm only teasing.'

She sighed.

'So having had my advances cruelly rejected,' he said, still grinning, 'I think I'll be off.' He picked up his jacket. 'Are we still on for tomorrow?'

'I hope so,' said Sarah. 'But I don't really know, I need to sort this thing with Colin out first. He might not be able to have the boys.'

He nodded. 'You know that this bit of it isn't yours to sort out? He's a big boy.'

'I did tell his new girlfriend to change the locks.'

'His ex-new girlfriend?' said Shaun.

'Oh, don't. He can hardly have the boys if he's homeless.'

'She was the one looking for a way out and she was the one who changed them, not you, and I'm sure she didn't do it lightly. Now I'm going. Ring me about tomorrow and let me know what's going on. Okay?'

Sarah nodded. Shaun smiled and leaning in close, brushed his lips on hers. 'Night, night,' he said. 'Sweet dreams.'

Sarah opened the door and watched him heading back towards the road. Sarah thought that Shaun waved as he made his way down the footpath that would lead him back to the village, but it was so dark she couldn't be sure.

Sweet dreams, Sarah thought as she locked up and turned off the lights; hardly likely under the circumstance. But she was wrong. Within minutes of snuggling up under the duvet and closing her eyes she fell into a warm dark dreamless sleep.

Mixed Cheeses on Toast

Per person:

Ingredients:

2 slices of bread of your choice, thickly cut

Choose around 3 cheeses from your favourites:

Cheddar

Applewood smoked

Blue cheese

Wensleydale

Double Gloucester

Mozzarella

Manchego

Cream cheese (either plain or one of the added flavour varieties.)

1 small red onion sliced into rings

1 dessert spoonful of mayonnaise

1 tsp of Dijon mustard.

Black pepper

Method:

In a small bowl combine the mustard and mayonnaise.

Using the 'shavings' blade on your grater, grate any hard cheeses of your choice into a small bowl. Crumble blue cheese.

Combine but don't squash cheeses together.

Grill bread to your preferred colour on one side only.

Remove from grill and spread with mayonnaise and mustard mix on the ungrilled side of the bread.

Heap cheese mix onto the mayonnaise and mustard. Be generous and go right to the edges of the bread. Don't press down. If using cream cheese now is the moment to add a few tsp of it to the toast – dot it around rather than leave in one big heap.

Add two or three onion rings to the top of the cheese and a twist or two of black pepper.

Return to grill and cook under a medium heat until the cheese is bubbling and golden.

Allow to cool a little before cutting into quarters and serving.

Chapter Twenty-Six
Going Swimmingly

Sarah was woken by the sound of the phone ringing. She was instantly wide-awake and, sitting up, picked up the receiver. 'Hello?'

'It's me,' said Kit. 'I was wondering if the boys might like to come up and have breakfast? We've got cornflakes, lots of toast and jam, maybe porridge and a fry-up and then we'll take the dogs for a walk and go swimming. What do you think?'

Sarah rubbed her eyes. 'What on earth is the time?'

'Half past seven. And Colin is up.'

'Really?' said Sarah, incredulously.

'Oh yes,' Kit said, with a cheery laugh that suggested Colin was there with him, and probably not as enthusiastic as Kit about the prospect of being up so early on a Sunday morning.

'And what about Magda?'

'Funny thing. I haven't seen her this morning.'

Sarah waited. There was just bound to be more.

'When we all got back last night I thought Colin looked as if he could use a drink, and have a bit of a chat, you know, man to man, and Magda went up to bed. She was sound asleep when I got upstairs. I thought it was rude to disturb her, after all it had been a long day.'

'Well done,' said Sarah.

'I thought so,' said Kit brightly. 'Anyway I'm going to start cooking in half an hour if they want to come up and join us. I was thinking maybe we should have kippers. Ah, and there we go; Colin's just popped off somewhere – not sure where, but he does look a bit peaky this morning.'

Kit paused, his tone less bright and forced. 'Actually, it would be lovely if you could join us too, but I suppose that's out of the question?'

The way he said it made Sarah smile. 'That's lovely, Kit, but I can't. I don't want to spend any more time with Colin than I have to.'

'I can see why,' Kit whispered.

'If you like I'll go and see what the boys say and call you back.'

'Righty-oh and don't worry, I can hold fire on the grilling till they're up and about. Wonderful thing, this new cooker, although there are moments when I really pine for my old microwave.'

'You can still use it,' said Sarah. 'For old times' sake. Just don't let Magda see you.'

'Unfortunately I can't. Mrs Oates threw it out in her big clear-up,' said Kit sadly. 'Said it was a health risk.'

Sarah smiled. 'Never mind.'

And with that he was gone. Sarah sat with the phone in her hand thinking, but not for long. Seconds later Alex came running in and jumped onto the bed, giggling, clutching Big Bunny.

'It's not a school day, is it? I heard you talking,' he said. 'Are we late? I thought Kit was here.'

'No, it's not school day,' said Sarah, as he snuggled up under the duvet with her, his tiny cold feet scrambling for purchase on her legs. 'And Kit was on the phone. He rang to see if you want to go and have breakfast with him and Daddy.'

Alex's eyes widened. 'Daddy's with Kit?'

Sarah nodded.

'Is Peony there?' asked Alex, cautiously, clutching Big Bunny a little tighter.

'No, she isn't. I think the plan is for you to go swimming later.'

'What, all of us?' asked Alex.

'No, just you and Harry and Daddy.'

'And Kit?'

'I don't know, darling, but it sounds as if he might be going.'

Which was when Harry appeared. 'Can we have a dog?' he said.

'No,' said Sarah, as he sat down on the end of the bed, and slipped his feet under the duvet. His feet were freezing too.

'We're going to go swimming,' said Alex. 'And having breakfast with Kit and Daddy.'

'Are we? Do you think Dad will let us have a dog, Mum?'

'No, but Kit will,' said Alex confidently.

'Okay, if you want breakfast up at the hall you need to do your teeth and get dressed while I find your swimming things and then I'll ring Kit. Okay?'

The two boys nodded. Sarah got out of bed and pulled on her dressing gown. Through the window, she could see that the day was crisp and sunny, the sky the brightest cloudless blue. A perfect summer Sunday. While they got dressed Sarah put on the kettle and opened the back door to let the garden in, only to find Kit on the doorstep, his hand raised as if he was about to knock.

'Oh, that was good,' he said.

Sarah laughed. 'I said I would ring you.'

He shrugged. 'I know, but I didn't want to leave it to chance,' he said. And then something very odd happened. As their eyes met Sarah felt a little flutter of attraction, so unexpected that she made a peculiar squeaking noise. Kit frowned. 'All right?'

Sarah nodded. This was mad. She was supposed to fancy Shaun. Hadn't he kissed her? Hadn't she felt a little tingle of lust?

'Nothing,' she said. 'I thought you were up at the hall playing host to my husband and your...' Sarah hesitated, searching around for the right word to describe Magda.

'My producer?'

Sarah nodded.

'I thought I'd leave them to it for a little while. Colin isn't feeling very well and Guy has been on the phone to Magda this morning already, apparently someone important –' Kit mimed quotation marks '– saw that little bit we filmed that went out on Harts and Holmes, and they are really keen to take a look at the pilot they shot yesterday.'

'Really?' said Sarah. 'Already? Do you know who they are?'

Kit shook his head. 'No, but Guy and Magda obviously did. They're already talking about commissioning a series. And she is all busy and buzzy and engines set full ahead. Terrifying.'

Sarah felt a great surge of delight. 'Oh, Kit, that's wonderful. I'm so pleased for you. For us. And Magda must be delighted.'

'Let's say it took the edge off sleeping on her own last night,' he said grimly.

Sarah laughed. 'So what's the plan now?'

'Wait to see if they want to buy it presumably.'

'Actually I meant up at the hall.'

'Oh, I see. Well, currently it's all about breakfast, and then we're all going swimming.'

'Including Magda?' said Sarah in amazement

'I did invite her, said we could pop into Cambridge and buy her a swimming costume just as soon as the shops open, but she didn't seem that keen. Asked me to drop her off at the station so she can go home to Guy instead. No fun, that woman.'

Kit waited, aiming for a little dramatic tension, and then grinned. 'Worked like a charm. I may have to borrow your ex-husband again.'

'Please don't. What's he going to do about somewhere to stay?'

'He said he's going to ring someone called Ms Goold and then talk to Peony about counselling. He said she might be able to help.'

Sarah nodded. She had no doubt Ms Goold would have the answer, at a price.

'And he needs to talk to Peony about his things and his precious book. When I left he was on the phone begging forgiveness.'

Sarah raised her eyebrows but said nothing.

'So, are the boys all up and ready for breakfast?' Kit asked.

'No, but they soon will be.'

Kit nodded. 'Good, and then you can get yourself all – you know – all spruced up and ready for your date with Shaun.' He shifted his weight. 'Lucky man. He's a good chap.'

Sarah smiled. 'Yes he is.' But she got the feeling that there was something else that Kit wasn't saying.

'I thought he was married?' he asked after a moment or two.

'He's getting a divorce.'

Kit nodded. It was odd how awkward it suddenly felt. 'Shame,' said Kit and then aware of what he was saying, added, 'What I mean is she was very lovely, his wife. Naomi – that was her name, red-head, very feisty.'

'You knew her?'

'Not really. I saw her about the village, you know.'

'Feisty?'

He laughed. 'Mrs Oates and I caught her in the lane shouting at some chap who had hit his dog with a stick. I thought then she was a bit of a handful. And she introduced herself.'

'So you approve of me seeing Shaun then,' asked Sarah, jokily, not altogether certain why she said it.

To her surprise Kit reddened. 'I'm not sure, you know it's not really any of my business who you see, is it? He seems nice enough. But I—'

Sarah stopped him. 'It's all right, Kit. It was meant as a joke. I don't need your approval.'

'Well, no, of course not,' he blustered. At which moment the boys came thundering down the stairs.

'Can we go and see the puppies?' asked Harry. Alex meanwhile grabbed Kit round the legs and hugged him tight.

'No,' said Kit to Harry, scooping Alex up onto his hip. 'We're having breakfast and then we're going swimming with your dad.'

'Not straight away,' said Harry. 'It's not good for you.'

'No, not straight away. I thought we'd walk the dogs.'

Picking up their bags and coats and jackets Sarah guided them all out of the door.

'If you need me,' Kit said, 'I've got my mobile.'

'Are you sure you'll be all right with them?'

Kit nodded. 'Of course.'

And with that the three of them were heading out of the door and up the lane towards the hall. Sarah watched them go, the boys chatting away, happy as at any time she could remember.

The house suddenly seemed extremely quiet and empty once they had gone. Sarah tidied and put the washing in the machine, watered the hanging baskets and felt a little lost and full of random thoughts about Kit and Shaun and how much life had changed over the last few months, which was why by half past nine she found herself lying in the bath, surrounded by bubbles, eyes closed, soaking away the bizarre events of the last twenty-four hours.

Her phone pinged to announce the arrival of a text message; drying her hands Sarah picked it up from where she had left it on the sink. It was from Shaun and read: 'Hope you slept well, just checking to see if we're still on for today?'

Sarah realised that she had forgotten all about letting him know what was going on, in the fuss and rush of the morning.

'Yes, all okay,' she typed and pressed send.

Seconds later a text pinged back: 'See you @ 12? I'll pick you up?'

'Looking forward to it,' Sarah replied, although as she pressed send she wondered if that was strictly true. It was like her sense of expectation had subtly changed and she wasn't altogether sure why.

*

Shaun arrived a few minutes early; Sarah was out in the garden dead-heading the hanging baskets. He smiled. 'They look fantastic. Fred'll be pleased to know his babies have all gone to a good home.'

Sarah smiled. 'Well, thanks for that. And thank you for last night.'

He shrugged, but she noticed something about him also seemed subtly different.

'Everything okay for today?' he asked.

She nodded. 'Yes, thanks. Kit came and picked the boys up and everyone is going swimming. Including Colin.'

'Okay. In that case we'd better be off. I booked us a table at this little pub I know on the river and...' He stopped.

'What?'

'I've been thinking,' Shaun said. He sounded serious. 'When I got home last night I was thinking about you and Kit and Colin and—'

Sarah smiled. 'And how complicated it all is?'

Shaun nodded.

'And how very messy?' she added.

'And I've been thinking a lot about you and me and what we could have at the moment. My own life is pretty messed up too. I'm spending a lot of my time supporting my ex-wife and her mum.'

Sarah smiled again. 'That's not messed up, that's goodness and kindness.'

'That's kind of you to say so. But the thing is...'

'The thing is,' said Sarah, picking up the conversation before he could say any more, 'is that in reality neither of us are really ready to get involved with anyone at the moment and while it would be lovely to be with someone maybe it wouldn't be fair, at least not right now.'

Shaun stared at her. 'Because life is messy?'

'It's always messy, but sometimes it is more complicated and messy than others and you're too nice and too good to be caught up in the mess,' said Sarah.

'At the moment?'

Sarah nodded. 'At the moment.'

His smile widened. 'That is such a relief.'

She slapped him teasingly. 'I think you're lovely, Shaun, but the thing is if I'm honest I don't really know what I want at the moment. What I don't want to do is lead you on or hurt you because I really like you, Shaun – and you deserve better.'

He nodded. 'Likewise. I don't know whether I'm coming or going at the moment.' Shaun paused. 'So this is weird, are we breaking up even before we've started going out?'

'I think we might be,' Sarah said.

'Sounds good to me. But friends though?'

Sarah nodded. 'Friends and I hope we stay friends and get to be better friends.'

'So what shall we do now?' Shaun asked.

'Well, we could go out to lunch and go to the pictures or go for a walk.'

'Brilliant idea. And you're not upset, or hurt? Or horribly disappointed or thinking that I've wimped out?' He watched her face carefully.

Sarah shook her head. 'No. How about you?'

'No, not at all. If anything I feel relieved.'

Sarah smiled. 'Me too. I'll just lock up and get my handbag.'

'Okay.'

Shaun headed for the car.

Their day was close to perfect. They talked about everything from the TV show to Sarah's new freelance career, they talked about Shaun's new job and his plans for the school and his house, they talked about gardening and puppies and the rigours of divorce and joy of new beginnings, and then, as they drank coffee and watched the boats go by on the river, the conversation turned to Kit and Roseberry Hall.

Shaun grinned. 'You know Kit told me about you.'

Sarah stared at him. 'What? When?'

Shaun nodded. 'A few weeks ago. I didn't realise it was you until yesterday. He came down to buy bedding plants from Fred. Actually I don't think I've seen him since.'

Sarah nodded. 'He was the one who told me about Fred's.'

'Uhuh. We got talking while I was helping him load up the plants, and he said he'd met this amazing woman.'

Sarah stared at him. 'Hang on, Shaun. It might not have been me.'

'True. It might not have been, but I think it was. He said that she was going to be renting a cottage from him, and that she was just about to move in.'

'Kit's got lots of property.'

'He said she was going through a rough time and that she was gorgeous.'

Blushing, Sarah shook her head and looked away. 'Oh, stop it. It could have been anyone.'

Shaun smiled. 'Have you ever heard the expression, "the lady doth protest too much, methinks"?'

Sarah's colour deepened. 'But it's true. The estate owns lots of houses.'

'Probably does, but then yesterday when I saw the way he looked at you while they were taking the photos, I knew it really was you.' Shaun drained his coffee. 'And I've been thinking about that a lot since yesterday. When you get right down to it, it wasn't just the way he looked at you, Sarah, it was the way you looked at each other.'

Sarah felt her heart lurch.

'Your life may well be a mess at the moment, but don't make it any messier by choosing the wrong man when life straightens itself out.'

'Kit?' gasped Sarah, and even as she said it she knew deep down that Shaun was right. How was it she hadn't seen it before?

Shaun nodded. 'When you think about it you'll know that I'm right,' he said. 'Now come on, let's go for that walk. You can go right along the river here on the towpath. It's a great place to come when you get your dog.'

'Who said we're getting a dog?'

'The boys told me yesterday when we were at the tea party. Apparently Kit is going to get them one.'

*

Shaun dropped Sarah off at the cottage around four. The day was far from over, but she wanted to be back in good time for the boys. As she opened the gate to the cottage Kit's two dogs appeared from the shade and ambled towards her, tails wagging. Sarah bent down to pat them.

'What are you two doing here?' she said, and then she spotted a familiar figure lying at full stretch on the scrubby grass that passed for a lawn. Kit had on a straw hat, which he had down over his face. Sarah thought there was a good chance he might be asleep.

'And how about you?' she said, shading her eyes with her hand. 'Who invited you to sleep on my lawn? Are the boys with you?'

'No,' said Kit, from under the hat. 'They went off to have tea with Colin.' He peeled himself off the grass, sitting up slowly, and their gaze met. Sarah suddenly felt self-conscious.

'Did you have a nice time?' he asked.

Sarah nodded. 'It was lovely.'

'Good.'

There was a slightly uncomfortable silence and then Sarah said, 'We've decided not to see each other again, well, not not again but not as a couple.'

'Oh, really,' said Kit.

Sarah nodded. 'It's too soon for both of us.'

Kit got to his feet. 'Are you upset? Do you want some tea or something? I think I've got a hankie here somewhere.' Kit patted his pockets.

Sarah shook her head. 'No, I'm fine.'

'But I thought you liked him?'

'I do,' said Sarah, taking out her keys and heading for the back door. 'But both of our lives are really complicated at the moment and we didn't want to rush into anything, make a mistake or maybe make things messier than they already are. But we'll stay friends.'

'Oh, good,' said Kit, nodding vigorously. 'That's very good. He's a good bloke.'

'Did Colin mention what time he would be dropping off the boys?'

'Six, I think. We had a nice time at the pool.'

'Good,' said Sarah, pushing the door open. 'So what exactly are you doing here, Kit?'

He sniffed and put his hands into the back pockets of his jeans, the epitome of discomfort. 'I wanted to talk to you, but maybe now isn't the right time.'

'Well, you must have thought it was pretty much the right time given you were camped out on my lawn, waiting for me.'

'The thing is,' said Kit, 'I'm really glad that you're going to be friends with Shaun.'

'Me too.'

'No, what I meant was I'm glad you're going to be friends and not – not...' Kit's expression suggested that he was in pain.

'Not making a mess of each other's lives?'

'That's right. Because I want to be that person.'

'What, the person who makes a mess of my life?' said Sarah.

'No, well, hopefully not. What I mean is...' Kit paused and looked at Sarah, his eyes bright. 'I think I might accidentally have fallen in love with you.'

Sarah's eyes widened. 'What?'

'You have to believe me, I didn't mean to. It wasn't my plan. It's just that when I saw you with Shaun last night it made realise I had to say something before it was too late. I don't want you to get your life sorted out and be with Shaun. I want you to sort your life out and be with me.'

'Oh, Kit,' she began. 'I—'

He held up a hand. 'Don't say anything. It's fine, if you don't want to, all you have to do is say so and we can carry on just like we are now, with you as my friend, but if you do then please let's try – maybe not now – maybe not until you're healed and happy and have sorted out the mess, because I so don't want this to be a rebound thing. Tell me we can try, Sarah.'

'What about Magda?' asked Sarah.

'I told her this morning that I couldn't see us together, that it wasn't fair on Guy and that although I thought she was lovely, she wasn't my type and that I didn't want to hurt her.'

'Bloody hell, Kit. What did she say? Is she going to pull out of the cookery show?' said Sarah, thinking about how much it meant to him.

Kit shrugged. 'I don't know and to be honest I don't care. If having the show means that I lose you, Sarah, I'd rather lose the show. But my instinct is that when it comes right down to it Magda is a realist. If it's a toss-up between me and making a shed load of money I think she will be following the money.'

'So,' said Sarah.

'So, what do you think?' said Kit quietly.

She looked at him and felt her heart melting. 'Oh, Kit,' she said.

He grinned. 'Is that a yes?'

Sarah nodded and with that he lunged forward.

'But not yet,' Sarah said, stopping him midstride. 'Let's take our time. There are things I need to sort out.'

'Like what?' asked Kit.

Sarah smiled. 'We don't have to rush. I'm not going anywhere. If this is meant then it will just grow, but at the moment I need to deal with Colin and sort out my work and—'

'And be with me,' said Kit.

'What if it's too soon? What if I hurt you?'

He grinned. 'It's a risk I'm prepared to take. I think we are meant to be together.'

And with that Kit kissed her and she kissed him back and the whole world stopped still and Sarah thought she might faint and she knew for certain that Kit was right.

Chapter Twenty-Seven
Set aside in a cool place for a year to mature

'This thing is,' said Magda, finishing off the last of the bread and butter pudding Sarah had made for dessert, 'we could add a short segment into Harts and Holmes each week. Sarah's little arty-crafty money-saving upcycling tips. Even get people to email them in. It's a great idea. What do you think?'

Sarah smiled. 'We've been here before, Magda.'

'I know, poppet, and just look how well Kit's done. Bestselling cookery book, his own show. New wife and a ready-made family. I know you like to help him all you can but you're very marketable in your own right, you know. You've seen the mail we've been getting. People love you and what you and Kit have got here, and what you're doing to the house, all that lovey-dovey happy family thing, all those hideous painted jam jars and homemade candles. All that love – amazing. We could do something with that, darling, we really could. There's a book in it if nothing else. At least think about it, sweetie.'

Not So Bread and Butter Pudding

Ingredients:

150ml whole milk
150ml double cream
1 tsp good vanilla essence
3 tbsp Baileys
Butter
4–6 slightly stale butter croissants
3 large eggs
3 tbsp Demerara sugar
Sultanas (optional)

Method:

Preheat the oven to 180C.

Grease a large ovenproof dish with butter. Tear each croissant into large pieces. Layer in the ovenproof dish with the sultanas (if you're using them).

Beat the eggs, cream and milk together, along with 2 tbsp of the sugar and Baileys until everything is well mixed. Pour the mix into the ovenproof dish, trickling it all over the croissants. Allow to stand for half an hour before baking to allow mixture to soak into croissants.

DON'T be tempted to press the croissants down into the mixture as this will make the pudding heavy.

Sprinkle the top of the croissants with the remaining sugar.

Stand dish in a large roasting tin. Half-fill the roasting tin with warm water – this helps the pudding cook evenly.

Cook for 35–45 minutes until golden brown.

Allow to stand for 10 minutes before serving.

The End

Recipes

Vanilla Ice-Cream

Ingredients:

4 medium egg yolks
2 tsp of good vanilla essence
1 can sweetened condensed milk (about 300g)
500ml of double cream (one large carton/tub)

Method:

Whip egg yolks with vanilla essence. Add condensed milk and then, using an electric whisk, beat well until everything is incorporated.

In a separate Pyrex bowl (or similar) whip cream until it thickens and holds soft peaks. Scrape yolk mix into cream, whisking until well incorporated. Cover with cling film and put into freezer.

After an hour remove bowl from freezer and whisk again to break up the ice crystals and keep the mixture silky smooth. Cover and return to freezer.

Whisk again after another couple of hours. An hour later whisk again and then pour into suitable container with a lid for freezing. Allow to freeze.

Remove ice-cream from freezer 10 minutes or so before serving to allow to soften slightly. (This isn't soft scoop.)

Alternatively pour the mixture into an ice-cream maker and freeze according to manufacturer's instructions.

As this recipe uses raw egg yolks it is not recommended for babies or the elderly.

Green Shoots Oven-Baked Risotto

Serves 4 as a main course

Ingredients:
6oz (175g) risotto rice
3oz (75g) butter
1 onion, peeled and finely chopped
1 small glass (3oz or 75ml) of white wine
1pt (500ml) vegetable or chicken stock
1 bundle of asparagus, approx. 6oz (175g) – choose a bundle with similar diameter stems. Cut into 1-inch (25mm) lengths
3oz (75g) frozen peas
1 bunch spring onions, trimmed and chopped
4oz (100g) Pecorino cheese (you can use Parmesan or even a crisp very mature Cheddar at a push), grated finely
1 bunch of chives, washed and chopped (scissors work really well)
Salt and black pepper

Medium-sized ovenproof dish, baking tray

Method:

Heat oven to 150C, 300F or gas mark 2

Melt butter in a saucepan, add chopped onion and cook very gently for 5–7 minutes until soft and golden (don't brown).

Add the rice to the saucepan, stirring gently until all the grains are coated in butter.

Add white wine and stock, bring to a simmer and then tip the whole lot very gently into the ovenproof dish (I find it easier to handle if you stand the dish on a baking tray to make it easier to lift in and out of the oven).

Add a good pinch of salt and freshly ground pepper.

Stir and then slide the dish on its baking tray into the centre of the oven.

Cook uncovered for 20 minutes.

Remove risotto from the oven, stir in the chopped asparagus, the spring onions and two heaped tbsp of Pecorino cheese.

Stir the rice gently to distribute all the goodies.

Slide back into the oven, uncovered, for a further 12 minutes.

Take out of the oven and add frozen peas, stir gently and return to oven for another 3 or 4 minutes till the peas are cooked but not wrinkly.

Remove the dish from the oven and sprinkle with chopped chives, gently stir through the rice.

Serve straight away with the remainder of the grated Pecorino, some crispy bread and a glass or two of the remaining white wine.

How to Cook the Perfect Poached Egg

Ingredients:

Eggs (use the freshest you can)
2 tsp of vinegar

Method:

Heat water in a frying pan until fine bubbles just start to form on the bottom of the pan.

Add vinegar to water.

Crack the eggs into a cup one at a time, and getting it as close to the water as you can, drop each egg into the water.

With a spoon ease the white close to the yolk to make a tidy shape and help the whole thing stay together.

Allow to simmer gently for a minute.

Turn off heat and allow the eggs to sit in the water for up to 10 minutes.

Using a slotted spoon remove the eggs. Drain well.

Serve with lots of hot buttered toast

Gnocchi and Spinach Bake

Serves 4-6

Ingredients:
1 chistorra de Pamplona cut into ½–1-inch slices
2 cloves of garlic, finely chopped
400g can of chopped plum tomatoes
300g fresh spinach
500g gnocchi cooked and drained as per manufacturer's instructions
1 buffalo mozzarella
Salt and pepper to taste (optional)

Method:
Heat oven to 180C, 350F, gas mark 4.

In a large pan – a wok is ideal – gently dry-fry the sliced chistorra and garlic over a medium heat, allowing the oil to seep out. Cook for around 3–5 minutes without browning.

Add the can of chopped tomatoes. Gradually add spinach, a handful at a time, allowing it to wilt before adding another handful. Stir between handfuls.

Cover and simmer for a few minutes on a low heat, stirring occasionally. Allow to reduce and thicken a little.

Take off heat and gently fold in the cooked gnocchi.

Adjust seasoning. (Sometimes I add a grind of pepper but the chorizo adds most required seasoning.)

Pour into a large ovenproof dish.

Cut buffalo mozzarella into slices and then tear into chunks. Dot the top of the dish with mozzarella.

Bake for around 30–40 minutes until the top is golden brown.

Serve piping hot.

This is *fabulous* reheated in a frying pan the next day, served with eggs and bacon.

Recipe from Freddies Deli
www.freddiesdeli.co.uk

The Ultimate Bacon Sandwich

For each sandwich:
2–3 rashers of your favourite bacon
2 slices of bread (it has to be said that thick white sliced works just as well as any other)
Ripe tomato (enough to cover one slice of the bread), very thinly sliced
Good mayonnaise
Freshly ground black pepper

Method
Grill bacon to your preferred interpretation of 'done'.

On a small baking tray or ovenproof plate arrange tomato slices, sprinkle with a little pepper, slide under grill towards end of bacon cooking time so they are cooked, but not to a pulp. Tomatoes may be cooked in the microwave if preferred.

While bacon and tomatoes are cooking, toast bread until golden brown. Spread both slices with mayonnaise.

Arrange tomatoes on one slice, add a little more pepper.

Top with piping hot bacon and second slice of toast. Cut into two (or four).

Serve with a napkin and a mug of tea or coffee.

Flapjacks

Ingredients:

Note: use butter for this. I've never found a margarine that works.
150g butter, plus a little bit extra for greasing
50g golden caster sugar
4 tbsp golden syrup
275g rolled oats

Method:

Preheat the oven to 190C/ 375F/ gas mark 5.

Grease and line a shallow 20cm-square tin with baking parchment or greaseproof paper.

Heat the butter, sugar and syrup in a small pan over a low heat and stir until the butter has melted. Add the rolled oats. Stir. Press the mixture into the tin and bake for 20 minutes, or until just golden at the edges.

Remove from the oven and cool for 10 minutes. With a knife cut into 10–12 portions while the flapjack is warm and still in the tin. Cool completely before turning out and cutting again with a sharp knife.

Store in an airtight tin.

Melting Moments Biscuits

Makes around 20–24 biscuits

Ingredients:
180g unsalted butter
60g icing sugar, sifted
60g custard powder or cornflour (if using cornflour add a tsp of vanilla essence to the butter when mixing)
1 tsp baking powder
180g plain flour
2 or 3 glacé cherries, washed and cut into small pieces

Method:

Preheat oven to 180°C. Line two baking trays with baking parchment.

Cream the butter for 2 minutes in an electric mixer.

Add in the icing sugar and custard powder and mix until combined.

Sift the baking powder and flour together then add to the dough and mix well.

Divide dough into 20–24 small balls.

Place balls on lined baking tray, leaving plenty of room between each.

Prick each ball once with a fork, and add a fleck of glacé cherry to the top of each.

Bake biscuits for 12–16 minutes or until light golden (they are still slightly soft when taken from the oven and crisp up as they cool).

Watch carefully in the last few minutes as the edges can brown.

Remove from oven and leave to cool in the baking trays for 5 minutes and then transfer to a wire rack to cool completely. (A fish slice helps.)

These are *fabulous* sandwiched together with buttercream and jam.

Summer Fish Pie

Serve 4-6

Ingredients:

For the pie

250ml vegetable or fish stock (Knorr cubes are fine)
100g undyed smoked haddock
250g salmon
250g Pollack fillets / firm white fish
150g raw or cooked prawns
75g frozen peas, defrosted
Small bunch parsley chopped
150ml /1/4 pt white wine
100ml double cream
1 heaped tbs cornflour

For the Topping:

1kg new potatoes; cut large ones in half so they are all same size
2 tbs olive oil
Small bunch salad onions, roughly chopped
70g cheddar grated
1 bunch chives, chopped
White pepper

Method:

Boil the potatoes in salted water until tender, (10-15 mins) Drain well before returning to the pan with the olive oil, chopped spring onions and half the cheese and the chives. Crush lightly with a fork or potato masher. Set aside while you make the sauce.

Heat the stock in a small pan. Pour the wine and cream into the pan and simmer to reduce a little. Mix the cornflour to a paste with 1 tbs of the sauce pour into the sauce whisking to ensure there are no lumps. Simmer gently until thickened. Leave to cool a little, adjust seasoning (remember smoked haddock can be quite salty – I usually just add pepper at this stage)

Next remove any bones and skin from the raw fish. Cut the Pollack, salmon and smoked haddock into chunky bite sized pieces. Layer with the prawns and peas in a deep ovenproof dish.

Pour sauce over the fish. Using raw fish makes it a much more succulent and chunkier pie.

Spoon the crushed potato mixture over the fish. Sprinkle on the remaining cheese and chives.
Put ovenproof dish into a preheated oven (200C /gas 6) Cook for 35 - 40mins until the topping is golden and filling bubbling.

Serve piping hot with green salad and chunky bread to mop up the sauce.

Based on a recipe given to me by the ladies who run the fish stall on Downham Market.

Summer Pudding

Serves 8
Ingredients

4 ozs (225g) strawberries
8 ozs (225 g) red currants
4 ozs (110g) blackcurrants
1 lb (450g) raspberries
5 ozs (150 g) golden caster sugar
7-8 thick slices of good white bread from a large loaf, cut so that they are around half an inch thick, crusts removed.
1 ½ pint (850ml s) pudding basin which has been lightly buttered
Cling film.

This recipe works well with any berries. You can substitute chopped fresh apricots, plums, peaches or nectarines but whatever combination you chose make sure you have a good proportion of dark berries to colour the juice.

Method

Wash fruit and dry on kitchen paper

Remove leaves from strawberries and slice or if small cut in half.

Set strawberries to one side.

Strip red currants and blackcurrants from stems by holding the stem firming, then sliding stem between tines of a fork and pulling the fork down gently but firmly. Discard stem.

Check raspberries and discard any that are mildewed.

Carefully line pudding basin with cling film allowing a generous overhang at the top. It's easier to use two pieces and overlap them by about 6" rather than try to work one sheet around the curves of the bowl.

Put sugar and 3 tbs water into a large pan.

Heat gently until all the sugar dissolves. Stir occasionally.

Bring to a boil for 1 min. Add all the fruit (except for the strawberries).

Cook for 3 mins over a low heat, stirring very gently 2-3 times.

The fruit should have softened, but remain reasonably intact and be surrounded by dark red juice.

Drain the fruit well and save the juice
Set fruit aside.
Taste the juice. If it is too sweet add a little lemon juice.
Allow fruit and juice to cool.

Cut the crusts from the bread.

Dip the slices one at a time into the juice, (just for a second or two) and neatly line the basin, beginning by lining the bottom.

Cut the bread to shape as you work.

Overlap the slices to get a nice seal & press the pieces firmly together.

Don't worry if the slices are not totally covered with juice as you will be adding more juice later.

Use off cuts of bread to fill any holes. You're aiming for a totally lined bowl, with no gaps.

When the basin is lined carefully spoon in the fruit, adding the sliced strawberries a few at time so they are evenly spread through the rest of the filling.

Fill the basin right to the top.

Carefully spoon the juice over the fruit, saving around 2/3 of a cup of juice for later.
Save any spare fruit for garnish.

With remaining bread cover the whole of the top of the basin, cutting of any overhanging bits.

When the top is covered fold the overhanging cling film over the bread.
Place a large saucer or tea plate over the cling film and then add a weight –
Tins work well.

Chill in the fridge for at least 6 hrs or overnight.

To serve, remove tea plate, unpeel the cling film, put a serving plate upside-down on top of the bowl and flip over. Slide bowl off and carefully remove the cling film.

Use the leftover juice to colour any patches that haven't soaked up the juices.
Serve with leftover juice, extra berries and cream or good vanilla ice cream.

Canadian Lemon Loaf

Ingredients:
One-third cup of soft butter
1 cup of white sugar
2 eggs
1½ cups of self-raising flour
1 tsp baking powder
dash salt
½ cup of milk
grated rind of a lemon
To decorate: a third of a cup of sugar and juice of the lemon

Method:

Preheat oven to 350 Fahrenheit

Put butter in mixing bowl, mix thoroughly (use an electric beater), slowly add sugar, keep beating.

Meanwhile in a second bowl mix (by hand) the flour, salt and baking powder. Then grate the lemon rind into the 'flour' bowl. Mix.

Back to the electric mixer bowl. Add the eggs one at a time and mix well.

Add the milk a little at a time, alternating this with a little flour, add each in turn, finishing off with the last of the flour, all the while beating slowly. Mix well.

Pour into a well-greased loaf tin and bake at 350 degrees for about 45–50 minutes. Test by sticking a long pin or skewer into it. If mixture sticks, give it another 5 minutes.

When loaf is baked, take from oven and while still warm, with a toothpick or skewer make some holes and pour the following mixture over it: one third cup of sugar mixed with juice of lemon.

Let cool before trying to remove from pan.

This recipe was sent to me by author, Debbie Viggiano
www.debbieviggiano.blogspot.com

Lemonade Cordial

Ingredients:

8 lemons, plus more for cutting into slices as a garnish if desired
12 ozs Sugar or 340grm of golden or ordinary granulated sugar or honey (this can be adjusted to taste)
500 mls or 1 pint water
Fizzy or still water to dilute to taste

Method:
Wash lemons thoroughly.

Roll lemons firmly on a hard surface until they become soft. This will make them easier to juice.

Carefully remove the zest from 3 lemons.

In a pan over medium heat, add the sugar, the lemon zest and 500ml (1pt) of water.

Simmer gently for about 5 minutes or until sugar has dissolved and the mixture has a light yellow colour. Do not boil.

Remove from heat and allow to cool.

Squeeze the juice from all the lemons.

Strain the lemon juice into a jug.

Strain the sugar mixture into the jug, stir.

Fill chilled glasses with ice and pour in a little of the lemonade cordial.

Top up with still or fizzy water to taste.

Garnish each glass with sliced lemons and a sprig of mint.

Serve.

Store any unused cordial in the refrigerator.

Banana Bread

Ingredients:
3 ripe bananas (the riper the better)
2oz brazil nuts (chopped)
2oz dried apricots (chopped – I often cut mine up with kitchen scissors)
8oz wholewheat flour
6oz sugar
2 eggs
2 tsp baking powder

Method:

Preheat oven gas mark 3 (170C)
Mash bananas, add beaten eggs, sugar, baking powder, nuts, and apricots, then mix together and slowly add the flour.

Grease a 1lb loaf tin and bake for one hour.

This tastes fine without the nuts and you can replace the apricots with dried cranberries or any other dried fruit you have about.

An excellent way to use up over-ripe bananas!

Recipe from my fabulous friend, Sarah Allen.

Grilled Haloumi and Sugar Snap Peas

Serves 4 as a starter, 2 as a supper dish
Ingredients:
250g haloumi
1 large lemon
1 tbsp olive oil
1 knob unsalted butter
Approx. 1 tbsp water
180g sugar snap peas
Generous tsp of freshly chopped mint

Method:
Cut lemon into 6 wedges, longways.

Cut haloumi into ¼-inch thick slices and place, along with 4 lemon wedges, under a preheated medium-hot grill. Retain two lemon wedges.

Grill haloumi and lemon wedges for 2–3 minutes on each side, or until golden brown.

While haloumi and lemon are cooking, heat oil, water, and butter in small pan over a medium heat. When mixture is bubbling add sugar snap peas. Cook for 3–4 minutes, shaking pan frequently, so the sugar snaps are sautéed but retain their snap. Add chopped mint to pan. Cook for further minute. Take off heat, while you:
Arrange haloumi slices on a warm plate.

Pile sugar snaps peas onto each slice, spoon over some of the juices from the pan.

Squeeze lemon juice from retained wedges over each slice, garnish with grilled lemon wedges.

Serve with warm pitta bread.

Real Cream of Mushroom Soup

Serves 2

Ingredients:
4 tbs butter
8oz mushrooms (field mushrooms and open mushrooms have a better flavour than button mushrooms)
1 tsp salt
1 medium onion, chopped
1 pint of chicken or vegetable stock
1/8 tsp ground nutmeg
250ml double cream
Salt and pepper
Chopped parsley for garnish

Method:
Clean mushrooms with piece of kitchen roll and chop roughly.

Gently fry onions without colouring in the butter till they are soft – stirring frequently. Stir in chopped mushrooms and fry for a minute or two. Add a pinch of salt and a little pepper.

Add stock, bring to the boil and simmer for around 10 minutes. Remove from heat.

Pour the double cream into a blender or liquidiser and add soup. Whizz for 30 seconds or so. Return soup to pan and bring back to the simmer (don't let it boil). Adjust seasoning. Pour into two bowls, sprinkle with nutmeg and parsley. Serve.

If you haven't got a liquidiser, take pan off heat and add cream, using hand blender to liquidise.

If you don't want to liquidise the soup you might want to cut your mushrooms and onions more neatly.

Flowerpot Bread

Ingredients:
1lb strong white bread flour or your favourite bread flour
2 tsp sugar
1½ tsp salt
½oz. fresh yeast or 2 tsp dried yeast
½pt lukewarm water

Optional Extras

2oz poppy seeds
2oz mixed seeds
2oz pumpkin seeds
2oz chopped walnuts
2oz grated cheese
2oz chopped olives
2 garlic cloves, peeled and crushed
2 tablespoons mixed herbs
2 tablespoons chopped chives
½onion, peeled and grated
2 tbsp sun-dried tomatoes, drained and finely chopped

Preparing your flowerpot
You'll need:
vegetable oil
lard
butter

Directions:
Before using your flowerpots they need seasoning. Take two to six traditional earthenware/terracotta flowerpots (3 to 6 inches in size). Wash thoroughly and grease them inside and outside, with lard, butter or oil. Use *new* flowerpots.

Put directly onto shelves in a preheated oven at 190C; 375F, gas mark 5, for 25–30 minutes, with a baking tray under the shelf to catch any drips. Switch off oven. Open oven door and allow to cool in the oven or remove and stand on cooling rack.

Repeat the process two or three times to create a good seasoning and non-stick surface to your flowerpots.

Before using them to bake with, line the base with greaseproof paper or baking parchment.

Method:
If you are using dried yeast, dissolve one teaspoon of sugar in the warm water then add the dried yeast. Leave until frothy (about ten minutes). If you are using fresh yeast, blend it into the warm water.

In a large mixing bowl put flour, salt and sugar. Add any of the smaller extras you wish to use at this stage.

Add the yeast liquid to the dry ingredients and mix to a soft sticky dough.

Turn the dough onto a floured work surface and knead the dough by folding towards you, then pushing down and away from you with the heel of your hand. Give the dough a quarter turn and repeat the action. Knead until smooth, satiny and no longer sticky. This takes around 10 minutes. If you are using larger extras add them at the end of the kneading process. Stretch the dough out on the work surface, scatter your extras on the surface and knead briefly to spread them through the mix.

Arrange your flowerpots on a baking tray. Cut the dough into evenly sized pieces and place in the prepared and well oiled/buttered flowerpots. Glaze top of dough with milk or salted water and sprinkle with mixed seeds.

Place each pot inside a large oiled polythene bag, leave in a warm place until the dough doubles in size (around an hour).

Remove the polythene bags and bake pots on the middle shelf of a hot oven at 230C (450F) or gas mark 8 for 10 to 30 minutes, depending on the size of your flowerpots, or until the bread is nicely browned and sounds hollow when tapped.

Remove the bread from the flowerpots and allow to cool on a wire rack.
Once they are cool you can slip them back into the flowerpots to serve.

Alternatively if you are using a breadmaker follow the manufacturer's instructions, remove when mixed and allow to rise in flowerpots as before.

Simple Sea Bass

Ingredients:
2 medium sea bass (1 per person, cleaned and scaled)
4 garlic cloves, crushed
2 tbsp good olive oil
1 tbsp Italian seasoning or 1tbs fresh parsley leaves
2 tsp fresh coarsely ground black pepper
1 tsp sea salt
1 lemon cut into wedges for garnish
1/3 cup white wine (optional)

Method:
Preheat oven to 220C/450F.

In a small dish, mix the garlic, olive oil, salt, and black pepper.

Place fish in a shallow glass or ceramic baking dish.

Rub fish with oil mixture.

Pour wine over fish.

Bake the fish, uncovered, for 15 minutes. Sprinkle with parsley or Italian seasoning and continue to bake for 5 more minutes (or until the thickest part of the fish flakes easily).

Drizzle remaining pan juices over fish and garnish with lemon wedges.

Easy Summer Pickle

Ingredients
500g courgettes
3 shallots
Salt

For the pickling liquid:
500ml cider vinegar
140g golden caster sugar
1 tsp mustard powder
1 tsp mustard seeds
1 tsp celery seeds
½ dried chilli (crumbled up)
1 tsp ground turmeric

Method

Draw a fork down from top to bottom on the outside of each courgette to make ' stripy skins' Go all the way round each courgette. Slice very thinly (using a sharp knife, the slicing blade of a food processor or a mandolin.)

Chop shallots.

Place the courgettes and shallots into a glass bowl and sprinkle with salt.

Cover with cold water, stir to dissolve the salt and leave for 1 hr.

Drain the courgettes very thoroughly and pat dry using kitchen roll or a clean tea towel.

Meanwhile put all the remaining ingredients into a pan and bring them to a gentle simmer. Simmer for 3 mins, making sure the sugar has dissolved.

Set aside to cool until the liquid is still warm but not hot. Add the courgettes to the pickling liquid and stir.

Spoon the mixture into 2 x 500ml sterilised jars

Seal the jars and leave for a few days in the fridge to mature.

Kept chilled, this pickle will keep for a couple of months.

How to sterilise glass jars.

Wash them in hot, soapy water, then dry in an oven heated to 170C/150C fan/gas 3 for at least 10 minutes. Always put your pickles, jams and chutneys into jars while the jars are still warm.

Alternatively you can sterilise glass jars in the microwave; wash well in the normal way, rinse, but leave them 'wet'. Pop them into the microwave for about a minute, use while still warm.

Tiramisu

Ingredients:
568ml pot double cream
250g tub mascarpone
75ml Marsala, rum or brandy
5 tbsp golden caster sugar
300ml strong coffee, made with 2 tbsp coffee granules and 300ml boiling water
1–2 packs sponge fingers
25g chunk dark chocolate
2 tsp cocoa powder
1tsp vanilla essence

Method:

In a large bowl whisk the mascarpone, double cream, caster sugar and vanilla essence in a bowl until it has the consistency of thick cream.

Mix around the coffee with spirit of your choice and allow to cool (taste and adjust strength). Pour in a small flat dish (this dish is just used for dipping).

Dip the sponge fingers quickly into the liquid in the small flat dish and then arrange a layer in your serving dish. (Dip one side in the liquid for a second or two then the other. Don't leave them too long –you don't want your sponge to be too soggy.)

Spoon half of the mascarpone mix over the sponge fingers.

Using a coarse grater, grate a layer of chocolate over the mascarpone mix.

Repeat process, ending with a layer of the mascarpone, so that you have 2 layers of sponge fingers and 2 layers of the mascarpone mix.

Cover with cling film and chill overnight in fridge.

Before serving, sieve cocoa powder over the top and then finish by grating the remaining chocolate.

Will keep for up to two days in the fridge.

Homemade Hot Chocolate

Ingredients:
300ml milk
225ml single cream
2oz dark chocolate, coarsely grated
2oz milk chocolate, coarsely grated
½ tbsp golden caster sugar
1 tsp pure vanilla extract
1 tsp instant coffee (optional)
1 tsp cocoa powder

Method:

Heat the milk and cream in a saucepan on medium heat to just below the simmering point.

Remove the pan from the heat and add the chocolate.

Stir until the chocolate has melted, add the sugar, vanilla extract, and coffee (if desired) and whisk vigorously until frothy.

Reheat gently, pour into two mugs.

Sieve cocoa onto top.

Serve immediately.

Optional extras: canned 'squirty' cream, marshmallows, extra grated chocolate.

Idiot-proof Sponge

Ingredients:
6oz (175g) self-raising flour
1 heaped tsp baking powder
3 large eggs
6oz (175g) butter (at room temperature)
6oz (175g) caster sugar
1 tsp good vanilla essence
1 tbsp strawberry jam or lemon curd for filling

Method:
Pre-heat oven to 170C, gas mark 3, 325F

Lightly grease two 8" diameter x 1½-inch deep (20 x 4cm) cake tins. Line each with a circle of lightly greased baking parchment.

Sieve the flour and baking powder together into a large mixing bowl.

Break 3 large eggs into the flour, add the caster sugar and room-temperature butter and the vanilla essence.

With an electric hand whisk, beat the ingredients together until you have a smooth, well-combined mixture (which as long as the butter is nice and soft should take you around a minute). If you haven't got an electric whisk you can use a wooden spoon, but it will obviously take a little longer.

Divide the sponge mixture equally between the two cake tins. Smooth the surface lightly with a palette knife.

Place them on the centre shelf in a preheated oven and bake for 30–35 minutes.

Don't open the oven door until 30 minutes have passed!

To test if they are cooked, very lightly touch the centre of each sponge with your finger. If it leaves no impression and springs back, the sponge is cooked.

Take sponges from the oven and allow them to rest for 5 minutes. Turn them out onto a cooling rack and carefully peel off the baking parchment.
Leave the sponge to get completely cold before you add the filling.

Cheat's Strawberry and Vanilla Gateau

Take two ready-made sponge flan rings and, using the base of a spring-form tin as a template, cut out a disc from the centre of each. Discard the rest.

Whip a carton of double cream with a little caster sugar (to taste), and a tsp vanilla and a shot of Drambuie (or similar) until it is stiff, and then fold in a small carton of ready-made luxury custard.

Place one sponge disc in the bottom of the spring-form tin.

Take some large strawberries, cut off the green end, and cut in half lengthways. Line the ring with the strawberries, cut side against the metal.

Spoon the cream and custard mixture in the centre of the ring and spread gently to the edges.

Smooth out then place the second sponge disc on the top.

Chill for a while then remove the tin by first warming around the edges with a hot cloth.

Dust the top with icing sugar, and using a metal skewer heated over a gas flame, quickly score a diamond pattern into the sugar. (Optional!)

Decorate with mixed berries and mint leaves.

This little gem came from Pat, at Palmers Restaurant, as a dinner party standby for anyone looking for an easy but impressive dessert. www.palmersrestaurant.co.uk

The Perfect Sausage Sandwich

Serves 2

Ingredients:

2 nice crusty bread rolls, halved and toasted
or alternatively 4 thick slices of bread cut from a crusty loaf
6 good quality pork sausages (or veggie sausages)
1 large thinly sliced onion
1 tbsp clear runny honey
1 tbsp Dijon mustard or English mustard
A good splash of balsamic vinegar.
The sauce of your choice: piccalilli, HP, tomato, Branston, burger relish – whatever

Method:

Heat a little olive oil in a heavy frying pan and slowly cook the sausages for about 15 minutes over a medium heat, turning over occasionally. Don't prick them.

Take out and put to one side.

Into the same pan put the onions and cook until caramelised. Stir in the balsamic vinegar add the mustard and honey.

Return sausages to pan to warm through.

Put 3 sausages and a pile of onions in each sandwich. Add sauce of choice.

Serve.

Kit's Basic Quiche

Ingredients:

1 packet of chilled ready made shortcrust pastry
2 large eggs
4 rashers of unsmoked streaky bacon
1 small tub of double cream (around 250ml)
3 tbsp of mature cheddar, grated
1 heaped tbsp of grated parmesan
1 small bunch chives, chopped
Salt and pepper to taste

Method:

Grease a 9-inch loose-bottomed tin.

Roll out the pastry – don't over-work or press too hard – and ease it into the baking tin. Trim away excess pastry. Leave in fridge to rest for 15 minutes.

Heat the oven to 350F, 170C, gas mark 4.

Cover the inside of the pie crust with baking parchment or tin foil and add baking beans or something like dried haricot beans so that the pastry crust can't rise during cooking. This is called baking blind. Make sure the beans cover the whole surface of the quiche base right up to the sides of the tin.

In the same oven spread the bacon out on another small baking tray and cook until crispy (7–12 minutes). Remove bacon and allow to cool.

Bake the pastry case for 20 minutes. Remove the beans and parchment. Bake for another 5 to 10 minutes until the pastry is just starting to colour. Remove from the oven and allow to cool.

Preheat oven to 180C, 375F, gas mark 5.

In a jug beat the cream and eggs together until well combined. Add salt and pepper.

Sprinkle the base of your pastry case with cheddar cheese, crunch up and add the cooked bacon and then chopped chives.

Pour the egg-and-cream mixture into the pastry case and sprinkle the grated Parmesan over the surface.

Place quiche in the centre of the oven and bake for 35–40 minutes until golden and firm in the centre.

Leave to rest for 10 minutes before serving.

Serve with salad and new potatoes.

Mixed Cheeses on Toast

Per person:

Ingredients:
2 slices of bread of your choice, thickly cut
Choose around 3 cheeses from your favourites:
Cheddar
Applewood smoked
Blue cheese
Wensleydale
Double Gloucester
Mozzarella
Manchego
Cream cheese (either plain or one of the added flavour varieties.)
1 small red onion sliced into rings
1 dessert spoonful of mayonnaise
1 tsp of Dijon mustard.
Black pepper

Method:
In a small bowl combine the mustard and mayonnaise.

Using the 'shavings' blade on your grater, grate any hard cheeses of your choice into a small bowl. Crumble blue cheese.

Combine but don't squash cheeses together.

Grill bread to your preferred colour on one side only.

Remove from grill and spread with mayonnaise and mustard mix on the ungrilled side of the bread.

Heap cheese mix onto the mayonnaise and mustard. Be generous and go right to the edges of the bread. Don't press down. If using cream cheese now is the moment to add a few tsp of it to the toast – dot it around rather than leave in one big heap.

Add two or three onion rings to the top of the cheese and a twist or two of black pepper.

Return to grill and cook under a medium heat until the cheese is bubbling and golden.

Allow to cool a little before cutting into quarters and serving.

Not So Bread and Butter Pudding

Ingredients:

150ml whole milk
150ml double cream
1 tsp good vanilla essence
3 tbsp Baileys
Butter
4–6 slightly stale butter croissants
3 large eggs
3 tbsp Demerara sugar
Sultanas (optional)

Method:

Preheat the oven to 180C.

Grease a large ovenproof dish with butter. Tear each croissant into large pieces. Layer in the ovenproof dish with the sultanas (if you're using them).

Beat the eggs, cream and milk together, along with 2 tbsp of the sugar and Baileys until everything is well mixed. Pour the mix into the ovenproof dish, trickling it all over the croissants. Allow to stand for half an hour before baking to allow mixture to soak into croissants.

DON'T be tempted to press the croissants down into the mixture as this will make the pudding heavy.

Sprinkle the top of the croissants with the remaining sugar.

Stand dish in a large roasting tin. Half-fill the roasting tin with warm water – this helps the pudding cook evenly.

Cook for 35–45 minutes until golden brown.

Allow to stand for 10 minutes before serving.

About the Author

Sue Welfare lives and works in Norfolk with her husband, Phil, and dogs, Jake and Beau.

Sue has written around 30 books as herself, and under various pen names, including Gemma Fox and Kate Lawson.

When not writing Sue enjoys gardening, singing, cooking - lots of cooking - and making things.

Made in the USA
Charleston, SC
08 May 2013